The Darktouched

Book 1 of the Darkness Rises series

A novel by Dave Haywood

Copyright 2024 - Dave Haywood
Reader discretion is advised.

This book is a work of complete fiction but details some instances that readers may find difficult or uncomfortable. A full list of possible triggers is at the end of this book.

Introduction

Well, this is new. I'm writing a new genre. Gone is all the death and destruction of my previous novels, and I've replaced it with death and destruction, but this time, with badgers. So you're either reading this because of my other books or you're a new reader to my world. Or... you might be following the series that this is all part of... You might even be a new YA+ reader, so I'd like to officially welcome you aboard Team Dave. (If you're under 18, it might be best to wait till then, as there are some gruesome bits and naughty stuff).

Who am I though? I'm just a writer who loves telling stories. I love hearing what you, the reader, think and especially enjoy hearing your thoughts on where my tales go. I like to write books with the story in mind first so when "The Darktouched" came to me, I wanted to tell this one just as much as my previous work. Don't get me wrong though, it's a screeching handbrake left turn from my psychological thriller/horror before, but has the same humour, twists, turns and 'WTF!' moments you'll hopefully love.

So how did I get here then? I simply followed a dream. If you don't know me already, I'm Dave and I love to tell a tale or two, but I wasn't sure if I could do it. I have a day job where people were screaming at me to write a novel but I wasn't sure I had the skill. Was I actually a good writer or was I just a great blogger? When the reviews started flooding in for my first novel "What We Leave Behind," I had my answer, not that I believed them at first...

So on to the dedications.

First, as always, I want to say thank you to my family as without them, I wouldn't have you, my readers. Thank you for bearing with me when I disappeared upstairs to tippy tap the hours away.

To Shreen, my awesome misses. You never miss. Thanks beautiful.

The #Booktok / #Bookstagram community is a thing of beauty too and should never be forgotten from any thank you list. You and all the readers are the lifeblood of the publishing industry and the most integral part an author needs. Everything else is just filler if we don't have readers! I appreciate you! From Tyronne's dressing gown army to the booktokkers being my unpaid PR team. Unpaid yes, but unloved? Never! In no particular order;

- Instagrammers - Kim, Leigh, Jessi, Becky, Sarah, Tyronne, Jade, Emily, Louise, and Linzie. (And another Stacey, but more on Tiktok).
- The Bound by Books club - Stacey, Eilidh, Scott, Amanda, Sophie, Rae, Tammy, Laura, Jade, Sadie, Dannie and never forgetting Chloe.
- Authors - Phoebe, Russell, Oliver and Sara.
- And a special shoutout to Mikko. Woof. Good doggo.

Again, thank you for pushing this little guy.

Stacey, Eilidh, Scott and Amanda from the above club. You are awesome and truly my people. You deserve the world.

And then there's Kaleigh. My hard taskmaster. My editor. My proofreader. My champion. You helped me get the book into the world, and I'll never forget your 5 STAR REVIEW! But seriously, you started as a mountain I wanted to best. The ultra perfectionist that knew her shit. I thought, if I can challenge myself and listen to her constructive critiques, as a writer, I'll better myself. And then she became my editor. And then a friend through hardships untold. I could not have wished for a better champion on my side. What she's done for me, will never, ever be forgotten.

I'd also like to thank my Dungeons and Dragons team who have supported me since my first book. You are all my favourite people. This one, especially, is for you. (Yes, I know in D&D, Elves don't have wings, but mine do, so hush up. No, I don't know what her AC is either).

Readers: You are amazing people. I'm forever grateful. Read lots, love loads.

Now, brace thyself.

Here we doth go.

Author's Additional Note...
(Just because I can)

Wait! Brakes! Stop and check this little bit out, even if you skimmed the introduction, because if you stop and read this, you'll find something I've hidden within these pages.

The Darktouched is split into three internal books: Part One - The Three Paths, Part Two - The Convergence, and the cataclysmic final Part Three - The Sealed Tower. Sounds typical for a fantasy novel, right? Scene setting and ooooh dun-dun-dunnnnn suspense! However, each part can be read slightly differently than a typical novel. You can follow the story of Kyriss the Druid, Ansel the village elder of the Wildling community - who just so happens to be a highly evolved badger, or you could even follow the grump-filled Grind and his dark discoveries underground.

Each chapter set is in threes. They start with Kayriss, then Grind, then Ansel. If you want to follow the sweet druid, skip ahead to her chapters up until Book Two. Then, skip back for badger-based action and back once more for the Mine Folk mysteries.

You can also read it like a 'normal' book, whatever you fancy. However, since all three are very different, you might want to follow each journey separately.

Part two is the dark / light back and forth between the two "sides," which is the best way to put it. This is probably best read alternating, but I'll leave it to you.

Part three? Well... You'll have to wait and see.

One last thing. Promise. Then I'll let you crack on.

I made a complete soundtrack for this book, so scan the below and listen to your hearts content. (Please like and subscribe too).

Enjoy, and welcome to the New World.

Prologue

It began when the first aberration was born.

To some, it was a cursed child. To others, an irregularity to be studied.

A winged freak of nature, the doctors could not explain. It was tested, prodded, probed, and left as an unexplained anomaly to be viewed as a mystery. Not the wind of change it was to become.

She was the first. Of many. Of everyone.

Distortions of humanity became the norm whenever a child was born, an entire generation different, accursed by the majority to be 'not human.' Humanity slowed and started succumbing to this new breed, a race replaced. It was vastly different, even to each other.

Many were killed. In hate. In fear. Many were raised in secret.

Parents moved their offspring into camps of the same new races. Entire communities sprung up, consisting solely of one of the new aberrant breeds.

'Safe spaces for different races,' they were called.

As the aberrations were the only babies being born, humanity began to dwindle—to fall. Life was finding a new path, and the now dominant race of misfits rose—not to fight but to exist freely among the fading human communities. Nature's new choice was finding its footing in a world on the brink of collapse and rebirth.

Humanity was not being shown the path.

Human nations attacked others for resources as their workforce dwindled. They would not accept help from the new races. Forgotten bigotries from millennia gone by that humanity had driven away rose back up as they had a new enemy to hate. To fear. Even though most of the new races wanted nothing but simply to exist, hate and racism were rife against them—fear of an unknown that wanted to be known.

No Animals
No Elves
No Mine Folk
No Night Ones

Or simply "Humans only."

Until, one day, no one was left to enforce the archaic, defunct rules. No more of the human society that had dominated the histories. No more of the Kings and Leaders. No more Prime Ministers or Dictators. No more of their wars, their killing for pride or prejudice.

No more humans.

The world changed with the abyssal emptiness humanity left behind. Where homes had been made to support families, the winged ones took to the air. Where workplaces once stood, the Night Ones took control. Other aberrations followed, and even the animals of their yesterdays evolved into something new as they had been left to be free from humanity's encroaching, stifling presence.

After many years, nature became the new order, forever changing the world. The buildings of the humans were swallowed up by the nature the concrete tried to suppress. Humanity vanished from their Earth, and peace reigned for sixteen hundred seasons.

That is until Kayriss found him.

PART ONE
The Three Paths

Chapter One
Kayriss
The healer.

    A young woman sat high in the branches of a silver birch tree. She looked around, through dense foliage, passed branches and trunks creaking under their weight. From the canopy high above, the forest below unfolded like a living tapestry of vibrant greens and golden light. The dense treetops swayed gently with the breeze, their leaves shimmering in the sunlight as beams filtered through in patches, creating a mosaic of shadow and glow on the forest floor. The light that danced with shadows often lulled the woman into a blissful calm; she watched their endless caress of each other. The birds that remained from old flitted between branches, their calls echoing through the air, while the distant rustle of leaves hinted at the presence of hidden creatures below. The scent of pine and fresh earth rose on the wind, mingling with the soft whisper of the trees. They swayed in unison, painting a picture of serenity and untouched wilderness.

She loved the silence in the canopies and would spend many a day just listening. Letting nature's scents caress her as she heard and felt all of life just living around her.

She was one of the few winged races left in the new world, so she cared not for her height. They had been called Elves by people long departed, and the race name had stuck around long after they did. This particular Elf had been alive for sixteen hundred seasons, making her one of the oldest beings alive to her knowledge, bar the trees themselves. Each of the four seasons was markedly different from each other, but she preferred the spring when her plant friends would either return or bud anew.

From what little she remembered from her hu-man mother, there were four seasons to one of their years, which would make her a mere four hundred or so, and due to her slowed ageing process, she looked to be in her twenties, in human years. Age mattered little to the Elf, as all she cared for was here in her forest. The greens, browns and delicate yellows were where her passion lay.

Growing up had been difficult. She had lived through much but remembered little due to the fact she was only a baby through the worst of it. She could barely recall her mother now. All she had was a vision of flowing gold. The memory was like sunlight woven through the golden fields, but all it was was a soft breeze, whispering through time. The memory used to bring grief, but through the years, she had learned to control it, to stifle it down, and even embrace it. Self-imposed isolation from the other Elven clans helped, too. They had appeared much after her, leaving her with a sense of being caught between the old ways and the new world, never seeming to find her home.

Her heart always longed for something more.

It ached in its emptiness, but she doused the void with care for other creatures in the forest. She had seen the land and its people change dramatically as seasons passed. Nature had reclaimed the planet, and with it, her powers rose, giving her incredible healing magic and other natural spell-casting abilities. Kayriss thought she had the natural world at her fingertips some days, but there was a disconnection on others. She was filled with the haunted memories of lives lost.

She sniffed at the air through a slender nose as the wind wafted through the high branches once more. It brought news of a change. Something was different and disrupting the forest's natural weave. Nature was uneven in its balance, making it all too prominent in Kayriss's senses. She looked out at the sea of greens as they swayed and moved with the winds, looking for an answer to the unsettlement. Placing a hand on the rough bark of her tree, she closed her eyes to better hear, to feel what nature was trying to inform her. Smells assailed her nostrils as the flow of the wind moved and jostled her position. The Elf of the Wood held firm and concentrated, letting the forest's natural life speak to her.

It gave her direction.

Kayriss jumped down effortlessly, opening her eyes only halfway down the tree, although she could've covered the descent in darkness as she knew each branch well. Each tree was family to her, as she'd lived among them for most of her life. Like following the veins in her body, she reached the forest floor, placing one hand in the dew-rich grass in appreciation of the thick woodland floor. She licked the moisture from each digit, her senses flooding with the tastes of nature, each dewy droplet a library of natural information.

During her descent, she hadn't even needed her wings. Rarely now would she even bother unfurling them, opting to keep them covering her back, liking how their silken feel tickled the patches of bare skin in her threadbare clothing. The sun would heat them, and on cold mornings, they'd steal away the heat, giving her the feeling of a constant warm embrace.

On the forest floor, her keen eyesight brought her gaze to the dark eyes of a muscular, mean-looking dog, possibly a mastiff in breed, she surmised, who was on edge and ready, as if guarding a precious morsel of food. Its shoulders were tensed and stiffened in a stance that could only signal defiance. Kayriss held a hand low in a calming gesture to not entice the animal into combat. Body language was vital when dealing with the animal kingdom as some roaming wildlife did not speak the usual words of the hu-manoid races.

Staying low, she approached, showing no signs of aggression to calm the wary beast. She knew it to be a fighting dog, used to guard one of the enclaves the various races lived in, by the leather armour around its shoulders and flanks. The defensive garb was enlaced with overlaying metallic diamond shapes, which gave the dog extra protection over its more vulnerable areas. Kayriss thought it must have looked highly prestigious when created initially, but now, it is worn and dirty in places.

'And what are you doing all the way out here?' Kayriss thought to herself.

Quietly, she cast an incantation to allow her to converse with the animal on its terms and in its language so that she could firstly asway any animosity and offer any assistance if needed. The druidic spell would allow her to talk to the animals whilst not outwardly barking when any passersby happened upon their conversation. She was always thankful to the nature spirits for their forethought. They blessed her with powers for which she was also grateful.

"I mean no harm, four legs," she said sweetly and submissively, still staying low, keeping her eyes fixed but non-confrontational. She called it a descriptive name as she had not yet reached that stage of canine pleasantries. Although she thought there was no chance in hell she would ever allow it to sniff her behind as dogs generally prefer. Also, she chose to keep her sentences simple, as the sudden realisation that the two creatures could talk to each other could sometimes frighten the animals she conversed with. Kayriss didn't use words much herself these days, either.

The dog gruffed in confusion and tilted its head as if the different angle would answer why he could suddenly understand this thing in front of it. Having heard the 'two-legged bird thing' speak in a language it could understand, the mastiff visually relaxed slightly.

Not entirely, but at least some. Kayriss realised that this was helping, so she risked a smile. 'It was tough to bite the face of something smiling at you', she thought.

"Hungry. Master hurt," it said in a gruff voice laced with concern but soldier-like and dutifully spoken. To any bystander, it would be the regular gruff barks a dog would make, but Kayriss understood.

She kept her body language open and transparent, reaching into her pouch for food. She laid the dried meat on the ground and stepped backwards as an offering of friendship and a sign of respect. The large dog cautiously approached, driven on by a gnawing, desperate hunger and warily, he sniffed at the strip of dried venison. Realising what it was, the dog gulped it down eagerly, without as much as a chew or savour, still with one eye on the new stranger. He looked down at the ground, hoping more would be placed before it. The dog looked up at Kayriss, who acknowledged with another offering. She held it in her hand this time, and the mastiff gingerly took it with its teeth.

"Four legs. I am a healer. Can I help your master? Also, may I be gifted with your name?" Another smile, more comprehensive this time. The dog wasn't convinced of her motives yet, in any case.

At that, and with hunger somewhat abated, he looked up, nodded and motioned for the Elf to follow. Risking the burgeoning friendship, Kayriss stood at her full height of five foot, five inches and travelled after the leading mastiff. It kept looking back at her for its defence and to see that this new person was still following it.

Kayriss was still unsure of its name but followed anyway, hoping to prize it out later. It wasn't long before the pair stepped into a copse of trees that had become a temporary home to the dog and its master for what she could guess would have been only a few days.

The two legs in front of her were lying down, his breathing laboured and failing. His skin was tanned by the sun's rays, having been stuck in the same position for a while. Kayriss went into healing mode, and it took over her senses as she raced towards the prone man. But before she could get to his side, the mastiff, who was quicker, positioned itself between the two.

"Your master needs my help; I mean you both, no harm. He is not long before his sleep becomes permanent." Kayriss added a hint that time was of the essence, although she knew dogs had no concept of clocks besides the one in their stomachs. The four-leg, realising that help was needed beyond his guarding duty, cautiously stepped to one side but was ever wary of her actions, ever watchful. Kayriss started her incantations and spells, calling on the spirit of the moon for her healing magic. It would be enough to stem the flow of his life ebbing away, and while she could heal cuts, abrasions and even breaks if any, long-term disease still took recuperation time. Also, terminal damage was not allowed, as Kayriss had found out when an overzealous woodpecker caught something from the old world in one of his incessant head-banging sessions. It had plopped down in front of her one morning; and no magic would revive it. Death was apparently, terminal.

showed none of the telltale aspects of being an Elf of the Wood. She thought through the other clans and races of her world that she knew of. His skin was not the colour of the Night Ones, and he was far too tall for a Mine Folk. Also, he was above ground, too, and neither of those races liked the sun's brightness. While the Night Ones resembled Elves, they lacked the wings. They were also darker in both skin tone and outlook. They also didn't tend to live as long either. Kayriss continued ticking through the list, eradicating all choices, leaving her with the thought that he was some aberration of none of the known clans.

Was he something old or something new? ...

Something about him was nagging at the back of her mind, but she had never seen anything like this since the hu-mans walked the earth. Surely? This could not be one of those. She did not know how long she had treated the curious creature, but he stirred in the morning of one of the long days. Still, without a name, the mastiff had taken up residence by her side and licked at Kayriss's hand in both thanks and affection.

As the sun shone through the trees one bright day, the creature awoke.

Chapter Two
Grind
Meeting the Mine Folk.

The underground smelt of the dampness that the Mine Folk had grown to love.

"The rain on the stone is a perfect cologne," Grind said, chuckling as he chomped through the flank of a sizeable, barbequed rat. It had been a particularly feisty catch, but it made for a hearty meal at three feet long. Mine Folk were not known for their speed as they were, at heart, almost muscular squares. They averaged in height, four feet, and width, much the same. They also matched their stature by being mostly made up of beards. It was a problem for their race that Mine Folks only knew who was talking due to the various braids and beard thatches quivering as any words were uttered.

Grind had been tasked with clearing out the historic garbage that the old race had left behind so that they could repurpose areas to fit their territorial needs better. His team was making good progress, too. They would soon be retasked to another location so that more families could prosper in the dark of the underground. He looked across at the diligent workers all lifting various detritus into their assigned removal boxes, ready to be cast up into the sunlight, away from their sweet, sweet darkness. He thought about what the Upsiders must feel when they found the boxes of rubbish that the Mine Folk had discarded as they appeared through the ground.

He mused that it was like an above-ground marker that Mine Folk lived below. The two levels didn't have much time for each other and traded sparsely as it was far too bright up there to be comfortable for his clan. As they searched and excavated, the mining team would scour the area for anything they could take back home. Metals they kept, and sometimes the odd trinket, but the rest was considered useless. The Mine Folk were happy and had all they needed as the world and nature provided. Smiling, he continued to munch through the rat as workers carried on their endless task, humming to himself to the rhythmic tippity-tap of the water drips.

The Mine Folk cave was an underground vast, echoing chamber of something none knew or cared to know. All they cared for was that it was underground. Its rough stone walls were slowly being shaped by their steady hands, the sound of chisels and picks tapping away at the rock. The sound resonated through the space as the cave was hollowed out for their use. Pale, luminescent moss clung to the jagged stone, casting an eerie, soft green light that flickered across the cavern, illuminating its craggy surfaces in a ghostly glow.

Here and there, torches sputter in iron sconces, their warm, flickering flames adding bursts of amber light to the cool, mossy radiance. Green and yellow lights vied for dominance, giving the cave a lime or chartreuse colouring. Shadows danced in the flickers, creating a sense of quiet, patient industry as the Mine Folk worked to transform the cavern into their home deep beneath the earth.

Brushing a rat foot from a rather intricate braid, Grind noticed one of his new workers scurrying around. He was a new digger called Dront and was recently assigned to Grind's unit. However, he wasn't as described by the manager of the area. He was a landlord's son who wasn't bright enough to be on the comfy city watch job and did not learn enough for the council. He would, however, move into the position where he would have jurisdiction over their area when his father passed, such as the Mine Folk way. So, Grind would have to tolerate him as best he could, even though he was an idiot in waiting. He even tried to teach him the basics of being a good Mine Folk, like;

- Look after each other.
- Never eat the rat's tail.
- Check behind the beard before mating.
- (Then check again. Just for good measure).

Most of it was falling on deaf ears, and he had eyes with the wild look of no one in control behind them. Grind thought that Dront probably wasn't even considered for the cooking quarter as they were masters in all their realms, as their food made them local celebrities. Pickings underground were sometimes slim, but what they could make from one of the many cats that crossed into their homesteads would sate any of the Mine Folk's hunger. Toss in some locally sourced mushrooms, and Grind would visibly salivate, even through his dark beard. It would become clearly, and quite obviously moist, such was his hunger.

Even the clothiers and leather workers were agog at how they could skin a cat. Brix, the master chief skinner, could even do it one-handed, and how was a mystery to all. Grind scratched at his costly cat hat, made from one of the black and white beasts that had once been a dinner for his family. It was an extravagance, but he worked hard and deserved it. Plus, cats were all vicious gits that deserved everything that was coming to them. Such was the Mine Folk way.

"Carry on with the... work." Grind said in an effort to keep Dront from approaching. The younger Mine Folk habitually engaged Grind in idle nitter natter that drove him insane. Grind was not one for talking to anyone but his family, especially not idiots born with a silver pick in their teeth.

Dront smiled back at Grind, waving over exaggeratedly as a section of the concrete ceiling above him collapsed, crushing him underneath.

Chapter Three
Ansel
Snuffles are banned.

"There be less of the snuffling, young one. We haven't snuffled in many a moon cycle." The loving eyes of the elder looked down upon the playing children who were filthy, from both mud and adventure. He smiled down at the pair, who laughed playfully and ran off, chasing each other with sticks too big for them to carry.

Ansel stroked the black and white fur of his face from snout to ear, careful not to knock off his hat with his claws. Seasons ago, their long dark claws had been used for burrowing, and the badgers and other animals who had evolved after the old race disappeared, still had some ancestral traits. Snuffling was one he wanted long gone. No animal needed to beg nature to fill their bellies, as their community provided food plentifully.

Those days were past, and the Wildling communities were thriving. The otters had taken to shipping, and their newfound watery freedom had created wonderful trade routes for the forest dwellers. Although they did think they were some swarthy pirates of old, even though they traded fairly and freely, the personas were still enticing. Saying "Aaaarrrrrrr" always got a good discount at the market when the otter clan were involved, but never, ever call them 'sea dogs'.

Foxes plagued the old cities, running whatever shady deal they could. "A fox is just a wolf in sheep's clothing. Best avoided," Ansel would always warn the children. Their crime syndicates were the scourge of the land but only a minor annoyance this deep in the forest.

Their community of Wood Haven, though, was filled with life that worked together in natural harmony. In the heart of the ancient forest, the village thrived, nestled quaintly in the wood's own heart. The hu-manoid animals dwelled harmoniously amidst towering trees and murmuring brooks, with air filled with the sweet scent of oak trees and wildflowers. The captivating sunlight danced through the lush canopy above, casting dappled patterns upon the forest floor. At the centre of Wood Haven stood the sturdy oak tree, its branches reaching towards the sky like protective arms. Wood-crafted steps circled the trunk, leading up to the village meeting place, high in the canopy, where the inhabitants gathered to trade goods, share stories, and celebrate the changing seasons.

Wood Haven was led with wisdom and kindness by Ansel, the eldest badger, his black and white fur now tinged silver with age. Yet through his years, his eyes shone bright with knowledge earned through ancestral seasons of life in the forest. He was revered by all who called Wood Haven home, as his gentle demeanour and sage counsel guided the community through both joyous times and cycles of hardship, mainly brought on by fierce seasonal weather.

Whether it they did.

The villagers of Wood Haven were a diverse array of creatures, each with unique talents and quirks. Among them were the ever-industrious Squirrels, the builders of the community who constructed most of what the village was now, as all homes in Wood Haven were of squirrel construct and design, stamped and approved. So, the squirrels would be there the next day if a family needed an annexe or extension due to a new youngling. Ansel tried to remind all the villagers that it would be good to remind the builders, especially the architect, that all the other animals were considerably taller than they were. He would've thought they would have learned after Agnes, a rather portly hedgehog, got stuck to a ceiling beam after falling backwards. But no, size was always an issue with particular creatures. They did good work, blending dwellings seamlessly with the surrounding landscape. Moss covered cottages nestled among the ancient tree's roots, while cosy burrows dotted the forest floor, their entrances hidden beneath fern and bramble-covered doors.

Alongside their industry were the owl folk, who watched over the village from their perches high in the trees. They formed the closest thing to a city watch that Wood Haven needed, as crime was a thing of the old race's past, mainly keeping a watchful eye on the interlopers and explorers who happened upon them. Ansel had told them to all relax, take up fishing or do another hobby, but they persisted, wanting to be the security the village might need one day. He was grateful for the owls, even if they were not required daily or even seasonally. Or ever. 'Better to have than have not', Ansel thought.

Many more races lived there, blending seamlessly with each other. Life in Wood Haven revolved around the rhythms of nature, the villagers living in harmony with the land and its other denizens. They'd celebrate the turning of the seasons joyously with festive gatherings and rituals, honouring the earth and giving thanks for its bounty, with bellies always full and grateful to bursting.

Wood Haven was not without its dangers, even if they were far away and did not plague the village directly. Beyond the borders of Wood Haven, dark and mysterious forces lurked in the depths of the Under-veil, a place where the lower aberrations lived. They were the stories to scare the children at night, tales of the Night Ones who come in darkness and steal your toes—myths and mysteries mainly, but dangers possibly. Yet, under Ansel's wise leadership and the community's collective strength, Wood Haven remained a bastion of light and hope amidst the shadows of the ancient woods.

That is, until the Wildlings found her.

Chapter Four
Kayriss
Home is where the hearth is.

Kayriss looked down at the man thing as his eyes opened again that fresh spring morning. She noticed they fluttered more awake this time as he regained consciousness from the many days he'd been asleep. After the brief flicker of life in the clearing, he'd fallen back asleep as the effort was too much.

He had blearily tried to focus on the surroundings as he awoke, and his gaze rested on the young Elf first. Their eyes pierced through each other; his were sea blue, and hers dark and brown. They had a depth to both colours that the pair immediately fell into. Kayriss swam in oceans azure, with warm water lapping her skin, and the man fell into the warmth of nature's hazel. He picked out all the wild flecks of fiery orange as he lost sight of the world around him.

The moment was brought to a crashing stop when the large mastiff in the room broke eye contact between them. He was rampantly licking at the male's face, happy that he was much more alive.

Kayriss took the time to cast an enchantment to speak with the dog as she was unsure what language this creature lying in her bed spoke, if at all. She hoped the spell would also work on the beautiful man thing.

"Master awake. Thanks you, thanks you! Edgar now has a master like the ancestors!" Kayriss picked up on the name and remembered to call the dog that rather than 'four legs' from now onwards. She held her hands up to the hu-man to show she was not a threat. He was still lying down but now covered mainly with the dog, which was handy because when she finally managed to get him into the bed, she'd stripped him due to the filth on his clothes. Most of it was caused by her in fairness as his muscular frame had to be dragged to her home some way away from where she'd found him.

That first night, she had examined him thoroughly for wounds or what had caused his unconsciousness but found nothing but muscle, sinew and, to her amusement, his manhood. She'd initially thought it some snake and poked at it, such as its girth and length. It was definitely different to the normal Elven appendages used for mating. They were small and efficient, whereas this was large and thick-veined. After realising the boa would not bite her, she'd lifted it inquisitorially, trying to get her finger and thumb to meet on the diameter. It had stiffened to look at her, its weight making its one eye lean towards her. Scared, she'd thrown a fur over it, and as she stepped back, she heard the snake slap on his thigh.

On this new day, she stepped backwards again, the man looking at her as her wings involuntarily unfurled. They matched Kayriss's defenceless posture, showing him safety, but he was not ready to see them. He shuffled back slightly as best he could with a mastiff on him, with a look of shock and bewilderment. After a second, though, his view turned to wonderment at the beauty of the winged creature in front of him.

The wings were delicate and transparent, only visible by the dark brown veins holding the translucent membrane in place. They'd catch the light as they moved, and a rainbow of colours would dance between the veined wings. The fore and hind wings had the same markings, which was standard among her Elven kind.

Realising his revelation, she pulled them behind her and stored them under a hastily grabbed cloak. The man almost seemed upset that their glory had been hidden away.

Disturbed by the sudden movement, Edgar went to the front of the cottage and took his usual stance of guarding his now awake master's resting place. He plopped his bottom down with a thud, clearly annoyed at being made to move. He harumphed a bark not covered by the spell, so Kayriss knew it to be a noise of sheer disgruntlement. Edgar returned to surveilling the forest for threats he knew not of, sliding his hind legs out for comfort.

Isaac, realising his nakedness, moved the blanket further up his body to protect whatever dignity remained.

Kayriss moved to the cooking pot, preparing an aromatic stew and ladling some out in an earthenware bowl for her patient. She knew he must be weak, having had little food or water for the days she'd been watching over him, her nature-based magic keeping him stable. Its smell had not registered with him until now, but it was hearty and full of natural aromas. His stomach also acknowledged the incoming food and grumbled in appreciation. Gingerly, he tested it and then gulped it down as its broth was filled with natural flavours and large lumps of vegetables and herbs.

"Just in thyme," he said, smiling, trying to converse with the winged chef in front of him. She looked quizzically at him.

"I could not feed you whilst unconscious. Unless your kind needs me to chew food first?" Kayriss took a mouthful of food and began mulching it in her mouth, ready to feed it to the man. She did not remember them eating this way if he was actually a hu-man. She was happy to help her patient.

"No, no! It's fine! I meant Thyme. Like the herb," he said, explaining his joke. Swallowing, she confirmed that it was rosemary, and the man laughed for reasons unknown to Kayriss.

"You like it? It is good?" Kayriss asked, hoping her cooking skills were up to his tastes. He nodded back, holding a thumb up, and his mouth was filled with food again. She smiled and waved her thumb back at him, hoping it was the correct gesture.

"What is your name, man thing?" She asked, wanting to know after his mouth was empty and belly full.

He'd stopped eating but looked outwardly confused as he investigated the empty bowl.

"I... I don't actually know."

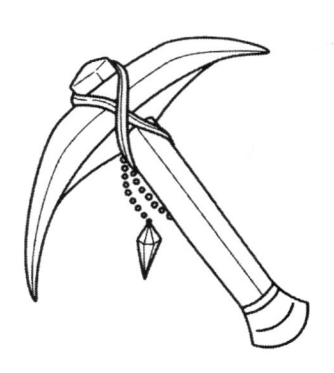

Chapter Five
Grind
Pitter patter.

Luckily for everyone, the cave-in had been localised, and no one else had been hurt except Dront. Mind, he was injured beyond repair.

The young worker had luckily felt no pain, though, because of the force and speed of the impact. Either he'd been squashed before he knew what was happening or crushed completely before his brain engaged. Grind thought that the latter was more probable. However, he was more annoyed that he'd just lent him his best hammer.

'Never getting that back', he thought grumpily as he finished the last of the rat. If it were anyone else, he'd have been more upset. He'd lost his hammer due to Dront. A crowd quickly gathered at the crash site, hoping beyond hope that their clan colleague was alive somehow. Five or so of the

Mine Folk were massed now, looking for any more structural weaknesses and finding none. One was trying to lift the rock ceiling for some reason, and Grind thought that the only reason for doing so was to spatula Dront into a bucket. It most definitely wasn't to get his hammer back.

There was no rhyme or reason for the collapse, so the group looked up at the new opening before them. Some wondered if this could be used for housing or other trade places, with the architect already drafting ideas for the newly found space. Grind wondered if this led to the surface, for the Upsiders to throw their rubbish down in revenge. The architect was hastily scraping old plans and drawing new options for stabilising the area from the paper roll on his belt. 'Quite heartless,' thought Grind, who believed he was the most unsympathetic in the clan. Clearly not, apparently.

He grumbled more unintelligible gripes through his beard as he stood up.

Pitter patter.

The sound caused the group to stare upwards at the mouth of the dark tunnel as a cold shiver of apprehension ran down their spines. It sent a wave of goosebumps cascading across their hairy skin, mostly hidden by the amassed beards. The air inside the cave was heavy with an oppressive darkness, thick and suffocating, enveloping it in a cloak of uncertainty. It was not the normal dankness that they all loved, as a dry air wafted through to them from the darkness beyond. With each passing moment, the sound grew louder, a distant echo reverberating through the tunnel like a haunting melody of impending doom.

Pitter patter.

It was a familiar and alien sound, sending a chill of primal fear coursing through their veins. Grind noticed they were all looking up into the gloom above. None were thinking about their fallen colleague now, distracted totally by the sound.

Which was growing louder.

Pitter patter. Pitter patter.

And faster.

Pitter patter. Pitter patter. Pitter patter.

Their hearts began pounding in their chests, and Grind took a few steps backwards. The rhythm of the sound began to quicken with each echoing footstep drawing closer. More steps back.

Pitter patter. Pitter patter. Pitter patter. Pitter patter.

Every shadow seemed to stretch and contort, twisting into grotesque shapes that danced malevolently along the tunnel's walls. A flicker of panic flashed in their eyes as they strained to see through the inky blackness, searching for any sign of what approached. The darkness remained impenetrable, concealing whatever lurked within its depths.

A darkness that seemed to be moving up the tunnel now, creeping ever closer.

Pitter patter. Pitter patter. Pitter patter. Pitter patter. Pitter patter.

And then, just as suddenly as it had begun, the sound ceased, leaving behind an eerie silence that hung heavy in the air like a suffocating fog. The Mine Folk team stood frozen in place, their breath caught in their throats, consumed by a sense of dread that seemed to seep into their very beards. Their instincts screamed at the group to flee from whatever unseen horror lay ahead, but even as they considered turning to run, a nagging curiosity tugged at the corners of their minds. It whispered of the mysteries and opportunities that lay hidden within the darkness of the tunnel.

A single rat, although somewhat larger than normal, plopped down from the gap and sat watching them. Collectively they sighed with relief, chuckling at their misplaced fear. It hissed violently towards the gathered group, swatting at them with a small clawed paw.

Then, the sound of the thousand giant rats emerging from the tunnel became a cacophony of skittering claws, scraping against rough stone and packed earth. As the rats surged forward, the five miners disappeared entirely under the throng of their sheer mass, all but disappearing from view.

Grind threw himself backwards, away from the scuttling and scratching mass covering his kinsfolk. Amidst the chorus of claws, there was a low, guttural chittering as the rats communicated, their sharp teeth gnashing and their whiskers twitching as they ate the poor Mine Folk within their number. Grind knew they were lost already, taking steps backwards away from the sea of verminous death.

A hand appeared from the furry, pendulous mass, and Grind could see that most of the flesh of the hand had been stripped, the whites of the bones poking through. It was suddenly yanked back inside as vomit filled Grind's mouth.

He swallowed it down and moved as fast as he could. As the horde drew closer to Grind, the tunnel towards his home village beckoned with the light of safety.

Pitter patter. Pitter patter. Pitter patter. Pitter patter. Pitter patter. Pitter patter.

He ran as fast as his legs would carry him, and Grind snatched up a large hammer during his escape. It was typically used for hammering support beams into stone, but he needed to do something, anything, to help the village. He couldn't let the rats get there.

Pitter patter. Pitter patter. Pitter patter. Pitter patter. Pitter patter. Pitter patter. Pitter patter.

Turning for a second, he saw a rat leaping at his throat, but his pivoted swing allowed him to bat the rat away with a crunching finality. They were a second behind him now.

He could feel their breath almost upon him, their stink filling his nostrils. Grind entered the tunnel and, in his flight, smashed at the support beams overhead, causing the tunnel to crash down.

Chapter Six
Ansel
Female found.

Ansel pushed past the gathered group of animals, wanting to see what the clamour was. This was a kerfuffle of the grandest nature, and the hubbub was awash all over the village. Gossip was chattering through the village, mainly by the hedgehogs who loved a natter. When the elder badger first saw the woman, he was unsure of what he was looking at, although a thought, deep within him, gnawed at the back of his mind.

No wings, so not an Elf... Taller than the Mine Folk and no facial hair... No fur, so not of the Wildling clans... No whiskers, so definitely not one of the scourge foxes... Her snout was squashed into her face like the Elven folk they sometimes traded with, but there weren't the delicate wings they all had.

'Maybe they had been cut off somehow? That would be cruel, but fit what he was looking at,' thought Ansel, trying to find a solution to the person. Though something was nagging at the back of his mind, he couldn't place the reason. It couldn't be, could it?

When she rose from the grass, the assembled mass took an audible step backwards alongside a shockwave of squeaks, gasps, chirps and whispered murmurs. 'The gossips were to have a field day', thought Ansel, thinking immediately of house hedgehog.

She was propped up on one arm joint, and Ansel could see that the woman's hair was short but the deepest brown of the darkest burrow, with eyes at the greenest depths of a flourishing forest. Their glinting beauty matched the alabaster skin perfectly, which was unblemished and looked smooth to the clawed touch of the collected animals. 'She would've been classed as beautiful if she had more animal traits', thought Ansel wistfully.

At his knee level, one of the dormice from the lower oak levels sniffed in the woman's direction and looked up quizzically at Ansel. He shrugged, raising one side of its snout, indicating a clear 'dunno' perspective on the situation. Ansel thought this one was Jonathon or maybe John, or it could've been Jon. He was never sure which one from the dormouse clan he was talking to as they all looked very much alike. Ansel nodded in agreement for a reason he was unsure of. Dormice hadn't evolved as much as some of the animal races from the old times, who all became more bipedal in appearance. The mice were still nonverbal and communicated with a sort of interpretive hand gesture and a collection of squeaks, thinking they were fitting in. Most of the community nodded and agreed with them, whilst not knowing what the hell any of them were on about.

Ansel never knew why some animal races evolved as they did and others didn't since the old race had died out. During the quiet years following the last hu-man one's death, many animal species seemed to change with the new space available. Squirrels, foxes, badgers, and otters all developed speech early and then moved to walk upright as if knowing that the world needed a new dominant hu-manoid species.

Most of the facts of what happened were lost in time, though, as it had been many a cycle since one of the old races had walked this island. There were more of them than the Elves and other amassed aberrations left combined from the old years, that was for sure. Those races had settled into separate factions and clans mostly, some above ground, some below in what everyone called the Under. He wasn't sure who or what was dominant now, but he knew that as long as there was peace, it did not matter.

The Elf clans were the quietest, calmest ones and mixed freely with the animals of the new world as they had a mutual respect for nature. If reports were accurate, they were the first to be born, but nothing from the old world much remained now to confirm it. There was talk of the first baby Elf being a female, but again, talk and whispers were hidden as time passed.

The Mine Folk followed, but they quickly fled underground, hiding among the tunnels of the time. They were ridiculed by the old race as 'funny-looking', so they had little to do with the people of the day. Shortly after, the water-born Oceanids sprang up near the extensive coastlines of the island, and then the Night Ones came, but not one Wildling had seen the latter for many a season now. Rumours swirled that they were the cause of the old races' downfall, and their disappearance was welcomed faction-wide. They had a turbulent nature, an apparent gift from their predecessors. Ansel heard talk that the Mine folk had eradicated them in the underground war years ago, but it could not be believed or trusted as this was animal-to-aberration gossip. As Ansel rattled through the different races that could be close to this female, she stirred and pulled herself further upright. She rubbed at her eyes and brought herself awake as a hush descended over the amassed animals.

Ansel could not shake the feeling that this woman was somehow not of this realm as she started looking around at the collected breeds, not seeming to understand who or what she was looking at. The old badger was realising what she was, filling him with dread.

As the woman's eyes began to focus entirely, she looked around, screamed, and passed out once more.

Chapter Seven
Kayriss and Isaac
Isaac be thy name. Now.

She had named him Isaac as he seemed to resemble one, confidently giving him the monicker after he couldn't remember his own. He was grateful as being called 'man thing' and 'hu-man' had gotten old extremely quickly. Isaac could be up and about more each day, and his newfound mobility allowed him to take in his immediate surroundings. As Kayriss busied herself with various balms and concoctions for his 'good health', as she would say, he surveyed the room.

It was a space without inner walls made of the rawest materials. There was a door to the outside world, which Kayriss would cover each night with a large drape of weeping willow directly from the branches above. It kept the home warm and sealed it from the world, leaving it in sheer darkness except for the raging hearth and occasional torch. Isaac was sure there was a fire risk, surrounded by wood and all, but the sconces did not produce heat from the flickering flames, which confused him. He might be unable to remember his name, but he recalled, 'fire equals hot'. He could also see actual trees growing through walls from his vantage point, giving the look that nature herself had created the abode. And he wasn't far wrong.

On the third day, Isaac asked, "Who built this house?" Kayriss pointed excitedly at herself, proud of the architectural achievement.

"I asked the nature spirit to help, and when I called, he helped. Do you like it?" She wanted to know excitedly.

"Yes, it's lovely," Isaac said, smiling. Kayriss beamed and sat back down in an intricately woven wooden chair as she sewed another garment for him. She made a selection of items to replace the ones she found him in, from natural materials stitched with care.

"It's a he. He's called Hovel," she continued, waving at the ceiling. Isaac was more confused now than when he started and decided to leave the line of questioning for a later date, content with his continued examination of the natural home. He was confused as to how a magical home had come into existence, so Isaac asked if there were more like her that helped, hoping the question would bring him more down to earth. And he'd just received a smile in reply, confirming little.

If nature herself had woven this dwelling, it had crafted a sanctuary that harmonised seamlessly with the surrounding wilderness that he had seen so far. The entrance to the house was concealed externally behind an ivy veil, which parted gracefully to allow Kayriss access, and a doorway carved into the trunk of multiple trees entwined with each other. It had an earthy scent, and a gentle breeze whispered through the canopy above. The main chamber was constantly bathed in a soft, dappled light filtering through the leafy canopy overhead. The walls were alive with creeping vines, their tendrils stretching and curling like reaching fingers, holding the home in a safe embrace. He was even sure he had seen the vines pass items without a word to Kayriss as she needed them—a cooking herb or another ingredient for another concoction. Moss carpeted the floor, offering a soft and springy path underfoot. The furniture appeared grown rather than built, with chairs and tables crafted from intricately woven branches and roots, each piece uniquely shaped by the hands of nature. Throughout the house, natural elements blended seamlessly with magical enchantments as a bubbling stream meandered through the living space, its crystal-clear waters alive with colourful fish and aquatic plants. Sunbeams danced upon the water's surface, creating ever-shifting patterns of light and shadow.

The open room nestled within the embrace of the trees, its walls formed by intertwining branches and fragrant blooms. A cosy nest of leaves and feathers served as the bed Isaac was in, cradling him in comfort as he recovered. As he recuperated, he studied the youthful woman, who he discovered was sixteen hundred cycles old, which in old race years was about four hundred. Isaac could not believe the woman in front of him was more than mid-twenties, nearer than he felt to be his age. He'd never seen anyone like her before, and he could not remember much of his life before waking up here.

Never known anyone even close.

Not anyone that had beauty such as hers.

She seemed to glide on air wherever she went, silent with every footstep. He found himself astounded by her appearance, too, as her delicate features carried the definition of beauty under the occasional smear of mud, of course. Her hair was long and flowing, the colour of sun-dappled leaves which cascaded down her back. The chaotic tangle flowed wildly with each step, flowing like a stream over hidden rocks. Her eyes danced through various natural colours, depending on her mood. Today, they were the colour of moss-kissed emeralds, shining with an inner light that reflected the obvious depth of her soul and the boundless love she held for the natural world. They were windows to a spirit as wild and untamed as the forest yet tempered by a serene wisdom far beyond her years.

Everything she wore was created from natural colours, but she favoured greens, from the garland she always wore on her head to the various cloaks and dresses he'd seen. Adorned in garments woven from the finest natural fibres and adorned with intricate patterns inspired by the flora and fauna of the forest, she appeared as though she were a part of the landscape. A cloak of forest green draped elegantly around her shoulders every time she left her home, its hem trailing behind her like the train of a woodland queen. She seemed to have an undomesticated beauty, a lush landscape unleashed into the woodland.

Those wings.

Straight from a butterfly, the translucent membrane was only visible due to the dark brown veins holding their form. They had a remarkable beauty, even though they had no place on such a small woman.

A woman Isaac felt himself falling for with each day passing.

Chapter Eight
Grind
Bront lays blame.

      Grind stood, dusting himself off as a large rock bounced off his broad shoulder. Shaking the dust from his beard, he looked back to see the total collapse of their recently expanded tunnel. The dust had begun settling as a pebble bounced from the top of the rubble pile. It clattered down and came to rest at his foot. Grind pressed his ear to the rockslide to listen for any sound of the encroached death rat horde but heard nothing but the settling of the rocks grating against one another. The 'siss' of small granules reminded him of a timer, the sand slowly running out

      The clan elder Bront would not be pleased with the destruction, even though it was to save the village. Grind wasn't even sure if anyone would believe the horde of rats that had appeared out of nowhere, and they would definitely not understand their almost hive-like actions. It was a thronged mass that moved as one but solely intended to eat everything in their path. Grind shuddered at the thought of it reaching the Mine Folk home as some of his clan gathered to see what had happened, the noise still ringing in his ears. A wave of murmurs rippled through the crowd as Bront pushed towards the front of the clan, his nose reddening with anger.

"Grind! What the onyx have you done, you quartzite slag heap! Where is your crew, you utter shiteslate!" Roared the town elder. The collected shock from the amassed people was evident as they gasped in unison at the shocking, swear-filled rant coming from the ordinarily polite council member. Grind watched as the wave of beards moved like flowing water, and they all started gasping and muttering behind the mix of braids. One of the Mine Folk picked up their child's beard and stuffed it in their ears so they would not hear more of the horrendous expletives. Taking a breath, Bront continued as the politician in him returned.

"A section of our meticulously crafted passage has collapsed, cutting off vital access to our resources, you complete rockrotter! And all that's left here is you, a pile of basalt-brained pepplepiss! Explain yourself at once!" Bront wanted answers, so Grind gave them without holding back, especially since he did not deserve such obscenities.

Bront, the venerable elder of the village, his beard a cascade of silver, twitched with no emotion as the moments before the cave-in were detailed. He was surveying the wreckage as Grind's story unfolded with a furrowed brow and a heavy heart. He was a great leader but sometimes quick to rile, his stern countenance betraying his deep concern for the safety and prosperity of his people. As Grind finished his tale, Bront stood motionless as the crowd considered the events, hushed chatter ruffling both beard and braids.

"If what you are saying is true, and I sincerely doubt the crag-crapper is telling it how it actually happened. I am concerned we have lost some of our brothers to the actions of this stone-cursed granite grumbler. We must convene the rest of the council immediately." And with that, he turned and stormed off, bomping past the other Mine folk, who were beginning to disperse.

Grind looked out at his village, safe from the horde behind the rock fall.

Stonemarsh, their current living district, captured the sturdy, enduring nature of the Mine Folk community, nestled amidst the rugged terrain of the Under cavern. Beneath the earth's surface, a labyrinthine network of tunnels opened into the sprawling underground village, the bustling heart of the Mine Folk clan. Here, amidst the cool embrace of the stone walls, artisans plied their trade, their skills passed down through generations. The cool, earthy, and slightly musty air was alive with the clang of hammers on anvils, the hiss of molten metal, and the rhythmic scrape of leather against wood.

Traders bartered their wares in bustling market squares, their voices echoing off the cavern walls as they haggled over precious ores and finely crafted goods. It was not just the industry that captivated the senses; the village was bathed in the ethereal glow of iridescent light emanating from veins of luminous minerals that snaked their way through the very rock, casting a shimmering rainbow of colours across the stone walls. This natural illumination served to brighten the underground expanse and inspired awe and wonder in all who call this subterranean enclave home, making it a hub of activity at all hours. When joined with the many hearths and fired sconces, this lit the vast cavern as bright as the Upsider's daylight.

Here, amidst the flickering hues of the underground world, the Mine Folk thrived, their ingenuity and craftsmanship illuminating the darkness with the brilliance of their creations.

However, Grind worried.

What else was down here if the rats were more giant and now a pack animal when attacking?

Was there something worse yet to come? Was his clan in further trouble?

Chapter Nine
Ansel
The pirate raid/trade.

Ansel looked down at the female and instinctively knew she did not belong. She matched nothing from the other, more traditionally hu-manoid races. He tried to put the fact that she resembled one of the old olds from his mind as he took his references from stories handed down. Tales of their callousness, their hatred, their willingness to kill. He perished the thought that they were coming back.

This woman looked like she would barely hurt a dormouse.

Ansel paced anxiously beneath the dense canopy of the ancient oak trees as the woman slept, his fur bristling with worry like autumn leaves caught in an unrelenting wind. His gnarled claws tapped nervously against the tree bark, a rhythmic echo of his troubled thoughts. He realised he was clawing at the wood and had begun to leave large scratch marks under the repetitious clawing.

For many cycles, too many to remember, tales of the hu-mans, or the old race had been whispered among the elders, stories steeped in shadow and warning, their presence feared and revered in equal measure. And now, as the spectre of their return loomed over Wood Haven like a gathering storm, Ansel's fears threatened to consume him whole. He pushed the feeling down, trying to keep his outward appearance the epitome of serenity.

He fretted over the implications of her being here. Were the hu-mans resurging? He feared the violence and upheaval they might bring to their tranquil village. In the depths of his worry, he wondered if her arrival spelt the unravelling of the peace his kind had safeguarded for generations.

Yet she slept. Soundly. They could not wake her.

The various Wildlings tried everything they knew to bring the female around, but the sleep state would not break.

As she slept, her long brown locks cascaded like a river of molten chocolate onto the down-feathered pillow. Both looked as soft to the touch as each other, but the woman's hair caught glimmers of sunlight that filtered through the enchanted canopy above. When they were briefly open, her eyes shone with the hue of a clear summer sky and sparkled with an almost gem-like brilliance.

She must've stood feet above all the gathered animals and, at Ansel's best estimate, must be at a height of five foot eight inches. What little movement she did make was fluidic in its grace, akin to one of the woodland Elves.

She'd been found dressed in an attire foreign to the wildlings as it was not functional in nature. It was a tapestry of ethereal elegance, woven from fabrics unseen by claw and paw. The white and blue of the cloth were hues borrowed from the dreams of sleeping stars and draped her in a flowing dress that shimmered with the iridescence of moonlit dew.

**

The sun had dipped low over the treetops, casting long, golden beams across the shimmering river. The waters were calm, gently cradling the small flotilla of boats manned by the most daring crew ever to sail these waters, or so the crew told everyone they met, at least. The rivers were the domain of the Otter Pirate Clan, the rowdy band of river otters who had taken to the grand and noble art of pirating, though their version was more playful than perilous.

Captain Browntail, a spry otter with a bright, mischievous gleam in his eye, stood proudly at the helm of the lead boat. His whiskers twitched with excitement as he shouted orders to his crew, a dozen or so equally enthusiastic otters who eagerly responded with a chorus of "Aye, aye, Captain!"

"Steady as she goes, crew! Keep yer eyes peeled for the flag of Ansel the badger, our ally on these treacherous waters! Aaaaarrrrrrrr!" Browntail called out, brandishing a wooden spoon like a cutlass.

The otters scrambled about, adjusting the sails made from a material weaved by the Wildlings of Woodhaven, their home from home. They secured the barrels of fresh fish and shiny trinkets they had gathered during their latest "raid" on a nearby town. They said 'raid' as it sounded much more piratey than 'trading'. Each one of the otters was dressed in their finest pirate garb. Bandanas tied haphazardly around their heads and fashioned belts made of purest cat hide holding up pouches full of river stones, which they liked to imagine were precious gems.

They weren't true pirates in the dangerous sense. The River Otter Clan was more about the spirit of adventure than actual marauding. Their raids were harmless affairs, exchanges of fish for stories, shiny stones for berries, and occasional help to those they visited along the way. They were headed to Wood Haven and had their regular trade raid with Ansel today. He had always welcomed the otters' playful antics with a warm smile.

As they rounded the bend, the village came into view, and they immediately saw that it was a hubbub of activity. Something seemed afoot, and Captain Browntail knew he could help. They clearly were in dire need of some piratey otter action.

"Cutlass, me lass! Ready the..." he paused, forgetting what he was saying as he became briefly distracted by one of their arch enemy circling above. They were all soggy feathered scoundrels to the otter pirate clan. The vicious, thieving seagulls. Scurvywhiskered clamshell crackers! Browntail pointed a paw to his unpatched eye and then to the circling seagull, making sure it was aware that he had seen it. Cutlass smiled back at her captain and got about, making ready to dock. Or whatever he was going on about.

The otters could see Ansel, a giant, grizzled badger, standing on the shore, his paws crossed over his chest. A bemused grin appeared on his face as he spotted the familiar sight of Browntail and his crew approaching.

"Prepare to dock, ye scallywags!" The captain bellowed, thrusting an arm merrily across his chest, fist-pumping high. His voice was filled with exaggerated bravado, and the crew sprang into action, paddling furiously with their webbed paws until the boat bumped gently against the soft, muddy bank.

Browntail leapt onto the shore with a flourish, landing gracefully before the elder.

"Ansel the badger, ye ol' sea dog! We've come bearing treasures from the far reaches of the river!" he declared, holding out a paw full of shiny pebbles and a particularly huge fish.

Ansel chuckled, his deep voice rumbling like distant thunder, but immediately, the otter knew something was amiss.

"Welcome back, Captain. It's always a pleasure to see you and your crew. The villagers will gladly trade, I mean, succumb to your raiding party as always."

Browntail's playful demeanour shifted slightly as he straightened up, a serious look crossing his face.

"Aye, but ye seem troubled, Ansel," Browntail said, dropping the pirate act out of concern for his old friend. "Can we help ye at all?" he offered.

"No, don't worry at all. Something has come up, but we are awaiting a solution. I think it is above your station, my swarthy friend." Replied Ansel, trying to asway the obvious concern in his friend's face.

"Ok, but we've got news too that's not as shiny as these pebbles, I'm afraid. On our way here, we passed by the underground settlement of the Mine Folk, those sturdy moles who dig in the hills just beyond your woods. There be trouble brewing there."

Ansel's eyes narrowed with concern. "What sort of trouble?"

Browntail motioned for his crew to gather around, and the otters huddled close as he recounted what they had witnessed. "The river was low near their settlement as if their floor below had shifted, and not for the better. When we passed the area above where their tunnels were, we saw that many of their rubbish holes had collapsed. The ground around them was cracked, and the trees around the area looked withered, like something's poisoned the earth. We don't speak to them, as you know, but it looked horrid from our viewpoint."

Ansel listened intently, his brow furrowing. The Mine Folk were known for their resilience but would struggle even if something had gone wrong with the earth itself. "Did you see any signs of what caused it?" he asked. Browntail shook his head. "No, but there was a strange smell in the air, like burnt wood, but earthier, if that makes sense. It was strongest near the biggest tunnel."

Ansel stroked his chin thoughtfully. "This is troubling news indeed. The Mine Folk's tunnels run deep, and if something's gone awry down there, it could affect more than just their settlement. Thank you for bringing this to my attention, Browntail."

The otter captain nodded solemnly. He ushered Ansel away from his crew and motioned for the larger Wildling to bend down. Whispering in his ear, he said, "We might just be playin' at being pirates, Ansel, but we know when somethin' serious is afoot. We'll keep an eye on the river in case anything else strange happens."

Ansel patted him on the back, his large paw almost knocking the otter off balance. "You may be playing pirates, but your hearts are in the right place. I'll send word to the elders and possibly gather a group to go and offer our help to the Mine Folk. Perhaps with all our heads together, we can figure out what's going on. After we've sorted out our little issue, that is," he whispered back.

Browntail wanted to pry but left it alone as he had never seen Ansel so worried. With the gravity of the situation hanging over them, the otters and villagers set about their trades as usual. However, the usual jovial atmosphere was tinged with an undercurrent of concern. The otters exchanged their fish and shiny stones for baskets of berries, bundles of herbs, and bolts of cloth for their sails.

As the sun set and the evening stars began to twinkle above, the thought of the Mind Folks' plight lingered in everyone's minds.

The River Otter Clan prepared to depart; Ansel stood by the shore, watching them load their boats. "Browntail, if you or your crew spot anything else strange on the river, come back and tell me right away," he instructed.

"Aye, aye, we will, Ansel," he promised, waving his wooden spoon in a mock salute. "The River Otter Clan never shies away from adventure! Or from helping those in need!"

With that, the otters pushed off from the shore, their boats gliding smoothly onto the starlit river. Immediately, the crew burst into song, filling the night sky with cries of pirate adventures.

♪ Down the river fast we glide
Otter crew by my side
Trading pebbles tales of fun
Life beneath the golden sun

♪ Sails unfurled wind in fur
Chasing dreams as waters stir
Whispering wind tells our fate
Each pebble's a treasure great

♪ Pirate otters brave and free
Riding waves of mystery
Pebbles clink and stories flow
Adventures where the rivers go...

The village of Wood Haven slowly faded into the distance as the otters began their journey back upstream, their playful banter receding into the night air as they disappeared.

Ansel returned his attention to the female. Even awake for the second she was, she carried herself with a regal poise that bespoke strength and serenity. But he couldn't shake the feeling of coincidence of her arrival and the darkness rising above the Mine Folk.

Ansel urgently needed the woodland healer they often traded with, as their knowledge of medicines was not effective enough to bring the woman around. Despatching one of the messenger ferret folk would be the quickest way, as Ansel needed answers. He chose the fastest of their number, a ferret called Ferris.

"Please fetch the elf druid Kayriss, post haste."

The ferret saluted and diligently obeyed, sensing the urgency of the ask. Ansel would have answers soon when Kayriss arrived.

Chapter Ten
Kayriss
Two become one.

Kayriss felt pleased with herself as she looked at Isaac, who was fully healed and ready to venture forth. She had grown to like his lumbering size as he stood seven clear inches taller than her.

Isaac felt like a towering oak tree next to her slight form, even though they seemed similar in age. His sturdy limbs would have given him a commanding presence were it not for his gentle nature, which appealed greatly to the smaller Elf.

His long brown hair cascaded down his broad shoulders like the branches of a mighty tree swaying in the wind, each strand resembling the rough bark of an ancient oak. He often tied it back, and the ponytail was equally as attractive as it showed his full facial features and his smile. It would make Kayriss almost swoon, and the first time she saw it, she giggled audibly at its beauty. His muscles rippled beneath his skin, showing their powerful strength like one of the bear clans, giving him a formidable power reminiscent of nature's most majestic creatures. His piercing blue eyes gleamed like the deep, clear waters of a tranquil lake, reflecting both care and determination behind his lost memory. Now healed, his every stride moved with the grace of a prowling panther, his steps as silent as the whispering breeze through the forest. In essence, he embodied the wilderness's raw power and timeless beauty.

Kayriss fell.

At the beginning of the second week, she woke in the deepest night with an urge she'd not felt before. Moving to his side, she carefully pulled back the furs covering him to reveal his naked form. She heard a murmur of question from Edgar as the mastiff was roused from his sleep. He looked over at the pair quizzically, wondering what was happening, but felt no threat from either.

He looked on as Kayriss unfurled her wings, not fully understanding what the two masters were doing. He slumped back down to the floor and fell asleep, happy they were both safe.

Kayriss ran her fingers delicately up his thigh and took him in her hand, raising him to full arousal until he stood at full standing. This time, she did not feel shock and surprise, but a hot wanting that stirred inside her. She felt the blood in his member warm to her touch, and it excited her further.

Fluttering her wings excitedly, she removed her clothing, exposing her form underneath. Isaac stirred in her grip but stayed asleep as she let him go briefly. An immediate sadness at the lost touch filled her, and she unfurled her wings to full spread.

The rapid buzzing that accompanied flight gave the room sound, but not enough to bother the sleeping male. She rose on her delicate wings and flew over him, slowly lowering herself.

Onto him and into her.

She had never felt anything like it before. She had played around with the other scattered Elves, but they had more slender appendages and never gave her the joy she'd heard about. As she took Isaac inside her, she realised that no longer would she need the Elven boys.

The feeling of warmth around his penis roused Isaac from his slumber, and he was shocked that his vision was filled with the now-naked Kayriss. In her nudity, she wore the innocence of nature itself, unencumbered by the constraints of mortal cloth. She was a vision of purity and beauty, a manifestation of the magic that breathed life back into Isaac days before. She was captivating with her otherworldly charm, her breathtaking elegance, astride him.

Like the finest porcelain, her skin was untouched by the mud and nature. Isaac was accustomed to seeing smudges on the skin, which he could see daily. The bareness of her body glowed with a delicate luminosity, kissed by the gentle caress of the moonlight filtering through the forest canopy. Every curve and contour of her form was a testament to the harmonious balance of grace and strength. She looked down at him, and her long, entanglement of hair cascaded down her front, covering her bare breasts. Their eyes met, and Isaac felt her look deep within him as he was deep within her.

Moments passed.

Isaac noticed that winding up over her pubic mound was a subtle yet intricate pattern of delicate tattoos that seemed to dance across her skin like vines in a sunlit glade, moving as she breathed with fluidity and poise that was both mesmerising and ethereal. It snaked up and around her body, a vine with lush leaves budding at various places. Isaac felt her presence as an intoxicating elixir as the fragrance of wildflowers in bloom assailed him.

Gently, he reached up and moved her hair away from her breasts, exposing her entirely once more. Following the line of the tattoo up and around her body, she shivered as his touch found a nerve long left unfelt. It wracked through her form, and he felt her internally clench as nerve endings fired.

Shocked that he'd been taken but aroused nonetheless, he arced his hips up, almost instinctively, gaining a deeper purchase within her.

Moaning, Kayriss began rhythmically moving up and down his length with the aid of her wings to lift her to the brink of releasing his penis, but then sliding back down the shaft, feeling both his sheer size and girth within her.

It wasn't long before Isaac and Kayriss cried out with blessed release.

Chapter Eleven
Grind
The council of beards.

Grind stood before the council, regaling them again with the details of the terminal incident an hour ago, the gravity of which had finally hit him.

When he reached the part where the rats ate his crew, he stopped, taking a moment to recover his train of explanation. They were a good team; he kept describing them in the current tense as if a rat swarm had not just eaten them and about the other one that was crushed.

Mine Folk were strong, and if he broke in front of the gathered council, they would debate that more so than the terrible deaths of his team. Of his co-workers. He snorted the feelings down and thumped his chest in defiance against the rising outburst of despair, sending his beard into a ruffled frenzy.

In the heart of the cavernous hall, amidst the echoing caverns and the flickering torchlight, Grind stood with as stout a frame as he could as the council deliberated. The nine-strong council were discussing animatedly as Grind watched all their beards quiver with conversation. They spoke over each other as the crowd in the gallery waited for the wise decision to come. Occasionally, Grind would pick up an expletive from Bront, who'd fire him a look of anger and annoyance.

Dirt-eater... Copper blooded coward... Magma mouthed ore for brains... were all slung in Grind's direction.

Grind was burdened by a weight far more significant than any mere stone, and his grizzled beard, once a badge of honour and resilience, now hung heavy with the dust of grief, each strand a silent witness to the depths of his sorrow. And still, he fought to show the strength of his people. If he showed the internal weakness, Bront might assume that he'd made up the entire sorry state of affairs, as he had nothing to actually prove his story physically.

With furrowed brow and eyes as dark as the depths of the earth, he stoically stood as a witness, his foot tapping an echo of the hollowed cadence of loss. Once, he had been surrounded by kin and comrades, family and friends, their laughter ringing through the halls like the chime of hammers on anvils. But now, in the council chambers, their voices were but whispers carried away on a chill mountain breeze, leaving behind an emptiness that gnawed at his soul like a hungry beast. Standing alone amidst the silent stone, memories of the rat attack and lives lost flickered like fading embers in the recesses of his mind, each a bittersweet reminder of what had been lost. He clenched his fists, feeling the weight of his grief settle like a leaden cloak upon his shoulders, threatening to crush him beneath its unbearable burden.

Yet, even in the depths of his despair, a flicker of determination burned within him like a stubborn flame refusing to be extinguished. With a heavy heart and eyes glistening with unshed tears, he vowed to honour the memory of his fallen colleagues, to carry their legacy forward through the darkness that now enveloped him. Though the road ahead was fraught with peril and uncertainty, he knew he would not face it alone, for the bonds forged in calamity and tempered by loss were more substantial than any hardship fate could throw his way.

He hoped. Bront hushed the collected beards again and rescinded the voices to a mixture of hairy, muffled guffaws.

"Grind. You are to reopen the tunnel and continue the excavation. If everything you said is true, then all the rats must have gotten squashed in the tunnel as you ran away. If not, then you will be tried for crimes against our building code."

The words stung him to his very core as shock rippled through the beards of his clan folk. He had not 'ran away' like a coward. He'd run to save them all. Yet he did not feel like the hero he believed himself to be.

"I saved you all! You'd all be dead by now if they'd got in here! Bront, listen to me you, mossbacked crag dweller!" Grind bellowed. The gathered masses gasped again, and a sea of murmurings began, such was the shock at Grind's outburst.

Bront was about to scream at him when the first rat fell from the ceiling.

Chapter Twelve
Ansel
Attackers at the gate.

The ferret had left a full day ago, and Ansel was worried for the female, who was still sleeping unnervingly quietly.

As darkness fell, he heard the first hoots from the knight owl patrols in the middle of the night. He jumped up and threw on the nearest robes to see what they were clamouring about. The moon hung high in the sky, a pale crescent casting a ghostly glow over the village. An ominous stillness pervaded the night, broken only by the rustle of leaves as a cold wind swept through the narrow streets. The villagers slept soundly, unaware of the malevolent shadows that had begun to creep toward their homes.

Ansel stood, his old bones aching from the chill, but his keen eyes remained sharp as he scanned the darkness beyond his door. The owls pointed into the night while flying down towards him. Landing with an audible thump, Hooth, the youngest of the owl guards, pointed low into the woods.

Four hu-manoids were making their way, tree to tree, towards the village. Ansel knew instinctively that they were not the friendly woodland Elves they knew of. They were Elves, but not like the benevolent, nature-bound kin the villagers occasionally traded with. The Night Ones were a twisted breed, corrupted by the unknown and driven by a hunger for chaos and blood. Their skin was ashen, their eyes black as the void, and they moved through shadows like phantoms. No one knew why they had turned to evil, but their legend was one of fear, spoken of only in hushed tones.

He also knew that more would follow.

Ansel tightened his grip on the ancient staff passed down through generations of village elders. It hummed with a faint light, its protective wards a small comfort in the face of what was to come. Behind him, lying on a simple bed, was the woman the community had found. The Night Ones seemed to be aiming directly towards her. She slept peacefully, unaware of the danger closing in.

Outside, the first Night Ones slipped into the village, their movements nearly silent. They spread out, fanning through the village as the rest of the owls swooped down.

The Night Ones below seemed unaware of their descent as their claws gleamed in a streaking attack run.

Blades gleamed in their dark Elven hands, and their black eyes shone with malice. They moved with preternatural speed, cutting down the few unlucky villagers who crossed their path. The air began to fill with the scent of blood and the sound of muffled cries.

Hooth got to one of the invaders and slashed his claws down his back. The weight of the giant owl brought the Elf crashing to the ground where he lay still, the rented back gushing with dark blood. Hooth moved with a quickness born of ancestral hunting but was not fast enough to see the second attacker approach. Watching from above, Ansel muttered a prayer under his breath and touched the staff to the ground. The wards around the village flared into life, an invisible barrier rising like glistening walls. It would hold for a time, stopping any more of the attackers from getting to his townsfolk, but he knew it wouldn't be enough to stop them.

A further prayer and the staff glowed into life once more.

Hooth saw the Elf fly at him; a dark glistening blade raised high above his head. He knew that there would not be time to dodge this and prepared for the worst. A glowing silver protective disc flared into life between them, and the Elf bounced off it harmlessly as Hooth raised his wings in defence.

"Thank you, Ansel!" He cried up, aware that his life would continue.

A loud crash sounded outside, followed by a low, guttural chant. The barriers surrounding the village were being assaulted; they flashed and trembled with each blow. More Night Ones began assaulting the wards as Ansel turned back to the door, the staff glowing brighter in his hands. The badger stood tall, his back straight, and his staff alighted with power. He knew he would fight to the last breath to protect his village, but he also knew the odds seemed against him.

Hooth and other owllings were fighting furiously below as a barrier to their left exploded outwards, the ward shattering in a burst of sparks. The Night Ones poured into the village, their dark forms filling the area. Ansel met them with a cry of defiance, his staff blazing as he unleashed a wave of magic that sent the first of them crashing into the walls of a hut.

The Night Ones were relentless. They moved as one, a swarm of shadows that flowed around Ansel's defences, their blades flashing in the dim light. Ansel fought with a ferocity that belied his age, his staff spinning and crackling with energy. Each strike landed precisely, felling one of the twisted Elves, but two more took the place of everyone he cut down.

A blade slashed across Ansel's arm, drawing a line of blood. He gritted his teeth against the pain and struck back, but the injury slowed him. The Night Ones pressed their advantage, driving him back step by step. Ansel roared, summoning the last of his strength. He raised his staff high, and the ground beneath the Night Ones erupted in a blaze of holy light. Screams of agony filled the air as the Dark Elves were incinerated, their forms dissolving into ash.

It was just not enough.

A larger Night One, taller and more fearsome than the rest, stepped forward. His black eyes glittered with cruel amusement as he dodged Ansel's desperate attack.

He drove his sword through the elder's chest.

Ansel gasped, the world dimming around him, as the elf twisted the blade, a satisfied sneer on his lips. "Foolish animal," he hissed. "Your efforts are in vain. We will find her."

With a trembling breath, Ansel collapsed, his staff falling from his grasp. The light within it flickered and died, plunging the area into a slick darkness. The leader of the Night Ones stepped over Ansel's body, his gaze turning to where the female was still sleeping.

He started to climb towards her, blooded sword in hand.

Chapter Thirteen
Kayriss
Hovel awakens.

Kayriss had never slept so soundly.

Isaac had fallen asleep with her cradled in his arms after their night time activities. He'd watched her fall asleep as he stroked her hair and wings as she snuggled into him. He'd watched as the delicate wings retracted and furled themselves up against her back. They felt soft to touch and he'd traced the darker veins for a while before he himself fell deeply asleep.

Isaac groggily awoke hours later as the sunbeams broke through the room's natural ceiling. Looking around, his eyes were brought directly into someone he wasn't expecting. A large furred creature standing on its hind legs was looking at him quizzically, its head tilted to one side. It stood about two feet tall and was dressed in clothing that was woven into a tunic and shorts.

Isaac blinked a few times, thinking he was still in some sort of weird dream, brought on by the druidic soup he'd been living on.

"Message for Kayriss!" chirped the hu-manoid furry thing, reaching to prod at the still-sleeping elf.

"What are you? A stoat? A weasel?" Asked Isaac, who really wanted to know at this point. Plus, it was a way of confirming that he had, indeed, not gone completely insane.

"I'm a ferret! We're stoatally different and weasily recognised!" Laughter exploded from the fluffy thing and it fell about crying with guffaws at his joke. Kayriss stirred and looked over at the ferret, not worried about showing her, or Isaac's nakedness.

"Well, hello, little furred one. How are you today?" Kayriss said as she sat upright. She reached high and stretched to her full length to ease the morning awake. Isaac smiled at the sight of her and placed a hand tenderly on her hip. As Kayriss's hands lowered, she placed one of hers on his.

"I have a message from Wood Haven! They are in need of a..." His words were cut short as a noise outside disturbed them all. It was slight, but to the druid, a difference in the wood she lived in. Jumping off the bed, she placed her hand on the woodland floor and closed her eyes. To Isaac, she seemed to be listening to something unseen, and he glanced at the ferret, who was shrugging.

"Get dressed. There may be trouble coming. I sense footsteps." The anxiety in her voice was audible, so Isaac did as he was ordered, a building concern in himself, too. Kayriss stood and threw on her clothing, unfurling her wings as she did. She moved with the same delicate grace but with an urgency to each step this time. When she reached the door, it opened without her touching it, leaving it wide open. Isaac could not see what was through the door, so he followed after her, one boot still in hand. As he left her home, he heard the words;

"Let us take him, Druid. This need not end in a fight." Ten armoured warriors stood before the young elf, the metal of their dark suits sending glimmers of purple bouncing around the tree line. They looked out of place in the natural environment, a direct colour contrast to the world they were standing in. As Isaac tried to get more detail, an arrow flew over his head. It was a clear warning to them both that trouble was expected and, more so, threatened.

"Why do you want him? Actually, you need not answer. He's mine." Her words bore a force and security that Isaac appreciated, as he had no intention of leaving her side.

"Fine. We'll take him ourselves. We warned you, Elf of the Wood." And all ten of the knights advanced in synchronicity. Kayriss flew upwards immediately, casting a spell as she left the ground. The warriors levelled their gazes at her, and some raised bows to fight. Before they could, though, the floor around their feet rumbled as roots ripped from the earth and entangled them, stopping their advance. A few arrows were loosed at Kayriss, but she could easily dodge them due to the imbalance of the earth below the archers.

"Hovel, time to move!" she shouted, and Isaac wondered who she was talking to. It wasn't long before he had an answer he could not comprehend.

"I was sleeping quite soundly, thank you, although your moans and murmurs kept me awake!" boomed a voice from around them. It had the sound of bark scratching against stone and the flowing of water along a riverbed.

Isaac turned to see Kayriss's home begin to lift from the floor.

Chapter Fourteen
Grind
Infestation.

Grind's breath hung in the chilly air as he watched the rat snarl towards the council. The ceiling of the underground tunnels seemed to press down on them now, and Grind waited for a possible collapse—the very earth would be lost. Bront looked over at Grind, who returned a look that said, 'I did say, but not now,' to the older Mine Folk leader.

Bront stood and leaned heavily on his gnarled staff; his eyes narrowed with the wisdom of his years, but he could not recall anything close to this situation. He was a city councillor, not a warrior. They had no need of them in Stonemarsh. He stood solid, though, and stared down the vicious rat. To his side was his son, Granite, who, without warning brought his stone chair crashing down upon the rat, squelching it dead almost immediately.

"They're coming," Grind muttered, his voice as gravelly as the stones beneath their feet.

A distant, rumbling noise echoed through the tunnels, like a thousand claws scraping against rock. Grind's heart quickened, knowing that familiar pitter-patter and what it brought. He exchanged a grim look with the elder. The warning he'd tried to offer had come too late; the sea of rats was already coming.

"Hold fast, lads!" Grind shouted, his voice ringing through the darkened caverns, rallying the dozen or so Mine Folk standing with him. "We give not an inch of our home to these cursed vermin!"

He motioned to his wife to move the children safely away as Grind and the few around him formed a tight defensive arc, blocking the main thoroughfare to the homestead. They were picking up anything they could use as a weapon, but fortunately, most were the artisans who carried their tools. Hammers, knives and the occasional axe appeared, and they gleamed in the faint light of the glowing moss that clung to the walls. The tunnels were eerily silent for a heartbeat, the only sound the steady breathing of the Mine Folk.

Grind snatched a spare pickaxe from a nearby miner and stood ready.

Then, the darkness seemed to move.

The first wave hit like a flood. Rats, each the size of a small dog and with eyes glowing a sickly red, surged forward, their fur matted and slick with some foul substance. They moved as one, a living tide driven by a single, malevolent will.

Grind roared and met the onslaught with a mighty swing of his new pickaxe. Its sharpened point cleaved through the thick hide of the lead rat, sending it sprawling with a shriek. For every rat that fell, three more surged forward, their teeth gnashing and claws scrabbling for purchase on the stone.

"By the Stone Fathers, there's too many of 'em!" one of the gathered Mine Folk yelled, his voice tinged with panic as he hacked at the endless wave. Grind saw one of his clan swing too early and was swallowed up in the furry throng, his screaming echoing through the hall.

"Hold your ground!" Grind barked, his pickaxe flashing in the dim light. But even he felt a tremor of fear. The rats didn't fight like animals; they moved with eerie precision, their attacks coordinated as if directed by a single, unseen hand.

He had seen this before, but not so close.

Grind watched as another of his clan tried to run, but his legs gave out beneath him as he stumbled on a loose stone, his makeshift weapon crashing to the floor. He clawed at the ground, desperate to rise, but it was too late. The rats were upon him. First, a trickle, then a flood of fur and gnashing teeth. His screams echoed through the cavern, rising in pitch as the swarm engulfed him, their sharp claws tearing at his flesh, their relentless jaws gnawing through leather, skin, and bone. His voice choked into a gurgling gasp as the weight of the horde buried him, his body lost beneath the writhing sea of vermin.

Swamped and swarmed. More fell, and they kept coming.

Grind steadied himself, choosing to fight to the death rather than run and fall like that. He looked over at Bront as the council leader raised his staff, the carved runes along its length glowing with a deep, earthen light. With a guttural chant, the elder slammed the staff down, and the ground beneath the rats rippled. Stone spikes shot up from the floor, impaling several of the creatures in an instant. The sheer mass of rats simply flowed around the spikes, unfazed, their numbers seemingly endless.

"I can't hold this spell long. Do something!" Bront warned, his voice strained with the effort of maintaining the incantation. "Think of something! It's like they know what we're planning before we do!"

Grind gritted his teeth, his mind racing. "Then we outthink them," he muttered, scanning the tunnel they had come from. The rats were pressing closer, forcing them all back step by step.

If they reached the village...

No, they couldn't let that happen. His people had lived in these tunnels for generations, carving their homes from the rock, thriving in the deep places of the earth. He wouldn't let a swarm of oversized vermin take that from them.

"Bront, we need to collapse the tunnel behind them," Grind called over the din of battle. "It's the only way to stop them from overrunning us! Bring down the ceiling of the council chamber!"

The elder hesitated, his eyes flicking to the carved stone archway leading to a neighbouring village. "If we do that, we trap ourselves in here with no access to the other villages!"

"Aye, but if the rats have come from that village, there may be little left..." Grind's words hung momentarily in the air, and Bront knew he could be right. "Better we fight them here, in the open, than let them crawl into our homes and slaughter our kin."

Bront nodded, grim resolve settling over his features.

"Then let's make it so."

As Bront began to chant another incantation, Grind rallied the remaining Mine Folk. "Pull back toward the village! Give Bront room to work!"

The Mine Folk changed the fight from a most desperate battle to a fierce, controlled retreat. Their weapons flashed in the dim light as they hewed down the rats that pressed too close. The air was thick with the stench of blood and fur, and the ground was slick with the remains of the fallen. Grind felt his muscles burning with the effort, but he fought on, every swing of his pickaxe fueled by the thought of his people, of the village behind them. He would not let them down. Granite was doing a solid job at his side of stomping the rats into the ground, so they pressed their luck and put their plan into action.

"Now, Bront!" Grind yelled as they reached the archway, the rats surging forward with renewed fury.

With a final, powerful chant, Bront slammed his staff into the ground. The tunnel the rats were coming through shook violently, cracks spiderwebbing up the walls. Then, with a deafening roar, the council chamber ceiling collapsed, and tons of rock crashed down to seal the hall off. The rear ranks of the rat swarm were buried beneath the rubble; their shrieks cut off abruptly. The Mine Folk continued to swat and slash at the scattered rats and seemed disconnected from whatever was controlling them. Bront had never thought to use the rock-shaping powers of his staff for such an aggressive move, but it seemed to have worked. Silence fell as the last rat was cut cleanly in half by the town leatherworker, broken only by the gathered Mine Folk's heavy breathing and the faint sound of distant, muffled scratching as the rats tried to claw their way through the collapse. Grind leaned heavily on his pickaxe, his chest heaving as he caught his breath. He exchanged a weary glance with Bront. "That was close."

"Too close," Bront agreed, his voice rough. "I... I should have listened..." Grind nodded, aware that he had tried to tell them, but realised now was not the time to be gloating. Grind thought there would never be a correct time for an 'I told you so' of such magnitude, so he nodded at Bront, closing the matter.

A grim determination had settled over him. "We've bought ourselves some time. But we need to figure out how to stop them for good."

Bront's eyes narrowed thoughtfully. "We'll need to delve deeper into the old lore and discover what's driving these rats. There's something unnatural about them."

Grind straightened, the fire of battle still burning in his veins. "Then let's get to it. These ratshite bastards came close to getting to our families, but we're Mine Folk. And we'll dig deeper, fight harder, and outlast them. For our clan. For our home."

The gathered Mine Folk began to regroup as the dismissed families ran back into what was left in the hall. Crying over the fallen started, echoing through what was left of the room. While the narrow victory had lifted their spirits, they'd still lost fathers, sons, and brothers to the rat attack. Grind had an unwavering feeling that this was somehow just the beginning. The darkness in the deep places of the earth was stirring, and the rats had tried twice now to get to them. Why though? What brought them? Who was controlling them? Whatever came next, Grind wanted to be ready. He would defend his people to the last breath, no matter the cost.

As they marched back toward the village, Grind glanced back at the collapsed tunnel, his grip tightening on the pickaxe he'd borrowed for the fight. The battle had been won, but he felt that the war had pitter-pattered that bit closer.

Chapter Fifteen
Ansel
Away into the night.

The wind howled through the towering pines as the sound of battle below continued to clash and clatter in the village. Tallin's blood was alight with anticipation, knowing his mission was near fruition. The filthy animals knew not what they hid in their midst; he and his Night One kinfolk would stop the coming resurgence. He crouched low, the shadows embracing him as he melded with the night. The village below was a cluster of rough-hewn huts, the faint glow of fires visible through the cracks in their walls. Animals were bolting and screaming from the clashing weapons, and the owls held their own. The dwellings were flimsy and temporary compared to the stone-built towers the Night Ones had hidden in the south. Nothing like the ancient stone halls his kind called home.

Tallin, leader of the Night One attack party, moved silently up the tree to the home he sought, as he could sense his prize lying within. There was no need for stealth now, as the raid was fully underway, but it came to him naturally, his senses sharpened to a deadly point. His breath misted in the cold air, the only sign of his presence. His dark eyes scanned the forest around him, every detail absorbed as he moved toward his target.

Elara.

She was in the village above, and Tallin's lips curled into a predatory smile at the thought. She would be his before the dawn broke. He'd called her that for ease, as hu-man female was an encumbrance in planning.

The trees, ancient and tall as they were, served as shields and pathways for him. He leapt upward, grasping a low-hanging branch with effortless grace. Climbing higher, he moved with the practised ease of a creature born in the forest. He was not, but his innate athletic ability was helpful anyway. From his perch, he had a clear view of the village below and the filthy animals unable to stop his ascent.

The Night Ones had been watching these Wildlings for days, observing their routines, strengths, and weaknesses. Tallin had grown to admire their tenacity, these... 'people' who earned a living from the northern woodlands. But admiration did not equate to mercy.

Tonight, the Night Ones struck. While Elara, the hu-man woman who had captured Tallin's interest, would be taken. His keen eyes picked where they took her, near the largest tree-lined huts. She was unconscious and carried to a place of rest, her face a picture of sleeping calm.

In their defence, the Wildlings were trying to assist her recovery; that much was clear. They were unaware of the evil in their homes, and he cursed the filthy, disgusting animal mutants. Tallin saw through the veneer of beauty she wore like armour. He knew the weight of responsibility that bore down on her shoulders, even if she was unaware herself. It would come to her, and that is what he feared most. She was a beacon to the old ways, and it made her all the more intriguing to him.

Tallin's thoughts were interrupted by the rustle of movement below. His second in command, Raithe, appeared at the base of the tree, his eyes glowing faintly in the dark. He was fending off a colossal owl thing as it attempted to lift off the ground on substantial snowy, coloured wings. Striking fast, he cut through one with a shriek from the owl man.

"She's up there," Raithe shouted, his voice louder than the sounds of battle. "The others are in position. We await your command."

Tallin's gaze flickered back to the village. "Gather the remaining and meet at the river; this will take but moments."

Raithe disappeared as quickly as he had come, melting back into the shadows. Tallin remained in the tree for a second before leaping and climbing to his target. Arriving at the balcony floor, Tallin landed soundlessly, his long fingers brushing against the smooth wood. The remaining Night Ones gathered in the darkened wood, awaiting his return. They were his family, his pack, bound together by blood and vengeance. Tallin raised a hand, and the Night Ones fanned out, disappearing to the rendezvous point Tallin had ordered.

He moved forward, his steps measured and silent, until he reached the doorway. He could hear the sound of large wings beating to get to his position, and he turned, readying himself for an assault. He could smell the incoming owl, its scent heavy in the air.

As the feathered knight breached the door, Tallin surprised it with a swift boot, sending it spiralling backwards off the ledge. The whoosh of air and the accompanying thwump signalled that he had incapacitated the guard. Smiling, he returned to his prey.

Elara's scent was the strongest, like fresh earth after a storm, with a hint of something sweeter beneath. It drew him, beckoning him closer. He slipped into the room, his movements a blur of speed and precision. He breached her hut, the largest hut, its walls thicker than the others. He could hear her breathing inside, steady and calm.

As he entered, more minor of the creatures bolted to hide in various boxes and behind pillars, but they were of no concern to Tallin. He glared contemptuously at a small orange-furred... 'thing' with a large bushy tail and a small yellow hard hat. He glared at it, and the creature cowered further behind the post.

For a moment, Tallin hesitated. This woman, this hu-man, had stirred something in him, a curiosity he hadn't felt in centuries. That curiosity would not stay his hand.

Tallin produced a thin, sharp blade with a flick of his wrist.

Elara lay on a bed of furs, her auburn hair spread like a halo around her head. She looked peaceful in sleep, her features softened, but Tallin knew better. This was to be a woman forged by hardship, a leader to her people, a worthy prize.

He moved to her side, kneeling to study her face up close. Her breathing hitched, a sign that she sensed something amiss. Before she could wake fully, Tallin clamped a hand around her neck and mounted her, his face inches from hers. Her eyes flew open, panic flashing across them as she struggled against him. The knife moved slowly to her eye as she tried to scream under his grip. Adrenaline coursed through her, urging her to fight, but when the blade moved in even closer, she stopped bucking under the more prominent man on top of her. Tallin was strong, far more robust than any hu-man, and he pulled in close, his voice a whisper in her ear.

"I should kill you now, Elara. But I'm compelled to bring you back to the citadel for reasons above your understanding. Are you going to fight me on this? Or should I reconsider...?" His voice embodied a calm command, and Elara nodded under his hand. "Do not scream, Elara. Not yet, anyway. It will only make this harder for you."

She stilled, her eyes locking onto his. There was fear there, yes, but also defiance. Tallin felt a surge of admiration for her spirit. But he could not let it sway him. She laid back, following his orders. Elara's free hand shot up, nails raking across his cheek, but Tallin barely flinched. He tightened his grip around her throat, pressing her closer to him.

"It's no use," he murmured a hint of regret in his tone. "You're coming with me."

With a final, swift movement, Tallin lifted her into his arms, the knife disappearing from her view. Elara struggled, but her strength was no match for his. He carried her out of the hut, slipping through the village like a shadow. The Night Ones had done their work well. There was no one left to fight them, no one left to help the woman.

Tallin made his way back into the forest, the darkness swallowing them whole. Elara's struggles grew weaker, exhaustion and fear sapping her strength. Tallin moved with purpose, his destination clear. With one last look at the squalid little village, Tallin hoisted Elara over his shoulder and disappeared into the night, leaving nothing but the whisper of the wind in his wake.

Elara had gone limp in his arms when they reached the river's edge. He'd been moving her position around for his comfort, and now she was in his arms again. She wasn't unconscious, but she had stopped fighting, at least for the moment. Tallin paused, looking down at her. Her eyes were open, and she looked up at him, her breathing shallow. He set her down gently, his hands lingering on her shoulders. "You'll be safe with us," he said softly, though he wasn't sure if she could hear or understand him. "No harm will come to you, so long as you don't try to escape."

Elara didn't respond, her silence unnerving him more than he cared to admit. There was no turning back now. He'd gone against orders to kill her where he found her as he felt compelled to keep her for himself.

She belonged to him now.

Chapter Sixteen
Kayriss
Home advantage.

 The early morning sun twinkled its rays, highlighting the darkness of the armoured warriors advancing towards Kayriss. They had all but broken free of her vines and were continuing towards Edgar and Isaac. The sun burned with a fiery yellow hue, through the towering trees, their bark shimmering with an ethereal glow, whispering secrets only the wind could decipher.

 One secret was in the process of revealing himself.

 Still unaware of where the last words had come from, Isaac looked around for the owner of such a booming voice. Kayriss would've laughed had the situation not been so dire and pressed her advantage as she fluttered on the precipice of battle. Her breath came in slow, steady intervals, the only sign of the tension coiling within her like a serpent ready to strike. Her wings beat with an intensity that made them even more translucent, and she looked down at Hovel as he began to raise himself from the woodland floor.

Her home was an ancient elemental of nature known only to her as Hovel, and she was forcing him to move. He was not one for walks, choosing to sit and settle for years at a time. Moving his great mass, the ground stirred beneath Isaac's feet, Hovel's roots trembling as he awakened from his slumber. Kayriss felt that she must move him to assist, as she herself had moved from healer to protector, and she steeled herself.

She must protect what is hers.

The Night Ones advanced in a militaristic formation, clad in armour forged from shadows and obsidian. Their darkness was entirely out of place in the lush greens and browns of the nature around them. The largest among them raised his hand, halting his legion at the edge of the forest clearing as if it were a sacred boundary. They, too, were watching as the very land rose, seeming at this Elf's command. A couple of his warriors shifted, wearying of the fight they were being ordered to undertake, not ready for the large mass in front of them. The larger Night One shot them a steely glance, and their resolve returned. A purple glass-fronted helmet mostly concealed his face, but the glint in his eyes betrayed a hunger, a longing to consume the life force of everything around him and leave nothing but desolation in its wake.

"Kayriss!" the voice of Hovel rumbled through the earth, vibrating up through Edgar's legs. He woofed uncertainly, unsure of what was going on in the poodle. The sound was like the grinding of stones, old and unyielding. "Must I move? These roots have been comfortable for a decade!" The ground quaked, and Kayriss could feel the irritability of the ancient elemental. Flying over, she placed a hand against the nearest tree, feeling the pulse of life within, calming it as best she could. "Yes, old friend," she whispered, "but only for a time. The Night Ones seek to destroy us, so we must fight.

A deep, grumbling sigh emanated from the forest floor. Hovel began to shift, roots snapping free from the earth with a sound like thunder. The ground rippled as the immense form of the forest guardian rose from its ancient rest, a towering behemoth of living wood, vines, and earth. Hovel's face, rough and chiselled like stone, emerged from the bark of an ancient oak. His eyes, pools of molten gold, blazed with a deep-seated annoyance.

"I despise movement," Hovel grumbled, shaking the air around them. "Do you want me to bring these two small things? I smell you on one of them. I assume they are yours."

"If that's ok, Hovel. I've grown quite fond of the both. Be careful and not squish either, please." Kayriss asked, a smile crossing her face.

An audible sigh filled with annoyance followed, and Isaac and Edgar were raised as Hovel stood. The night elves froze at the sight of the colossal elemental, their courage clearly faltering. Their leader stepped forward, his gaze locking onto Kyriss. "You think this tree bastard thing can save you, Elf?" he spat, his voice dripping with venom. "The darkness devours all."

With a swift motion, he signalled his forces to attack. What once was a handful became many as The Night Ones surged forward, their bodies melting from the shadows as they rushed through the forest. Their weapons, forged from dark metal, gleamed wickedly in the warm sunlight. Kayriss dodged through the air, her wings unfurling in a burst of emerald and gold. She soared above the treetops, her eyes scanning the battlefield below. With a wave of her hand, the forest responded. Thorns rained down, conjured from the trees themselves, impaling many of the encroaching attackers, the large wooden barbs making short work of the Night Ones. Vines erupted once more, but this time, they were targetted, snaring fewer of the Night Ones in their grasp, squeezing life from them as they struggled.

Hovel roared, a sound that echoed for miles, causing the very ground to shudder. His massive arms, formed of intertwining roots and thick trunks, swept through the ranks of the Night Ones, scattering them like leaves in the wind. Trees uprooted themselves, lashing out at the invaders with branches as sharp as spears. The attackers fought back against nature itself fiercely, their swords slicing the life from the branches.

The forest was alive, and it was angry.

Hovel easily swatted any fired arrows aside, his golden eyes narrowing in irritation.

"Be gone, piss ant pests!" he bellowed, his voice resonating with the fury of an earthquake. The ground split open beneath his feet, instantly swallowing a dozen Night Ones. He stomped, and the earth trembled, sending shockwaves that knocked the invaders off their feet.

Kayriss, high above, continued her magical assault, raining down thorns infused with her druidic magic. Each shot found its mark, her aim unerring. The missiles burst into brilliant green flames upon impact, consuming the Night Ones in purifying fire. Their screams filled the air as Hovel continued his literal ground assault, his massive form ploughing through the enemy forces like a hurricane.

The Night One leader was not so easily cowed. He raised his sword, channelling a bolt of searing darkness into a concentrated beam of shadow that streaked toward Hovel. The blast struck the elemental in the chest, sending a shockwave through his body. Purple light cracks emanated from the impact, spiderwebbing across the giant's chest. For a moment, Hovel faltered, his movements slowing.

Kayriss saw the momentary weakness and dived toward the Night One leader. With a swift motion, she summoned a gale of wind, knocking him off balance. She landed before him, her eyes burning with fury.

"Leave this place!" she commanded, her voice ringing with authority. "This wood will never fall to the likes of you."

"Wood? We give not two curseborn shits about your fucking nature. We are here for him." The Night One sneered, but Hovel unleashed a roar of pure rage before he could respond further. His form surged with renewed strength, the forest around him coming to life in a frenzy. The trees bent and twisted, their branches lashing out with relentless fury. The ground erupted in a mass of roots and vines, ensnaring the remaining Night Ones in an unbreakable grip.

"Begone."

With the final word, the vines tore themselves downward, dragging, cutting, slicing whomever they held. The clamour abruptly ended with the squelching sound of bloodied bodies hitting the floor.

With a single, mighty swing, Hovel struck the leader of the Night Ones, sending him crashing into the earth with bone-crushing force. Audible bone cracks echoed through the treeline, followed by the silence of the dead. The shadows that seemed to cloak him dissipated, leaving his broken form exposed and vulnerable. Kayriss stood over the fallen leader, her wings outstretched, casting an ethereal shadow that danced with light and colour. It covered him entirely. "This is your end," she whispered, her voice cold as the night.

With a final, swift motion, she summoned the last of her druidic power, a spear of pure natural energy forming in her hand. She drove it into the heart of her would-be attacker, and his body dissolved into ash carried away in the wind.

Hovel let out a long, rumbling sigh, the golden glow in his eyes dimming slightly as he began to settle back into the earth. "That was... tiring," he muttered, his massive form sinking slowly back into the ground.

"Hovel, before you sit, could we possibly travel to Wood Haven and see if we can get to the root of the problem?" Kayriss asked as politely as she could. She fluttered up to check his wound, but it was already sealing itself, moss flooding into the cracks made. Kayriss watched as the forest guardian looked at her, seeing him consider her words.

"Root... Very funny." He seemed to smile, but it soon disappeared to his resting brook face. She landed softly beside Isaac, placing a hand on his waist.

"I bet you've never travelled by house before, have you?" She said, smiling broadly.

The ground beneath her rumbled gently as Hovel began walking towards Wood Haven. Isaac and Edgar had the same confused look, making Kyriss laugh. She smiled, the tension in her shoulders easing as the forest around her quieted, the whispers of the trees turning soft and peaceful once more. She looked over the battlefield, now littered with the remnants of the Night One's failed assault. The forest had survived but left questions.

Why did they want Isaac? What had happened at Wood Haven? She hoped Ansel would be able to answer those and possibly more.

**

The ferret messenger walked gingerly back to Wood Haven, wholly traumatised by the battle he'd just witnessed.

Chapter Seventeen
Grind
You were right.

The once thriving village of the Mine Folk lay in sombre silence, the echoes of the attack still reverberating through the winding tunnels and stone corridors. Fallen bodies of the brave miners, leatherworkers, and artisans, their faces etched with the final expressions of struggle and pain, were scattered across the cavern floor. Most had been covered due to the extent of their injuries. Bront had not wanted to scare the children or scar their wives.

The glowing crystals embedded in the walls, which once provided warmth and comfort to the community, now cast an eerie, pale light over the scene of devastation. The moss, which normally casts its luminescent glow, seemed to be dimmer, as if in mourning for the devastation.

Families huddled around whatever remained of their loved ones, their grief raw and unrestrained. The wails of mourning mothers, fathers, and siblings filled the cavern, a chorus of sorrow that tugged at the hearts of all who heard. Children clung to their parents; their young minds could not fully grasp the tragedy that had befallen their village, but they sensed the gravity of the loss. The Mine Folk were a hardy people, accustomed to the dangers of the deep, but nothing had prepared them for this. The giant rats had come like a plague, a swarm of teeth and claws that seemed driven by something more sinister than mere hunger.

Bront stood at the centre of it all, wondering if he had listened to Grind, this outcome would've been different. His broad shoulders slumped under the heavy weight of responsibility, and he second-guessed everything he did since the first tunnel was brought crashing down. His ordinarily stern face was lined with exhaustion, and his grey eyes, usually sharp with authority, were clouded with sorrow. He had fought alongside his people, his staff being used for violence, no construction, and had smashed through the ranks of the monstrous rodents, but the battle had been costly. Too many lives had been lost, and the village was on the brink of despair.

Grind approached him, his face a mask of grief and determination. He wanted to smack Bront squarely in the beard but knew it would serve no purpose other than making him feel slightly better. Bront had lost a brother in the assault, and Grind knew that lashing out would only add to the pain not helpful. He was gruff and grumpy but not a stoneskull. The pain in Bront's eyes was evident, but he stood tall, ready to do what needed to be done. Sighing heavily, he looked out over the broken bodies of his people.

"We cannot let this happen again," he said, his voice rough with fatigue. "The village is defenceless. If those beasts return, we won't survive another attack. We've lost too much already."

Grind nodded, his gaze hardening. "We need to understand why they attacked in the first place. This wasn't natural. The rats have never come at us like this before, not in such numbers, not with such fury."

Bront turned to him, a glimmer of hope in his tired eyes.

"You're right. We need answers, and we need them quickly. We can't afford to wait for another assault." He paused, thinking deeply. "There's an Elf—a druid. I've heard she can commune with nature," he said finally. "She has a way with creatures. If anyone can understand the minds of those cave maggots, it's her."

Grind's expression shifted to one of cautious optimism. "She lives up on the surface, doesn't she? In the forest, near the mountains."

Bront nodded. "Aye, and that's where you come in. You and Granite will go. You're both strong, quick on your feet and our best shot at locating her. Find Kayriss and bring her here. We need her to speak to the animals, find out what drove them to attack us, or tell them to crack their skulls on someone else's anvil! But she might also be able to find out if there is something more to this than we know."

Grind glanced back at the grieving families, his resolve strengthening. He was about to decline, having not been surface side since his youth.

"We'll leave at dawn," he said firmly. "Granite and I will find Kayriss, and we'll bring her back. If there's a reason for this madness, she's the one to find it."

Bront placed a hand on Grind's shoulder, his grip firm.

"Be careful. And, if it helps, you were right. I... should've listened sooner." Grind smiled under the beard, careful not to make it move much. Smugness had a time, and this wasn't it.

"Nay, worry. I'm not sure what we could've done. The tunnels here are everywhere; we'd never have had the time to secure them all." Grind said, thinking that would help the older Mine Folk, who he could see was balancing on a chisel's edge.

Grind nodded, his eyes meeting Bront's in a silent promise. "We'll return," he said, his voice filled with determination. "And we'll make sure this never happens again."

As Grind turned to prepare for the journey ahead, Bront remained where he was, watching the flames of the first funeral pyres begin to flicker to life. The scent of burning incense mixed with the smoke, rising to the high ceilings of the cavern, where it lingered like the ghosts of the fallen. It then slipped through any crack, drifting upward to the Upside world. The village would mourn its dead, but it would not falter. There was work to be done, and Bront knew that the future of the Mine Folk depended on the success of Grind and Granite's mission.

But he knew the pitter-patter sound would haunt him throughout the rest of his days.

Chapter Eighteen
Ansel
The broken badger.

    Wood Haven lay in almost ruins. The once-vibrant village, nestled deep within the ancient forest, had been a sanctuary for the Wildlings. A place where they could live in harmony with nature, safe from the dangers of the outside world. Now, that harmony had been shattered, and the village was a shadow of its former self. The ground was littered with the fallen, brave creatures who had tried in vain to defend their homes from the Night Ones. The bodies of rabbits, hedgehogs, and the occasional deer lay scattered among the broken remains of their simple dwellings, their lifeless eyes staring into the void. Blood stained the forest floor, soaking into the earth and mingling with the fallen leaves. The air was thick with the scent of death, a heavy, suffocating reminder of the horror that had descended upon them. The Wildlings had been unarmed, their peaceful existence leaving them ill-prepared for such violence. They had fought with tooth and claw, with the desperation of those who knew they had little chance, but it had not been enough. The Night Ones had come like a shadowed storm, their blades flashing in the moonlight, cutting down all in their path. There had been no mercy, no chance for the Wildlings to defend themselves.

At the centre of the village, where the fires still smouldered and the last cries of the dying had faded into silence, Ansel lay broken. His thick, coarse fur was matted with blood; the badger clung to life by a thread. His once powerful form was crumpled on the ground, a deep wound in his chest where a Night One's blade had struck true. His breath came in ragged gasps, each one a struggle, his dark eyes glazed with pain and the knowledge that his time was running out. Hooth stood over him, his feathers ruffled and his sharp talons digging into the ground in anguish. They curled into the wood as the rage inside him shone out. The owl's wings hung low, reflecting the guilt that weighed heavily on him. He felt as if he had failed them all, but most of all, he had failed Ansel, the elder who had guided the village through countless hardships, the one who had always been there to offer wisdom and strength.

"I should have been there," Hooth muttered, his voice thick with self-reproach. "I should have saved you, Ansel. I should have saved them all."

Ansel's eyes flickered open, the pain evident in every movement. His voice was weak, barely more than a whisper.

"Hooth… you… you did your best, my lad," he managed, each word a labour. "No one… could have known… the Night Ones would come. They are not… creatures of this forest."

Hooth shook his head, the shame and anger burning in his chest.

"But I was a knight owl. I was supposed to guard! To be ready for such an assault! It was my duty to protect us and to keep watch for dangers. And I failed. I wasn't strong enough." Anger bubbled to the surface, and the last words were more screech than vocabulary. Ansel reached out with a trembling paw; his grip surprisingly strong as he took hold of Hooth's hand.

"You... were strong, Hooth," he said, his voice growing fainter. "Strong enough... to fight when others would have fled. But you cannot... bear this burden alone." Hooth lowered his head, his sharp beak nearly touching Ansel's hand.

"But now... what will become of us? Without you, Ansel, the village is lost. And there's more..."

A sudden realisation struck Hooth like a lightning bolt, and his eyes widened in horror.

"The woman," he breathed, his voice filled with dread. "The one we found in the woods... where is she? The Night Ones... they must have taken her." He looked around, and on a branch was one of the squirrel builders, coming to see if he could help with anything.

"Hooth, I saw the one who took her," he said, his voice wavering and showing his fear completely. "He called her Elara. I think he must've known her to know her name?" Hooth nodded and cursed himself under his feathers, feeling yet more failure of his station.

Ansel's grip on Hooth's hand tightened momentarily, then weakened as the elder's strength faded. "She is hu-man... One of the old races. I wasn't sure, but it's the only answer." he rasped, his eyes clouding over. "She... she must have been what they were after. You... must find her, Hooth. Protect her... she may hold... the key... to this darkness."

Hooth's heart sank as he realised the gravity of the situation. The woman had been an enigma, a mysterious figure who had metaphorically stumbled into their village only days before, unconscious, lost and frightened. They had taken her in, nursed her, and given her shelter. Now, it seemed that her presence had drawn the Night Ones to them, bringing death and destruction in her wake. Hooth was filled with conflicting emotions of duty and hatred for the woman who had brought such destruction upon them.

As Ansel's paw slipped from Hooth's hand, the old badger gave one final, shuddering breath and was still, his breathing barely moving his chest. The village elder's movement was all but gone, leaving Hooth alone in a world that had suddenly become far more dangerous. Hooth rose slowly, his wings spreading as if to shield the village from further harm, though he knew it was a futile gesture. The Night Ones had come and gone, leaving only ruins in their wake. But the owl knew what he had to do. Ansel's words echoed in his mind: "You must find her... protect her..."

The hu-man woman, whoever she was, was in grave danger. And if she was indeed the reason the Night Ones had attacked, then her fate was tied to that of the entire village. Hooth could not bring back the fallen but could still fulfil Ansel's final request or bring the vengeance he craved. He would find the woman, and he would uncover the truth behind the Night Ones' assault. With a final, mournful glance at Ansel's still form, Hooth spread his wings and took to the sky. The forest stretched out before him, dark and ominous, but he did not hesitate. He flew swiftly, his sharp eyes scanning the ground below for any sign of the Night Ones or their captive. He vowed that none of them would return to his village; he would be the protector he thought he once was.

He took up a perch and waited as the trees in the far distance began to crash apart.

Something significant was crashing towards them.

Chapter Nineteen
Kayriss
Travels with her home.

The forest was alive with the quiet stirrings of the wood. Hints of sunlight filtered through the thick canopy, casting dappled patterns of light and shadow on the forest floor. The ancient and towering trees swayed gently in the early morning breeze, their leaves rustling like a whispered conversation.

However, Hovel was crashing through the wood, careful not to stomp on anything below his massive feet. They were a mix of wood and stone, with intricate pathways snaking up his body. He looked as if a mapped landscape had somehow got up and started moving. A small brook flowed impossibly up and around him, with water streaming at unnatural angles. From his position, Isaac could see fish swim up the stream as if it were flat on the ground and not hindered by gravity. Hovel's steps were heavy and deliberate, each a deep reverberation in the earth, as were his grumbles of protest at having to move.

"Bloody druids, and they're asking nicely. Hhrumpf..." he bellowed under his breath. Kayriss smiled and patted his hand she sat in affectionately.

Hovel was a creature of the forest, and his body was formed from the elements around him. His skin was the rough texture of tree bark, his limbs were thick like ancient roots, and his eyes were deep hollows glowing with the golden light of life itself. Kayriss thought that they resembled the sun herself, shining down on the very nature that made up Hovel. Moss and lichen clung to his form, and small creatures darted in and out of the hollowed spaces in his body as he moved, unbothered by their enormous host. He moved purposefully, his massive frame swaying as he trudged through the woods.

Nestled in a cradle of vines and branches formed by Hovel's arms were three passengers: Kayriss, Isaac, and Edgar, and the latter was not best pleased with the height. The elemental's presence comforted Kayriss, who felt the hum of nature's energy flowing through Hovel like a river. The journey was fascinating and strange, an experience he would never forget. Edgar, however, was a bundle of nerves.

The dog, a sturdy, muscular creature with fur the colour of freshly tilled earth, sat stiffly in Isaac's lap. His dark eyes darted around, and his ears flicked at every creak and groan of the elemental carrying them. Edgar was usually the picture of calm, his protective instincts honed over the years and through his ancestry. Being taken by a giant, living embodiment of the forest was an entirely new experience that Edgar was still trying to come to terms with.

"It's all right, Edgar," Kayriss murmured softly, her slender fingers scratching behind his ears. She moved closer to Isaac as both comfort to Edgar and the urge to be with him once more. She gave the large dog a head scratch, and he moved slightly, crushing Isaac's lap even further.

The spell she had recast allowed her to speak with all animals, but the magic had deepened her bond with Edgar since they had first met. "Hovel means us no harm. He's just carrying us to Wood Haven."

"Yes. But very high," Edgar replied, his voice gruff but wavering. To Isaac, his voice sounded rich, a deep tone that always carried a hint of concern. It was an unintelligible mix of barks, huffs, growls, yelps, and yips. "I don't like not being on the ground. It feels... unnatural. And now, the ground is moving." Kayriss interpreted everything to Isaac, who gave Edgar a reassuring pat, even though he quietly echoed the sentiment.

Kayriss smiled, her eyes green and soft with understanding. "It's only for a little while longer. You're doing so well, Edgar. You're a good boy."

Edgar straightened at her words, his tail wagging just slightly, thwacking against Isaac. "I'm a good boy," he repeated as if reminding himself. "I'm protecting you and Isaac. Good boy."

"You are," Kayriss said, leaning down to kiss the top of his head. "You're protecting us all."

Isaac, who had been quietly observing the interplay between the elf and the dog, chuckled. "You're braver than I am, Edgar," he said, running a hand through his tousled hair. "I've never seen anything like Hovel before. It's amazing, but also... a bit overwhelming."

Hovel, though silent as ever, seemed to sense the conversation. The vines and branches holding them shifted slightly, adjusting their positions to provide more comfort as if the elemental was attempting to ease their journey.

Edgar seemed to relax as a fish jumped out of the nearby river. The small stream was running up Hovel's body, and Isaac noted that the fish was defying all gravity with its movements. To it, they were wrong, not it.

The forest around them was dense, with trees so tall their tops were lost in the mist that clung to the morning air. The path ahead was little more than a faint trail, but Hovel moved with certainty, knowing the woods as intimately as a heartbeat. The further they went, the quieter the forest became, as if all of nature held its breath in reverence for the great being walking among them. Trees seemed to bend and move out of the great giant's footsteps, returning to their original position with a creak.

"Hovel," Kayriss called softly, her voice carrying the gentle authority of a druid. The elemental turned his head slightly, the hollow glow of his eyes fixing on her. "How much longer until we reach Wood Haven?"

Hovel's voice, when he spoke, was like the grinding of stones deep within the earth, a sound that was felt as much as heard. "Not far now, young druid. The village lies beyond the river, at the edge of the forest."

Isaac looked out over the landscape, trying to see through the thick trees where the village might be. "I wonder what the people there will think of us arriving like this," he mused.

"I think you might be more shocked than they were. Magic is known around here," Kayriss replied with a grin. "Not many can claim to have travelled with a nature elemental as their guide, though."

Isaac smiled at that, though Edgar's brow furrowed. "Will there be other dogs in Wood Haven?" Edgar asked, his tone hopeful but tinged with worry.

"I've not seen one; I'm sorry," Kayriss replied. "But if there were, they'd be amazed by your bravery."

Edgar nodded, settling down a little more comfortably in Isaac's lap. He was still nervous, still wary of the unnaturalness of being carried so high off the ground, but her words calmed him. He was a good boy, and good boys did what they had to do to protect their family.

The journey continued in peaceful silence for a time, with the occasional rustle of leaves or the distant call of a bird breaking the silence. Kayriss noted that one of the chirps said, "Bloody great tree walking towards us, Gladys! Get the kids!" making her chuckle. As they walked, the forest began to thin, the trees growing less dense, and the light of the sun finally breaking through in warm beams. The air grew fresher, carrying the scent of water and rich earth.

Finally, they reached the edge of the forest. Ahead, the river Hovel knew led to Wood Haven sparkled in the light, its waters clear and swift. Beyond it, nestled in a comprehensive clearing surrounded by grand oak trees, was the village of Wood Haven. Smoke rose gently from the chimneys of the tiny wooden houses, and the distant sounds of a bustling village reached their ears, a far cry from the deep quiet of the forest. It was not the typical village clatter that Kayriss had heard before; there was something darker, more grief-stricken, in the air. The trees themselves seemed to be bowing in a sort of reverence to why, she did not know. Hovel stopped at the river's edge, carefully lowering his passengers to the ground. Kayriss, Isaac, and Edgar stepped down onto the soft grass, feeling the cool breeze that swept off the water.

"Thank you, Hovel," Kayriss said, the worry evident in her voice alongside the gratitude. She touched the elemental's arm, feeling the rough bark beneath her fingers. "We couldn't have made it here so fast without you. Find somewhere on the outskirts and rest, old friend."

Hovel inclined his head, a gesture of respect. "The forest watches over those who walk in harmony with it. You are welcome, Kayriss of the woods."

Edgar looked up at the towering elemental and let out a small, respectful bark. "Thank you, Hovel," he added. "For not dropping us on our heads."

The glow in Hovel's eyes softened, a silent acknowledgement of the dog's bravery. With a great hand, he reached up, and small vines from what was loosely his hand reached into the stream and plucked out a small fish. The vines twisted down to Edgar, offering him a tasty meal. A bark and a chomp followed, and he woofed it down.

The great elemental turned and began to walk back into the forest, his form slowly blending into the trees until he was no longer distinguishable from the woods. Isaac wrapped an arm around Kyriss, pulling her close as they looked at the village. "We made it," he said, his voice full of relief and anticipation.

"Yes," she agreed, her eyes shining as she gazed at their new home. We made it," Isaac noted, noting that her eyes now shone a deep blue and that there was worry in them that he had not seen before.

Edgar, now happily back on solid ground, sniffed the air, his tail wagging furiously. The nervousness was gone, replaced by curiosity. "Come on," he urged, bounding ahead. "Let's go see the village!"

Kayriss and Isaac followed their loyal companion toward Wood Haven. The long journey through the forest was behind them, and ahead lay new adventures, new challenges, and something far darker than either could imagine.

Chapter Twenty
Grind
Into daylight.

Grind stood in the hollow of his stone-carved dwelling, the air thick with the mingled scent of damp earth and the lingering smoke of the torches that lined the walls. His heart was heavy with the weight of what had come upon them. The walls of Stonemarsh, once a safe haven deep beneath the mountain, had been breached by a tide of ravenous rats, their numbers too great for the miners to repel without losing some of their community. His strong hands, calloused from years of labour, trembled slightly as he placed them on the shoulders of his wife, Paura, and their young son, Toric.

"We'll rebuild," Puara said, her voice strong but laced with sorrow under her full, beautifully platted beard. Her eyes, though, betrayed the fear she harboured for her husband and their people.

Grind nodded, not trusting his voice to remain steady. He knelt to meet Toric's gaze. The boy's face was smudged with dust, but his eyes were bright, even in the dim glow of the underground lights. His beard was still growing, but one his father was proud of still.

"Be strong, Toric," Grind said, ruffling the boy's thick hair. "I'm only going up for a spell. I'll find help and be back before you know it."

Toric nodded, clutching the small, wooden figure of a miner Grind had carved for him last winter. He handed a pouch to Grind, and it clinked as it moved.

"My painted stones, father. For luck." Grind smiled and held his son tighter than he ever had before. Paura touched his beard cheek, guiding his gaze back to hers with a soft tug. "Save some of that fer me!" She said and returned the grasping hug. "Keep safe, yer brick biter. We need you back here." she whispered, the words barely more than a breath.

Grind pressed a kiss to her brow, a final, lingering touch, and stood tall. He turned, slinging his pack over his shoulder, feeling the weight of his pickaxe resting comfortably against his back. His eyes met those of Granite, son of Bront, who had been waiting outside of his home. His expression was as stoic as ever, though Grind knew there was steel beneath that calm.

"Ready?" Grind asked, his voice rough.

Granite nodded, his hand resting on the hilt of a massive hammer slung across his back. He had been Grind's battle companion in the last assault, and the attack had drawn them a little closer. Granite was glad to have the company as he had never set foot in the Upside. He always thought it was too bright up there for a Mine Folk, so he would gladly take Grind's help as they faced the unknown above. What perils would they meet first? He gripped the handle of his hammer closer, still at the thought of the terrors above.

The two Mine Folk left the warmth of the hearth behind and headed deeper into the winding tunnels, the path taking them ever upward toward the light. Many Mine Folk villagers lined the glowing crystal paths, their faces illuminated by the soft glow of bioluminescent moss. Elders, with eyes gleaming with wisdom, offered blessings, while the younger Folk stood in awe of the pair who would soon journey to the surface, a place of myth, danger and bright lights. Voices hummed with an ancient song, wishing strength, courage, and protection, for they knew the perilous path ahead. Grind and Granite, hearts heavy with the weight of expectation, nodded solemnly, carrying with them the hopes of their people as they ascended toward the unknown.

As they walked, they left Stonemarsh behind, and the air grew cooler, the shadows lengthening. The darkness seemed to pull at them with every step. The last time Grind had ventured this far up had been in his youth, but even then, he had not dared to open the door that led to the surface. The tales of what lay beyond were enough to keep most Mine Folk rooted deep in their stone burrows.

Now, there was no choice.

At last, they reached the end of the tunnel, where a great metal slatted door stood, sealing the Upside world out. The door was ancient, its edges lined with runes of protection. To Grind and the rest of the Mine Folk, they were ancient incantations sealing the door closed. He traced the letters with his eyes;

'Times Square Cark Park, Newcastle,' was all he could make out; although he understood it, he did not. Whatever spellcaster had laid the runes there was long dead now, but they had served their purpose. With a strength borne of determination, he pulled and lifted as hard as his arms would allow.

A grating sound followed, screeching the opening of the portal.

Immediately, light shone in, blinding the two Mine Folk who did not realise how brightly that light could shine. It took them moments to acclimate; even then, the brightness seared their vision. Both pulled their hats down low, shielding their vision.

The pair waited as long as needed so that they could see, and when they could, they saw that the world they were finally witnessing was made up almost entirely of the lushest greens—colours his kind had never indeed seen in this intensity. Blinding light flooded the tunnel, causing both dwarves to shield their eyes, their skin unused to the sun's unyielding glare. Grind squinted, his vision adjusting slowly to the world above. The sky was a vast blue expanse stretching endlessly above them, and the air smelled of earth and grass, rich and unfamiliar. Granite audibly gasped at the life he was seeing in front of him. Grind hesitated, his hand hovering over the hilt of his pickaxe, memories of Bront's words ringing in his ears.

"Follow the river," the elder had said, his voice grave and lined with age. "It will lead you to Wood Haven. There, seek out Kayriss, the druid. She is the only one who might help us."

Grind took a deep breath and stepped into the greenery.

"Never thought I'd miss the dark so much," Grind grumbled, clearly not a fan of this new world. His voice was low as he blinked against the brightness.

"Aye," Granite agreed, forcing himself into the light. His eyes were still struggling to adapt, but the rushing water caught his attention, drawing him toward it.

The clear and swift river cut a path through the dense forest surrounding them. Its banks were lined with moss-covered stones, and the air around it was cool and fresh. Grind felt a twinge of homesickness as he looked at the stones, similar to those of his underground home yet so different in their setting.

"We follow this," Grind said, primarily to himself, his voice rough with emotion. Granite merely nodded, his eyes scanning the surroundings warily.

They walked silently, the river guiding them southward through the dense trees. The sound of rushing water was a constant companion, mingling with the rustling of leaves and the distant calls of birds. It was a peaceful place, but Grind could not shake the sense of unease prickling at the back of his neck. The world above was vast and open, lacking the comforting confines of stone walls.

Terrors could be around any corner.

As they rounded a bend in the river, the peaceful sounds of the forest were shattered by a raucous chorus of voices, all shouting in a language that was half garbled and entirely strange. Grind's hand instinctively went to his pickaxe, and Granite's grip tightened on his hammer.

A group of creatures Grind had never seen emerged from the trees. They were standing on two legs and dressed in mismatched cloth and leather garments. Each one carried a weapon of some sort, ranging from swords to spoons. Although armed, their faces were split in wide, toothy grins rather than grimaces of hostility. Their bodies were covered head to foot in beard hair somehow, making them look like tall, elongated rats in clothes.

"Well, well, what 'ave we here?" the largest of the group, a burly furred thing with a patch over one eye and a tail tipped with brown fur, stepped forward, his voice thick with a strange accent.

"Looks like a pair o' lost moles, it does!" another cackled, tipping his tricorn hat. Most of the creatures behind the lead one were saying "Aaarrrrr!" an awful lot.

"We be Mine Folk," Grind said, his voice low, fighting to keep his temper. "We seek passage to Wood Haven. Also, we are not moles."

"Wood Haven, eh?" the leader said, scratching at his whiskers. "We might just be headin' that way ourselves. Ain't that right, lads?"

A raucous cacophony of 'Aarrrrssss' flooded out of them, bursting into a chorus of agreement, some nodding eagerly, others already launching into a bawdy sea shanty that made Grind's ears burn.

"Hush now, crew, there be time for songs on the open waves." He said, and the song was brought to a crunching stop. "We be the mighty otter pirates of the seven seas! We be the terror of the land and waters!" The taller one announced.

Granite shot Grind a sidelong glance that spoke volumes. Neither of them relished the idea of travelling with these strange, noisy creatures, but they had little choice. The river was the quickest route, and the otters seemed to know it well.

"What's your... What are you?" Grind asked, crossing his arms over his chest.

"The name's Captain Browntail, aaaarrrrr. I be Cap'n of the great ship ye see before you," the leader said with a flourishing bow that seemed out of place in the middle of the forest. Grind and Granite looked over at a rickety, but at least afloat, boat. "She be called the Nautical Majesty of The Moonlit Waters. Isn't she a beauty?"

Grind nodded somewhat begrudgingly as he did not want to offend his would-be travel companions.

"And these be me crew, the finest lot o' river pirates ye'll ever meet."

Granite let out a low growl, clearly unimpressed. "Pirates, is it? What'd you be doing this far from the sea?"

"Ah, the river's our road, matey," Browntail said with a grin. "We knows these waters better than the fish what swim in 'em. And if it's Wood Haven ye be wantin', then we be yer best bet. Aaaarrrrr."

Grind sighed, the thought of listening to the otters' incessant chatter for days on end already wearing on him. But Bront's words echoed in his mind, urging him forward.

"Fine," he said at last. "But we travel quick and without delay. We've no time for yer shanties or games."

"Aye, aye, no delays!" Browntail agreed though Grind suspected the otter's word was worth little. "But ye can't rush the river, friend. She takes her own time; she does."

Grind gave a curt nod, resigned to his fate. Moving forward, Browntail waved a hand up in front of him.

"And how ye be paying for this very trip, m'lad? Asked the captain, a webbed paw outstretched. "We only be taking the finest treasaarrrrr."

Grind sighed. Audibly.

"And what are you classing as treasure then?" Grind said through gritted teeth, his patience wearing the thinnest of thin.

"Do ye have any, shall we say, pebbles?" Browntail asked, wanting to know.

"Pebbles. As in small stones?" Grind tried to confirm.

"Aye! Pebbles be the food of life, the apples in our eyes! The..." Grind cut him off with a raised hand. Looking at the floor, he picked up several small stones and dusted them off. He handed them all to the captain, hoping this would be enough to pay for the trip.

"Well now! We have a rich merchant ere! Aaaarrrr!" Grind sighed at the clearly crazy otter but handed them over. They disappeared into a belt pouch with a clink.

The two Mine Folk were led to what was little more than a raft with grandiose additions to it hidden amongst the reeds. It was a strange craft, made of rough-hewn wood, its sides adorned with carvings of waves and fish. Browntail climbed aboard, offering Grind and Granite a hand, though both ignored it and clambered in.

"Settle in, lads!" Browntail called as the other otters took their positions, readying the boat for departure. "Next stop, Wood Haven! But first, a shanty to lighten the load!"

Grind sighed and stuffed his beard in his ears as the otters broke into a raucous chorus.

♪On the waves we ride with might
Pirate otters sail by night
Pebbles trade beneath the sun
Every day's a search for fun

♪In the morn we catch the breeze
Shanties sing to rolling seas
Pouches full of pebbles bright
Otters' joy a wondrous sight

♪Heave ho away we go
Otters on the sea
Pebble trade and endless play
Adventure wild and free

♪Thieving gulls and playful fights
Sandy toes in moonlit nights
Fearless crew of furry pride
Friends forever side by side

♪Heave ho away we go
Otters on the sea
Pebble trade and endless play
Adventure wild and free

♪Treasure maps drawn in the sand
Journeys planned by otter hand
Pebble trading tales we tell
Every port a wishing well

♪Heave ho away we go
Otters on the sea
Pebble trade and endless play
Adventure wild and free

As the boat glided into the river's current, the otters launched into another raucous song, barely finishing their first, as their voices carried across the water. Grind groaned inwardly, glancing at Granite, happily tapping his foot to the beat. Grind's mood deepened by the second, as this was clearly not the epic mission that had been described.

It was going to be a very... very... long journey...

Chapter Twenty-One
Ansel
Ansel's Alive!

The village was quieter than usual. The conventional hum of life in the Wildling settlement had faded to a tense, worried murmur. People huddled in small groups around the fires, their faces etched with fear and sorrow. Ansel had been laid in his bed and barely moved to eat or drink a morsel. He'd been cleaned from his bloodied state but was still deathly pale. Everyone knew he was clinging to life after the Night One assault; even the village healers were at the end of the herbalist's talents. They had managed to stabilise him but not save him, as the wound was deep, the blade possibly poisoned. Every breath Ansel took was shallow, each a struggle that sounded too much like a whisper of death. The air inside the small hut where Ansel lay was thick with desperation. The Wildling elders stood around the narrow cot, exchanging anxious glances. Ansel's skin had gone almost grey under his fur, and his once-bright eyes were dull and unfocused. His chest rose and fell slowly, agonisingly, with each shallow breath.

"This cannot be how it ends," whispered Yara, one of the village healers, her voice trembling. "He has fought so hard. We cannot lose him like this."

The others nodded, but they all knew their skills were insufficient. The Night One's blade had been infused with a poison none knew how to counter.

Ansel was slipping away from them, and they could not stop it. A sharp, urgent cry rang out from the edge of the village. All eyes turned towards the source of the sound, and there she was, running from the edge of the woods, the greens of her cloak billowing behind her, such was her speed.

Kayriss, the druidic woman, was the village's last hope, and everyone knew it. She burst into the hut, breathless and wild-eyed, her auburn hair tangled from the sprint. Her green eyes scanned the room quickly, taking in the dire situation. Without a word, she knelt beside Ansel, her hands hovering above his wound. The smell of death hung heavy in the air.

"This is beyond healing," one of the elders said softly. "Even for you, Kayriss."

She ignored the comment, focusing all her energy on Ansel. Her hands began to glow with a soft, golden light. She closed her eyes, murmuring an ancient incantation under her breath. The light grew brighter, illuminating the dark hut and casting strange, flickering shadows on the walls.

"Hold on, Ansel," Kayriss whispered, her voice trembling slightly as the glow intensified. "Just hold on a little longer."

The magic began to flow from her hands into Ansel's body. His breathing grew even more laboured as if his spirit were fighting the healing, struggling against the pull of life and death. Kayriss gritted her teeth, pouring every ounce of strength into the spell. Her hands trembled with the effort, and sweat beaded on her forehead.

For a moment, it seemed as if nothing would change. Ansel's chest stilled, and a cold silence filled the room. The light from Kayriss's hands flickered, nearly going out.

Slowly, the poison began to recede. The black veins that had snaked across Ansel's skin faded, returning to a more natural colour. His breathing deepened, and colour began to return to his coat. It was working but at a cost.

Kayriss's breath hitched as she felt the spell's toll on her body. She had to finish it; she couldn't stop now, but the power required drained her, pulling her deeper into an abyss of exhaustion.

Outside, the village was in a calamity of motion.

The otter pirates had arrived, their ship docking on the riverbank just as the healing climaxed. Grind and Granite of the Mine Folk leapt from the ship, their faces creased with worry at the signs of chaos in the village. They rushed through the streets, following the murmurs and pointing fingers that led them to the small hut.

Just as they entered, the light from Kayriss's hands flared once more, brighter than ever, before finally dimming. Ansel's eyes fluttered open, his breath steady, his skin warm. The room was silent, stunned by what had just occurred.

Kayriss, however, had nothing left. The last of her energy spent, she swayed where she knelt, her vision blurring. Isaac, who had been standing behind her, watching in silent awe, moved forward just in time to catch her as she collapsed. He pulled her into his arms, his face a mixture of relief and deep concern.

"Kayriss?" he whispered, his voice breaking. "Kay, can you hear me?"

She nodded weakly, her eyes barely open. "He's... he's safe," she murmured, her voice faint. "Ansel... he'll live."

Isaac held her closer, his heart aching with gratitude and fear. "Please be alright," he whispered, his voice thick with emotion. "I need you."

Grind and Granite moved forward, their usually stern faces softened with concern. They'd walked from the darkened depths to otter pirate sea shanties to this. Grind knelt beside Isaac, his large hand resting gently on Kayriss's shoulder.

"I believe she saved him," Grind said quietly, his voice rough with emotion. "She saved him, but at what cost? She is the one we are searching for."

Kayriss's breathing was shallow, her body limp in Isaac's arms. She had given everything she had to bring Ansel back from the brink, and now she was teetering on the edge herself.

"We need to get her to a bed," Isaac said, his voice urgent. "She needs rest. Now."

Together, the group carefully lifted Kyriss and carried her to a nearby hut. Isaac stayed by her side, his hand never leaving hers. The others gathered around, their faces reflecting the relief and worry that had settled over the village.

Sitting up in his cot, Ansel looked around at the concerned faces. His gaze finally settled on Isaac, who was holding Kayriss with a look of raw, unguarded emotion. He tried to speak, but his voice was hoarse, his throat dry.

"Another hu-man...?" Ansel rasped, his voice barely a whisper. He noticed Kayriss was unconscious next to him and tried to move, but the effort was far too much. "She... she saved me."

Isaac nodded, his eyes locked on Kayriss's pale face. "She did."

As the night deepened, the village remained on edge. Ansel was out of immediate danger, Kayriss still lay unconscious, her breathing shallow, her body drained of all energy. The Wildlings, the otter pirates, and the Mine Folk kept a silent vigil, their hopes and prayers focused on the woman who had given so much to save one of their own.

Isaac never left her side, his heart heavy with fear for what the morning might bring. He knew Kayriss was strong, a woman stronger than he could have believed, but even the strongest had their limits. He held her hand tightly, willing her to fight and return to them. As the first light of dawn broke over the village, the only sound filled the air: the soft, steady breathing of a healer who had given everything to save another.

**

Isaac woke early, alone in the hut next to the sleeping Kayriss. He ached from falling asleep in an uncomfortable position but realised that he was still holding her hands. Looking down at them, he noticed something he was sure wasn't there before.

From her fingers, lacing up her arm and under her skin, was the delicate outline of a thin vine where her veins once were.

PART TWO
The Convergence

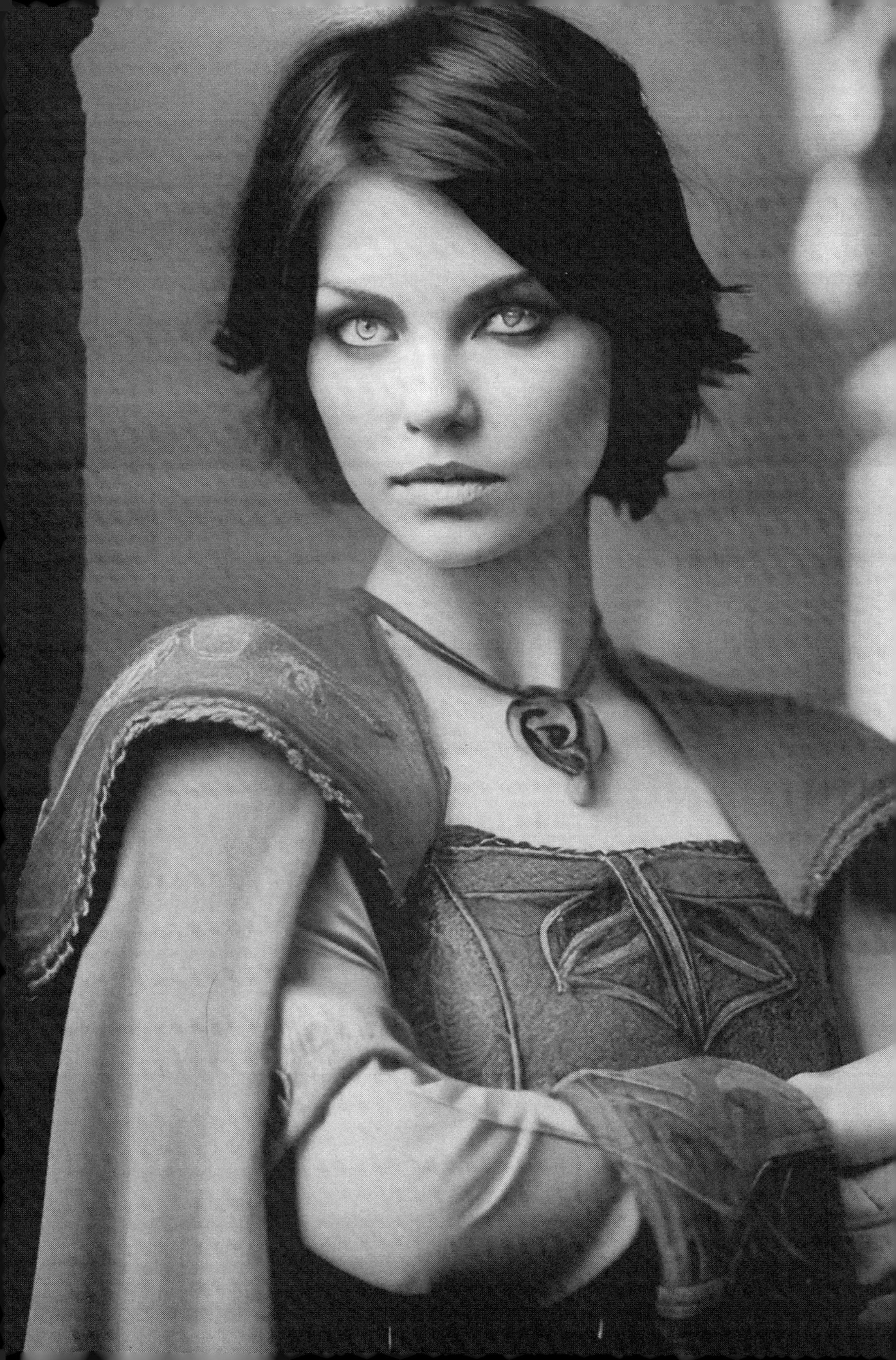

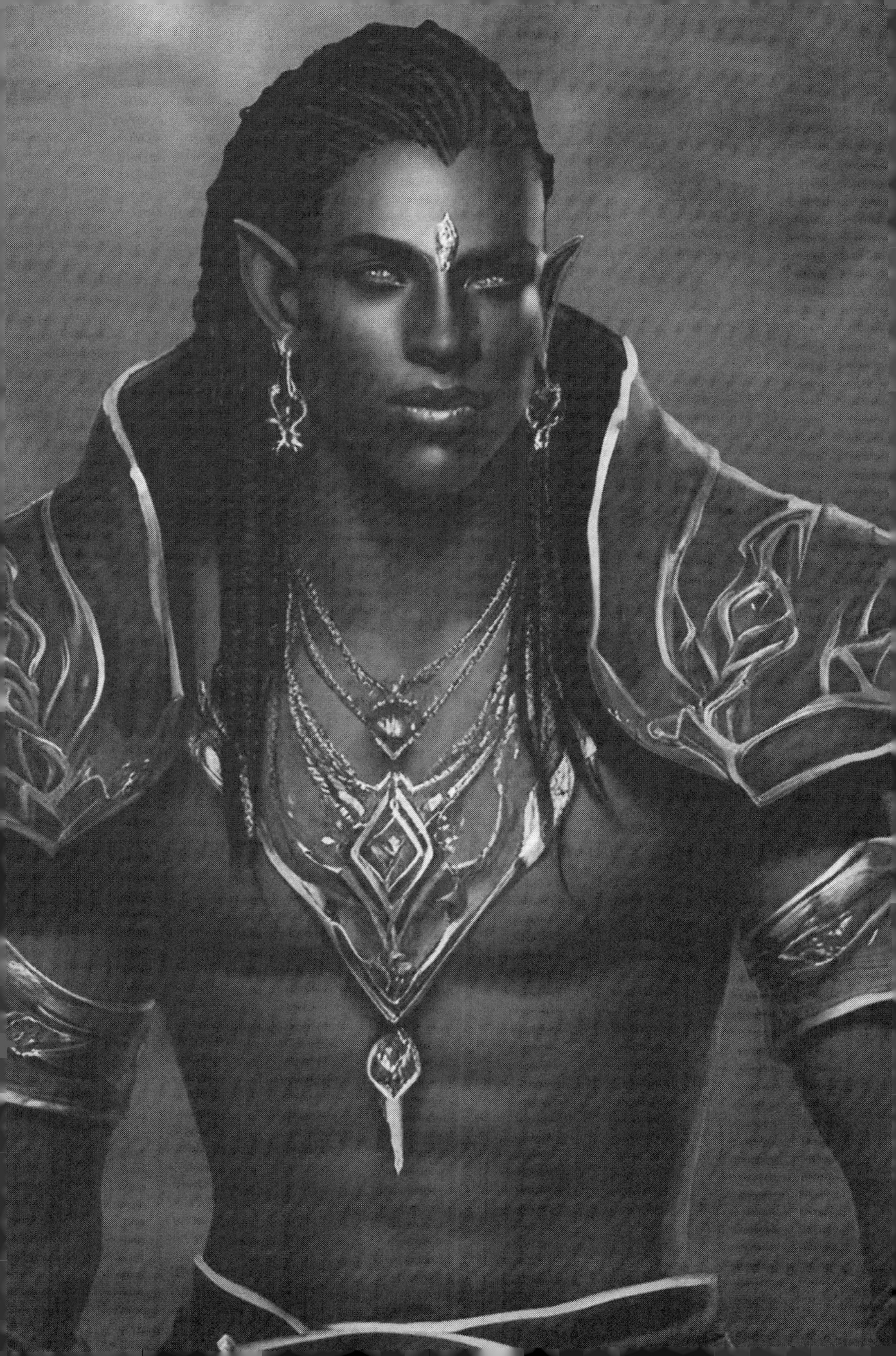

Chapter Twenty-Two
Kayriss
New friends.

It took Kayriss three days to recover from the spell. She drifted in and out of consciousness, unable to focus on anything except the feeling of a hand in hers.

It never left.

She knew it was Isaac's. She knew he was there. Somehow, she felt like he was part of her now, an unrippable part of her soul. When she came back to alertness, the first thing she noticed was the myriad of smells that assaulted her senses. Firstly came Isaac. His was a warm smell, the essence of what strength would smell like. She cradled that in her heart for a while, which made a warmth in herself grow. Edgar was close by, too; his usual dog aroma, laced with the same old leather, brought the beginnings of a smile to her face.

Then there was the collection of animals—otters, badgers, and the occasional dormouse. A new, different aroma assailed her, too. It was stonelike in its nature, one she had never smelled on a person before.

Opening her eyes, she met the most interesting group of people she'd ever encountered.

"You are awake, my dear." Ansel's voice came, and he was now fully standing and back to his normal self. "I, we, owe you a great deal. Myself especially, of course, though. You have my thanks." He smiled an expression of someone whose life had been saved and placed a large, clawed hand on her shoulder in thanks. An excited dormouse ran to his side and squeaked something unintelligible. Ansel nodded serenely, still unsure what John, Jon, or Johnathon had said.

As she panned around, his eyes came to rest on two small-sized beings, as wide as they were tall, their features hidden under a mass of facial hair. They smiled at her; at least, she thought they were. It was hard to tell.

"Such power in such a small frame. You are quite the marvel, young druid," Ansel continued. "When you are ready, I think we all have a lot to discuss."

**

The Wildling village was bathed in the soft golden light of the setting sun, casting long shadows through the trees that towered like sentinels around the settlement. Kayriss and Isaac had spent the day helping the Wildlings with various tasks as her strength returned. She would tend to wounded animals, collect herbs, and share advice with the healers for better concoctions. Isaac, however, was mainly stared at by any of the villagers that wandered past. He was a full head and shoulders above even the tallest among them, which just so happened to be the ever-watchful Hooth. He'd not left Isaac's side, watching the newcomer closely. Isaac felt some tension there but did not understand why.

The village bustled with life now, which gave Kayriss the feeling that Ansel was not only the village leader but also its emotional anchor. It warmed her that she had given so much for him. She'd felt her depleted powers return slowly, but she was trying not to use them as much, currently relying on tried and tested herbalism where possible.

As evening fell, Kayriss and Isaac were slipping away from the crowd, drawn by a mutual desire that had simmered beneath the surface all day. A look. A glance. A smile. Kayriss led Isaac through a winding path that twisted deeper into the woods, away from the village's eyes and ears.

Isaac followed closely, aware of her thoughts and what she had planned. His heart was pounding with a mixture of excitement, nervous anticipation, and pure wanting.

The air was thick with the scent of pine and damp earth, the forest alive with the distant calls of night creatures beginning their evening rituals. Kayriss moved with the grace of one born to the wild, her lithe form almost blending into the foliage. She glanced back at Isaac with a mischievous smile, her emerald eyes sparkling with a promise of what would come. With a wave of her hand, she called the surrounding animals to give them space, and Isaac was sure that a pair of rabbits smiled at him.

They soon arrived at a secluded glade, a small clearing surrounded by ancient oaks whose branches intertwined overhead, creating a natural canopy. The ground was carpeted with soft moss and dotted with tiny wildflowers that glowed in the fading light. It was a place of peace, untouched by the outside world, a perfect hideaway for two lovers seeking a moment alone.

Standing in the middle, she shrugged off her clothing, and he took in her beauty. He drank her in as a parched, deserted man would. Without a word, they came together, their bodies pressing close as Isaac shed his clothes in a hurried, silent dance. Kayriss's pale skin shimmered in the twilight as her long, auburn hair cascaded down her back like a waterfall of moonlight. Isaac's rough hands found her smooth curves, his touch gentle yet hungry. She wrapped herself around him, pulling him down onto the soft earth where they became a tangle of limbs, lost in the sensation of skin on skin, the world beyond forgotten.

The forest seemed to hold its breath, the usual sounds of the woods muted as if in reverence to the pair's secret union. Their soft laughter soon grew louder as the sheer absurdity of their sneaky rendezvous took hold. They were a curious pair, a druid with a deep connection to nature and a hu-man with a head missing its memories. Yet, here they were, laughing like children as they gave in to their passions in this hidden corner of the world.

Just as their laughter and pleasure peaked, a tiny rustling noise interrupted their moment. From a nearby thicket, a small dormouse emerged, its round eyes wide with shock at the sight before it. The little creature froze, its tiny paws clutching a berry as it stared at the naked couple with an expression of utter disbelief.

Kayriss, astride Isaac, turned and waved at the agog dormouse. The gesture resulted in it dropping the berry and its jaw. She pointed at the tiny witness, her laughter bubbling up uncontrollably. Her internal muscles spasmed around him as she did, and he gasped at the feeling.

"Look, Isaac! We're being watched..." She said playfully.

Isaac turned and saw the dormouse, its tiny mouth still agape in what could only be described as a scandalised surprise. He thought to protest, to stop their union, but Kayriss turned and placed her hand on his chest.

"If he's going to watch, then a show he'll see."

She started rhythmically moving up and down his length, enjoying the sensation as if she had not a care in the world. All that mattered at that moment was the feel of him inside her.

As if realising the situation's absurdity, the dormouse let out a tiny squeak and darted back into the undergrowth, leaving the pair alone once more.

Kayriss continued her motion, unfurling her wings, which shone in the natural light. As she orgasmed, Isaac saw the flush of pleasure ripple up her wingspan in a glorious rainbow of colours. They danced an electric pattern across the sheer membrane, and Isaac could not hold himself back anymore. He burst within her, the heat filling her to a gasping point.

Kayriss rolled onto her back as the feeling subsided, bringing her wings safely in as she did. Staring up at the canopy of leaves overhead, she said,

"Oh, the stories that little one will tell," her voice breathless from mirth. "If anyone could actually understand him. Poor thing."

Isaac, lying beside her, propped himself up on one elbow and looked down at her, his expression softened by affection. "Let them talk. Or squeak," he said with a grin. "We've got nothing to hide."

Kayriss turned to meet his gaze, her laughter fading into a contented smile. She reached up to touch his face, her fingers tracing the lines of his jaw. "You're right," she whispered. "Let them talk."

The two lay there for a while longer, basking in each other's warmth. The earlier rush of their secretive escape had now mellowed into a quiet, shared peace. The forest around them resumed its nighttime symphony, the sounds of crickets and owls filling the air once more as if the world had resumed its normal rhythm.

Isaac looked down at her naked form, seeing the intricate tattoo of vines and nature just under the surface. Given her closeness to the world around her, was this normal?

Eventually, they gathered their scattered clothes, dressing slowly, their playful mood still lingering in the air. Hand in hand, they made their way back toward the village, leaving the glade as they had found it—untouched and tranquil, save for the memory of their laughter that lingered among the trees.

Chapter Twenty-Three
Tallin
Old rivalries.

    The dark horse and its shadowed rider drifted through the forest like a whispered omen, their presence warping the very air, as if the trees themselves feared to watch.

    Through the tangled grasp of ancient trees, the black horse moved silently, its hooves barely stirring the mist that clung to the forest floor like breath from the underworld. Atop it sat a rider cloaked in shadow, face obscured by a hood that swallowed the last light. The air trembled with something unseen, like the woods recoiled from their passage. No birds sang, no creatures stirred, and the leaves themselves seemed to shrink away, whispering warnings that went unheard. The rider's eyes, though hidden, felt like they pierced the soul, and the path ahead seemed to twist in unnatural ways, leading ever deeper into the unknown. There was no escape, only the weight of impending doom that hung thick as the night itself.

Tallin rode ahead, his steed's hooves pounding the earth relentlessly, each thud reverberating through the twilight as if the land feared his approach. Behind him, bound and defiant, Elara bounced along, her wrists chafing against the rough rope that held her tethered to his saddle. Her legs hung over each side of the horse, causing her dress to ride up.

The dusk settled over the world like a shroud, casting long, eerie shadows across the landscape as they approached the southern citadel. It had taken them days to reach the Night One's home, and when it finally came into view, Elara gasped at the sight.

Her heart pounded with a mix of fury and dread. She had spent the journey stewing in her hatred for Tallin, the Night One who had torn her from the animal village. On the journey, he had 'graced' her with the name he had chosen for her, telling Elara it was a gift he had bestowed.

It is a privilege almost.

He told her that Elara would be her given name and that she should appreciate the gift if she survived. She noted that he kept saying that the prophecy she was chosen for would never come to pass and that the Alter would never be broken. She knew not what he meant, leaving him to listen to the sound of his voice, which he clearly loved. Elara chose to keep the name, not because he had chosen it but because she couldn't remember her actual name.

She had never imagined she could harbour such a deep hatred for another being. However, this Night One, this villain in her midst twittering on, she hated him.

The citadel rose before them, a monstrosity of architecture that defied the very nature of the earth it was built upon. It was as though the ground had been ripped open and twisted into this abomination of stone and shadow. A sprawling complex of buildings, each laced with veins of gleaming obsidian ore, created the illusion that the entire fortress was a single, living entity, a beast of blackened stone, coiled and ready to strike. Nature did not even encroach upon Night One land and held back from the boundaries.

The citadel's walls were not merely defensive structures; they were statements of power, bristling with sharp edges and jagged spires that clawed at the sky. The obsidian veins that ran through the stone glowed faintly, a dark luminescence that seemed to pulse in time with the fortress's life force. Elara could feel it, a cold, malevolent presence that pressed down on her spirit as they drew nearer.

It felt alive.

Tallin felt nothing but grim satisfaction as he surveyed his home. This was his domain, forged from the very essence of the darkness he commanded. The citadel had stood for centuries, long before his time, but under the rule of the King in Shadow, it had become something more... a symbol of his power, his dominance over the land. He relished in its cold embrace, in the fear it inspired in all who dared approach.

No one did.

Elara glanced down at the mist-filled abyss below as they crossed a sizeable dried-up river bed that surrounded what she could see of the citadel. She could see the bottom, which reminded her of a river, but this one was filled with a writhing, oozing fog that swirled and concealed whatever horrors lay within. The thought of escape flashed through her mind, throwing herself into the rent, letting the fall or whatever fate allowed to take her life before Tallin could. But she quickly dismissed it. There was no guarantee the fall would kill her instantly, and even if it did, she refused to give Tallin the satisfaction of seeing her surrender to despair.

"Why are you taking me here?" Elara wanted to know. Tallin merely looked straight ahead without gracing her with an answer.

The massive gates of the citadel loomed ahead, etched with ancient runes that seemed to writhe and pulse with dark magic. As they approached, the gates groaned open like the dying breath of some great beast. Tallin led his steed through without a glance back at Elara, who followed, her hatred for him burning hotter with each step.

Inside, the citadel was a maze of shadows and stone, the air thick with the scent of iron and damp earth. The walls, lit only by sparse torches, cast flickering shadows that twisted and contorted in the dim light. Elara felt the oppressive atmosphere close around her, suffocating in intensity. Every stone seemed to hum with dark energy; every shadow seemed to harbour unseen eyes watching her every move.

Focusing, she saw people moving about as if actually living here. There was a market selling meagre goods. A person dressed entirely in black approached one stall. The stall operator handed him small shiny coins and gems, and he turned to see Elara. She gasped at the sight of the orange fur covering his face. The long snout turned upward in a constant sneer.

"The scourge foxes. They run the streets down here. They won't bother you, though, as you are quite clearly with me," Tallin offered through a sneer of his own. "They are no ordinary creature but a sheer embodiment of cunning and malice. This is why they work for us. They are not like your fluffy little bastards…"

Elara looked over at the fox, his tall, lithe frame cloaked in black clothing. He seemed to blend in and out of the many shadows, making him nearly invisible at various times. His fur was a deep, smoky red with a flash of white running through it, and was the only way to catch a fleeting glimpse at times. Sharp, amber eyes glow faintly beneath the hood of his cloak, reflecting the distant torchlight with a malevolent gleam. His eyes were constantly in motion, scanning his surroundings with a predator's intensity, calculating every possible threat and opportunity. The fox's clothing was finely crafted yet functional, designed for stealth and speed. His tunic, made of supple leather, was adorned with intricate, swirling patterns that seemed to writhe like serpents when caught in the light. The fabric is thick enough to offer protection but flexible enough to allow swift, silent movement. A belt, studded with small, sharp daggers, wrapped around his waist, each weapon within easy reach of his clawed hands.

This was the first time she had taken in one of the Wildlings, having been unconscious most of her time in Wood Haven. As she walked and, at times, dragged by the rope tied to the horse, she noticed the fox's hands, covered in fingerless gloves, were tipped with claws that glinted like the obsidian in the walls. Every inch of this scourge fox exuded an air of menace and danger, a creature born of the night and the secrets it holds. But Elara saw something else in his eyes.

Was it fear? Regret?

Tallin dismounted and yanked the rope holding Elara, momentarily jolting her eyes away from the fox. When she looked back, he was nowhere to be seen. Tallin handed the reins of his horse to a waiting servant. She nodded obediently and smiled towards Elara. Tallin turned to Elara, his expression unreadable, but his eyes glinted with the satisfaction of victory.

"Welcome to your new home," he said, his voice a cold, cruel whisper that sent a shiver down her spine.

"Home?" Elara spat, her voice filled with venom. "I would sooner die than call this place my home."

Tallin's lips curled into a smirk.

"That can be arranged."

Before Elara could respond, a shadowy figure approached, dressed in the dark armor of the Night One soldiers. His helmet obscured his dark Elven face, but his posture spoke of urgency.

"My Prince," the soldier said, his voice low and tense. "The other raiding party has not returned. They were due back hours ago." Tallin's smirk vanished, replaced by a frown. "What do you mean they have not returned?" His tone was sharp, laced with a dangerous edge.

"They were tasked with capturing the hu-man male from the elf druid, but there has been no word from them. We fear they may have been lost."

Tallin's eyes narrowed.

"Let me rephrase that for you. They were tasked with capturing the hu-man male from the single elf druid female. I faced an entire village of curse-born filth-bloods!" Tallin's backhand swipe hit the knight with a clang reverberating through the courtyard.

"The loss of a raiding party is not just an inconvenience; it was a sign of weakness, a crack in the armour of our power. One fucking Elf girl should not be such an inconvenience." The knight nodded quickly, desperately trying to prepare for the next assault.

"Send out a scouting party," Tallin ordered, his voice cold and commanding. "Find out what happened to them. I want to know if they're dead, captured, or worse. See to it yourself."

The soldier bowed and hurried off to carry out the order, leaving Tallin and Elara alone once more. Tallin's gaze lingered on Elara, his eyes narrowing as if he were considering something. Elara smiled back at him.

"I think I like this Elf druid. She sounds sassy," Elara quipped, also preparing herself for Tallin to strike out.

It did not come.

Elara met his gaze with defiance, refusing to let him see the fear that gnawed at her insides. She would not give him the satisfaction of knowing how much his citadel unnerved her, how the very air seemed to sap her strength and will. But beneath her defiance, a flicker of hope stirred. If the other raiding party had been lost, perhaps it meant there were forces out there stronger than Tallin, forces that might one day bring his dark reign to an end.

"Take her to the dungeons," Tallin finally said, turning away. "I will deal with her later."

Two guards stepped forward, their hands closing around Elara's arms. She struggled briefly, but their grip was ironclad. As they dragged her away, she cast one last look at Tallin, burning his image into her memory. She vowed then that she would escape this place and find a way to break free from his clutches, no matter the cost. As she was led deeper into the bowels of the citadel, the walls seemed to close in tighter, the darkness growing more suffocating with each step. Elara held onto her anger, letting it fuel her determination. She would not be broken. She would not be defeated.

The citadel may have been a fortress of nightmares, a spiked castle of epic proportions, but Elara was determined to survive it. If the other raiding party was truly lost, it meant there was still hope.

A hope that somewhere out there, someone was fighting against the darkness.

She hoped they would come for her.

Chapter Twenty-Four
Kayriss
"A quest ye say!"

Wood Haven was a village unlike any other, but it still held some strong traditions in its veins. For example, "never give a job to someone you wouldn't do yourself" and "treat others how you'd like to be treated," so the Council of Animals was called upon for all significant decisions.

The canopy overhead was thick, with shafts of sunlight filtering through the leaves, casting dappled patterns on the ground below. Every tree seemed to hum with its tune, every burrow and den a sanctuary for those who called this place home. All of the homes were empty now, though, as all the creatures had gathered in the main meeting hall to hear the plan's next step. The room was abuzz with activity; creatures of all kinds were chatting at the top of their voices. Isaac could understand all of them except the dormouse, as they all seemed to speak the same language.

"How can I understand them?" Isaac wanted to know.

"It's only the less evolved ones I have to cast a spell for. Back in the old days, some of the creatures you see here were actually a lot smaller..." She reported offering too much information that Isaac had to process now.

Ansel stood at the head of the assembly. His fur, greying with age, gave him an air of wisdom and authority that few would dare question. His eyes were as sharp as ever, and he scanned the faces of those who had come. He knew the time for decisions had arrived, and every creature in the village sensed it, too.

"Friends, we face a dilemma," Ansel began, his deep voice carrying over the crowd's murmurs. "The hu-man woman, who we now know that the Night Ones are calling Elara, has been taken, and we do not yet know why. But what we do know is that she is important. More important than we could have imagined. Her disappearance is no mere accident; it is a calculated move by forces that we must uncover."

The crowd quieted as Ansel spoke, each creature keenly aware of the gravity of the situation. A small blue bird flew in, landing on one of the rabbit's more prominent ears. This was the only thing anyone wanted to hear right now.

Isaac reasoned that his arrival was about the same time as Elaras's, concluding there must be a connection. He stood beside Kayriss, feeling judgement on himself from all around for simply existing. The weight of eyes on him felt like he was tarnished with the same brush, that his being there would bring the Night Ones back again. Kayriss pulled him closer and smiled at the gathered masses, and their eyes seemed to soften as if she, the healer of Ansel, allowed Isaac to be there. He was with her, so he deemed it okay.

A dormouse sniffed at the pair, smelling the same scent. Another, next to him, pointed with a clear 'I told you so' look on its face to the other.

Kayriss smiled at both and nodded, making both dormice drop their berries and mouths.

Ansel turned his wise eyes to Isaac, a soft sigh escaping him. "Isaac, while you are here now with Kayriss, I believe that it is right that you walk a different path. If the Night Ones are searching for hu-mans, then handing them another might not be the best ploy."

Isaac heard the reason in the words, but his connection to Kayriss threw logic and caution in the same bag to be thrown into the river. Ansel continued;

"Your connection to Kayriss is strong, but it is precisely because of that bond that you should leave her and us. This village may not survive another assault, and your connection weakens Kayriss as her love for you is evident."

Kayriss, who had remained silent until now, was considering all options. She knew Ansel to be correct; he was the wise elder for a reason, but her heart... It longed, needed, and yearned to be with Isaac. She stepped forward. "Where Isaac leaves, I follow. We are stronger together, and I will not leave him behind. But I understand the importance of finding Elara. We need to prioritise her safe return."

The crowd murmured in agreement, though some, like Grind and Granite, seemed less concerned with their love and more interested in another path.

"This hu-man's safe return is obviously a priority, but our village was also attacked. And not by a few Night Ones." Grind said, his voice gruff and unwavering. "Let's not forget those cursed rats who attacked my Stonemarsh. If we leave them unchecked, they might return with even greater numbers."

Granite, his stout travelling companion, nodded in agreement. "Aye, those vermin need to be dealt with. Who knows if this Elara even wants to be saved." A wave of murmurs rippled around the room. It was hard to judge, but all gathered had mixed thoughts.

Captain Browntail, seeing the opportunity for adventure, straightened his coat. It was a rich and dark red, having cost him many a pebble at the markets to handcraft. He stepped forward with a flourish, his first mate Cutlass beside him. The pair had an air of confidence and danger about them, tempered by the mischievous glint in their eyes. Cutlass cleared her throat to get everyone's attention on Browntail.

"If the seas have taught us anything, it's that timing, ye be everything," Browntail said, his voice smooth and persuasive. "We find Elara first, as a maiden cannot be left without a rescue." As he finished, he stomped his small paw down on the floor, and his first mate shouted a triumphant "Aaaarrr!"

"Wise words from someone so small," Ansel confirmed, smiling at the captain. "Let's say we travel to save Elara but try to speak to whomever we can about the rat situation en route. Kayriss, can you question the wildlife on your travels?"

Kayriss nodded, already resigned to partaking in this rescue. She, too, wanted the answers as to why these two hu-mans had appeared. More so, what it meant going forward, she had some memories of the old race, as her mother was one of them. That happened when she was much younger than her current sixteen hundred cycles. Long had most memories been forgotten.

"Kayriss, you have already done so much for us, and I hope you understand the weight of the responsibility that I am placing upon your small shoulders," Ansel asked genuine concern in his voice.

"I will speak to the rats when the time comes and any we may find along the way," she said. "But I agree, Elara must be found first. We don't know what danger she might be in."

Hooth, the owl city guardsman, who had been listening quietly from a low-hanging branch, jumped down, adding his assistance. His voice was a deep, resonant hoot but understandable in their dialect.

"The nights grow longer, and the darkness spreads. I will go with you, Lady Kayriss. My eyes see what others cannot, and I will be needed when we search for Elara." The assembly murmured approval. Hooth was known for his keen vision and unerring sense of direction, traits which would be invaluable on their journey.

The two Mine Folk stood and moved to the owl's side, and he looked down at them approvingly, aware that they had strengthened their mission.

Edgar wagged his tail slightly and padded forward, his deep brown eyes filled with loyalty. He moved to sit next to Hooth, and his bark confirmed that he, too, was joining the rescue party. Kayriss quickly cast her animal-speaking spell.

"Where she goes, I go. We are pack, and we protect our own."

Browntail and Cutlass leapt to the front of the gathered party, landing together and striking as imposing a stance as possible. "Ye not be questing without us!" He boomed, followed by Cutlass's obligatory "Aaaaarrrrr!".

Ansel nodded, a hint of a smile on his face.

"Very well, then. It seems we have a group ready to venture out. Captain Browntail and Cutlass, you will lead us on any water your group may come across. Grind and Granite, your strength will be crucial when we face the dangers of the land. Hooth, your eyes will guide us through the night and the skies. And Kayriss, your skill with words and healing may be our saving grace."

He paused, looking at Isaac and Edgar. "And Isaac, if you are determined to go, then you must stay close to the group. Edgar, I trust you to keep him safe. But remember, this is not just about finding Elara; it is about understanding why she was taken. We must be prepared for anything."

The council nodded in agreement, and the decision was made. Despite the uncertainty of what lay ahead, they shared a sense of purpose.

The group began their final preparations as the sun dipped lower in the sky, casting long shadows over Wood Haven. The journey ahead would be dangerous, but they knew they could not turn back now. Elara's fate hung in the balance, and possibly the Wildlands' fate.

**

    Ansel moved through the quiet village, happy that it was returning to a semblance of normal. He'd been worried about jeopardising the group but knew someone had to go. If he were years younger, he'd have gone himself, but he would hinder their speed. In recent days, he'd recast his protection glyphs, doubling their size and strength, reassuring him that the village would be safe from further attacks. Deep down, he knew there would be none as the Night Ones had their prize. However, he wondered if sending Isaac was giving them an extra bonus but knew Kayriss would not leave his side. They had a bond everyone could see.

    It was a bond strong enough to reshape their world, and he was not going to interfere with it.

    Rounding a corner, he noticed Kayriss sitting on a high branch, her wings gently keeping her balance. She seemed lost in thought, unaware of his presence. Ansel coughed to get her attention. She fluttered down to him with the gentle buzz of her wings.

"Everyone's asleep, but I have troubles, Ansel." She said, and he placed a large paw on her shoulder in support. "I have always felt of both times, and when I found Isaac, he completed me. But with Elara, too... What if she was meant for him? What if he falls for her? I think I want to find her to asway my fears." Ansel considered the words.

"You say you are from the old times. Do you read their words?" Ansel asked, changing the subject.

"Yes, I do, but have never found more than a few small books. It helped me understand a some of the ways from the old times, but never the full picture."

Ansel sighed and placed a large paw on her shoulder. He looked visibly greyer in the light. Kayriss saw something weighing down on him, a burden born many years ago.

"Come, child. I have something you must see."

Chapter Twenty-Five
Tallin
The Prince and the Prisoner.

    The steps descended into a maw of eternal night, each cloaked in shadows that seemed to writhe and breathe like a living thing. As the Night One approached the flight, the stone felt cold beneath his feet, as though the void itself had kissed it. The deeper he went, the more the air thickened, heavy with the weight of forgotten whispers and the lingering scent of damp, ancient decay.

    The darkness wasn't merely an absence of light; it was a presence, a creeping shroud that clung to skin like the tendrils of some unseen creature. Every footfall echoed, swallowed by the abyss as if the very dungeon waited hungrily for the final step, eager to consume all hope.

The stone steps leading to the dungeons were slick with moisture, worn smooth by the centuries of feet that had passed over them. Tallin crept, his footfalls barely audible as he descended into the depths of the Night One's fortress. The further he went, the colder the air became, thick with the scent of damp stone and the faintest trace of something sweeter, Elara's perfume, a delicate, hu-man fragrance that lingered despite the gloom.

He reached the bottom of the stairs, hesitating before the heavy iron door that separated the world above from the darkness below. It was an ancient door that had seen countless prisoners pass through its threshold, and now it held the last, or first, of her kind. The hu-mans of old used the dungeons for some other long-lost reason, but they sufficed with Night One additions. Tallin's hand hovered over the latch, his mind warring with itself. He had no reason to be here, no duty that called him to this place.

He was here, and he knew why.

Her name, Elara, echoed in his thoughts as he pushed open the door. The hinges groaned in protest, the sound reverberating through the empty corridors. A guard at the far end of the hall stiffened at his approach, quickly lowering his gaze in deference as Tallin entered.

"Leave us," Tallin commanded, his voice steady despite the unease that churned within him.

The guard hesitated only momentarily before nodding and retreating down the corridor. When the echo of his footsteps finally faded, silence fell, broken only by the faint drip of water seeping through the stone walls.

Tallin approached the cell that held Elara, his steps slow, almost reluctant. She was the only prisoner currently held here, so he knew she'd be expecting a visit.

She was sitting on the cold stone floor, her back against the wall, knees drawn up to her chest. Even in the dim light, her presence was unmistakable. Her hair, once a cascade of dark waves, was now tangled and matted, but her eyes... her eyes were as piercing as ever, burning with defiance and something else, curiosity perhaps, or recognition of his inner conflict.

Her presence was a strange, blinding contradiction in the dim glow of the cell. To Tallin, she was both a burning flame and a shadowed figure, radiant in her defiance yet cloaked in the darkness of her captivity. She was a fragile blade, beautiful yet dangerous, reflecting a light that did not belong in such a place, and yet, like the cell's flickering torch, there was a frailty to that glow. She was both the dawn he despised and the night he could not escape, a reminder that his darkness would be starkly revealed in her radiance.

The cell that held her had seen centuries of rot and ruin. It was a forgotten relic of a world long dead, the walls thick with grime and stained by the slow passage of time. The stone, once strong, had grown slick and crumbling in places, though its core remained impenetrable, a prison designed to hold even the fiercest wills. Rusted chains dangled from the walls like relics of forgotten cruelty, and the air was damp, thick with the scent of decay and mildew. A single barred window let in a sliver of dull, suffocated light, illuminating the cracked floor where puddles of stagnant water had long ago made their home. Though squalid, it had a security that only age could grant. Unforgiving and as cold as the bones of the dead who had once rotted away in this tomb.

"You again," Elara said, her voice hoarse but unwavering. There was no fear in her gaze, only a challenge. "Come to gloat over your prize?"

Tallin felt a pang of guilt at her words, though he masked it with the stern expression he had learned to wear so well. "I came to ensure you are being treated... adequately."

"Is that what you tell yourself?" she asked, a wry smile tugging at her lips. "Or did you come because you can't stay away?"

He stiffened at her boldness but could not deny the truth in her words. Every time he resolved to distance himself, something pulled him back. It was like an invisible thread connected them, tightening each time he tried to pull away. He should have been repulsed, should have felt the hatred his people harboured for the hu-mans who had destroyed their world.

Instead, he felt something entirely different.

"You think yourself clever," Tallin said, though the heat in his voice was not anger but something far more dangerous. "But you are still a prisoner, Elara. Do not mistake my visit for kindness."

She laughed softly, the sound echoing off the walls like the chime of a bell. "Kindness? No, I don't expect that from you. But I wonder... do you even know what you expect from yourself anymore? I thought you were supposed to kill me, yet here I sit."

Her words cut more profound than he would ever admit. Tallin clenched his fists at his sides, his long nails digging into his palms. He had never been one to question the decisions of the Council. The prophecy was clear. Two hu-mans would return, ending everything the Night Ones had fought to rebuild. Elara was a threat, the first sign that the prophecy was beginning to unfold. The Council was right to want her dead.

Why couldn't he bring himself to order her execution? Why did the thought of her death twist his insides with a pain he had never known before?

"I do not need to justify myself to you," he said, his voice low and dangerous, though the words rang hollow in his ears.

"No," Elara replied, her gaze never leaving him, "but you do need to justify it to yourself. How long will you keep pretending?"

Tallin's breath hitched, and for a moment, he could not look away from her. Her eyes were like mirrors, reflecting all the doubts and fears he had buried deep within. He had been taught to believe that hu-mans were nothing more than remnants of a past best forgotten, that they were the cause of their destruction. Those teachings seemed fragile in her presence like cobwebs easily brushed aside.

"I am not here to debate with you," he said, forcing the words out with more conviction than he felt. "The Council has made its decision. You are to be executed."

There. He had said it. The words hung between them like a death knell, and yet, rather than fear, he saw a quiet resignation in her eyes.

"And you?" she asked softly. "Is that what you want?"

Tallin faltered, his breath catching in his throat. He had never been one to question his duty, to doubt the path laid before him. Standing here in the cold, damp darkness, with Elara's gaze piercing through every barrier he had erected around his heart, he was at a loss.

"I..." His voice trailed off, the words he wanted to say slipping away like sand through his fingers. He didn't know what he wanted anymore. All he knew was that the thought of her death filled him with a dread he couldn't explain.

"Tell me, Tallin," Elara whispered, leaning forward just enough that her words brushed against his senses like a caress. "What do you fear more? The prophecy coming true, or the possibility that you might be wrong?"

Her question lingered in the air, heavy with implications he wasn't ready to face. Without another word, Tallin turned on his heel and left the cell, the iron door clanging shut behind him. As he ascended the stairs back to the world above, Elara's voice echoed in his mind, unravelling the certainty he had clung to for so long.

For the first time, Tallin realised he was no longer sure of anything.

And that terrified him more than any prophecy ever could.

Chapter Twenty-Six
Kayriss
The library of the old race.

    Kayriss was led through the village of Wood Haven to the massive oak tree in the centre. It was enormous, and she wondered why Ansel was bringing her here. He'd mentioned books before, which excited her, but she'd not seen any in her days here so far. The tree was the heart of the settlement, towering over everything, even matching Hovel in size. It was ancient and sprawling but did not hold any books.

    The oak's massive roots wound deep into the earth, and it was at the base of this great tree that Ansel brought her.

"Here, child. What do you see?" Ansel said, his words dripping in playful mystery. Kayriss looked closer, but she could only see a large wrap of blackberry vines. "Look closer. With your magic."

Kayriss gently, with a druidic enchantment, politely asked the bush to part, showing what was hidden beneath. The thorny branches circled and undulated at her affable ask, creating an opening through the bramble. A warm green light shone as the spell completed.

Below the tangle of vines and plants was a metal door. It was set into the floor, covered in moss and plant growth cycles. The door was out of place in the natural surroundings, and Kayriss looked quizzically at Ansel.

"Open it," he said, smiling.

Another incantation followed, and a gust of wind took hold of the handle and breezed it open. Immediately, a waft of stale air flushed out from the darkness below. The entrance led to a stone staircase, spiralling down into the dark, musty depths. It was completely out of place in the surroundings, but Kayriss was lost in her own inquisitiveness.

The air grew cooler as they descended, and the smell of old paper and damp earth filled Kayriss's senses. At the bottom of the stairs, they entered a vast, underground chamber. Darkness filled all their senses until Ansel called forth a light source.

She watched in awe as he raised a handle, and the large room filled with an otherworldly light. Kayriss was unsure what magic was being used, but the globes hanging from the ceiling buzzed with a slight hum. Their glow was a sickly yellow, barely illuminating the room.

"I do not know how it works either, child," he said, anticipating the question.

Kayriss stepped cautiously into the strange, dimly lit chamber, her eyes wide with curiosity and apprehension. She had been led to this place, deep underground, through a narrow, rusted metal hatch hidden beneath the roots of an ancient tree. The air inside was thick and stale, carrying the scent of time long past, of metal, dust, and something else she couldn't quite place. This all brought on a wild entanglement of emotions but I pressed forward.

The chamber was unlike anything she had ever seen. The walls were made of cold, smooth metal, reinforced with thick beams that crisscrossed overhead, creating a low ceiling that made the space feel claustrophobic. The floor was solid and unyielding. Her footsteps echoed softly as she moved deeper into the unnatural cavern. Lining the walls were rows upon rows of strange objects. Books, yes, more than she had ever seen in one place, but also other things she couldn't immediately identify. The books were stacked on metal shelves that reached from floor to ceiling, their covers worn and faded, some titles barely legible. The pages were yellowed with age but were intact, preserved by the dry, airless environment.

The books were just the beginning. There were boxes, many sealed and stacked haphazardly in corners, covered in thick layers of dust. Some were open, revealing their contents. Strange devices made of metal and glass, with wires and dials, their purposes unknown to her. She reached to touch one, feeling the cold, lifeless surface under her fingers. It was heavy, solid, and seemed to hum faintly as if it still held some dormant power. Kayriss was used to feeling the life in everything she touched, but here, deep down below the surface, there was nothing. It was devoid of life.

In another part of the weird tunnel, Kayriss found what looked like furniture, though it was unlike anything she had ever seen. There were chairs made of a smooth, shiny material, their legs and backs curving in odd, unnatural shapes. A table stood nearby, its surface cluttered with more books, papers, and objects she couldn't name. One of the papers caught her eye; its surface was covered in a blotched shape, which she faintly remembered. The symbols and lines drew something.

It was a map.

It showed the outline of a couple of islands and a single 'X' marking something she was unaware of. She continued rifling through the papers, seeing the word 'shelter' repeated many times. She concluded that the old race called their caverns this. Turning the next page, she saw what looked like a handwritten note.

When Humanity Falls, Darkness Rises.
A poem by Luke Jones.
24th August 2044

Shadows cross the faces painted grey
Dreams fall and shatter in the nightless day

Hope crumbles no place left to stay
Whispers echo in a world of decay

Cities burn while the spirit dies
Lost voices scream wicked lullabies
Broken hearts and empty skies
Tears fall like rain no one denies

When humanity falls, darkness rises
In the void of our own disguises
Feel the cold wind no compromises
Ash and smoke are our only prizes

Wander through the ruins of our fate
No saving grace too little too late
In the silence of a lifeless state
Bound by shadows endless weight

When humanity falls, darkness rises
In the void of our own disguises
Feel the cold wind no compromises
Ash and smoke are our only prizes

Guitar wails a cry in the dark
Fingers bleed leaving a mark
Echoes haunt every empty park
Lost souls fade away no spark

It seemed written with some writing implement and not printed like the other pages.

"Who wrote this?" Kayriss enquired.

"Many years ago, we found this place. There was a body. Something we haven't seen before. We buried it and then thought of leaving this place as it was from the time before. We Wildlings like to look forward, not back." Ansel explained. He moved his large form awkwardly in the confines, opting to sit on one of the off chairs. It creaked under his weight but held.

Dropping the notes back on the table, Kayriss continued her search.

Along one wall, she discovered rows of what looked like containers, all identical, each sealed tightly with metal lids. She pried one open, her fingers struggling against the stubborn seal, and inside, she found a strange, powdery substance. She sniffed it cautiously, recoiling slightly at the unfamiliar, musty scent. 'What could this have been used for?' she wondered. As she continued exploring, she noticed a section of the wall with large, square doors, each with a round handle in the centre. She twisted one open, revealing a small, enclosed space inside, almost like a box, lined with soft material. There were more of these in the shelter, some more prominent, some minor, each a mystery to her. They seemed too small to be rooms yet too big for simple storage. One area of the shelter was filled with an assortment of clothing, strange garments made from materials she couldn't identify. The colours were dull and faded, the fabric stiff and brittle with age. Some were hung on hooks, others folded neatly in piles. She lifted one. It was heavy, with thick padding and a large hood, unlike any clothing she had ever seen. What kind of environment requires such protection? Dropping it back down, she picked up another. This one was thinner, a single layer of cloth. It had short arms and the word 'ACDC' on it. Kayriss tried to sound it out, but it wasn't a word she was used to.

There were remnants of a time long gone and a thousand questions everywhere she looked. The objects held no meaning to her, yet spoke of a civilisation far more advanced, yet long vanished. She realised this place, this fallout shelter, had been built to withstand something terrible. It was a refuge, a final stronghold for those who once lived in the world above. They had filled it with everything they thought necessary to survive. A library of knowledge, tools, food, and clothing, but the world had changed, and the purpose of this place had been forgotten. As there was a dead body here... Kayriss knew that this shelter had faltered somehow. Kayriss stood in the centre of the chamber, her mind reeling from the weight of what she had discovered. This was a relic of the Hu-man age when they faced unimaginable dangers and went to great lengths to protect themselves. Yet, despite all their preparations, they were gone, their knowledge and artefacts left behind, buried in the earth. Cycles later, she was the one to uncover them truly, left to wonder what stories these silent walls could tell. Ansel and the other Wildlings, who had come to see the place as nothing more than a relic of a time they had no connection to, could not read the old texts. The books had been left to rot, their knowledge deemed irrelevant by the inhabitants of Wood Haven. To them, the Hu-mans were a distant memory, their language and wisdom buried alongside their bones.

But Kayriss had questions. She could read the forgotten language of the Hu-mans, a gift passed down from a mother she could not recall, though she had never expected it to be useful. As she stepped further into the library, her fingers brushed the spines of the books, feeling the rough texture of their worn bindings. One of the tomes called to her and urged her to read it. She concluded it was the spirits that powered her, helping once more. Pulling it free from the shelf and carefully opening it. The pages crackled as they turned, brittle with age. The words, though faded, were legible, and as Kayriss read, consuming the volume with a speed she didn't know she could achieve. She was desperate to learn more about the Hu-mans, where her mother lived, and uncover the dark history buried within. The text spoke of a time when the Hu-mans faced great evils, creatures born of chaos and darkness that terrorised the world. These abominations spread fear and death wherever they roamed, threatening the very existence of the Hu-mans. The Hu-mans, resourceful and resilient, fought back. They waged wars against the evils, using their cunning and strength to survive. Werewolves, evil spirits, vampires and other monsters had risen as their numbers decreased, making the fights harder by the day. In the beginning, they had tried to survive, not believing the growing stories of the wondrous and the malignant devils that were slowly killing them off, as they were more worried about the falling birth rate and the new aberrant babies being born.

Over time, these monstrous beings were mainly eradicated, either by the Hu-mans' hands or by the passage of time. They didn't realise their numbers were dwindling as fast as they were until too late. The relentless battles and the encroaching dominance of the aberrant races reduced their numbers. Their children were birthing them out of existence. The pages continued, mentioning the first of the aberrants.

Born to a mother called Victoria Doherty. A father committed to the line of duty, named Jack Wright.

And a baby, they called Kay.

Chapter Twenty-Seven
Tallin
The grand entrance.

The grand hall of the Night One Council was a place of shadows and secrets, its high vaulted ceilings echoing with the whispers of ages past. Braziers lined the walls, their flickering flames casting an eerie glow over the sombre faces of the Council members seated around the massive stone table. At the head of the table sat the King in Shadow, Marus, his presence commanding and cold, his eyes sharp as they bore into the figure of his eldest son standing before him.

King Marus, the King in Shadow, was a figure carved from the deepest reaches of the night. His skin, as dark as obsidian, reflected no light as if the very essence of shadow had been woven into his flesh. His face was sharp and regal, with high cheekbones and eyes that glowed faintly with a cold, silver light, like distant stars barely visible through a stormy sky. His presence was one of quiet dominance, a king who did not need to raise his voice to command absolute obedience. His silver hair, falling in stark contrast to his dark skin, cascaded down his shoulders like molten moonlight, a crown more imposing than any metal or jewel could craft. King Marus's beard was a silvered cascade of fine strands, sharp and neatly trimmed, framing his jaw like the gleam of a moonlit blade against the void.

There was something ancient about him, as though time itself recoiled in his presence, and he moved with the grace of one who had walked through centuries of darkness, untouched by age or weakness.

Marus ruled with a hand both steady and merciless. His voice, when he spoke, was soft but carried the weight of a thousand forgotten deeds, each word a shadow cast over those who dared to meet his gaze. His clothing, black as midnight, seemed not to shine but to absorb all light around it, an extension of his very being. He was a king of secrets and whispers, ruling from behind the veil of night; his power felt in every dark corner of his realm. To his people, he was a saviour who understood the darkness better than any living soul; to his enemies, he was a phantom… unseen, untouchable, but ever-present. In the silver of his hair and the abyss of his skin, he embodied the paradox of his reign: a ruler of shadow, born from the lightless depths yet crowned in the gleam of silvered power.

King Marus's throne was a monument to shadow and power, carved from a single slab of obsidian so black it seemed to ooze night from every line of its creation. Jagged edges rose from the base like the peaks of a dark mountain, towering behind him in twisted spires as though the very night had been sculpted into form. The seat was smooth but cold as death, with intricate silver inlays that spiralled like veins of moonlight through the stone, hinting at ancient runes of dominion. The arms of the throne were adorned with polished onyx, shaped into the heads of snarling beasts long forgotten, their eyes glimmering faintly as if watching all who approached. Positioned in the deepest corner of his hall, the throne seemed less a seat of comfort and more an extension of the shadows, as though Marus himself was merely a darker reflection of the void upon which he ruled.

Chairs smaller but similar in design flanked each side, fanning out to fill the room, and on each was another of his Night One council, waiting to hear what news was to befall upon them.

Prince Tallin stood tall, though inside, he was a whirlwind of conflicting emotions. The weight of the decision he was about to make pressed down on him like a mountain, yet he knew he could no longer hide his doubts. Elara's presence had stirred something within him that could not be ignored—also something he knew he must keep secret.

"Speak, Tallin," King Marus commanded, his voice a deep rumble that reverberated through the hall. "You have requested this audience with the Council. What is it that weighs so heavily upon you, my child?"

Tallin took a deep breath, steeling himself. "Father, members of the Council," he began, his voice steady and respectful but laced with the moment's gravity. I have come to question the prophecy that we have long held as truth—the prophecy that foretells the return of two humans who will repopulate the Earth and bring about the downfall of our kind."

A murmur immediately rippled through the room, the Council members exchanging glances, some shocked, others sceptical. At the far end of the table, Tallin's younger brother, Prince Kaelen, leaned forward in his chair, a faint smirk playing on his lips as he watched his brother's boldness with calculating eyes.

King Marus' expression hardened. "You dare question the prophecy, Tallin? The very prophecy that has guided our people for centuries?"

"I do," Tallin replied, meeting his father's gaze with a resolve that surprised even himself. "Elara, the human we have imprisoned, is unlike anything I expected. She is not the monster our legends portray. She is just as much a person as any of us. I cannot help but wonder if we have misinterpreted the prophecy. If we have allowed fear to blind us to the truth."

Kaelen's smirk widened, though he remained silent, content to watch as his brother dug deeper into what he saw as a grave mistake. He sat further forward in his seat, eagerly awaiting the next misstep.

"And what truth do you believe we have missed, my son?" King Marus's voice was icy, and his patience was clearly wearing thin.

Tallin hesitated, aware of the delicate line he was walking. "I believe there is a possibility that the prophecy is not as literal as we have taken it to be. Perhaps it is not the humans who will bring about our downfall, but our actions against them. By destroying them out of fear, we may set ourselves on a path to ruin. Much as they themselves once did."

The silence that followed was suffocating. The Council members exchanged wary glances, unsure of how to respond. Finally, one of the elder members, a wizened woman with piercing blue eyes, spoke up.

"And what do you propose, Prince Tallin? That we simply allow this human to live? To risk everything we have built on the hope that your interpretation is correct?"

Tallin opened his mouth to respond, but before he could, Kaelen stood, his voice cutting through the tension like a knife. "My brother's sentimentality is admirable," he said, his tone laced with feigned respect. "But it is dangerous. The prophecy has been clear for centuries, and our survival depends on adhering to its warnings. To question it now, on the basis of a single human, is foolish. We cannot afford such risks."

Tallin shot his brother a sharp look, but Kaelen met his gaze calmly, calculatedly. The younger prince had always been ambitious, and Tallin could see the wheels turning in his mind, the opportunity he was seizing. If Tallin lost the Council's favour, Kaelen would benefit the most.

King Marus raised a hand, silencing both of his sons. He turned his gaze to Tallin, his expression unreadable. "You have always been my most loyal son, Tallin," he said slowly, each word heavy with meaning. "But loyalty to the crown means loyalty to our people, to the laws and prophecies that have protected us for generations. I cannot ignore your doubts, but neither can I dismiss the wisdom of the Council."

Tallin felt his heart sink as his father's words hit him like a blow. He had known this would be difficult, but he had hoped... perhaps foolishly, that his father might see the truth in his concerns.

King Marus turned to the Council, his voice booming. "The Council will deliberate on this matter. In the meantime, Tallin, you will be entrusted with the care of the human. You are to keep her under close watch, and you are responsible for her actions. Should she prove to be the threat the prophecy warns of, it will be on your head."

Tallin's breath caught in his throat. He had not expected this. To be given charge of Elara meant that his father was neither dismissing nor accepting his doubts but instead testing him. It was both a burden and a strange kind of trust.

Kaelen's smirk faltered slightly, but he quickly masked it with a look of concern. "Father, is that wise? What if Tallin's... compassion leads him to make a mistake?"

King Marus shot Kaelen a sharp look, silencing him. "Tallin will do what is necessary," he said firmly. "And he will bear the consequences if he does not."

Tallin bowed his head, accepting his father's decision. "I understand, Father. I will not fail."

"See that you don't," Marus replied, his tone final. "This council is dismissed."

The Council members began to rise, some casting wary glances at Tallin, others with expressions of curiosity. Kaelen lingered a moment, catching Tallin's eye with equal parts challenge and warning look. He was not finished with this, and Tallin knew it.

As the hall emptied, Tallin stood alone momentarily, the weight of his new responsibility settling over him like a cloak of lead. He had asked for this, he reminded himself, and now he had to see it through.

**

Tallin's quarters starkly contrasted with the cold, dark dungeons where Elara had been kept. The walls were lined with tapestries, and the floors were covered in rich, woven rugs. A fire crackled in the hearth, casting a warm glow over the room as Tallin stood by the window with a glass of wine. The deep red liquid swirled in the goblet as he stared out into the night, lost in thought.

He had ordered Elara to be brought to his quarters, knowing that it would raise eyebrows among the servants, but he cared little. He needed to keep her close, understand her, and perhaps... protect her.

The door creaked open, and two servants entered, leading Elara between them. She was still dressed in the ragged clothes she had been captured in, her hair tangled, her skin pale from her time in the dungeons. Her eyes, those bright, defiant eyes, were as sharp as ever as they locked onto Tallin.

"Prepare her," Tallin ordered, not turning from the window.

The servants moved quickly, leading Elara toward the bathing chamber. She resisted initially, her instincts still tuned to survival, but Tallin's presence seemed to calm her, if only slightly. She glanced at him as she was led away, a silent question in her gaze.

Tallin watched her go, his grip tightening on the glass. He wasn't sure what he was doing or why he felt the need to see her treated with dignity. She was still his prisoner, and yet...

The sound of water splashing from the adjacent room reached his ears, and he imagined Elara stepping into the bath, the water's warmth chasing away the dungeon's chill. He could see her in his mind's eye, the grime and fear melting away to reveal the person beneath.

A person, not a monster.

He moved to the door, pushing it aside. He leaned against the frame with his glass, enjoying the sight before him.

The two servants, both Night One females, were dutifully cleaning Elara as she stood naked in the metallic bathtub in the centre of the room. They sponged her down carefully as if she was made of glass and she was not to be injured.

Elara's eyes met Tallin's, and a fire raged behind them, lighting the ember inside him. She did not flinch or try to hide her nudity from him, but she let him drink her in. When she was finally brought back into Tallin's main room, she was dressed in a simple but clean gown, her hair washed and brushed. She looked different, almost like someone from a time long forgotten, a reminder of what the world had once been. The servants bowed and moved to leave the room, but Tallin held one back, ushering the other to close the door and leave the three of them alone. Tallin motioned for Elara to sit.

"You've been given a reprieve," he said quietly, his voice softer than he intended. "But don't mistake this for mercy. I am bound by my duty, and I will do what I must if you prove to be the threat the Council fears."

Elara looked at him, her expression unreadable. "And what do you believe, Tallin? Do you really think I'm the monster your people say I am?"

Tallin held her gaze for a long moment, the weight of her question pressing down on him. Finally, he spoke, the words slipping out before he could stop them.

"I am all-powerful here. The people bow to my whims."

With those words, the servant moved to the bed and unrobed.

Chapter Twenty-Eight
Kayriss
The first of her kind.

Kayriss's breath came in ragged gasps, each colder than the last, as if the air around her had turned to ice. The revelation played on a loop in her mind, a grotesque cycle she couldn't escape. The first aberration. The words echoed, taunting her with their finality. She pressed her hand against the cold, metal wall of the fallout chamber as if searching for something solid, something tangible to cling to.

Nothing felt real anymore.

The room spun around her, a suffocating whirl of confusion and disbelief. Kayriss's legs buckled under the weight of it all, and she crumpled to the floor, a marionette with her strings cut. Her fingers brushed against something smooth and cool, drawing her attention away from the dizzying spiral in her head.

Another book.

She picked it up with trembling hands, the childish illustrations on the cover jarringly out of place in this sterile, haunting environment. The title was faded, almost illegible, but the pictures were clear enough. They depicted animals. Owls, wolves, and deer, among others. Their wild eyes were full of life and primal energy that made her heartache. The pages turned slowly under her fingers, each a revelation and another knife twist. The drawings showed all the Wildlings in the times of the hu-mans. These unfamiliar forms of what the Wildlings once were were beautiful in their strangeness, a twisted echo of what once was. Some stayed as they were, though, while others became the Wildlings of today.

To the humans...? They were kept in cages. They were kept as pets. Some were eaten as a delicacy.

The blood drained from her face as the pieces fell into place. Her lineage lay bare in the innocent pages of a child's science book. 'Had her birth caused all this?' Kayriss wondered, her stomach lurching. She had not been the miraculous survivor of an unknown cataclysm as she had believed. She and all the races she knew were mutations, accidents born from the collapse of a dying world.

The first aberration.

A silent scream lodged in her throat. The room seemed to close around her, the walls pressing in with the weight of her discovery. How could this be? How had they kept this from her? From all of them?

Ansel. The thought of him gave her a flicker of hope, the one person she could rely on in this madness. She lifted her head, eyes searching the room for him, expecting to see the same shock and horror reflected in his face.

He sat there as if awaiting her to find this revelation. His expression was calm and unreadable as ever. He looked down at her, his eyes cool and distant, as if he had expected this as if this was just another inevitable part of their journey. Kayriss's breath caught in her throat, disbelief warring with a growing sense of betrayal.

"You... you knew," she whispered, the words barely audible, her voice cracking under the weight of the realisation. Her fingers tightened around the book as if she could somehow squeeze the truth from its pages.

Ansel didn't flinch, didn't shift his gaze. "I did."

The simplicity of his answer sent a shiver down her spine. A flood of questions filled her mind, each more frantic than the last. "How long? How long have you known?"

His silence stretched, a tangible thing between them before he finally spoke. "Since we found this shelter. I sealed it from the others who may have taken this badly. But not before I saw everything you have."

The room seemed to tilt under her, the floor unsteady beneath her feet as she tried to stand. "You've known all this time... and you never told me?" Her voice grew louder, edged with hysteria. "How could you keep this from me? From everyone?"

"I kept it from you to protect you, to protect everyone," Ansel said, his tone infuriatingly calm, as if discussing the weather and not the shattering of her entire reality. "From yourself. And from the others."

"Protect me?" Kayriss spat, the words laced with bitterness. "You let me believe I was... I was something special. But all this time, I was just... a freak!"

"No," Ansel said sharply, moving closer, his calm demeanour cracking just a fraction. "You were the first, yes. But not a freak. You were the beginning of something new, something stronger."

Her laugh was hollow, empty of any genuine mirth. "Something new? We're all just... mutations! Wildlings evolved because the hu-mans died? Because we replaced them. Us freaks of nature. Us aberrations!" She threw the book at his feet as if that could somehow make the truth disappear.

Ansel sighed, the sound heavy with years of unspoken burdens. "I didn't want the others to find out. I didn't want them to see you, us, as anything less than what we are. Leaders. Survivors. Not relics of a past that no longer matters."

It mattered to her. Her entire life had been built on a lie: that her very existence resulted from some catastrophic failure, not some divine intervention or natural evolution. Now that she knew the truth, the floor beneath her felt colder and more hostile, as if rejecting her presence.

"You sealed the fallout chamber," she said, the realisation dawning on her like the slow creep of dawn. "Not to protect us from what was outside... but to protect the secret from getting out."

Ansel nodded, and the confirmation felt like a punch to the gut. She wanted to scream, to cry, to lash out at one of the only beings she had ever truly trusted. All she could do was sit there, staring at the badger who had lied to her, who had let her live a life of ignorance while he carried the weight of the truth alone.

"What now?" she asked, her voice barely a whisper.

"Now," Ansel said, his voice firm, "you know why we can never go back. Why we must look forward, Kayriss. We are what's left in this world and must make it better than the previous one. I believe that starts with finding Elara."

But as she looked into his eyes, she wasn't sure she believed him anymore. The truth had fractured something deep inside her, something she wasn't sure could ever be repaired. She had been the first of her kind, but now she felt like nothing more than a ghost of what could have been, a relic of a past that was as dead as the world that created it. Kayriss turned away from him, letting the coldness of the chamber seep into her bones. She didn't want to think about the future anymore. She just wanted to escape the present and the unbearable weight of knowing who she was in the past.

There was no escape, not now.

Not ever.

Chapter Twenty-Nine
Elara
The Prince on show.

    The night was deep, and the fire in the hearth had burned to glowing embers by the time Elara finished her forced bathing. She sat in the chair Tallin had placed by the fire, her body still tense from the forced incarceration. The gown she had been given clung to her damp skin, the heat from the bath still lingering on her flushed cheeks. She stared into the fire, trying to make sense of the strange mixture of fear and curiosity that had taken root inside her since Tallin had brought her to this room.

    Tallin stood by the servant, who was naked now but expressionless, as if nothing was wrong with the situation. She was a young woman, similar in age to Elara, who she thought was in her mid-twenties. She had soft, delicate features, wide, doe-like eyes, and skin darker than Tallin's. It glistened with a darkness she'd not seen before, and the lines of her lithe body flickered against the light. She was scintillating to watch, an ebony marvel, smooth as silk, that coruscated with a dazzling brilliance.

He looked at Elara, his gaze lingering momentarily before turning to the servant. He placed a hand on her shoulder, smiled and nodded slightly. Elara noted that she returned his smile and moved to the bed, where she positioned herself on all fours.

"Elara," Tallin said, his voice smooth and commanding, "You are to understand that here, in this realm, I am the one who holds power. You may have questioned it before, but I will leave no doubt in your mind."

Elara's eyes flicked up to meet his, a shiver running down her spine at the intensity of his gaze. There was something dangerous in his voice, a challenge wrapped in silken tones. She opened her mouth to respond, but the words caught in her throat were silenced by the tension thickening the air between them.

Also, because Tallin was removing his clothes.

Standing in the dim, flickering light of the chamber, his presence was undoubtedly commanding and magnetic. As he began to disrobe, the air around him grew heavier, charged with an almost palpable energy. His hands moved with deliberate grace, unfastening the clasps of his dark, intricately woven garments. The fabric slid off his broad shoulders, revealing skin the colour of polished obsidian, smooth and unmarred. His musculature was flawless, every contour sculpted precisely like a living statue of perfection.

Elara held in a gasp at the sight of him.

His chest was broad and robust, tapering down to a chiselled abdomen that rippled strength. Each movement of his body revealed his sheer physical power, yet there was an effortless fluidity to his motions, a testament to his agility and control. The light caught on the subtle sheen of his skin, highlighting the contours of his muscles and the ridges of his veins that snaked across his forearms and biceps. His arms were strong and capable, yet there was an elegance in how he moved as if each motion was part of a silent, ancient ritual.

Elara had not taken in his features before, as her only thought was to escape, but now, she pulled her gaze to his face. It was a masterpiece of masculine beauty, with sharp cheekbones, a strong jawline, and full, sensuous lips set in a knowing, almost seductive smile. His eyes were a piercing shade of darkness, with a hint of amber laced through them, glowing faintly in the dim room. They shone with an intensity that was both alluring and dangerous. His ears pointed like all the other Night Ones, adding an exotic, otherworldly charm to his features, marking him as something more than mortal.

As he continued to undress, revealing more of his powerful physique, the air seemed to hum with the raw energy of his presence. His long and muscular legs were perfectly proportioned, every sinew and tendon visible beneath his onyx dark skin. Even in his undressed state, there was nothing vulnerable about him. He exuded a primal, unassailable strength that made it clear he was not a man to be trifled with.

Tallin, in his entirety, was the epitome of manliness. He was a dark, formidable figure of unrivalled beauty and strength, radiating an aura of dominance that was impossible to ignore.

He stepped closer to the servant, who stood quietly, her gaze cast downward in submission. Without taking his eyes off Elara, he gently lifted the servant's chin, forcing her to arch her back. The young woman's breath hitched, but her eyes showed no fear.

Only a strange mix of reverence and anticipation.

"You see, Elara," Tallin continued, his voice low and measured. "My people exist to serve me, to please me. They would do anything I ask, without hesitation, without question. As they know, I have their best interests at my heart."

He slid his hand down the servant's cheek, tracing the line of her jaw, and she leaned into his touch, her lips parting slightly. Elara watched, her heart pounding in her chest, unable to tear her eyes away from the scene unfolding before her. There was an undeniable pull in the way Tallin commanded the room, a magnetism that both repelled and fascinated her.

Tallin's hand moved to the servant's shoulder, and she closed her eyes, her breath quickening as she yielded to his touch. Elara's pulse raced, her senses heightened as she took in every detail: the way the firelight danced across Tallin's chiselled features, the taut muscles of his arms flexing as he moved, the way the servant responded to him with a mix of obedience and desire.

Her eyes moved down Tallin's body, and she realised he was fully ready for what he was about to do. Elara gasped at the breadth of his member, and with a fluid motion, showing both force and care, he entered her.

She gasped, a soft and full of need-sound, and Tallin's lips curled into a satisfied smile.

"You see," he said, his voice barely above a whisper as he finally looked back at Elara, "This is what it means to hold power. My people are always ready for my every need."

Elara's breath caught in her throat. She had never seen anything like this. A display of dominance so blatant, so unashamed. There was something deeply primal about it, a raw energy that shocked and intrigued her. Her eyes roamed over Tallin's body, tracing the lines of his muscular form as he slid in and out of his servant. His movements were smooth, controlled, and undeniably commanding.

The servant responded eagerly to Tallin's every touch, her body arching toward him as he explored her with hands that were both firm and gentle. Elara felt her cheeks flush, her body reacting in ways she couldn't fully understand. There was an undeniable intimacy to the scene, a connection between the two that Elara envied despite the circumstances.

More than that, she realised unsettlingly how easily she could be drawn into this world and lose herself in the power dynamics that Tallin so expertly wielded.

Tallin's gaze never left Elara, even as he brought the servant closer, deeper, guiding her with a steady hand. He was watching her, gauging her reaction, testing her resolve. Elara's mouth was dry, her heart pounding as she sat frozen in her chair, unable to look away.

The servant moaned softly, her voice thick with pleasure as she surrendered completely to Tallin's control. Elara's breath caught again, and she found herself leaning forward, drawn into the moment's intensity, despite herself. Tallin's smile widened as he noted this display's effect on Elara. He was not just showing her his power; he was pulling her into it and making her a part of it, whether she wanted to be or not. As much as she tried to resist, a part of her was captivated and wanted to understand the full extent of his influence. She wanted to know the entire length and breadth of his power.

Finally, Tallin released the servant, who collapsed against the bed, breathing heavily, a satisfied smile on her lips. He looked at Elara, his eyes dark and full of unspoken promises.

"Do you understand now, Elara?" he asked, his voice silky smooth, wrapping around her like a web. "Do you see what it means to be in my world?"

Elara swallowed hard, her voice barely a whisper as she responded.

"I see."

What she saw, she realised, was not just the power he wielded over others but the power he was beginning to wield over her as well.

That, more than anything, was what truly frightened her.

**

The Night Ones' scouting party moved in silence, their footsteps blending with the sigh of the waves that lapped at the rocky shore. The sea was a vast, endless black, mirroring the starless sky above. To the north lay the forest where Kayriss, the druid, was said to be hiding the other hu-man, but here, at the edge of the world, only the sea spoke—a hushed whisper that crawled into their bones, cold and invasive. The wind was as dark as their intentions, and the waves below, slick and glistening like oil, seemed to mock their every step. Six of them were seasoned hunters of shadow, trained to stalk the night. Their leader, Verik, walked at the front, his blackened armour reflecting nothing of the world around him. Behind him, his soldiers moved in a silent, practised line, eyes sharp, hands resting on weapons that had tasted the blood of many. They were the best of the Night One Guard, sent to track Kayriss and bring her head to Prince Tallin.

Something was wrong. The sea's whisper had changed. The rhythm of the waves was no longer a steady pulse; it became erratic, like the breathing of a predator waiting just beneath the surface.

"Stay close," Verik whispered, though no sound should have carried over the wind. He felt it, the creeping sense of something watching. The others must have felt it too, for their hands tightened around hilts, and their eyes scanned the horizon though there was nothing to see but endless night.

The first attack came without warning. A soundless crash, like a wave breaking upon a shore, and one of their number was gone. Just... gone. No scream. No struggle. Verik's head whipped around, but there was nothing there, only the faint saltwater spray in the air where his soldier had stood moments before.

"What was that?" Heren, the rear guard, hissed, her voice trembling in a way none had ever heard. She had seen countless battles and never flinched, but this... this was different.

Verik opened his mouth to reply, but the words died on his tongue as the sea itself rose before them. It was not a wave or a storm, but something else, something alive yet formless, a shadow given liquid form. It moved like water, faster than the eye could track, flowing across the rocky shore, silent and deadly.

Before any could react, it struck again. This time, the night was filled with the sickening sound of flesh and bone breaking; two more of his party were torn from the world in a rush of dark, watery limbs, their bodies dragged into the shadow of the sea before the air had even stopped moving.

"Shields!" Verik bellowed, but it was no use. He felt the cold embrace of water creeping up his leg, and when he looked down, there was nothing but blackness, curling and tightening around him. He swung his blade wildly, but it cut only air, not air, but something far worse: emptiness.

One by one, his soldiers were pulled beneath, their screams swallowed by the void. It wasn't a creature they could fight; it wasn't even something they could understand. The darkness of the sea had become a thing of malice; water turned to death. It flowed over them, around them, through them. It moved like a current with purpose, hunting each in turn.

Verik fell to his knees, the cold now up to his chest, the weight of the sea pressing down on him as if he were already drowning. He gasped for breath, but the air was thick with salt, his lungs filling with something more substantial than fear. It was water, but it was also something darker, something older, something that belonged to the deep, where no light had ever shone.

In the final moments, as his vision blurred and the last of his strength ebbed away, Verik understood. The sea had not been watching them. It had been waiting. Whatever hunted them now had always been there, lurking just below the surface, patient and eternal. His last sight was of the water rising to meet him, dark and seamless, as though it had claimed him long ago and had only now come to collect its due.

By morning, there would be no sign of the Night Ones along the western shore. The tide would erase their footprints, their bodies lost to the depths. The sea would return to its gentle rhythm, a vast expanse of indifference, as though nothing had ever disturbed it.

The darkness they had once called their ally had betrayed them, as it always does, swallowing them into the depths.

Watched on by a single, solitary figure.

Chapter Thirty
Kayriss
Confrontation.

Ansel watched as Kayriss struggled to process the revelation, her shoulders sagging under the weight of it all. He knew this moment would come and had anticipated it from the day he first realised what she was. Yet, as he watched the hope drain from her eyes, he couldn't suppress the pang of guilt that gnawed at him.

He had to do it, he told himself. There was no other way.

When the first signs of change appeared in the hu-man population, they documented it as best they could, and he found some of their ancient tomes here when he was much younger. Ansel had been among the few who recognised the gravity of the situation and suggested that they needed to seal this place as a relic of tragedies in the past. The council had agreed because they were blinkered by Ansel hiding the picture books from them. The fallout from the cataclysmic events the old race faced had not just reshaped the landscape; it had reshaped life itself. The mutations were not random. They were a response, nature's desperate attempt to adapt to a world irrevocably altered and shattered. The hu-mans who survived the devastation all died out with age. Kayriss... she was different. The first of her kind. The first Elf. The first to emerge from the hu-man era, not as a deformed relic, but as a new being altogether. The scientists had marvelled at her and debated her significance in hushed tones. Some saw her as a beacon of hope, a sign that life would find a way. Others saw her as an abomination, a mistake that must be corrected.

When Ansel became more intelligent with his evolved state, he had seen her for what she was: the future. His ancestors were mere animals that snuffled and begged for food or were kept as pets and playthings, and he knew that this one would break most of the Wildlings, eaten by the hu-mans.

He was not going to be reminded of that fact ever again.

He also saw the danger. If the Wildlings knew the truth and realised they were the product of a dying world's last gasp, it could destroy them. Ansel couldn't let that happen. They needed to believe they were strong, that they had risen from the ashes, not been twisted by them.

He had kept the secret, even as it weighed on him like a stone. He had sealed the fallout chamber, locked away the truth, and led his people forward with the promise of a new beginning. Ansel had known that one day, the truth would come out; he had just hoped it wouldn't be this soon.

As Kayriss turned her back on him, he felt a pang of something he hadn't felt in years. Doubt. Had he done the right thing? Could she ever forgive him for what he had kept from her?

It didn't matter, he told himself. The secret was out now, and there was no turning back. He would deal with the consequences, whatever they might be. One thing was certain: he couldn't let the truth spread. If the others found out, it could unravel everything they had built.

Ansel steeled himself and would do whatever it took to protect them, even if it meant lying or Kayriss hated him. The future depended on it.

**

Kayriss rose and fluttered out of the shelter, not looking at Ansel on her flight out. She had much to consider. Much to mull over.

She sat in the tree for what felt like days, but it was only for a few hours. They passed in a haze of numbness; her mind felt like a broken compass, spinning in circles as she tried to understand what she had learned. Every corner of the fallout chamber seemed to mock her, and every glance at Ansel was a bitter reminder of the secrets he had kept. As he clambered out and closed the hatch, she wanted to confront him, to demand answers, but the words always died in her throat, choked by the weight of the betrayal she felt.

Kayriss knew it couldn't go on like this. The secret she had uncovered was too monumental, too explosive to be buried again. Ansel couldn't be allowed to hide behind his calm, calculated exterior. The others deserved to know. She deserved to know why he had lied and chose to carry this burden alone.

The decision to confront him hardened within her like a blade being forged. It was only a matter of when not if. She went to him as he moved the brambles gently back into place. He had taken his time to cover it once more, hiding away the details of their past. The dim light cast sharp shadows on his snout, accentuating the fur lines that had deepened over the years, the silent testimony to this weight he bore. He didn't notice her at first, his attention entirely on restoring the camouflaged metal door.

Kayriss fluttered down, her movements deliberate and slow, as if she were stalking prey. She landed just a few paces behind him, her voice cutting through the silence like a knife.

"How long were you planning to keep this from me?"

Ansel froze. He didn't turn around immediately, but Kayriss saw the tension ripple through his shoulders. When he finally turned to face her, his expression was guarded, his eyes searching hers to hint at what was coming.

"Kayriss," he began, his voice low as if trying to placate her. "You need to understand—"

"I need to understand?" she interrupted, her voice sharp. "You've been lying to me, to all of us, for as long as I can remember. You let us live in ignorance while you kept the truth locked away. You made us believe we were something we're not."

Ansel sighed, running a hand through his fur, which made him seem suddenly older and more vulnerable. "I did it to protect you. To protect all of us."

"From what?" Kayriss demanded, stepping closer, her anger flaring. "The truth? You think we're so fragile that we couldn't handle it?"

"Yes. Maybe. I thought it was my burden to carry." Ansel said, the word coming out sharper than he intended. He caught himself, softening his tone. "The truth could have destroyed us, Kayriss. It could still destroy us if it gets out. But maybe I was wrong. You've shown such strength in the last few days."

She stared at him, disbelief warring with her growing fury. "You didn't trust us though. You never did."

"It's not about trust," Ansel replied, his voice firm. "It's about survival. It could tear everything apart if the others knew what you are and what we all were to the hu-mans. We've built a new life here, a new society. But it's fragile, held together by belief, by hope. If that belief is shattered..."

Kayriss shook her head, her mind racing. "So, what was your plan? To keep this secret forever? To let us live in ignorance while you played the wise leader?"

"Not forever," Ansel said quietly. "Just until we were strong enough until we could face the truth without destroying us."

"And who decides when we're strong enough?" Kayriss challenged, her voice rising. "You? Do you think you have the right to play God with our lives?"

Ansel's gaze faltered, and for a moment, Kayriss saw something she hadn't expected in his eyes. Regret.

"I didn't ask for this," he said softly. "I never wanted to be the one to make these decisions. But someone had to. Someone had to keep us safe."

"Safe," Kayriss repeated, the word bitter on her tongue. "You call this safe? Living a lie, pretending we're something we're not? Is that your idea of safety?"

"I did what I thought was right," Ansel replied, his voice strained. "I did what I had to. I see now that I should've relied on you, too. I would ask your forgiveness, but know that might take time."

Kayriss's hands clenched into fists, her nails digging into her palms. She could feel the anger, the betrayal, swirling inside her like a storm, threatening to consume her. Beneath it all was something else: a cold, calculating clarity. Ansel had burdened himself for the good of others, even though misguided.

"You don't get to decide what's right for all of us," she said, her voice calming. "You don't get to keep us in the dark just because you're afraid of what might happen."

Ansel held her gaze, his eyes filling with tears.

"It has been such a burden. I am so sorry Kayriss. You deserve better. I was just worried about what happens when they find out that everything they've believed in is a lie? Would you like to know that your ancestors were pets? Or lunch? Do you think they'll just accept it? Or do you think they'll panic, lose hope, turn against each other?" Ansel began to look smaller, the worry seemingly shrinking the typically giant badger's considerable presence.

Kayriss flinched at the thought, her mind flashing to the others. Their faces are falling, their trust undone. The delicate balance Ansel had maintained for so long. She knew he wasn't wrong. The truth could shatter them, could unravel everything they had built. Could she live with the lie?

"I don't know," she admitted, her voice barely above a whisper. "But they deserve the choice. We all did."

Ansel's expression softened, and for the first time, Kayriss saw the badger beneath the leader, the being who had carried this burden alone, who had sacrificed so much to protect them. That didn't change what he had done or taken from her.

"Kayriss..." Ansel began, but she cut him off.

"No," she said, her voice firmer now. "You had no right. We should've all known. This isn't just about me anymore. It's about all of us. And I won't let you keep this secret any longer."

Ansel's eyes darkened, and for a moment, she saw a flicker of something dangerous, something she hadn't expected. It was panic. "If you tell them... you risk everything."

"I know," Kayriss replied, her resolve hardening. "But it's a risk I'm willing to take. A risk you should've taken long ago."

They stood there, locked in a silent standoff, the air between them thick with tension. Kayriss could see the wheels turning in Ansel's mind, the calculations, the possibilities. She knew he was weighing the risks, considering his options.

Finally, he spoke, his voice quiet but filled with a dangerous edge. "If you do this, you'll have to be prepared for the consequences."

Kayriss met his gaze, her heart pounding. "I am."

Ansel nodded, a grim smile tugging at the corners of his mouth. "Then I hope you're ready to lead them when the time comes. Because once this secret is out, there's no going back."

Kayriss felt a chill run down her spine but held her ground. "I'll do whatever it takes."

Ansel's expression softened, and for a brief moment, there was a flicker of something like pride in his eyes. "I always knew you would."

With that, he placed the same reassuring paw on her shoulder.

"I was truly wrong to keep all this from you. You are nature's strength."

**

As she turned to leave, her mind was already racing, and she planned her next steps. She would tell the others, but she would do it on her terms, minimising the chaos Ansel feared.

She would be ready to face the consequences because she was done living in the dark. It was time for the truth to come to light, no matter the cost.

First, they had a hu-man to save.

Chapter Thirty-One
Tallin
Truths unfold.

Tallin finished and withdrew from the servant who stretched herself out of the bliss she had just experienced. She was about to snuggle into the silken sheets when he looked down on her.

"See? Happy and finished, " he said, standing in front of her, glistening. Turning to the girl, he said, "Now you may leave." She quickly snapped the euphoria away and gathered her clothes. She hastily padded out of the room, barefoot and smiling. Opening the door, she swished out, and Elara thought she caught sight of another Night One in the corridor, but the large wooden barrier swung shut. Was someone listening in? Elara returned her gaze and watched Tallin wipe the servant from his member with a silken square of cloth from the bedside table. He folded the damp moisture away, corner by corner and replaced it on the side. She watched as he gathered his clothes and began to dress himself. Tallin stood before the mirror, adjusting the intricate clasps on his doublet with a precise flick of his fingers. His clothes were woven from the finest silks, dyed in deep midnight blue and adorned with silver thread that caught the dim light of the room, making him look regal and aloof. They blended a mix of dark colours that swirled on him, highlighting the dark perfection of his skin. Elara sat on the chair, her arms crossed, watching him with disdain and wariness. She was determined to shrug off the intoxicating show he'd put on, making the tension between them thick, like a shadow that clung to the room's corners.

"Do you know," Tallin began, his voice smooth and deliberate, "I'm a prince like no other? My people adore me. They say there hasn't been a ruler like me in generations." He turned slightly, catching Elara's eye in the mirror, hoping to see some flicker of admiration. Her gaze remained cold and unyielding.

Elara said nothing, her silence a wall between them. She had no reason to trust him yet, knowing better than to let herself be swayed by his charms, no matter how desperately he tried to impress her.

Tallin cleared his throat, undeterred by her silence. "Even the scourge foxes appreciate my rule. Do you know how rare that is? The foxes don't submit to anyone. Wild, untamable creatures. Yet, they respect me. Maybe it's because all their families work in the obsidian mines for the Night One's prosperity, security and stature. Hard work, but fair. I ensure they are well treated." He smiled on one side. Elara was unsure what darkness lay laced into his last statement.

He turned fully now, facing her, as if expecting her to be moved by the information. Elara's expression didn't change. She could see through his carefully crafted words and hear the underlying arrogance in his tone. The Night Ones, the scourge foxes, the people—they weren't his concern—or hers, for that matter.

His concern was maintaining power and keeping control.

"And that's supposed to make you noble?" Elara finally spoke, her voice edged with bitterness. "You think that because they work for you, they love you? You think that makes you a good ruler?"

Tallin's smile faltered for a moment, but he quickly recovered, shrugging casually as he stepped closer to her. "It's more than that. It's about balance. The Night Ones see something in me, something powerful. Even they can't deny it. They recognise that I'm a leader who can keep the peace between all our worlds."

Elara's eyes narrowed as she leaned forward slightly. "The Night Ones," she repeated, her tone icy, "the same ones who've kept me locked in this castle, who've taken away my freedom. And you want me to believe they see you as some sort of hero? Just because you were born into it? Respect is earned, not given."

Tallin's expression darkened, but he kept his composure, his voice low and measured. "You're here for a reason, Elara. There's something about you, something… significant. The Council of the Night One King believe you're part of a prophecy. A prophecy that says two hu-mans will touch the darkness, and in doing so, will bring about a new era of humanity. One where humans have repopulated the world."

Elara's heart skipped a beat at his words, but she kept her face impassive, refusing to give him the satisfaction of seeing her fear. "And the Night Ones don't want that to happen."

"No… Clearly." Tallin said, almost sadly. "They believe hu-mans had their chance and squandered it. They're… protective of the new world now, in their own way. They don't want to see it fall back into hu-man hands."

"And you?" Elara asked, her voice sharp. "What do you believe?"

Tallin hesitated, his gaze dropping to the floor briefly before meeting hers again. "I believe in preserving what we have. But I also believe in power, and the prophecy... it could be dangerous, unpredictable. If it's true, it could change everything."

Elara stared at him, her mind racing. He was telling her the truth, or at least part of it. His motives were still shrouded in darkness, and she couldn't trust him. He might be charming and trying to impress her, but he was still her captor.

"And that's why I'm here?" she pressed. "Because you're afraid of what I might do?"

Tallin's smile returned, this time softer, almost genuine. "You're here because you're important, Elara. To them, to me. I'm not afraid of you, but I need to understand you. To know what you might become."

Elara felt a chill run down her spine but refused to show it. "You'll never control me," she said, her voice steady. "No matter what you think, no matter what you try."

Tallin chuckled softly, his eyes lingering on her face. "If you leave this palace, think about what you leave behind." He turned away, his demeanour shifting back to the confident prince's, adjusting the final clasp on his doublet. As he did, Elara saw something in his eyes, a flicker of doubt, of uncertainty. It was fleeting, but it was enough. Tallin might think he held all the power, but she knew better. The prophecy might be real, and the Night Ones might be afraid, but so was he. That fear, buried deep beneath his arrogance and charm, was something she could use. Something that might be her way out.

Chapter Thirty-Two
Kayriss
Adventure partytime.

The morning sun barely peeked through the dense canopy of the ancient trees as the party gathered at the edge of the Wood Haven forest. A light mist clung to the ground, swirling around their boots as they finalised the lengthy journey south. The air was crisp with the scent of pine and earth, but beneath the freshness lay an undercurrent of tension, a shared understanding that they were venturing into unknown territory, a land none had ever seen.

Kayriss stood apart from the group, her hand resting on the smooth bark of a towering oak. Isaac had seen that she was troubled and had asked numerous times for assistance. She had thanked him and held on a little tighter than usual when he embraced her. Aware that this was, in fact, the help she needed, Isaac gave her the warmth she craved. Now, he knew that she was somehow communing with the trees, seeking guidance from the ancient spirits of the forest. Her long, brown hair flowed as beautifully as always but had been combed through, a gift from one of the Wildling villagers. It gave her a different look, more polished and serene, but still, her hair flowed like a river down her back, and her eyes, sharp and green as the leaves, were closed in deep concentration. Isaac noticed that her hair had a slightly green tinge woven through the strands, which he thought only added to her beauty. She wore a cloak of living vines, and a wooden staff carved with runes was clasped in her other hand. The trees whispered to her, their voices filled with warnings and encouragement in equal measure.

"They say the way south is treacherous," she finally murmured, facing the others. "The forest will thin, and we'll face lands that are harsher, less forgiving. But they also say we will find what we seek, if we are true to our purpose."

Isaac nodded grimly. He was a tall, broad-shouldered man, but the only thing he wanted to carry on them were Kayriss's troubles. He secretly cared not for the journey, although he did not wish ill on this Elara; he just wanted to be with Kayriss. The Wildlings had shaped him into armour made from one of the knight owl's own who had fallen in battle, resized to fit his different frame. It shifted on his body, and Isaac cared not for the extra weight but welcomed its protection.

At his side hung a long sword, another gift from a fallen owl. Its hilt was worn smooth from countless unfought battles, and a bow slung over his shoulder with a quiver full of arrows. Having not used one before, Isaac wondered how he'd use such a weapon. "We'll face it all together," he said to Kayriss, his voice steady. "Whatever lies ahead, we'll handle it. Elara needs the rescue."

Beside them, Edgar, loyal as always, sat alert, his ears perked up and his brown eyes scanning the forest. He was a large, muscular hound, his coat a mix of brown and black, with a dark streak running down his front. He had been at Isaac's side since Kayriss found him, and his nose twitched as he sniffed the air, eager to follow any scent that might lead them to Elara. A group of industrious Wildlings had freshly polished his armour plates, and the metal and leather gleamed like new. Edgar had given them an appreciative woof in thanks.

Kayriss had spoken to him about why he was with Isaac, and she had found out that he was once a guard dog for one of the bear clans, much further up north, but they had mistreated him, and he'd run away. He'd stumbled across Isaac in the forest and said that something deep within him had told him he should be this man's best friend. He didn't know why; it just felt right, instinctual even. Kayriss had thanked him for everything he'd done to help Isaac and gave him many a loving stroke for being such a good boy.

Grind and Granite exchanged a look and grunted in agreement. They were short and stocky, with broad shoulders and powerful arms, their beards thick and braided with stone beads. Grind, the older of the two, bore his annoyance at travelling further away on his sleeve, but the druid was the only one who could assist, so travel they must. He tried to impress upon her the urgency of his people's need on the journey, hoping to sway the mission. Granite was less grizzled and hoisted his massive hammer over his shoulder, ready for the march ahead. His heart was filled with a wave of anger he was suppressing, having lost an uncle in the second wave of the rat's assault. He had buried the feeling from everyone but knew it was ready to burst forth in vengeance.

"The stones don't speak of the south," Grind rumbled, his voice deep and gravelly, "but our hammers will do the talking if need be." Granite nodded, his eyes gleaming with quiet determination. "Aye. No stone will stand in our way, and no enemy will stand long. We'll crush any shard shitters that get in our way."

Captain Browntail tightened the straps on his leather-padded armour hidden under his long coat. His clothes were a mishmash of various pieces of gear collected from countless voyages, and his eyes were a deep, solid brown, sharp and restless. At his side stood his first mate, Cutlass, a younger, leaner female with a wiry frame and quick reflexes. She wore a bandana tied around her head, and a pair of curved swords hung at her hips, their edges gleaming in the morning light.

"Southward, eh?" Browntail said with a grin. There was a sparkle in his eye, and he clearly relished the adventure to come. "Never been thar far inland before, but if the sea's taught us one thing, it's that there's no land too wild or too dangerous that can't be tamed by a determined crew."

"Aye," Cutlass added with a nod. "Oh. and... Aaaaaaarrrrr!" She added, noticing that Browntail was smiling broadly at the sound. "Also, think of the new pebbles!" She proclaimed over excitedly, jumping up and down on the spot.

The otters had brought with them an exceedingly large treasure chest, which they'd said was extremely important to keep locked at all times. It was down to the last member of the party to carry it, as it was too large for either otter.

"What in God's name are you bringing along here that I have to carry, otters? This best not be a box of pebbles!" Hooted Hooth, The knight owl and last member of their party.

"I can categorically confirm what ye be holding be a far greater treasure in thar!" Came the reply. Hooth perched the chest upon his back, and his large amber eyes blinked slowly as he surveyed the group. Hooth was a rare sight, one of the guardians of the Wood Haven that lived high in the canopies, with feathers as white as snow and a pair of sharp talons that gleamed like silver. His armour was crafted from metal and leather that had been found, many of the plates relics of the old ones. It was shaped to his avian form, and a small, intricate crest adorned his breastplate. His beak was hooked, and when he spoke, it was with a deep, resonant voice that carried a natural authority.

"South is unknown to all of us," Hooth said, his gaze sweeping across the party. "But the unknown is not to be feared. It is to be conquered. We have been charged with finding Elara, and we shall not fail." Kayriss saw behind his wide eyes that he seemed to be holding something back. She resigned herself to talk to him on the way about it.

With their resolve set, the party began their journey southward. They moved in a loose formation, with Kayriss at the front, her druidic senses attuned to the subtleties of the forest. Isaac and Grind walked close behind, their eyes scanning the surroundings for signs of danger. Granite carried the bulk of their supplies, his strength allowing him to bear the heavy load easily. Browntail and Cutlass took the rear, their hands never straying far from their weapons, constantly trying to start a sea shanty with the wandering crew. Hooth took up the rear, unable to fly under the weight of the mysterious chest on his back, yet his keen eyes were still scanning for any threats. They were brought to Edgar, who was bounding through the underbrush, seemingly having a fantastic time.

The forest was dense, the trees tall and ancient, their branches interwoven to form a nearly impenetrable canopy. Sunlight filtered through thin beams, casting long shadows on the forest floor. The underbrush was thick, with ferns and bushes crowding the path, and the air was filled with the sounds of birds and distant rustling. As they walked, the path grew narrower, the trees closer together, and the ground beneath their feet became uneven. The further south they travelled, the more the forest seemed to close around them as if it were reluctant to let them go. The forest was alive with movement, the occasional scurrying of the un-evolved animals, the distant call of a bird, and the constant whisper of the wind through the leaves. It was a place of life and mystery, a realm few had ventured into, and fewer still had returned.

Grind, the dwarf trudged through the dense forest, side-eyeing Isaac, who was staring up at the trees as if he'd never seen them before.

"You lookin' for birds, or just tryin' to remember where your head's at?" Grind muttered, kicking a root grumpily out of his path. Isaac blinked and glanced down at him. "I... actually don't remember ever seeing trees this big." He scratched his head. "I only remember things from the recent few weeks. Before that, nothing." Grind stopped in his tracks, eyebrow raised. "Weeks you say? So, what, you just woke up one day, decided 'Hey, I'm Isaac; I'll walk around forests with Mine Folk now?'"

Isaac shrugged, trying to keep pace. "Basically, yeah. I just woke up in a glade with Edgar by my side. No idea who I was, where I came from. It was then that Kayriss found me." Grind snorted.

"Kayriss found you? And then you two... started bashing boulders? You are though, aren't you? I've seen the way you two make eyes at each other."

Isaac smiled, and it was answer enough.

"You're playing in powerful fields there, lad. She's a force of nature from all I heard." He said. "You'll be getting more and more into plants and nature as she rubs off on yer!" Grind bellowed out a laugh, which brought a smile to Isaac's face.

The banter continued, and while there were clearly different motives for the group to be together, the hours and miles passed.

**

Tired and wearily, the party paused for a brief rest in a small clearing, the sun now high in the sky. Kayriss knelt by a stream that ran through the clearing, her hands hovering over the water as she murmured an incantation. The water began to glow softly, and she cupped her hands to take a drink, the enchanted liquid refreshing her instantly. She motioned for the rest of the party to drink, and they did, grateful for her concoction.

"The trees are thinning," she said, her voice thoughtful. "We'll soon leave the familiar woods behind and enter lands that are less forgiving." She moved to hold Isaac's hand as he wiped the sweat from his brow with the other. Nodding, he said, "You know best, Kay, we'll need to be more cautious from here on out. We're heading into the unknown."

Browntail, leaning against a tree, chuckled. "That's where the adventure lies, matey! Never fear the unknown! It's where the best stories come from." An 'Aaaarrrrr' cried out as usual next to him, but there wasn't the same confidence that Cutlass normally employed.

Hooth, perched on a low branch nearby, hooted softly in agreement. "The unknown is our trial. We must face it with courage." Flying down, he looked at the large chest he had been carrying as Cutlass walked over to him. She was considerably smaller than the giant owl, so she smiled at him. Without a word, she hugged his leg in thanks for his efforts. It was warm and surprised the owl. Cutlass then patted him on the hip and bounded back to Browntail.

Hooth was annoyed at carrying the awkward chest, but that little show of affection made it easier. He picked up the enormous chest once more as they resumed their journey, and the forest gradually began to change. The trees became sparser, the ground rockier, and the air took on a different quality. It was drier, with a faint hint of salt. They were leaving the comfort of the wood's haven and entering wild and untamed lands, where the rules of the forest no longer applied. The party moved with a heightened sense of awareness, each step taken with care. The further south they travelled, the more the forest seemed to be missed by them as it provided the safety and security they'd all been accustomed to. When they'd left its seclusion, the last vestiges seemed to close around them as if they were reluctant to let them go.

The path ahead had become less clear, overgrown with thorny bushes and twisted roots, and the light grew dimmer, the sun obscured by a growing cloud cover. What lay before them was a vast, open landscape. It stretched into rolling hills, thick with wild grasses that swayed in the breeze like an ocean of green and gold. Far larger than any they'd seen, trees towered over the landscape, dotted haphazardly, their roots twisting through the earth in a chaotic dance of nature reclaiming its kingdom. Vines hung in thick ropes from their branches, and bushes clustered around their bases, swallowing up what was once a road of the old world. The air was thick with the scent of blooming flowers, earthy soil, and the faint rustle of unseen animals moving through the underbrush.

Here and there, though, the wilderness whispered of the world that had come before. A cracked stone arch jutted from a hillside, half hidden by creeping ivy. Faded, rusted signs leaned precariously against trees, their letters long washed away by time, but the shapes were still vaguely hu-man, arrows pointing to what once might have been cities or travel warnings long forgotten. The remains of a bridge stretched over a dried-up riverbed, now a skeleton of steel wrapped in moss and tangled roots. It was as if the land had let these remnants remain, little hints of a forgotten civilisation. As the party gazed across the landscape, there was an eerie beauty to it all. The silence felt heavy, broken only by the occasional call of a distant bird or the rustle of the leaves in the wind. Where hu-mans once thrived, now nature ruled in absolute dominion. Yet, these quiet, decayed markers of the past poking through the wildness reminded them of the fleeting presence of humanity, swallowed by the earth in just a few centuries.

The world had moved on, but it hadn't completely forgotten.

**

By nightfall, they had reached a ridge overlooking a vast, sprawling landscape. Hours earlier, the forest had abruptly ended, giving way to rocky terrain stretching before them like a barren wasteland. Far in the distance, they could see the faint outline of mountains, their peaks shrouded in mist.

"This is it," Kayriss said quietly, her voice tinged with awe and trepidation. "We've crossed into the south."

Isaac stepped forward, his gaze fixed on the horizon. "Elara's somewhere out there. We'll find her, no matter what it takes."

The others nodded in agreement, their resolve as strong as ever. They were far from home, in a land none knew, but a single purpose mostly united them: to find Elara and bring her back safely. The journey ahead would be long and perilous, but they were ready to face whatever challenges lay ahead.

With the sun setting to the west of them and the unknown stretching out ahead, the party set up camp for the night, knowing that the true test of their strength and courage was coming the closer they got to Elara.

That is until night fell.

Chapter Thirty-Three
Elara
Your room. M'lady.

    Tallin led Elara down a long, dimly lit corridor, his footsteps echoing off the cold stone walls. The castle was a labyrinth of dark passageways and heavy doors, and Elara felt a growing sense of unease as they walked. Night Ones passed them immediately dissolved into hushed whispered gossip, making no effort to hide that they were talking about Elara. Tallin had been courteous enough, trying to ease her discomfort with small talk, but their underlying tension remained unspoken, a silent battle of wills.

    At last, they reached a door at the end of the hallway. Tallin pushed it open and gestured for Elara to step inside. "These will be your quarters. No more prison cell. Again, you see my leniency." he said, his tone polite but firm. "I trust you'll find them comfortable."

Elara entered cautiously, her eyes sweeping across the room. It was less grand than she had expected, especially after seeing the opulence of Tallin's chambers. The walls were of the same cold stone, though softened by rich tapestries depicting scenes of ancient battles. The pictured wars were from times past and depicted the old races in constant conflict. She thought these were to highlight the old ways and how they should not be discarded. The room was sparsely furnished. A large bed with a carved wooden frame and deep green velvet drapes, a sturdy oak wardrobe in one corner, and a writing desk near the balcony. The floor was covered with a thick, dark rug that muffled her steps as she moved further in. Though simple, the bed looked comfortable enough, with plush pillows and a thick quilt inviting rest. It was the balcony that drew Elara's attention. She crossed the room to the heavy curtains, pulled them aside, and stepped out onto the stone ledge. The view took her breath away, as far below, the land stretched out in a vast expanse of forests and rolling hills, bathed in the golden light of the setting sun.

Yet, as beautiful as it was, there was no mistaking the drop. The balcony was high… impossibly high. There would be no escape this way.

Tallin appeared beside her, wincing at the light, leaning casually against the balcony's edge. "Quite the view, isn't it? It's a long way down, though. I wouldn't recommend trying to leave this way." He smiled, but it didn't reach his eyes. "You'll find the room secure. You'll be well-guarded at all times. For your protection, of course."

Elara turned to face him, her expression guarded. "Of course," she replied, her voice devoid of warmth.

Tallin's smile faltered just slightly before he recovered, pushing away from the balcony and heading back inside. "If there's anything you require, just ask one of the guards. They'll make sure you're taken care of." His tone was almost gracious, but the underlying message was clear. She was still a prisoner, no matter how polite he was. Just with better pillows.

As he moved toward the door, Tallin paused and turned back to her. "I'll leave you to settle in. But remember, Elara, you're here because you're important. You're here because I commanded it. It would be wise to keep that in mind." With that, he left the room, the door closing with a heavy thud behind him.

Elara stood still for a moment, her gaze fixed on the door. She felt a strange mix of relief and anxiety at his departure. She was alone now but not truly free, and the guards stationed outside constantly reminded her of that.

A few minutes passed in silence before there was a soft knock at the door. Before Elara could respond, the door opened, and a younger Night One entered. He was tall and lean, with dark hair and eyes that seemed to sparkle with mischief. He bore a striking resemblance to Tallin, but there was something softer, more approachable about him.

"Hello," he said, closing the door behind him. "You must be Elara. You, m'lady, are the talk of the town, as the old ones say." His voice was smooth, with a hint of curiosity.

Elara regarded him warily. "And you are?"

The young man smiled, a touch of amusement in his expression. "Kaelen, Tallin's younger brother. The second prince of this realm. I thought I'd come to welcome you personally. Make sure my brother isn't being too… overwhelming."

Elara studied the Night One in front of her. He exuded a unique blend of playful charm and enigma; even she could tell that he stood before her in the briefest of moments. Like his brother, he had a tall, muscular build, his physique sculpted by years of what she assumed would be some combat training or royal discipline. His dark skin gleamed like Tallin's in the meagre light, complementing the smooth, sleek flow of his hair, which cascaded down his shoulders, much longer than his brother's. It was tied in places and braided with silver clips, each showing a different design. Kaelen's style was a stark contrast to Tallin's more functional regality. His clothing was almost over the top in its richness, woven with intricate patterns that seemed to shimmer with every movement. Embellished with silver and gold thread, his attire spoke of a young prince unafraid to display his status, perhaps indulgent in his desire to impress. Despite the excess, there was something calculated in his presentation, as if his appearance was just another layer of the mystery surrounding him. His sharp eyes gleamed with intelligence, and the faintest of smiles tugged at his lips, which could signal welcome or mischief. Elara could not thoroughly read him, and that worried her greatly.

Elara didn't relax, her eyes narrowing slightly as she continued to study him. "Overwhelming is one word for it."

Kaelen laughed softly, leaning casually against the desk. "I can imagine. Tallin has a way with people, doesn't he? Always so sure of himself, so convinced he's the best thing to happen to this kingdom." He paused, his tone turning more serious. "But you should be careful around him, Elara. My brother is... complicated. He's not always what he seems."

Elara crossed her arms, not entirely convinced. "And you're different? I'm supposed to trust you instead?"

Kaelen held up his hands in a gesture of surrender. "I'm not asking for your trust. Trust should be earned, not given. I just think you should know that Tallin isn't always as noble as he likes to appear. He has his own agenda, and it doesn't always align with what's best for others."

Elara studied him, trying to gauge his sincerity. "And what's your agenda, Kaelen? Why are you here?"

Kaelen's smile faded, and he looked almost serious for a moment. "Maybe I just don't want to see you get hurt. Or maybe I'm tired of living in my brother's shadow. Maybe I want to prove that I'm different."

Elara's gaze didn't waver. "Or maybe you're just as dangerous as he is."

Kaelen sighed, pushing away from the desk. "Maybe. But at least I'm honest about it." He turned to leave but paused at the door, glancing back at her. "Just... be careful, Elara. Tallin might seem charming, but he's still the one holding the chains. Don't let him fool you."

With that, he left, the door closing softly behind him.

Elara stood alone in the room, her mind racing. Kaelen's words had unsettled her, but she couldn't afford to trust him more than Tallin. They were part of this twisted world, connected to the Night Ones and their dark prophecies. She was caught in a game she didn't understand, with no allies to rely on. She was still unsure of her life before waking up in the woods. Elara thought back over the words Kaelen had said, and one part stuck out to her like a dagger.

"Trust should be earned, not given."

She had said almost the same thing earlier to Tallin. Was he listening in on the conversation? Who could she trust? Elara was now more guarded than ever, wanting to be far, far away now. Away from Prince's and stone buildings, and...

Everything.

She glanced around the room again, taking in the cold stone walls, the heavy furniture, the high balcony. This wasn't just a room but a cage, no matter how comfortable it appeared. Elara was determined not to let them break her. She would find a way to survive this: outmanoeuvre both brothers and the Night Ones. She just had to be patient and wait for the right moment.

When that moment came, she would be ready.

**

Far to the north, the waves settled and parted over the bodies of the scouting party. The woman moved silently through the carnage, her steps light but deliberate, like the quiet ripple of a stream cutting through a barren landscape. Bodies of the Night One scouting party lay scattered around her, their lifeless forms a testament to a battle fought in the shadows that they had no chance of winning. She weaved through them, not with reverence but with cold purpose, her bare foot nudging aside a limp arm here, a broken weapon there. Blood pooled beneath the fallen, dark and still as a moonless lake, but it did not slow her. She was hunting for something, and her patience ran as deep as an ocean trench.

Amongst the dead men's belongings, her hand found its way to a tattered satchel, half buried beneath the collapsed weight of a fallen warrior. She tugged it free, fingers slipping in and out of its contents with the fluid grace of water seeping through cracks. She drew a small piece of parchment from within, its edges weathered and stained. Her eyes flicked over it, and for a moment, the soft sound of her breath could be heard, like the faintest breeze over calm waters. A drawing revealed itself on the parchment—an elf woman with sharp features and a hu-man male standing beside her.

Below them, etched with stark simplicity, was a single word: Kayriss.

The name seemed to stir something within her, though she gave no outward sign of recognition. The parchment fluttered in her hand like the surface of a disturbed pond, but soon it was still, her fingers tightening around its edges. She slipped the drawing into the folds of her clothing with the quiet certainty of a river returning to its course. Without a glance back at the dead, she continued on her way, leaving the Night Ones behind as nothing more than flotsam in her wake. As she left, the waves moved over the bodies and dragged them all into the sea, leaving no trace.

"Kayriss," the female said. "Why are these dark ones after you...?" She mused over why as a distant storm gathered on the horizon.

Chapter Thirty-Four
Kayriss
Ribbet.

The campsite was quiet, the air heavy with the stillness of the night. The adventuring party had set up camp on the rocky ridge, the forest behind them and the barren landscape stretching out ahead. A small fire crackled at the centre of the camp, casting flickering shadows on the surrounding rocks and trees. The party was scattered around the fire; each lost in their thoughts as they prepared for the long night ahead.

Kayriss sat cross-legged near the fire, her hands gently weaving patterns in the air as she murmured a soft incantation. The flames responded to her touch, growing brighter and warmer, chasing away the chill of the evening. As the fire steadied, she glanced at Hooth, perched silently on a low branch nearby, his amber eyes fixed on the darkness beyond the camp. Deftly climbing up to meet him, Kayriss sat beside him, wanting to get to know him further and see what was behind his eyes.

"Something troubles you," Kayriss said softly, barely more than a whisper. She placed a hand on his back to soothe whatever was bothering him. Hooth turned his head slightly, his gaze meeting hers. "The night feels… different," he replied, his voice deep and resonant. "There is a presence in the air, something unnatural. I sense it lurking just beyond our sight."

Kayriss nodded, her expression thoughtful. "That is not what I was referring to, but I've felt it too. The forest behind us is quiet; the way ahead? I don't want to have to go further than we have. It's as if the very earth is holding its breath."

Hooth shifted on his perch, his feathers rustling softly. "We must remain vigilant. Whatever is out there, I feel it knows we're here."

As they spoke, Kayriss realised that Captain Browntail and Cutlass had dragged away their chest and were nowhere to be seen. Clearly, they were busy with their affairs, having made an effort to drag the large chest away from the party. They had whispered to each other in low tones, their eyes darting around nervously as they worked on moving the chest to a different location. The sound of stone scraping against wood echoed softly in the night, but none of the others had paid them much mind. Light barely reached them, but she could hear them nattering in the distance, reassuring them they were safe.

"You don't mind carrying that thing, do you? You know it's probably filled with pebbles, don't you?" Kayriss asked. Hooth turned to face her, a smile creeping across his face. "No doubt it does, but they put their paws up to walk into the unknown with us, so it's the least I could do." Kayriss patted him on the back.

"You're a good owl. I'm glad you're here."

Back at the campfire, Grind and Granite were setting the watch rotations. Grind, ever the cautious one, insisted on taking the first watch, but Granite, eager to prove himself, argued for the honour. After a brief but good-natured debate, it was agreed that Grind would take the first shift and Granite would follow immediately after.

The fire began to dwindle as the night deepened, its light flickering weaker as the cold night air closed in. Most of the party had settled down to rest, their forms huddled under blankets or cloaks, the weight of the day's travel heavy on their shoulders. Grind sat near the edge of the camp, his keen eyes scanning the horizon, his pickaxe resting on his lap. The land was silent, except for the occasional wind rustle through the grass. Hours passed, and the night grew darker still. When it was time, Grind roused Granite with a gentle nudge. The younger Mine Folk took his place, gripping his hammer tightly as he settled into his watch. The stars twinkled overhead, cold and distant, as Granite kept his eyes peeled for any sign of trouble. Even Hooth had nestled himself under a wing, shrinking his form against the branch for comfort.

Granite saw it. Saw them.

Faint movements in the long grass, just beyond the reach of the campfire's light. At first, it was barely noticeable, a slight swaying of the tall blades as if brushed by a gentle breeze. But there was no wind.

Granite's grip tightened on his hammer, his heart beginning to race. He narrowed his eyes, straining to see through the darkness. The movement was deliberate and controlled. Something was out there, moving closer. He stood slowly, not wanting to alarm the others but ready to wake them if necessary.

The movement continued, the grass parting in small waves as whatever it was drew nearer. Granite's breath caught in his throat as he caught a glimpse of something, a shape, low to the ground, hopping forward. His mind raced, trying to identify what he saw, but the darkness and the distance made it difficult. He felt a knot of dread forming in his stomach.

The hopping continued, and as Granite watched in growing horror, more shapes began emerging from the grass. They moved in unison, their numbers growing with each passing second, until the long grass was alive with the rhythmic sound of dozens, no, hundreds of creatures hopping toward the camp.

Granite's mouth went dry as he realised what they were facing. "Wake up!" he hissed urgently, his voice barely above a whisper as he shook Grind awake. "Something's coming. We're surrounded. Wake the others!"

Grind was instantly alert, his hand on his pickaxe as he sat up and looked around. The others also began to stir, sensing the tension in the air. Isaac was on his feet instantly, his sword already drawn, even though he had no idea how to use it effectively. While Kayriss rose gracefully, her staff in hand, her eyes wide with alarm. Edgar growled low in his throat, his hackles rising as he sensed the danger.

"What is it?" Isaac demanded, his voice low but tense.

Granite pointed toward the long grass, his hand shaking slightly.

"I don't know, but there seems to be quite a number of them!"

Isaac's eyes narrowed as he peered into the darkness. The first of the creatures were now close enough to be seen in the fire's dim light. It was a grotesque, hunched figure, its skin slick and glistening, mottled with sickly greens and browns. Its eyes were bulbous and unblinking, shining with a malevolent intelligence. It wore armour made of coral, the jagged edges giving it a twisted, almost unnatural appearance as if the sea had spat it out in disgust.

The creature held a spear made of bone and coral, the tip sharp and deadly. Behind it, more of its kind emerged, forming a wide circle around the camp, their numbers growing until the adventuring party was completely surrounded. The creatures moved with an eerie silence, their webbed feet barely making a sound as they hopped closer and closer. Their eyes were fixed on the party, unblinking and cold, their intentions clear. Kayriss stepped forward, her staff glowing faintly as she prepared to cast a spell. "We're outnumbered," she whispered, her voice trembling with controlled fear. "But we must hold our ground."

Hooth, who had taken to the air with a powerful beat of his wings, circled overhead, his keen eyes counting the enemy below. "There are too many," he said, his voice sharp with urgency. "We cannot fight them all."

Isaac gritted his teeth, his sword at the ready. "We have no choice."

The beasts advanced, making a sound that Kayriss thought sounded like the word 'ribbet', their spears gleaming in the firelight, their croaking breaths filling the night air. They moved with terrifying coordination, tightening the circle around the camp until the adventuring party could see the cruel glint in their eyes and smell the briny stench of their breath.

Captain Browntail and Cutlass reappeared from the shadows, their faces pale as they entered the scene. "We're surrounded," Browntail muttered, his voice uncharacteristically shaken.

The standoff was tense. The two groups faced each other across the small space of the campsite, the firelight casting long, flickering shadows on the ground. The adventurers stood back to back, their weapons drawn, ready to defend themselves. They were now close enough to strike and paused momentarily; their leader, a more prominent, bulbously menacing figure with a crown of coral atop its head, stepped forward, its eyes locked on Kayriss.

For a long, breathless moment, neither side moved, the tension so thick it felt like a physical presence in the air. The adventuring party knew they were outnumbered and knew that a fight could mean their doom. But they also knew they could not surrender now or ever. The leader raised its spear, aimed directly at Kayriss's heart. The time for words was over. The only thing left was the fight.

The night seemed to hold its breath, waiting for the inevitable clash.

With a croak that echoed through the stillness, the frogmen attacked.

Chapter Thirty-Five
Elara
Whispers before dawn.

The first light of dawn barely kissed the horizon when Elara was roused from a fitful sleep by a soft knock on her chamber door. She knew that she had only slept so well because the feel of the bed and its sheets were a definite upgrade to the prison cell she'd been kept in previously. She blinked awake, the remnants of uneasy dreams clinging to her like a shroud. Her mind was still foggy when she heard the knock again, firmer this time but still cautious as if the one seeking entry knew the hour was not meant for visitors.

"Who is it?" she called her voice husky with sleep.

"It's Meira, my lady. We... we met yesterday," came the reply, although it was unknown to her.

Elara sat up, pushing back the covers. Her pulse quickened. What could this servant want so early in the morning? She rose and crossed the room, opening the door just a crack to peer outside. There stood the servant woman Tallin had used in front of her as a show of power and control, her dark eyes wide and earnest, a thin cloak drawn tight around her slight frame.

"May I come in?" She asked quietly.

Elara hesitated only for a moment before opening the door fully and allowing the servant inside. She slipped through the doorway, casting a nervous glance back down the hall before Elara shut the door behind her. The young woman's movements were quick, almost furtive, as if she feared being caught.

"What's this about?" Elara asked, her brow furrowing. "It's not even dawn yet."

"I'm sorry to disturb you, my lady, but I felt we should talk," the servant replied, trembling slightly. She clasped her hands together, the knuckles white from the pressure. "There's something you need to know. Something I fear you won't learn from either Tallin or Kaelen."

The mention of the brothers' names made Elara's stomach twist. She had met them both, two striking Night Ones with charm and confidence in abundance, but there was something still unsettling about them, something she couldn't quite place.

"Go on," Elara urged, her curiosity piqued despite the early hour.

"I'm Meira, one of the many servants of Tallin. We met, of sorts, recently." Blushing at the words, she continued. "He is generally a good master, not kind, but at least we don't get used in the obsidian mines." Meira took a deep breath, steeling herself for what she was about to say. "Neither brother can be trusted, my lady. They have their motivations, and I fear neither has your best interests at heart."

Elara narrowed her eyes. "And what do you know of their motivations?"

Meira hesitated, glancing down at her hands. "Tallin is clever and believes that he knows what is right. At all times. He's always been the one to play the long game, to manipulate others to achieve his goals. Kaelin is no better. He's reckless, driven by his own desires. They've been at odds for as long as I've served in this house, each with secrets they guard jealously."

Elara's breath caught. She had sensed the tension between the brothers, but Meira's words hinted at something far darker. "What secrets?" she pressed.

Meira shook her head. "I don't know everything, only fragments. But what I do know is enough to make me wary. Tallin has dealings with those who walk in shadows and Kaelen... well, let's just say he's no stranger to dangerous liaisons."

The room suddenly felt colder, and the shadows lengthened as Meira spoke. Elara wrapped her arms around herself, trying to understand everything. "Why are you telling me this?"

"Because I don't want to see you hurt," Meira said, her eyes meeting Elara's with a fierce sincerity. "Actually, wait. I want you to trust me. I'm doing this for my own good. That's as straight an answer as you'll ever get. Kaelen in power is not something anyone wants. Especially Tallin. And you have a strength they don't understand, and that's why they're both interested in you. But that interest is a double-edged sword. I know I'm just a servant, but I've seen enough to know when something is wrong."

Elara studied Meira's face, unsure of what truth she should believe anymore. She searched for any sign of deceit in Meira's face but found none. Instead, she saw only a young Night One, frightened but determined, who had risked much to bring her this warning. There was something about Meira that Elara couldn't ignore. A vulnerability, yes, but also a spark of courage. Her eyes flickered over Meira, taking in the woman with cautious curiosity. Meira, like all Night Ones, was cloaked in the shadowy elegance of her kind. Her dark skin shimmered faintly in the dim light, a lighter shade than the brothers. It made her hair jet black, a contrast to her skin. It was also cropped short and neat, like the other servants Elara had seen. She stood straight, poised but not rigid, as if constantly aware of her surroundings yet unbothered by them. Though Meira was a servant to Tallin, there was a quiet dignity about her, a certain grace that made Elara hesitate to see her as merely subservient to him. Her eyes, sharp and deep as an evening sky, seemed to notice everything. Her gaze was calm, a steady intelligence that lingered beneath her reserved demeanour. Elara caught the briefest flash of something familiar, though she couldn't quite place it, a rare softness among the Night Ones. It was enough to make Elara trust her more than the others. Meira didn't exude the cold, distant aura so many of Tallin's kin did. Instead, they had an unspoken understanding, even if it was fragile and untested.

"As you can tell from yesterdays... example, I quite like Tallin staying in power." Meira blushed at the memory, aware of what Elara had witnessed.

"You could be punished for speaking to me like this," Elara said softly. Meira's lips quirked into a sad smile. "Perhaps. But if it helps you see the truth, it's worth the risk."

Silence hung between them for a moment, the weight of unspoken fears heavy in the air. Then, Elara made a decision. "You said you've seen enough to know when something is wrong. What if we helped each other?"

Meira's eyes widened, a flicker of hope breaking through her anxiety. "What do you mean?"

"If we're both careful, we could keep an eye on the brothers, share what we learn, and protect one another. I'll be your friend, Meira, and together, we might find a way to navigate this maze of secrets."

Meira blinked as if she hadn't expected such an offer. Slowly, she nodded, a small but genuine smile on her face. "I would like that, my lady."

"Then it's settled," Elara said, feeling a strange sense of relief. In Meira, she might have found an ally who knew the dangers of this place far better than she did. "We'll look out for each other."

Meira's smile grew, her earlier tension easing. "Thank you, my lady. I'll do my best to keep you safe."

Elara nodded, determination hardening within her. The brothers might be dangerous, but now she wasn't alone. With Meira by her side, she would uncover the truth, no matter how dark the secrets might be.

"So. Tell me everything about this place…"

Chapter Thirty-Six
Kayriss
Knight fight.

    The leader of the frogmen let out his guttural croak, and in that instant, the night exploded into chaos. The frogmen surged forward, their coral spears glinting wickedly in the firelight as they attacked from all sides. The adventuring party braced themselves, each member ready to meet the onslaught head-on.

    Isaac was the first to strike, his sword flashing wildly as he swung with no skill attached. It was more of a warning shot, but he was lucky to deflect the thrust of a spear at his chest. He pivoted smoothly, bringing his blade down in a mighty arc that cleaved through the spear's shaft and drove deep into the frogman's thigh. The clash of steel and bone echoed across the battlefield as the blade met flesh in a frenzy of sparks and blood. The creature let out a pained, gurgled croak and staggered back, blood oozing from the deep wound. The frogman landed on his behind with a squelch, his cries filling the night air. Another took its place almost immediately, its bulbous eyes filled with malice.

Kayriss moved with the grace of the forest, her staff spinning in her hands as she chanted a spell. The air around her shimmered with green energy, and vines erupted from the ground, snaring the legs of the nearest frogmen. They struggled against the bindings, their croaks growing frantic as the vines tightened, but Kayriss knew the spell would only hold them for a short time. They hacked and slashed wildly at the vines, pulling and trying desperately to free themselves. Kayriss noticed an urgency to them as if failure meant a worse fate, as one jabbed wildly with his spear, virtually severing his foot in the process. She would always start with pacifism first to give the attackers a chance to explain themselves, but unfortunately, most battles ended with more offensive spells or actions. However, she'd never seen such panic in the eyes of attackers.

Grind and Granite fought side by side, their weapons swinging in unison with the precision of repetitive miners, smashing against the rocks. Grind's pickaxe point disappeared head after head, felling the attacking frogmen easily. Spears whistled through the air, piercing the chaotic melee as both fighters ducked and weaved between the deadly shafts. Granite's weapon smashed into another, shattering its coral breastplate. On the backswing, it crushed through the armour of another frogman, sending it sprawling to the ground. The Mine Folk fought with a raw, relentless power, their bellows of effort echoing through the night. Neither was a seasoned warrior, but fighting for their home made them as good as.

Edgar, the loyal hound, darted between the legs of the frogmen, his teeth sinking into the exposed flesh of their ankles and thighs. His growls were fierce, his movements quick and lethal as he tore through the ranks of their enemies. He scuttled them as he ran, his size knocking many attackers over in his path.

Browntail and Cutlass fought with the reckless abandon of the seasoned imaginary pirates they were, having practised on their long river journeys. Their swords flashed in the firelight as they cut down any frogmen that came too close. They fought in unison, their snakelike bodies moving tidally through the ranks as they bounced off one another. Every frog that fell brought a congratulatory 'Aaaarrrrr' from Cutlass. Blood-soaked and battered, the two swarthy fighters surged forward, their weapons cutting arcs of silver and red in the dim light.

Above, Hooth swooped low, his talons grasping two or three warriors at a time and launching them across the battlefield, where they landed with a sickening plop. On his attack runs, he'd also slash down with his sword across the faces of the frogmen, slicing some in half. His aerial assaults were swift and precise, each strike designed to maim and disorient as he barrelled into the fray, scattering soldiers like leaves in a storm.

Even as the party fought valiantly, more and more frogmen poured into the clearing, their numbers seemingly endless.

Isaac's arm began to tire as he parried another blow, his muscles burning with the effort. He glanced around, his heart sinking as he saw the sheer number of frogmen still advancing. Despite their best efforts, the party was still being overwhelmed. The frogmen pressed closer, their eyes gleaming with the promise of victory, their croaking voices growing more confident.

Kayriss was surrounded, her vines no longer holding back the tidal assault. She had cast another spell, summoning a barrier of thorns around herself and some of the others, a wall made of pure thorns, but even that was being chipped away by the relentless attacks. Grind and Granite were back to back, fending off multiple attackers simultaneously, but their immense strength was beginning to wane.

The end seemed near, and Kayriss rattled through spells she could pull from, but Ansel's healing did not fully restore her magic besides the fact that there were an endless number of attackers. She moved to Isaac, their arms interlocking. No words passed between them, but Isaac implored her to fly upwards, to leave the battle and be safe, no matter the cost on the floor below.

There was no end. The croaks filled their ears to deafening, and they all readied for the attack that bit home.

Someone whimpered, and another grunted furiously.

Just as the situation seemed most dire, a figure emerged from the darkness at the edge of the camp. She moved with a fluid grace, her body seeming to glide across the ground like a ripple on the surface of a still pond. Her skin had a bluish hue that shimmered like the water's surface under the moonlight, and her hair flowed like seaweed caught in a gentle current. In her hands, she held a pair of blades that curved like the waves of the ocean, their edges as sharp as the coral of the combat divers.

Without a word, the mysterious warrior launched herself into the fray. Her movements were a blur, her body twisting and turning with an almost supernatural agility. She struck with the precision of a master, each blow finding its mark, each movement a dance of death. The frogmen, caught off guard by her sudden appearance, hesitated for a split second, which cost them dearly.

The warrior's blades flashed in the waning firelight as she spun through the ranks of the frogmen, cutting them down with effortless skill. Her strikes were like the tide, relentless and unstoppable, washing away the frogmen as if they were nothing more than driftwood caught in a storm. The party, momentarily stunned by the appearance of this new player, quickly regained their footing and pressed the attack with renewed vigour.

Inspired by the warrior's fluid grace, Grind and Granite fought with even greater ferocity, their weapons swinging with crushing force. Isaac and Kayriss moved to support her, cutting down any frogmen that tried to flank her. Edgar, sensing the shift in the battle, lunged at the nearest frogman with a renewed snarl, his jaws clamping down with brutal force. He shook it until it went limp in his jaws, so he shook it some more for dramatic effect.

The frogmen, once so confident in their numbers, began to falter. Their leader croaked in alarm, trying to rally its remaining troops, but the tide had indeed turned. One by one, the frogmen began to retreat, their courage broken by the ferocity of the adventurers and the mysterious new warrior. The leader let out a final, desperate croak before fleeing into the darkness, its forces scattering in all directions. They hopped into pools unseen and disappeared as quickly as they had arrived.

Kayriss managed to pick up one of the fallen tridents and looked around. There was a single frogman left who was wounded enough that he wasn't running or hopping his escape. With a precision born of her Elven senses, she threw the trident with enough force to nail the frogman to the floor; the gap between each prong filled with one of its legs. The fallen frogman croaked a squeal and pulled desperately at the weapon but to no avail.

Within moments, the clearing was silent once more, save for the crackling of the fire and the heavy breathing of the adventurers. The ground was littered with the bodies of the fallen frogmen, their blood darkening the earth. The party stood in the aftermath of the battle, their weapons still raised, their eyes scanning the surroundings for any lingering threats. Breathing was laboured and heavy, each breath a reminder that they'd bought themselves more time alive.

The mysterious warrior sheathed her blades fluidly and turned to face the party. Her eyes, the colour of the deep ocean, were calm and steady as she regarded them.

The water Oceanid Serafin looked directly at Isaac uneasily, levelling her gaze towards him.

Chapter Thirty-Seven
Elara
History before nine.

    Elara sat by the small, flickering fire in her chamber, the shadows dancing on the stone walls. The dim morning light cast long, eerie shapes, but the warmth was comforting against the chill that seemed to seep into the citadel from every corner. Across from her, Meira sat, her posture tense, hands clasped tightly in her lap. The servant had a solemn look on her face, as if the weight of the world rested on her slender shoulders.

    "So. Tell me everything about this place..." Elara began, her voice breaking the heavy silence. "About the Night One Citadel and the power it holds over this land."

Meira nodded, her gaze drifting to the window where the sky was just beginning to lighten. Moving to it, she pulled the curtains across so that a mere shard of light broke into the room.

"The Citadel is more than just a fortress, my lady. It's the heart of a kingdom built on shadows and blood. Its walls are not just stone and mortar; they are the very embodiment of fear and control. Even though the Night One Monarchy would not agree."

Elara leaned forward, intrigued and unsettled. "What do you mean?"

"The Citadel sits upon an obsidian mine, one of the largest and most dangerous in the new world," Meira explained, her voice barely above a whisper. "The obsidian mined here is not just any stone, it feels imbued with dark power, a remnant of the world before, when the Hu-mans ruled and their folly led to their own cataclysm. That stone is what is said to give the Night Ones their strength, and it is what binds this kingdom together in chains."

"Chains?" Elara echoed, her heart quickening.

Meira's eyes darkened. "Metaphorically speaking. The miners who extract the obsidian are not just criminals; they are prisoners in every sense of the word. Most are members of the scourge foxes' families. These Wildlings were once free as all animal folk are but have been moulded into fierce warriors in service of the Night Ones. Their families must give up one member of their litter to service the mines, and that causes them to be brutally loyal to protect their pack. These offered families are, however, little more than slaves, forced to work in the mines to ensure their loved ones above remain loyal."

Elara felt a pang of horror. "They're held hostage? And the foxes... they work for the Night Ones because they have no choice?"

"Yes," Meira confirmed, her expression grim. "The scourge foxes are the enforcers in the streets below the Citadel, keeping the peace, hunting down those who dare defy the Night Ones. But they do so knowing that if they fail, their families will suffer the consequences. It's a cruel cycle that keeps all of them in line."

Elara clenched her fists, anger bubbling up inside her. "And all for obsidian? For power?"

"For control," Meira corrected. "King Marus, the King in Shadow, understands that power is nothing without control. He rules with an iron fist, and his sons, Tallin and Kaelen, have inherited that same cold ruthlessness."

Elara's mind whirled with the implications of what she was hearing. She had sensed the darkness in Tallin, the way he wielded his charm like a weapon, but she hadn't imagined the depth of the cruelty beneath the surface. Kaelen? ... What was his part in all of this?

"Tell me more about Tallin and Kaelen," Elara urged. "How do they fit into this?"

Meira hesitated as if weighing how much to reveal. Finally, she sighed and began to speak. "Tallin and Kaelen are the sons of King Marus, but they are not just princes; they are heirs to an ancient legacy. Their family has ruled since the fall of the Hu-mans, ever since the old world crumbled into dust. Their power has been passed down through generations, along with certain… prophecies."

"Prophecies?" Elara repeated, a chill running down her spine.

Meira nodded, her expression grave. "Yes. Prophecies that have shaped the course of history, guiding the Night Ones in their rule. One of those prophecies speaks of a time when a new darkness will rise, threatening the fragile balance that has been maintained since the fall. It's said that the meeting of two Hu-mans will awaken this darkness... and their dark touch."

Elara felt a cold dread settle over her. "Two Hu-mans... like me?"

"Yes," Meira whispered, her eyes locking onto Elara's. "You, my lady, are one of the Hu-mans of that prophecy. At least, that's what they believe. If you were to meet another of your kind, the darkness within you would rise, bringing chaos and destruction. That is why Tallin and Kaelen are so interested in you. They see you as both a threat and an opportunity."

Elara's breath caught in her throat. "An opportunity? For what?"

"For power," Meira said, her voice trembling." If they can control and harness the darkness within you, they can reshape the world as they see fit. But if they fail... the consequences could be dire. That's why neither brother can be trusted. Their goals may differ, but the same ambition drives both. To seize the power that lies within you."

Elara stared at Meira, her mind reeling. She had come to this place seeking answers about her past, about a strange power she was unaware she possessed, but now she realised the stakes were far higher than she had imagined. She wasn't just a pawn in some game of thrones; she was the key to a prophecy that could alter the world's fate.

"Why are you telling me all this?" Elara asked, her voice barely a whisper.

"Because you deserve to know the truth," Meira replied, her eyes filled with fierce determination. "And because I believe you can break this cycle, my lady. You have the strength to defy the prophecy, to forge your own path. But you must be careful; Tallin and Kaelen will stop at nothing and use you for their own ends. You'll need allies if you're to survive."

Elara felt a surge of resolve, her fear turning to determination. She wasn't sure how she would do it, but she knew she couldn't let herself be used as a tool for destruction. She would find a way to control her power, resist the darkness that threatened to consume her and start by allying with the one person who had shown her the truth. "Thank you, Meira," Elara said, clinging to the servant's hand. "I won't let them win. Together, we'll find a way to end this."

Meira squeezed Elara's hand, her expression softening with relief. "I believe in you, my lady. And I'll do everything I can to help you."

As they sat together in the dim light, the shadows of the Citadel seemed less oppressive, the weight of its secrets lighter now that they were shared. Elara knew the path ahead would be fraught with danger, but she felt a glimmer of hope for the first time. She also thought she needed answers from the people and Wildlings below them in the streets.

She wasn't alone in this fight, and with Meira by her side, she was ready to face whatever challenges lay ahead.

Now, they needed to speak with a fox.

Chapter Thirty-Eight
Kayriss
Serafin.

"Who are you?" Isaac asked, his voice hoarse from exertion.

"I am called Serafin," she replied, her voice soft and melodic, like the sound of waves gently lapping at the shore. "I am an Oceanid, a daughter of the sea."

Kayriss stepped forward, her eyes wide with curiosity. "An Oceanid? I've heard of your kind but never thought I'd see one so far from the coast."

Serafin nodded, a slight smile playing at the corners of her lips. "We are rare on land, it is true. But I was drawn here by the water disturbance, a darkness reaching the ocean's depths. I followed the signs, and they led me to you. And, well, these..." The last part of her sentence was laced with a hatred born from contempt for these frogmen. "There is also much talk of the two newcomers in the world."

"Thank you for your help," Isaac said, lowering his sword. "We would have been overwhelmed without you."

Serafin inclined her head. "You fought bravely, newborn. But the danger is not over. The creatures you fought tonight are just the beginning. There is a greater darkness at work here, one that threatens both land and sea. And I want to know why they want *you* so badly..." She motioned towards Kayriss, who looked shocked at the line of questioning.

"The Night Ones are questing for Isaac, but he's mine. They cannot have him". The defiance in her words brought a raised eyebrow from Serafin, followed by a slight smile that lit her face.

"Yours?" She smiled. "I see..." With that, her demeanour seemed to soften, and as the party exchanged uneasy glances, they seemed to accept this newcomer's presence in their midst.

"We seem to have a common enemy," Kayriss said, her voice resolute. "And we could use your help, Serafin. Will you join us?"

Serafin's eyes flickered with something unreadable before she nodded. "For now, I will. But know this: the ocean calls to me always, and I will not stray far from its embrace. But as long as our paths align, I will fight by your side."

Grind and Granite looked at Serafin uneasily, unsure of her motives.

"The Night One prophecy talks of the hu-man uprising, and I see you have one in your midst. I have heard rumours, but please bring me up to speed with his arrival in our realm if you would."

Captain Browntail stepped forward before anyone could speak, Cutlass bustling in behind him. He looked up at Serafin with a longing in his eyes, but Cutlass quickly slapped it down and hurumphed in his direction.

"It be a story ye need water maiden! Then I be the one..." Browntail started to tell his tale but was politely interrupted by Kayriss.

"Searfin, allow me." She smiled down at the otter, who realised the gravitas of the situation was above a shanty. He also realised he hadn't been told everything, so the two otters plopped down together and listened. Kayriss explained the events of the previous couple of weeks, from her finding Isaac to the Wildlings locating the hu-man woman. She continued through the attacks on all their villages to the point of their meeting with the frogmen. Searfin listened intently, taking in the details.

"This matches with news that has reached us. We heard the Night Ones took a female. They were calling her Elara. Besides, we have nothing as their path to their citadel was mostly inland. Our sea-faring Wildlings are adept at picking up morsels of information for us."

Browntail and Cutlass took in the details of their new water-based party member as the stories unfolded. They were both completely enthralled by her appearance.

Serafin's skin shimmered as the surface of a calm sea kissed by moonlight, and the fire crackled its light onto her. The blue tint of her skin would blend seamlessly with any ocean, and the otters could see that her body was adorned with fish scales that rippled like the undulating waves, snaking up her form in an elegant, protective pattern. Each scale caught the light, reflecting hues of sapphire and cerulean as she moved with the fluid grace of a swift current.

Her armour, crafted from blue leather and strengthened with coral inlays, clung to her like a second skin. It was as though the ocean itself forged this protective shell, each piece of coral a testament to the strength and resilience of the reef. The armour was flexible and formidable, allowing her to move with the speed of a darting fish while providing the unyielding defence of the seabed. Her hair, a vibrant cascade of red seaweed, flowed around her like a living, breathing part of the ocean, tangling and swirling with the currents. Even on land, it moved as though alive and drifting in underwater currents. It framed her face like the tendrils of a deep sea anemone, a striking contrast to the cool blues of her skin and armour. Her eyes, deep and reflective like the ocean's abyss, held the wisdom of countless tides, and when she spoke, it was with the power of a storm brewing on the horizon.

The otters wondered if she was more fish than hu-manoid, realising they were hungry. As the stories concluded, they padded off to their packs to seek a bountiful feast.

Kayriss seemed to glimpse something behind Searfin's eyes and realised she was watching Isaac's movements. She thought of keeping an eye on this new ally as she hadn't been entirely convinced of her motives just yet.

"Ribbit."

The noise came off to one side, and Kayriss remembered the frogman she'd pinned to the floor. She moved over to it, followed by the party, their adrenaline flowing again.

"Hold your weapons, everyone." She approached the wounded frogman slowly and with open gestures. "I mean you no harm. Even though you attacked us. Let me help you..."

The frogman, she realised, was wounded gravely, his injury weeping blood through the lines of coral laced across his armoured chest.

"Allow me to heal you," she said, and a few gruffs of annoyance blurted out from the team behind. Looking back, she said, "If we do not make the first step, we are no better than our attackers. Peace must be worked on."

Still pinned to the ground, the frogman could not resist as his wounds were healed. His large eyes blinked in shock as his pain began to fade. When the spell finished, Kayriss removed the trident from its pinned position, allowing the frog to stand. He was only waist-high to Kayriss and shifted nervously as he tried to explain. His wide, amphibian eyes blinked slowly, and his throat ballooned out before deflating with a series of deep croaks.

"Ribbit... we... we no mean harm, Elf lady," he began, his voice a strange mix of guttural croaks and hisses. His webbed hands gestured wildly as he spoke. "Croak... darkness... came to our lands, felt deep in our waters. Ribbit... we scared, confused." He paused, glancing at Kayriss and her companions, and continued to murmur in low, anxious ribbits.

"Croak... we simple folk," he continued, throat inflating again. "Ribbit ribbit... no magic like you, no big wisdom. Croak... just water, just home. When darkness come, we think, ribbit, you bring it. We act... to protect. Croak-croak... no think well." He let out a slow, deep rumble from his throat, the sound almost mournful.

"Ribbit... wrong, we know now," he said, bowing his head. "Croak... but... still, the dark thing, it's here... We feel it watching these lands. Croak, ribbit... we fear what come next." His voice faded into a soft series of croaks as he looked up at Kayriss with wide, pleading eyes.

"We seek same. But we are friend. You need not be scared." Kayriss offered, trying to mimic his simple speech patterns. "You can be free. Tell your frogs that we are friend though. No more attack."

He looked up at her with wide eyes, smiled broadly and bounded off into the night.

**

With the alliance formed, the party gathered closer around the fire, their bodies weary but their spirits bolstered by the arrival of this mysterious new ally. Kayriss chose the final watch, and Serafin offered to sit with her. It allowed the others to sleep, so she agreed, as she did not want to sleep with her awake. The night was still dark; the journey ahead would be fraught with danger. They had survived this first trial and gained a new ally, and Kayriss felt they were a bit closer to facing whatever came next.

At least, that's what she thought.

Chapter Thirty-Nine
Elara
Schemes afoot.

    Elara paced the length of her room, Meira's words swirling in her mind like a storm. She'd left shortly afterwards under the guise of collecting old clothing for cleaning. Elara had realised she was unsure who this room belonged to previously, so she requested fresh bedding and other items. The revelations from their conversation had left her unsettled. She needed to speak with them directly if the scourge foxes honestly held more answers and possibly a means to escape. There was another reason she dared not admit even to herself... doubt. Meira's story had been too smooth, too convenient, and the only way to verify the truth was to hear it from the foxes themselves.

    She approached the door, her heart pounding in her chest. She turned the handle slowly, cracking the door open just enough to peek out. As expected, the guard stationed outside stood at attention, his sharp eyes snapping towards her as soon as the door moved.

Elara tried to sound casual, "I need some air. Could you please let me pass?"

The guard's expression didn't change. "I'm afraid I can't allow that, my lady. Orders from Prince Tallin."

Elara knew it would be as such but needed to leave if her plans were to begin. "I don't want to go far. Just a quick walk. Surely that's not too much to ask?"

"Apologies, my lady. I can't let you leave this room unescorted," he replied, his voice flat and final.

"Then escort me," Elara said, pushing the door wider. Pressing her luck, she stepped a foot outside.

"My lady. Please return to your room."

Elara retreated inside, frustration boiling in her veins. She was told that she wasn't a prisoner but held captive nonetheless, as every step she tried to take seemed to be shadowed by invisible chains. Elara considered her options, pacing back and forth. Waiting was not an option. Her resolve hardened. She would try again. Elara approached the door a second time, trying to feign nonchalance. She pushed it open with more force, hoping to slip by quickly.

"Please, my lady. I must insist you remain inside," the guard repeated, his tone more insistent now.

Elara's temper flared. "This is ridiculous! I'm not asking to leave the castle, just this room! I'm entitled to some freedom, am I not?" Her raised voice seemed to echo down the hallway, and the guard shifted uncomfortably. Elara could see the internal conflict in his eyes. Before he could respond, they both felt a presence walking towards them. The unmistakable sound of boots clicking sharply against the stone floor made their stomachs sink as they realised who was coming. Tallin appeared in the hallway, his presence filling the space. He was dressed in his usual dark attire, his eyes narrowing as he took in the scene. The guard stepped aside, bowing slightly as Tallin entered the room, gesturing Elara back inside again.

"Elara," Tallin's voice was calm, but there was a steely edge to it. "What seems to be the problem?"

Elara's frustration flared into anger. "The problem? The problem is that I'm being treated like a prisoner! I've done nothing wrong, and yet I can't even step out of this room without an armed escort."

Tallin's gaze didn't waver. "This is for your safety. We've spoken about this..."

"Don't patronise me, Tallin," she snapped, cutting him off. "I know you're worried about what they might do, but I can't stay locked up like this. I need to see more of the city and the castle... You said I wasn't a prisoner."

Tallin crossed his arms, his expression unreadable. "You are free. In here. I am still gauging the feelings of my people and what they'd think of a hu-man walking in their midst." Elara hesitated, her mind racing for an excuse that didn't betray Meira and what she had been told.

"But you're supposed to be all-powerful. Shouldn't they listen to you? Isn't that what your demonstration was all about yesterday?" She chided, trying to pull at his ego. Tallin studied her, his eyes piercing through her resolve. The tension in the room was palpable, a silent battle of wills. She could feel his suspicion, but there was something else beneath it, something she couldn't quite name. His silence stretched, and Elara felt her skin prickle under his gaze. She hated how he made her feel like he could see straight through her, past all her defences. There was a strange, electric undercurrent between them, an awareness that made her pulse quicken in a way she wasn't prepared to examine.

"Very well," Tallin said finally, his voice low and measured. "You may tour the city and the castle under my supervision. But if you think I'll allow you to wander into the scourge foxes' den alone, you're sorely mistaken."

Elara bristled at the implication that she needed his permission, but she bit back her retort. This was the best she could hope for, and she knew better than to push him too far.

"Fine," she agreed, though her tone was anything but pleased. "But I want to go now."

Tallin raised an eyebrow as if considering her request. After a moment, he gave a curt nod. "Now you demand? Fine. Get ready. We leave in ten minutes."

Elara's heart raced as she watched him turn and leave the room, the door clicking shut behind him. The tension between them lingered, a taut string ready to snap. She couldn't help but feel a mix of triumph and trepidation. As she prepared herself, she couldn't shake the feeling that she was walking into something far more complex and dangerous than she'd anticipated. Tallin's reluctance had told her one thing: there was more to this city, this castle, and these foxes than met the eye. Maybe Meira was telling the truth after all.

Elara was about to find out.

Chapter Forty
Hooth
The secret of the otter chest.
(Aaarrrr)

The night sky was a deep indigo blanket studded with a thousand shimmering stars. The air was cool, carrying the scent of damp earth and the lingering musk of the swamp where they had battled the frogmen earlier. The adventuring party had set up camp in a small clearing, the embers of their fire casting a warm, flickering glow across the group as they settled for the night.

Kayriss was tending to the wounded; luckily, just minor abrasions and the occasional slice. Granite seemed to have come off worse and tried to refuse treatment, but after receiving a look that hurt more than the wound, they stoically agreed. She bandaged his shoulder and dressed it with a herb that Granite found warming on his skin. Her sharp eyes glanced over the camp, taking in her companions' weary but satisfied expressions. They had fought well, and now it was time to rest.

Captain Browntail leaned back against a log, his whiskers twitching as he chewed on a piece of dried fish. He nudged his first mate, Cutlass, who took his meaning without a word. The two had been whispering and chuckling together all evening, and now, it seemed, they had a plan in mind.

"Hooth!" Captain Browntail called out, his voice carrying across the camp. "Be a good lad and help us with the chest, would ya?"

Hooth sat a little apart from the rest, his large, feathered form blending into the shadows. His golden eyes, sharp as a hawk's, narrowed slightly at the request. The chest in question was a heavy, ornately carved box that the otters had been guarding jealously since the trip had begun, but they had refused to reveal its contents. Due to its size and weight, Hooth had been carrying it for their journey, begrudgingly at first, but is now more interested in why the furry pair wanted it. They seemed to have everything they needed and never tried to open it during any rest stops.

Hooth rose to his feet with a resigned sigh, his armour clinking softly. "Why don't you carry it yourselves if it's so important?" he grumbled, his voice low and gravelly.

Cutlass grinned, flashing a toothy smile. "We would, Hooth, but yer strength is unmatched. We did try, but it needs to be further away from ye prying eyes. There's no need for ye land lubbers to see our tresaarrrrr! It'd be no trouble for a knight like you, though, eh?"

Hooth muttered something about lazy pirates but strode to the chest nonetheless. With one mighty heave, he lifted it, his powerful wings helping to balance the weight. The otters guided him to a secluded part of the clearing, away from the rest of the camp.

"Just over here," Captain Browntail said, pointing to a spot beneath a large tree with the thickest shadows. "Perfect, right there, matey!"

Hooth set the chest down with a thud, eyeing the otters with a mix of suspicion and irritation. "There. Now, what's in this thing that's got you two so secretive?"

"Ah, don't be nosy, Hooth," Cutlass teased, tapping the chest with her paw. "It's just treasure, nothin' more. But we appreciate yer help, mate."

Captain Browntail fished around in his pocket and pulled out a small, smooth pebble, polished to a shine. He offered it to Hooth with a grin. "For yer troubles."

Hooth stared at the pebble, his expression unreadable. After a moment, he took it, tucking it into his pouch with a curt nod. "You owe me more than a pebble for hauling that thing," he grumbled, though there was a hint of warmth in his tone. The otters chuckled, exchanging a knowing glance, before they shooed Hooth away with a wave of their paws. "Go on, get some rest. We'll guard the chest tonight."

Hooth returned to the campfire; his feathers ruffled in more ways than one. He sat back down, resuming his silent vigil over the camp as the others drifted off to sleep one by one. Despite his fatigue, something about the otters' behaviour nagged at him, and he found himself unable to relax.

**

Later that night, when the moon hung high in the sky, and the camp was quiet save for the crackling of the fire, Hooth decided to check on the otters. Grind was awake and on watch duty so that he could leave. He rose silently and returned to the secluded part of the clearing, his keen eyes picking out the shapes in the darkness.

As he approached, he heard soft splashing and the low murmur of voices. Curiosity piqued, he moved closer, keeping to the shadows. When he reached the edge of the clearing, what he saw made him pause.

The chest, now open, revealed its contents: a pool of clear, shimmering river water somehow contained within the ornate box. The otters, Captain Browntail and Cutlass, were inside, their sleek bodies moving gracefully through the water. It wasn't treasure they had been guarding—it was a bath.

Hooth watched as the two otters swam together, their movements slow and deliberate. There was no playful splashing, no banter. Instead, there was a quiet intimacy, a deep connection that spoke volumes in the stillness of the night. Their fur gleamed in the moonlight, the water rippling gently around them as they embraced, their heads resting against one another. Clearly, they were not just companions in adventure but in the deepest of otter love.

For a long moment, Hooth watched, his heart softening at the sight. He had known the otters to be mischievous, rowdy, and brave, but this side of them, this tenderness, was something he hadn't expected. It was a reminder that even in a world filled with danger and darkness, there was room for love and gentle moments like these.

Respectfully, Hooth turned away, leaving the otters to their privacy. He returned to the camp, his mind turning over what he had seen. He could have teased them about it in the morning, but something told him to keep it to himself. It was their moment, and he had been a silent witness to a rare glimpse of their true selves.

The following morning, as the sun began to rise and the camp stirred awake, Hooth returned to the secluded spot where the otters were closing the chest. The air was still cool, and the remnants of their night together were evident in the soft smiles they shared.

"Ah, Hooth!" Captain Browntail greeted him, slipping back into his usual pirate persona. "We've got the chest ready to move again. Care to give us a hand?"

Hooth, maintaining his gruff demeanour, nodded and lifted the chest without a word. As he did, Cutlass pulled out another pebble, this one slightly larger than the last, and handed it to him with a wink. "For yer troubles, matey."

Hooth took the pebble, his expression stern as ever, but he couldn't help the slight twitch at the corner of his beak. "I'll start charging you by the pound if you keep this up," he muttered.

The otters laughed, beginning another of their sea shanties to raise their crew. Hooth smiled as he listened to the lyrics.

> ♪On the briny deep, we sail
> Hearts entwined in the ocean's wail
> With each wave, our love does grow
> Pirate otters are bold, yo ho!
>
> ♪Golden sunsets we shall chase
> In your eyes my safe embrace
> Treasure found within your smile
> Sailing hearts mile after mile
>
> ♪Yo ho ho our love's the sea
> Boundless tides for you and me

Anchored strong in stormy tides
Together in the wild ride

♫Parrots squawk but we don't care
Pirate love beyond compare
Captain's hat upon your brow
In your arms, a blissful vow

♫Yo ho ho our love's the sea
Boundless tides for you and me
Anchored strong in stormy tides
Together in the wild ride

♫Cannonballs and treasures vast
But our love is everlast
On this deck or far ashore
Pirate hearts forevermore

♫In the moonlight
Soft and still
Pirate love
The greatest thrill
Map of stars will guide our way
Hand in hand
We'll never stray

When Cutlass was further ahead, Hooth looked down at Browntail and asked with a knowing smile,

"First mate?" Browntail caught his implication immediately, smiling broadly. Gone was the bluster of his pirate love, replaced with another.

"My only mate."

**

The rest of the party heard them before they saw them, immediately knowing who was coming. The song filled the group, and Isaac looked over at Kayriss, his heart filling with the warmth he felt for her. They were none the wiser about the night's events, and as they packed up to continue their journey, Hooth kept his silence. Heaving the box back up on his back, he motioned for the otters to sit on top while they walked. Immediately, their eyes lit up, and they darted up his body to sit on the ornate box. Bursting into song, they started munching through breakfast, happy not to be walking for a moment. As they moved through the forest, the sun breaking through the canopy above, Hooth felt a sense of contentment. He had seen something special last night that reminded him of the importance of loyalty and love, even in the roughest of times.

For that, the small pebbles in his pouch were treasures indeed.

Chapter Forty-One
Elara
Precious one...

Elara paced the small, dimly lit room, her boots scuffing softly against the cold stone floor. The space around her felt suffocating; the walls were too close, and the air was too still. She had been trapped in the castle for days, maybe the darkness causing her to lose track of time. The narrow window at the far end offered no clues, only the muted glow of a sky awake for another day. Her heart beat faster with each passing moment. She had ten minutes till she would be outside. She would make her move. She had to get out. Now, as the minutes stretched on, the weight of her plan began to press on her like the walls closing in.

Her eyes flicked across the room, searching for anything she could take with her—a weapon, a tool, even something small that might help. The room was barren, the stone walls offering nothing but cold and silence. The modest trappings were nothing that could easily be taken, even if they had an external use. Her fingers brushed over the worn wooden table beside the bed. She ran a hand along its rough edge, but it was too heavy and bulky to be used. The simple chair was no better.

The candle on the table flickered in the faint draft, its weak flame barely lighting the gloom. Elara felt her frustration growing. She had nothing. No blade, no way to defend herself if it came to that.

She crossed the room to the window and peered through the narrow slit. Outside, the fortress loomed; she imagined the shadowed Night One figure moving far below, guards patrolling in the distance. It was too far to call, and not that she would. Not that they'd help. Tallin had made sure her imprisonment was as complete as possible. She was a prisoner, but one kept in plain sight. She stepped back from the window, biting her lip. Her mind raced through possibilities; could she break the chair leg and use it as a club? Could she rip the bedding and make a rope to climb out the window? All absurd ideas. They would take time she didn't have, and she might be unable to muster strength.

Elara let out a breath, her hands shaking. She needed something more. Anything.

As she scanned the room again, her chest tightened. There was nothing. No weapons, no tools, no hope. Her body trembled with the weight of it, helplessness settling over her like a shroud.

She felt it.

A sudden wave of coldness, a creeping sensation crawling along her spine, was subtle at first, like a whisper of wind brushing against her skin, but it grew stronger and more insistent. Elara froze, a strange heaviness settling in her chest. Her breath caught in her throat, and the world seemed to tilt for a moment.

She reached for the table, steadying herself. The feeling grew deeper, like a shadow wrapping around her heart, squeezing just enough to make her aware of it but not enough to stop her from moving. Her fingers dug into the wood as she tried to shake the sensation, but it only intensified. Her mind began to cloud, her thoughts becoming fragmented and scattered. It was like a dark fog rolling in from the edges of her consciousness, swallowing her thoughts one by one.

What... is this?

She squeezed her eyes shut, willing herself to focus, to push the sensation away. It clung to her, thick and oppressive.

She heard it. A voice. Soft and distant but unmistakable.

"Not long now, precious one."

Elara's eyes snapped open, her heart hammering in her chest. The voice was a low murmur, barely above a whisper, but it sent a chill straight to her core. She whipped around, scanning the room for its source, but no one was there. The room was still empty, still silent, except for the sound of her ragged breathing.

She pressed her hands to her temples, trying to calm herself. 'It's just the stress. I'm imagining things. The confinement, the fear. It's getting to me.' Elara reasoned.

The voice had been so real, however. It had been so close, as though someone had been standing right behind her, breathing those words into her ear. The darkness inside her pulsed again, stronger this time, like a storm brewing beneath her skin.

Elara shook her head, swallowing hard. No. It's not real. I'm not losing control.

She couldn't afford to lose control now. She had to focus. She had to escape. She had to…

Another pulse of darkness surged through her, this time accompanied by a deep, aching hunger. It gnawed at her, primal and relentless, as though something inside her was waking up, something ancient and powerful.

"He's coming for you. Don't worry, dearest one."

The voice was unmistakable this time, closer.

Elara gasped, stumbling back, her hands trembling as she clutched her chest. The darkness was rising inside her, swirling like a storm, threatening to consume her whole. She wanted to scream, claw at her skin, and stop whatever was happening, but she was trapped in the storm, helpless to its pull.

And then, as quickly as it had come, the sensation faded, leaving her breathless and trembling. She stood in the centre of the room, staring at nothing, the eerie silence returning. The voice was gone, the darkness retreating, leaving only her pounding heart and the distant echo of whispered words.

Not long now, precious one.

Her knees nearly gave way as she leaned against the table for support. Was this just her imagination? Was there something more to the darkness she felt within herself? Before she could dwell on it any longer, the door creaked open, the heavy wood scraping against the stone floor.

Tallin stood in the doorway, his broad figure framed by the dim light behind him. His sharp eyes swept over her, taking in her pale face and trembling hands.

"Elara," he said, his voice calm but laced with suspicion. "It's time."

She straightened, masking her fear behind a steely resolve. She had no idea what was happening to her, but she couldn't let Tallin see. Not now.

"Let's go," she said, her voice firmer than she felt.

Tallin gave a curt nod, his gaze lingering on her a moment longer before he stepped aside, motioning for her to follow.

Chapter Forty-Two
Kayriss
The rat in the party.

    Kayriss and her companions were packing up the meagre possessions they'd brought with them after a break from the long slog through the marshalls. Everyone was still aching from the night's battle with the frogmen. It had taken a longer time than any wanted to move the corpses out of their camp the night previous, and Grind had wanted to pile them up and burn them, but Kayriss had told him that that would be a bad idea as it may attract more predators. Plus, nature would deal with the corpses as nature does, returning them to the earth where they lay. The air was cool, with a faint, musty scent that lingered in the nostrils, a reminder of the marshlands and nearby riverways. Browntail had wondered where they led to, clearly wishing he was back on the 'ocean waves' as he put it.

Kayriss was the first to awaken, her senses honed by years of living outside. The breeze brought nature's news to her, and her senses tingled with the direction they needed. The nature spirits drew her south, showing her the direction of Elara and her captors. She sat up slowly, the blanket slipping from her shoulders, and took a moment to gather her thoughts. Instinctively, she moved her hand to Isaac, who was still blissfully asleep. She looked at his peacefulness and wanted nothing more than to snuggle against his form, but the sun was up; the way was clear.

She reached for her pack, which rested against an old tree stump, and began to prepare for the day's travel. Her movements were deliberate and precise, born of habit and necessity. She pulled out a small, well-worn leather pouch and checked its contents: her collection of herbs, medicinal supplies, and a few rare crystals that could amplify her spells. Everything was in order.

Next, she took out a small, intricately carved wooden box. Inside was a set of enchanted runestones, each marked with a symbol that pulsed faintly with stored magic. She ran her fingers over them, feeling the familiar hum of power beneath her fingertips. The runestones were her safeguard, a way to channel energy quickly if they were ambushed or needed to perform complex spells on the move. Satisfied, she carefully wrapped the box in cloth and secured it back in her pack.

Kayriss's staff lay on the floor beside her. It had taken some knocks and gouges from the fight in the night, but she watched as it slowly healed itself as the rays of the sun touched each blemish. She reached for it, feeling the comforting weight in her hand. The staff had been with her for years, a reliable tool and a trusted companion.

As she finished her preparations, Kayriss glanced over at Grind and Granite. The two Mine Folk were still asleep, their heavy breathing wafting their beards upwards. She giggled as Grind belched a snore, and his beard fluttered upwards. They had insisted on taking as many watches as they could, preferring the night to the brightness of the day, despite her protests, and it was clear from the dark circles under their eyes that they hadn't gotten much rest.

Kayriss stood and walked over to where they lay, crouching beside them. She hesitated for a moment before gently shaking Grind's shoulder. His eyes snapped open immediately, alert and wary, a sign that he was still adrenaline-filled.

"Morning already?" Grind grumbled, sitting up and rubbing the sleep from his eyes.

"Close enough," Kayriss replied, offering him a small smile. "We need to get moving. The sooner we get moving, the sooner we get answers and help Elara." Grind mumbled something into his beard that Kayriss could hear but chose to leave the sentence unanswered. Granite stirred next, his deep voice rumbling as he stretched his thick arms. "Can't say I'm looking forward to another day of tramping through these marshlands or whatever is coming, but I suppose we've got little choice."

Kayriss nodded, her expression serious. Grind sighed, his shoulders slumping slightly. "Aye, you're right. Let's get to it then."

The two Mine Folk began their preparations; their movements were practised and efficient. Grind checked his pickaxe, inspecting it for nicks or dull edges. His weapon was an extension of himself, and he treated it with the respect it deserved. Grind knew that it was keeping him alive; without him, his village might be lost if it wasn't already. Granite, meanwhile, hefted his hammer, testing its weight in his hands before securing it to his back. He also took a moment to adjust the straps of his armour, ensuring everything was in place for whatever might lie ahead.

Kayriss took out a small metal flask and handed it to Grind as they worked. "Drink this," she said. "It's an energy elixir. It won't replace sleep, but it'll help you stay sharp."

Grind accepted the flask with a nod of thanks, taking a small sip before passing it to Granite. Being miners, they were used to pushing their limits, but they knew better than to refuse Kayriss's potions. Her knowledge of alchemy and herbcraft has proven helpful and effective.

Once they were ready, Kayriss looked around at the rest of her party.

Edgar was up and bounding after a small animal, clearly having remembered he was a dog. He leapt over the grass mounds, enjoying the freedom of the morning. Both otter pirates were awake now and straightening their clothing. Cutlas was smiling as she had found a new pebble during the night. She offered it to Browntail, who smiled back at her and slipped the small rock into one of his pouches. Hooth was already circling overhead, his eyes watching for any more attackers.

Their new party member, Serafin, was crouched low, her hand in a small brook. Her eyes were closed as if she was in communion with the water. Kayriss chose to leave her to her commune while they readied themselves.

The day had passed with only one incident, which, late in the evening, the party were still chuckling about. The stretch of land they covered was a murky, swampy marshland, leaving Grind feeling very much out of his element. His heavy boots were constantly getting stuck in the muck, and his grumbling was loud enough to scare off any would-be marsh predators.

Around noon, as the sun was at its apex, Grind stepped in a rather dubious patch of marsh while crossing a particularly thick patch of mud. He sank much faster than anyone else and called the party to a halt. Grind let out a low growl of annoyance but was stuck fast.

"By me beard, I'm stuck again!" Grind bellowed, attempting to pull his feet free. He tugged with all his strength, but instead of freeing himself, he got his boots firmly entrenched while his feet came flying out. The force sent him tumbling backwards, headfirst into a thick, squishy mud puddle behind him with a loud splat.

Covered head to toe in mud, Grind sat up, resembling a swamp monster more than a Mine Folk. His hat had been knocked crooked, and a swampy fern was sticking out from behind his ear like an accidental accessory. His beard was caked with layers of muck, and he glared at the rest of the party, who were trying and failing not to burst out laughing.

"Go on, laugh it up!" Grind grumbled, pulling off his hat and wringing a small newt out of his beard. "If I wanted a swamp bath, I'd have stayed in me grandmother's cabbage stew!"

With that, the party lost it, and laughter filled the air. Even Grind saw the funny side in the end and guffawed along with them. Serafin approached and called forth clean water from a nearby stream to wash the mud off. A long tendril of fluid arced up and gently cleaned off the laughing Grind, but at the sight of the magic, all surrounding him were brought to silence, in awe of the wonders they were beholding.

"Your magic is nature, mine is water," Serafin said to Kayriss, who nodded approvingly back to her, clearly impressed.

For the rest of the day, every squelch of the marsh reminded Grind of his earlier mishap, bringing a chuckle and much-needed merriment to everyone.

**

The next day was much like the last but without the merriment. All of the group was tired, their feet aching with each step. Camp breaks became a God-sent gift, and talking became an effort.

Long shadows began to retreat as the sun warmed them away, and Kayriss took a deep breath and looked toward the south. Their path seemed almost tangible, a living entity that beckoned them forward with promises of danger and discovery. The weight of their mission had truly settled on her shoulders, but she welcomed it. She felt they were close to something important that could change the fate of the Mine Folk and perhaps even the world above.

"Stay close," she instructed her voice steady but carrying the gravity of their situation. "We don't know what we'll encounter, and I don't want us getting separated."

Grind and Granite exchanged a glance, their expressions hardening with determination. "We're with you, Kayriss," Granite said, his deep voice echoing through his beard. "Let's see this through."

Kayriss led the way, with Isaac holding her hand. She smiled at him, and his glance back filled her with strength of resolve, even though she wished they were both away together somewhere else.

Grind and Granite followed in grim silence, their expressions tense. The Mine Folk, who had been through so much with their stout, muscular frames and rough-hewn features, usually embodied stoic endurance. Today, a shadow hung over them, one born of their recent tragedy and fresh wounds. Both felt they were walking away from their troubles, getting no closer to answers for their Stonemarsh. It had only been a few days since the attack on their village, a brutal onslaught by the swarm of giant rats. The Mine Folk had always coexisted uneasily with the creatures that lurked in the depths, but this time, the rats had come with such a terrifying ferocity, driven by a force that none of them could understand. Grind wanted to know how he could stop the attacks, but this trip they were on still needed to answer his questions.

As they ventured further south, Grind's voice cut through the silence, his tone laced with bitterness. "Remind me again why we're out here? Shouldn't we be tracking down the rest of those filthy rodents and finishing what they started?"

Granite grunted in agreement, his large hands clenching and unclenching around the handle of his warhammer. "Aye, they've taken enough from us. And we can't let them attack again. I hate them little cave maggots. I'm never eating another of the filthy verminshites."

Kayriss didn't respond immediately. She understood their anger, felt it herself even, but something was gnawing at her, a sense that the attack hadn't been as straightforward as it appeared. By the description of events from the two Mine Folk, the rats had seemed almost... frantic, as if they were fleeing something rather than hunting, which troubled her. Also, rats were not pack animals and definitely not hive-mind creatures.

"We'll find your answers, Grind, and save Elara," she finally said, her voice calm but firm. "Something drove those rats to attack, something unnatural. If we can understand what it was, maybe we can prevent it from happening again."

Grind muttered something under his breath, but he didn't argue further. They continued, the tension between them thickening with every step.

Up ahead, Kayriss saw it.

A lone rat.

It was matted and grizzled with age and strolled almost painfully. It seemed to be dragging itself across the grass with visible effort. It was clearly on its last legs, its breathing laboured, and its eyes dull with fatigue.

Grind and Granite both stiffened, their hands going to their weapons. "Should we finish it off?" Granite asked, his voice low as if the rat could hear them. He readied his hammer and stepped towards it, eager to end its life. Not out of mercy but sheer vengeance.

Kayriss raised a hand to stop them. "Wait," she said softly, stepping closer to the creature.

"Kayriss, what are you doing?" Grind's voice was sharp with incredulity. "That thing is vicious. Don't get too close." Kayriss shook her head. "No, this one's different. I want to know what it knows."

Ignoring the protests from her companions, Kayriss knelt beside the rat as she cast the incantation everyone was expecting. She whispered the incantation, her voice weaving through the minds of all creatures, and reached into the rat's mind. The rat's eyes flickered, its dull gaze sharpening slightly as it became aware of her presence in a new way. Kayriss felt a strange connection form between them, a thread of consciousness that allowed thoughts and images to pass between them. This was more than the animal-speaking spell; this was deep, and Kayriss felt that her powers were growing. She ignored it for now and conversed with the elderly rat.

"I mean you no harm, rat," she said, adopting calm and controlled body language. "Why did your pack attack the Mine Folk?" she asked, her voice gentle but probing.

The rat's thoughts were sluggish and fragmented but carried a deep, ancient sadness. Images flashed through Kayriss's mind: a vast underground world, the rat pack moving as one but with frantic urgency as if being pulled by an unseen force. The Mine Folk village appeared not as a target but as an obstacle in their path.

"We did not intend... to fight," the rat's thoughts came slowly, each word dragging itself to the surface. "We were... called. Something... in the south. We could not... resist."

Kayriss frowned, trying to make sense of the disjointed images and feelings. "What called you? What was driving your pack?"

The rat's mind shuddered, a wave of fear rippling through the connection. "Do not know. Just... felt it. A pull... a need. Madness. We... could not think. Only move... south. Must go... south."

The revelation hit Kayriss like a blow. The attack on the Mine Folk hadn't been out of malice or hunger; the rats had been driven mad, drawn by some powerful force to the south.

A force that was still calling to them.

A force that was calling to her.

Chapter Forty-Three
Tallin
Darkness encroaches.

Tallin stood beside the door, his imposing figure a constant reminder of the power dynamics. Yet, there was something different in his demeanour now, a slight relaxation of the tension that had characterised their earlier exchanges. He gestured her out of the room.

"This is the way to the city," Tallin said, his voice echoing softly in the vast chamber. "We call it the Under-Veil, though it once had another name."

Elara glanced at him, curiosity piqued. "What was it called?"

"Lon-don," he replied, the foreign word rolling off his tongue with a strange familiarity. "It was a city of the hu-mans, once vast and sprawling. But that was before their fall."

As they began their descent, Elara couldn't help but marvel at the sheer scale of the palace. Inside the citadel of the Night Ones was a breathtaking blend of ominous grandeur and shadowy elegance. The walls seemed constructed entirely of polished obsidian, their surfaces smooth as glass, reflecting dim, flickering light in twisted, distorted patterns. These walls seemed almost alive, absorbing the faint light and giving off a cold, eerie glow that bathed the entire citadel in a perpetual twilight. Massive, ornately carved pillars rose from the obsidian floor, towering towards a vaulted ceiling that stretched impossibly high above. The pillars were etched with intricate runes and ancient symbols, their edges sharp and precise, filled with a deep purple or inky blue luminescence that pulsed rhythmically, as if with a heartbeat of its own.

The floor was a vast mosaic of dark stones, some deep black and others rich, dark purple, arranged in complex, interwoven patterns that seemed to shift subtly when observed from the corner of Elara's eye. It was mesmerising and disorienting, as though the ground beneath her feet was alive with a dark energy.

Grand staircases of black marble spiralled both upward and downward, their bannisters wrought from a gleaming, silver-like metal that caught and reflected the dim light, creating an ethereal, ghostly effect. The steps were wide and imposing, leading to hidden chambers and shadowed alcoves that concealed their whispered secret collection.

Massive chandeliers, made of twisted metal and adorned with crystals that emitted a cold, pale light, hung from the various ceilings. Their illumination cast long, dancing shadows across the floor and walls, creating an ever-shifting tapestry of darkness and light. Throughout the citadel, heavy, velvet drapes in shades of deep crimson and midnight blue hung from arched windows and doorways, their surfaces embroidered with silver and black thread in swirling, arcane patterns. Elara noticed that all were pulled closed.

The windows that she could see, though, were narrow slits of obsidian glass, letting in no light from the outside world, only the ever-present darkness.

They walked in silence, Tallin not offering details of their tour. They moved past a grand hall, and Elara noticed a massive throne sitting atop a raised dais. It was forged from the same dark metal as the bannisters but adorned with spikes and twisted, thorn-like designs. The throne was draped in a cloak of shadowy fabric that seemed to ripple and flow like liquid darkness.

"Your father's chair I assume?" Elara noted, not expecting an answer. When none came, they continued walking down the large staircase for what seemed like many minutes.

The air inside the citadel was heavy and thick, almost tangible, filled with a sense of ancient power and a deep, pervasive cold that seeped into Elara. She noted that it had no noticeable effect on Tallin, assuming he had grown up here and had become accustomed to the stagnant environment. To Elara, it felt like she was inhaling the essence of night itself, a reminder that this was a place of shadow and mystery where the Night Ones reigned supreme.

Their pathway down was wide enough for several people to walk abreast, but as they reached the ground floor, a door barred their way.

"Are you sure you want to do this?" Tallin asked. Elara picked up something in his voice that she thought sounded like concern. "Yes. I.. I do. Open it"

The light hit them almost immediately as the doors creaked open.

**

Elara watched as the daylight shone in, the heat a wave washing over her. The outside was a stark contrast to the dim interior of the citadel, two sides of light's coin.

The stonework outside was worn smooth by countless years of use, but here and there, she could see traces of old carvings and faded inscriptions in a language Elara didn't recognise. It was an assault on her senses, and as such, she didn't see Tallin wearing a helmet. Elara looked at him and was taken aback by his new look. The helmet looked regal yet protective, and the face was mostly covered except for the visor, which was darkened glass.

Tallin looked down at her and gestured for her to go outside, but she was caught in amongst the million questions that now filled her head. The outside, though, called to her louder than hardware-based questions.

Stepping outside, she witnessed a world made of two.

Chapter Forty-Four
Kayriss
Nexus.

She released the spell, the connection severing as the rat's thoughts faded into the fog of its failing mind. Kayriss looked down at the creature, her heart heavy with the knowledge it had shared.

"Something's calling them," she said aloud, facing Grind and Granite. "Something from the south is driving them mad, forcing them to move. They didn't attack your clan by choice; they were compelled."

Grind's expression softened slightly, but his anger was far from gone. "Compelled or not, they still killed our kin."

Granite nodded, his brow furrowed. "Aye, but what's in the south that could do this? We've lived down there all our lives and never seen anything like it. Why the change now?"

Kayriss stood, her resolve hardening. She looked over at Isaac, and her thoughts went to Elara, the two hu-mans that had appeared in all their lives, and she couldn't help but connect the two incidents.

"I don't know. But we need to find out. If something can drive an entire pack of rats to madness, it's only a matter of time before it affects others. I believe that your village may be safe for now, though, as the rats have passed, going by this one."

The Mine Folk exchanged glances, their earlier annoyance giving way to a shared relief, knowing their village was likely safe. It didn't last long, though, as they realised that whatever was waiting in the south would soon be joined by the rat horde. Kayriss looked back at the old rat, now barely moving. She couldn't bring herself to leave it suffering. She cast a final spell with a soft word and a wave of her hand, ending its pain peacefully. The rat's body stilled it's suffering over.

"Let's move," she said quietly, "We have a long journey ahead, and whatever's calling the rats won't wait for us."

As granite passed the dead rat, he let his hammer fall upon its head, vengeance still burning bright in the forge of his heart.

**

The talk earlier that day had troubled Kayriss far deeper than she realised. She'd taken to walking off to one side, leaving the party to travel together. She'd told Isaac that she'd needed some time to consider everything, and he had dutifully agreed after some protest of wanting to help.

"Elf. You are troubled."

The words came out of nowhere, but Kayriss turned to see Serafin looking down at her. She never realised how tall she was until now, matching Isaac's height.

"Yes. I am. Everything seems to be coming to a nexus point, and we're walking right into it." Searfin nodded down at her, clearly on the same train of thought as the older elf.

"Some people talk of leylines down in the south, but no one could ever confirm this. The different races all seem to know something but don't talk to each other. We might be the dominant races, but we are not the cleverest." Her words pierced through Kayriss with the depth they carried. "The hu-mans might be extinct, but at least they talked."

Serafin smiled at her, hoping Kayriss would continue to engage in the conversation. Kayriss seemed wary of their new companion, so Serafin continued.

"The Nexus has long been a place of myth, known only to a few who talk in the shadows. They delve deeply into the mysteries of the new world but live in whispers and gossip. In ancient times, the Nexus was revered by a long-extinct civilisation, who built great structures around it to use its mystical abilities." Serafin now had Kayriss's full attention.

"What is it, though?" Kayriss wanted to know.

"No one fully knows. It is apparently directly under the Night One city, though." Serafin continued.

"And we definitely don't talk to them..."

Chapter Forty-Five
Elara
Old/New Worlds.

    They walked together, occasionally passing grand archways that led into darkened chambers, their purposes long forgotten.

    The city that had been hidden away from her gradually came into view, revealing itself as they walked closer. Elara's breath caught in her throat as she saw a sprawling labyrinth of buildings and structures, all with an ancient, almost haunted quality. The architecture was unlike anything she had seen above, with tall, narrow buildings that leaned slightly as if bowing under the weight of centuries. The stonework was intricate, with delicate patterns etched into the surfaces, though time had worn many of them away.

One sign was a worn-out red circle with a blue band through its centre. The letters formed the word 'Wandsworth Town' emblazoned through the middle of the circle. Elara knew not what it meant and hurried to catch up to Tallin.

The city was far from abandoned.

It teemed with life, the streets bustling with activity. Night Ones, hooded from the light walking around, stopped at the sight of Tallin and bowed their heads in reverence. He nodded to each of them, a gesture that surprised Elara due to the sheer scope of effort it would need to acknowledge them. Elara watched as figures moved through the narrow alleys and across the open squares, their shapes shifting away from the light. No scourge foxes yet, she mused. These were all Night Ones, their dark skin and sharp features unmistakable when glimpsed. They moved with the same graceful fluidity that spoke of elegance and danger as Tallin, yet with a poorer station in this world.

Rounding the corner, Elara saw her first scourge fox, its sleek, furred form slipping through the crowds with a predatory grace. The two species coexisted in a way that was both fascinating and unsettling. The Night Ones and the foxes moved around each other with an almost practised ease, as if they had long since learned the rules of this shared space. The Night Ones seemed to take advantage of the foxes' heightened senses, allowing them to scout and hunt, while the foxes benefited from the Night Ones' intelligence and resourcefulness. It was a symbiotic relationship that was clearly fraught with tension, a delicate balance that could easily be tipped into chaos.

Tallin noticed her lingering gaze and spoke as they walked. "The Night Ones and the scourge foxes have formed an alliance of necessity. We protect each other, rely on each other. But it wasn't always this way. There's still fear on both sides. A constant undercurrent of distrust."

Elara nodded, understanding the unspoken implications. "What happened here? How did this place come to be?"

"Lon-don was once a great city, one of the largest of the hu-mans," Tallin explained, his tone contemplative. "But that was before the world changed, before the great collapse. When the hu-mans fell, their cities crumbled, and this place was abandoned, forgotten by those before."

He paused, looking out over the city with something like nostalgia in his eyes. "But we found it and took it as ours. We were the most organised of the new races in the beginning, so it was right that we should take their capital as our home. It was a refuge at first, a place to hide from the dangers alive in the old world. Over time, it became our home, a sanctuary for those who could survive the dark."

Elara took in his words, her mind spinning with the implications. This place, this Lon-don of old, was a remnant of a world long gone, repurposed and repopulated by those who had inherited the earth after humanity's fall. It was both a sanctuary and a prison, where survival meant adapting to the shadows.

As they continued their walk, the sounds of the city grew louder—a mix of voices, the soft growls of the scourge foxes, and the distant clatter of metal on stone. Elara found herself both fascinated and unsettled by the atmosphere. There was an underlying tension here, a sense that the city was on the brink of something—whether it was collapse or change, she couldn't tell. The buildings grew taller in places, and in others, they were completely taken over by nature, swallowed in green. Some stood as silent monoliths, towering over the narrow streets like quite sentinels. Elara could see that many of them had been repurposed from the old hu-man structures. The architecture was a mix of styles, ancient brickwork reinforced with newer, cruder materials in the Night One style. Now, it looked like a shadow of what

Elara's imagination was conjuring up, its former self, a place where hu-mans roamed freely and in abundance.

Tallin led her through a maze of streets, the crowds parting slightly as they passed. Elara could feel the eyes of the Night Ones on her, their gazes sharp and assessing. She saw a group huddled together in a darkened alcove, whispering in low voices as they watched her with suspicion. The scourge foxes were less obvious in their scrutiny, but she could sense their presence, lurking just out of sight.

"Why did you bring me here?" Elara asked, her voice low, almost lost in the city's noise.

Tallin glanced at her, his expression inscrutable. "You said you wanted to understand. This is part of that understanding. This is our world, Elara, the new world they left us with. It's not just about survival; it's about finding a way to live with the shadows, to build something from their ruins."

There was a weight to his words, a depth of meaning beyond the simple explanation. Elara realised this wasn't just a tour; Tallin showed her the heart of their existence, where they drew their strength and fear. It was a world built on the remnants of the past but struggling to forge a future.

"You think me cruel. Unyielding. Because I kidnapped you from the animals. But I consider it a rescue. They do not know your potential. I do." Tallin looked down at her, his eyes clear behind the glass.

For the first time in all their interactions, Elara felt he was telling her the truth.

Chapter Forty-Six
Kayriss
Under the stars.

The campfire crackled in the cool night air, sending embers spiralling upwards to join the countless stars scattered across the clear sky. The heat from the fire was comforting, warding off the chill that crept in as the sun dipped below the horizon. They'd covered much ground in the daylight, finding a raised platform away from any of the night's denizens. It reached into the sky and ended in a crumbling end, the rest of the platform falling to the ground below. They noticed signs near their campsite, and Kayriss explained that one read 'M1', but most of the rest of the words had decayed with the elements.

Around the flickering flames sat the ragtag group bound by their shared trials. They had fought, bled, and laughed together, but the mood was different tonight. It was quiet and introspective, with the weight of unspoken thoughts pressing down on them.

Kayriss leaned back on a log, the flames reflecting in her sharp, green eyes. She had always been the most guarded of them, her mind filled with thoughts and worries. Tonight, even she felt the pull of the night's honesty. She glanced at the others, her voice barely above a whisper. "What do you fear losing the most?"

The question hung in the air, surprising them all with its suddenness. It was not like her to initiate such a deeply personal conversation. The silence stretched as they each considered their answer.

Finally, Isaac, who was matching Kayriss's gaze, moved to hold her hand. He said nothing but shifted closer to her. She held his hand back and laid her head in his lap, snuggling closer still.

There was a murmur of understanding from the group. Isaac and Kayriss's fear was palpable; they knew their love was something that could not be conceived of. He shouldn't even exist, and they still did not know how he came to even be in that forest. But she loved him so. It was as deep as the roots of the oldest tree.

Serafin looked at them both; her ordinarily cold exterior melted a little. She pulled her hand to her chest, and it was clear she realised their love.

"For me, it's losing the waters," Serafin said. Her voice rippled and broke like waves. "The seas, the rivers, and all the streams... They are the freedom I was born into. I do not know much about the land world, but I want to be in the water. Exquisite."

Grind rubbed his hands into his beard and sighed heavily. He was a Mine Folk of few words, but those words always carried weight. "I faced my fear. To see those accursed rats swarming towards my kin. I.. I felt lost." he said, his voice gruff but tinged with emotion. "My hands... they've always known the tunnels, every rock, even the caves themselves. But they betrayed me. They let in the rats. Mine Folk died. If I were to lose them, I would be losing everything."

Granite grunted in agreement. "Aye. I may be younger in years than my friend here, but seeing friends fall…? I fear losing more of them… of seeing the light go out in another friend's eyes. We fight, we survive, but… there's only so much loss a heart can take."

Kayriss looked behind his eyes and saw that Granite was going deeper with his words than he'd probably have liked.

"I think, after seeing those rats eat and consume my kin. To die like that?" He stood abruptly and turned away, clearly not wanting to show the emotions that had welled to the fore. Kayriss moved to him and round him, so he kept his secrecy. Bending, she held him, allowing his grief to flow.

Words hung in the air, and the mood hung lower.

There was a pause before Hooth, the massive warrior with a heart as big as his frame, spoke. "I fear losing, simply that." He said, his deep voice trembling with emotion. "When Ansel was struck down. I felt all the failures of history. That is not a legacy I want to leave behind. The thought of losing you all, of being alone with the weight of that failure to protect… it's unbearable."

Edgar, unable to converse at that second, made his unbarked words clear by nuzzling up to Isaac.

There was a deep silence after their words, the crackling of the fire the only sound in the night. Their shared fears hung heavy in the air but bound them closer together. These were their truths, raw and unfiltered, laid bare under the stars.

Cutlass stood, her typical pirate bravado all but gone. She removed her tricorne and looked down at Browntail, tears welling in her eyes.

"I fear losing you."

Browntail stood and moved quickly to her side, his hat falling away. He grabbed her and held her, their hands pawing each other lovingly. He grabbed her and held her so closely that tears were in his eyes. They were filled with pride and sadness. "I fear losing you too," he said.

"You're truly my first and only mate."

The fire crackled as they all fell into a contemplative silence, the night wrapping around them like a blanket. For a long moment, no one spoke, each lost in their thoughts, their fears laid bare under the watchful eyes of the stars.

Grind stood, walking over to the two embracing otters. From within a pouch hidden under his beard, he pulled out two stones, both painted with pictures of Mine Folk. He handed them to Browntail and returned to his seat, saying nothing. Browntail thought he could see a smile under the beard and nodded back at him.

Something shifted; the heaviness in the air lightened, replaced by a quiet determination. They shared their fears, and in doing so, they also shared their strength. Having faced darkness together, they had found a light that would guide them through whatever came next.

One by one, they settled down for the night, the fire's warmth and their companions' presence easing their minds. The fears they had spoken of were real, but so was the bond they had forged, which would carry them through the darkest times.

As the last of them drifted off to sleep, the stars above shone slightly brighter as if acknowledging the unbreakable connection formed around that campfire. The night was still and peaceful, and for the first time in a long while, they all slept soundly, their dreams untroubled by the fears of what they had left behind.

Chapter Forty-Seven
Tallin
Humanity falls...

Tallin could see the confusion behind Elara's eyes as they walked through the mixed world. Their city was part old world, part new, with the ornate tower seemingly in the centre of it all.

"You want to know how we came into being, don't you..." He said a matter of factly.

His dark cloak billowed slightly in the cool breeze that swept through the streets. His face, usually stern and composed, now carried a more profound weariness as he prepared to speak. Walking at his side, Elara could see the weight of history in his eyes; this was not just a story. It was the legacy of a fallen people. He began, his voice low, almost reverent, as if he were invoking a ghost from the past.

"There was a time, long ago, when the hu-mans ruled these lands. They were proud, and their bloodline was strong—so much so that they believed they were the chosen protectors of this world. But pride has a way of drawing attention, and not all attention is good. The hu-mans attracted the gaze of something far darker than they could ever have anticipated."

Tallin's eyes darkened as he continued, his words like a slow, relentless storm.

"The Great Darkness came upon them, creeping into their hearts, their minds, and their very blood. At first, it was subtle, like a shadow at the edge of their vision, easily dismissed. But over time, it grew bolder, until the hu-mans could no longer ignore its presence. This darkness twisted them, bringing forth their worst fears, their most desperate desires. Their bloodline, once pure and unbroken, was cursed."

Elara shuddered at his words. She had heard whispers of what had happened before, but nothing as chilling as this. Tallin's tone carried the weight of a history long buried in despair.

"The curse didn't just affect their bodies," he said. "It consumed their very souls, rising up in different forms to torment them. Each hu-man bore the darkness in a unique way, some manifesting it as madness, others as insatiable hunger, some even turning on their own kin. No one was spared. The hu-mans tried to fight it, but the more they struggled, the stronger the curse became whole."

He paused, glancing down at her to gauge her reaction. She was enrapt and noticed his face was etched with something close to sorrow, though he quickly buried it behind his usual mask of resolve.

"And it didn't end there," Tallin continued, his voice now heavy with the following tragedy. "The curse seeped so deep into their blood that it robbed them of the ability to bear their own children. No new hu-mans were born. Instead, other races began to rise from them, some twisted, all altered. Different from even each other. I believe that the Night Ones were first, then Elves, Mine Folk and others. Most say it was a single Elf, though. Wildlings evolved from the animals of old, which is where we met the scourge foxes. They weren't born from the remnants of the hu-mans, but because of their absence, they grew into what we know today as Wildlings. One race fractured from many. Personally, I would say that they had their time, and we were made to rule in their stead."

Elara listened to his mixture of sorrow and arrogance, a distinct concoction of the two differing emotions. The weight of his words hung over her like a shroud. He was recounting her people's history. Elara's mind raced as she tried to reconcile this tale with everything she had known, trying to remember what had happened before she awoke. These new races, these beings who now walked the earth, were all echoes of the hu-mans, products of the same ancient bloodline that had fallen to darkness.

"But the worst part," Tallin said, his voice now softer, almost a whisper, "was that the hu-mans couldn't accept what was happening to them. In their desperation, they sought answers, salvation, even power. They turned on the new races, on each other, on their own kin, believing that by purging the darkness from others, they could save themselves. Their panic led them to self-destruction. The very thing they feared. The end of their race, was hastened by their own hands."

He let the silence linger, allowing the gravity of his words to settle in.

"In the end," he continued, "the hu-mans died out. Slowly, painfully, over time. No more children, no more future. And with each passing generation, their numbers dwindled until there were none left. Only the 'aberrant' races remained, little in their numbers. Creatures born of the darkness, trying to survive in the world that had once been theirs."

Tallin's eyes met Elara's, a flash of something unspoken passing between them. To him, this was more than just history; it was personal. Perhaps it always had been.

"They were consumed by their own fear, their own darkness," he said, his voice a quiet lament. "And in the end, the hu-mans fell, not because of some great battle or cataclysm, but because of their own hearts. They were undone by the very thing they sought to escape. And we are what they left behind."

He turned away, letting the stillness take over. The sky above seemed darker now, even at this early hour, as though the shadows had heard his story and mourned the loss of a race long gone.

Elara swallowed, the story filling her with a sense of both dread and sorrow. The hu-mans had been powerful once but had been no match for the darkness within them. As she looked at the world around her, filled with the remnants of that ancient bloodline, she wondered if they were doomed to repeat the same fate.

**

It was a long time before either spoke. Elara felt the weight of the shadows pressing down around her, and Tallin allowed her the time he thought she needed to reflect on his words.

Stepping into a bustling marketplace, many of Tallin's people approached, offering him trinkets as a mark of respect. He graciously received them and talked to them as he would any member of higher ranking.

Elara realised that his attention had slipped from her.

That was precisely what Elara needed right now.

Hidden in an alcove of a crumbled archway, Elara shifted her gaze to a scourge fox she'd noticed following her. He was tall, his posture rigid and defensive, eyes glinting in the darkness. The orange fur of his face had dark markings, aiding in his stealth. They streaked from his snout to his high ears, giving him black stripes to obscure his bright colouring. His dark clothing was entirely leather and blended almost perfectly into the shadows, except for a faint shimmer of silver at the tips, like the last remnants of moonlight before dawn swallowed the night. His muzzle twitched as he sniffed the air, the sharp, pointed ears rotating slightly as if listening for any sign of betrayal.

"What do you want?" he growled softly, his voice carrying an edge of suspicion. "I've been speaking to one of the upper citadel servants. She spoke to me about the mines, and I wanted to know the truth."

"You're trying to trap me; say something against the Night Ones. Leave me be!" The fox turned to leave, already attempting to disappear into the shadows of the alleyway.

"I'm not trying to trap you," Elara said, her tone gentle but firm. "I needed to speak with you, away from him." She cast a glance to where Tallin stood, oblivious.

The fox narrowed his eyes, taking a step back, his tail flicking in clear agitation. "Then speak quickly, hu-man. My patience is thin. Remember, I carry all the risk with not a single reward."

Elara swallowed her hesitation. She had to approach this delicately. "Meira said something to me before about the scourge foxes, about what you're going through. She told me how your kind had been twisted, cursed, bound to a fate that was never yours to bear." Her voice was low, urgent. "I need to know if it's true. What she said. Are you being controlled? Forced to do these things?"

The scourge fox's expression hardened, his yellow eyes flashing with a warning. He said nothing at first, merely watching her, weighing her words as if waiting for a sign that she could not be trusted.

For a moment, Elara feared she had misstepped. Then, with a slow exhale, the fox spoke.

"She spoke the truth," he said, voice rough with something like resignation. "We were not always like this. Not always creatures of the dark." His eyes seemed to dim, and he turned away, staring into the blackness beyond the alcove. "Long ago, we were free. We roamed the forests, fierce but honourable protectors of the night. But then... they came. The Night Ones." His lip curled slightly, revealing sharp teeth. "They poisoned us. Twisted our minds and our bodies. We were bound to their will, forced to serve as their hunters, their enforcers."

Elara's heart clenched at the bitterness in his voice. While living in their midst, she had seen the scourge of foxes' control over the populace. Hearing this and hearing that they had once been something more, something better, was like a knife to the gut.

"But not all of you agree with this, do you?" she asked. "Not all of you want to serve the Night Ones."

He was silent again, his muscles tensing as if bracing for an attack. His eyes shifted toward her, cautious, suspicious. The fox's eyes narrowed, but his suspicion wasn't as sharp this time. There was doubt but also a flicker of something else: hope, perhaps or maybe desperation.

"You have to understand," he continued. "We foxes are not your enemy. I'm not here because I want to be. They have my family in the below. We want to be free as the other Wildlings, but unless our families are free, we have to stay, bent to their wills."

Elara reached out her hand, a sympathetic gesture to his plight. The fox recalled, wary of her touch.

"And why should I believe you are not the same as him?" he asked, voice barely above a whisper but laced with contempt directed completely at Tallin. "You stand with them, with him, don't you? With Tallin. With the Night Ones."

"I stand with him, but that doesn't mean I agree with everything he does," Elara said softly. "Tallin's... complicated. His mission was to capture and kill me because of some ridiculous prophecy. But here I stand. I don't trust him and risk trusting you, but I see that there's more to this than just us versus them."

Her words seemed to hang between them, fragile, waiting to be shattered.

"I don't expect you to trust me right away," she added, stepping closer. "But I need you to know that I am on your side. You may not have chosen this, but you don't have to suffer it alone. Let me help you."

The scourge fox's tail swished once, his body tense as though caught between instinct and reason. His gaze flickered again toward the crowd where Tallin stood, their voices still a murmur beyond earshot.

Finally, after what felt like an eternity, he spoke. "There are those among us who resist the Night Ones' control," he admitted quietly. "But we are few, and we are scattered. Their control binds us tightly... it's not so easily broken."

"Do you know how?" Elara pressed. "Is there a way?"

He hesitated, his claws scraping the stone beneath him. "Free our families, and we will fight with you. I don't know how you're going to do that. They are trapped in the below. I cannot see a way it could be possible."

Elara's pulse quickened. "So, free your family from the mine, and you'll help me?" She wanted to know.

"Mine? There's no mine..."

Chapter Forty-Eight
Isaac
Darkness rises...

Isaac woke in the middle of the night, frightened by a dream of Kayriss filled with rage. Something he couldn't see had caused her such anguish, and the pain of it ripped sleep from him.

She was still there, though, safe and asleep. Hooth nodded down at him from his perch on an old sign, his head turning around at unnatural angles. Isaac stretched and extricated himself from Kayriss's cuddle, much to her sleeping annoyance. She moved and managed to find Edgar, who was more than happy to receive her hug.

Isaac stood, stretching his aching body. The walk had been long, and he felt every step.

He strolled down the ramp to the earthen floor, scanning for any movement. He found none, so he sat on a large outcrop of rock. The remnants of the hu-mans were everywhere here. A protruding sign... what looked like a metal wheeled chariot, its horses long dead.

Was this his people? Why was he here? Why now?

These questions had been spinning since he awoke in the forest days ago with Kayriss. She quietened their noise and silenced their troublesome presence in his mind. The previous night's campfire talk had brought them to the forefront of his mind. He felt he had a purpose for coming into being, but he still wanted to know why. He did not know who could answer them in this strange new world, alien on all levels to him. He felt a man out of both time and creation. Was he of the hu-man world, or this one?

Isaac's mind was tumbling through options and evidence when he heard a voice.

"Isaac..." He looked around. No one was there. Up, down, all around. Nothing. "Isaac..." it said once more. There seemed to be no vocal direction for the sound as it appeared to be coming from within him. Taking stock of himself, Isaac felt an encroaching darkness rising within him. Coldness crept from his extremities, limbs, heart and mind. He felt his soul cloud over with icy tendrils clawing into him.

"Who... where are you?" Isaac wanted to know.

"Don't you worry boy. We'll meet soon." Immediately, Isaac stood, looking around for a voice he slowly realised was within his head. He rubbed his eyes, thinking he was still in a dream state. "Rub all you like, you'll not be rid of me. I brought you here. I mothered you."

Isaac turned to move back to the camp, but the words coaxed him to stop. He wanted answers, and the voice may have them.

"You don't need the Elf bitch, now do you… You want Elara. I made her for you. She is perfection. She is yours." The voice seemed to care for him, but the words were filled with malice and darkness.

"Who are you?" Isaac asked, thinking to start simply.

"Who I am is irrelevant right now, but you can call me Nyxsarathryn if you'd like. I have your best interests at heart, my dear Isaac." The words oozed into his mind, and while they spoke kindly, Isaac feared them again. "Come south. Meet with Elara. Save her from the disgusting Night One called Tallin. He wants to take her from you. Keep her from you."

Isaac felt an urgency within him that he could not withdraw from. Trying, he moved one step towards Kayriss and the group, but his body would not follow the most straightforward instructions. Opening his mouth to call to them, his voice was not his own and made no sound.

"While I would never dream of controlling you, dearest Isaac, I can mould your actions as you're getting closer to me. It's all in your best interest, of course." Isaac fought against Nyxsarathryn's control to no avail.

"You say you have my best interests at heart, but hold me trapped here? Your words do not match your actions." Isaac thought, knowing the intruder would hear him.

"True. Of course, you are right. I'll let you go because I trust you, sweet Isaac. Keep moving south, and we'll meet soon." With that, Isaac regained control, the dark feeling lifting.

Isaac collapsed in a heap and wept.

Chapter Forty-Nine
Elara
Not *mine.*

"What do you mean there's no mine? What are they doing down there?

The fox stared at her for a long moment, eyes glowing faintly in the dark. "He told you they were miners?" A genuinely confused look appeared across his face. "Our families serve Nyxsarathryn."

It was Elara's turn to be confused. The name felt familiar, almost parental, but she knew it had not been uttered since she awoke.

"Who's that?" Elara asked.

"There's no time, but I hope, for your sake, you're telling the truth, hu-man," he growled. "Because if you betray us, the darkness we carry will find you. And it will consume everything you care for."

Elara met his gaze without flinching. "I won't betray you."

The fox said nothing more. With a final flick of his tail, he turned and slipped into the shadows, vanishing as though he had never been there.

"What are you doing?" Tallin appeared at her side, grabbing her arm roughly; the anger was evident on his face. She wasn't sure if it was that she had slipped his clutches or something else.

"You were busy with your people. I was just looking around at the remnants of mine." Elara lied. Tallin's anger subsided slightly, but his grip on her arm did not.

"Come. You've seen everything I wanted you to see."

**

Elara's boots scuffed against the stone floor as she was led back to her room, the dim torches casting flickering shadows along the corridor. Tallin walked beside her; his presence was as steady as ever, but Elara could feel the tension radiating off him. He hadn't said much since they'd left the Under-veil, but she could sense his unease. It was there in the way his hand tightened on her shoulder and his jaw clenched when he thought she wasn't looking. They rounded a corner, and Meira came into view, her dark figure making herself busy with a tray of drinks, half hidden in the shadows. Her sharp, knowing eyes locked onto Elara as they passed, and Elara offered her the faintest nod, confirmation that she had spoken to one of the scourge foxes, which confirmed the details of Meira's story. The encounter had left Elara with more questions than answers. The fox's words haunted her still, the control, the whispers of resistance, Nyxsarathryn... It was clear that there was more at play than she had initially understood, layers of intrigue and manipulation that ran deeper than she'd anticipated. Most definitely more than Meira or even Tallin knew.

Meira's lips curved into a slight, satisfied smile, though her gaze remained sharp, assessing. In return, she inclined her head ever so slightly, a silent acknowledgement of their shared secret. Something in Meira's eyes, something unreadable, made Elara's stomach twist. Was she an ally in this, or just another player in a game Elara didn't fully understand? Tallin's steps quickened as they passed, his eyes flicking briefly to Meira before he looked away, his jaw set. He didn't say a word, but Elara could feel the tension between the Prince and his servant. One that he'd taken in front of her. The other that cleared enjoyed every inch of the decadent Night One. Once they were out of Meira's sight, the silence between Elara and Tallin deepened. He hadn't spoken since they began their ascent, but she could see it in his stiff posture; his eyes darted around the corridor.

He was shaken.

She had gotten away from him, which rattled him, even if it had been for a brief moment. Elara glanced at him from the corner of her eye. Tallin always projected an air of control, of calm authority, but now... now, he seemed unsettled—not just because of the day's events but because of her. She could feel how he moved, and his gaze lingered on her longer than usual, filled with something she couldn't quite place.

Was it fear? Or concern?

As they approached her room, the silence became almost suffocating. Tallin stopped in front of the door, opening it deliberately slowly as if giving himself time to gather his thoughts.

"Elara," he said quietly, his voice rougher than usual, "you shouldn't have wandered off like that."

There was no anger in his tone, no reprimand. Instead, his words carried a note of something far more unsettling. Worry. His hand rested briefly on the doorframe; his gaze fixed ahead as if he couldn't quite bring himself to look at her. He looked over at the guard and motioned for him to leave. Dutifully, he nodded and clanked off down the corridor, his armour audible in the silence.

"I didn't wander," she replied, matching his calm but with an edge of defiance. "I needed to see my history for myself. I didn't need to watch as your people fawned over you."

He flinched, just barely, but enough for Elara to notice.

"They weren't fawning. I've told you, the people are affectionate towards me because they love me," Tallin said, but his voice lacked its usual sharpness. "I'm protecting you. You don't understand the risks out there."

Elara folded her arms, staring at him, trying to figure out what was happening behind those storm-grey eyes. "Is that what this is about? Protection?"

Tallin's gaze finally met hers, and for the briefest moment, something raw flickered there before he quickly masked it. His usual unreadable expression returned, but it was too late. She'd seen it.

"I'm not the only one watching you, Elara," he said, his voice low, the edge of warning unmistakable. "Not everyone sees you the way I do."

Her chest tightened at his words. *The way I do.* It was an admission veiled in caution but an admission nonetheless.

"And how do you see me?" she asked, her voice barely a whisper, though she wasn't sure she wanted to know the answer.

Tallin's hand tightened around the doorframe, his knuckles whiter than his darker skin should have been. For a moment, she thought he might tell her, but then he shook his head as if dismissing the thought altogether.

"That's not the point," he said finally, his voice quieter now, less certain. "The point is... you're important—more than you realise. If you're not careful, they'll come for you, and I can't always protect you from what's out there. Or from what's within."

His words lingered in the air, heavy and full of implication. Elara swallowed, her thoughts flickering back to the darkness she had felt rising inside her earlier, the voice she had heard in her mind. She still didn't know what it was, but Tallin's warning made her wonder if he knew more than he was letting on. Tallin's gaze softened momentarily, and Elara could see the worry beneath his mask. He was shaken, not because of his pride or duty, but because he was afraid. Afraid for her.

"Rest tonight," Tallin said, his voice more measured now as if trying to regain control. "We'll speak more in the morning."

He pushed open the door to her room and stepped aside to let her in. Elara hesitated, feeling the unspoken tension between them and the weight of the conversation they weren't having. She stepped inside, and Tallin lingered at the threshold for a moment longer.

Before he closed the door, he paused. "If you'd like," he said, his voice softer now, almost hesitant, "you can join me for dinner tonight. We could... talk."

Elara blinked, caught off guard by the invitation. Tallin never extended personal invitations, which is not like this. She studied his face, trying to gauge his intentions, but he had already retreated behind his mask again, his expression unreadable.

"Perhaps," she said, her voice neutral, though her mind raced with curiosity. "We'll see."

Tallin nodded, though she could see the faintest flicker of disappointment in his eyes before he turned away.

"Until then," he said, his tone returning to its usual formality. He shut the door quietly behind him, leaving her alone in the dim room again.

Elara exhaled slowly, the events of the day swirling in her mind. The encounter with the scourge fox, Meira's cryptic approval, and now Tallin's uncharacteristic concern. There was more to this than she understood, layers upon layers of secrets she hadn't yet uncovered.

As she sat on the bed's edge, her thoughts circled back to the darkness she had felt earlier. The voice in her head. Tallin's warning.

What was happening to her?

She sighed, pressing her hands to her temples—dinner with Tallin.

It could give her some of the needed answers, or it could only deepen the questions.

Chapter Fifty
Kayriss
The light in the dark.

Kayriss awoke before dawn, the sky still painted in the deep hues of night, with only a faint hint of light on the horizon. The air was cool, and the forest below them was quiet except for the soft rustling of leaves in the wind. They could see for miles high on their platform, and Kayriss missed the trees she loved so much. She lay still for a moment, listening to the rhythmic breathing of her companions, but something felt wrong.

She turned to the space beside her and found it empty. Isaac was gone. Frowning, Kayriss rose quietly, careful not to disturb the others. She slipped on her boots, her wings tucked tightly against her back as she moved through the camp. The platform they had chosen to sleep on was raised, overlooking the vast, moonlit forest below. Isaac's absence gnawed at her. This was the first time she had woken not in his arms, and something about it felt urgent.

Her eyes scanned the area until she saw a figure at the base of the platform, sitting in the shadows—Isaac. Relief washed over her, but it was quickly replaced by concern when she noticed how still he was and how the tension in his shoulders seemed to weigh him down.

She descended the steps quietly, her footsteps barely a whisper in the stillness. As she approached, Isaac looked up, his blue eyes catching the faint light of the coming dawn. His expression was troubled, a heavy frown etched across his face. He seemed lost in thought, as though his mind were miles away.

"Isaac," Kayriss said softly, her voice gentle. She crouched beside him, reaching out to touch his arm. "What's going on? Are you okay, my love?"

For a long moment, Isaac didn't speak. His gaze shifted from the sky to the ground, searching for the right words. Kayriss waited patiently, sensing that whatever was bothering him was something he had been holding inside for too long. Finally, he let out a heavy breath, his voice quiet and filled with uncertainty. "There's... something I need to tell you. Something that's been haunting me."

Kayriss remained silent, her hand on his arm, offering him a quiet presence. She knew him well enough that he needed space to gather his thoughts before opening up.

"I heard a voice," Isaac continued, his tone strained. "It started as a feeling. It's been with me for a while now, urging me... calling me south. At first, I thought it was nothing—just my imagination. So I dismissed it. But it's getting stronger. Louder. And last night, I spoke to it." He paused, running a hand through his hair, his frustration evident. "And it told me that I'm not supposed to be with you. That I'm meant for Elara."

Kayriss stiffened at the mention of Elara, her heart skipping a beat, but she forced herself to remain calm. The weight of his words hung between them, thick and heavy.

"I don't want to listen to it," Isaac said, his voice cracking with emotion. "But the voice... it feels like it's inside me, tied to this darkness I've been feeling for so long. It tells me that I'm destined for something else, something I don't understand. And it scares me, Kay. I'm scared of what's happening to me. Of what I might become."

He looked at her then, his eyes filled with a vulnerability she rarely saw in him. "But the truth is, I love you. You're the one I choose. No voice, no darkness can change that. I don't care what it says. I want you. Only you."

His words were raw, filled with desperation that tore at Kayriss's heart. She could see the struggle in him, the battle he was waging against forces beyond his control, and it hurt to see him like this. He was lost, unsure, afraid.

For a long while, Kayriss said nothing. She sat beside him, letting the silence stretch between them as Isaac's confession hung. Her wings shifted slightly, a soft glow emanating from them in the darkness, but she didn't speak. Not yet. Isaac needed to let it out; she was willing to give him that space.

When he finished, Isaac released a shaky breath as though releasing a burden he had carried for far too long. Kayriss reached out, her hand resting gently on his cheek. Isaac turned his face toward her. Her green eyes met his, filled with warmth and understanding.

"You're not alone, Isaac," she said softly, her voice steady. "Whatever this voice is, whatever darkness you're afraid of, you don't have to face it by yourself. I'm here with you. We'll face it together."

Isaac closed his eyes, leaning into her touch. "But what if the darkness is inside me? What if I can't stop it?"

Kayriss's gaze softened as she stroked his cheek gently, feeling the tension in his muscles slowly ease beneath her touch. "Then we'll fight it together," she whispered. "You're stronger than you think. And I believe in you."

Isaac opened his eyes, and for a moment, the weight of his fears seemed to lift, if only slightly. He wrapped his arms around her, pulling her close as if anchoring himself to her warmth. He pulled her onto his lap so they could be closer and feel each other's bodies. The two sat together in silence, the first light of dawn slowly beginning to break through the horizon.

Kayriss rested her head against his, her wings glowing faintly in the early light. Their bond felt more potent in that moment, unspoken but undeniable. The weight of his fears and the darkness inside him were all real, but so was the love they shared. At that moment, that was enough.

As the sun began to rise, casting its warm glow over the open forest, the two sat together silently, the light breaking through the darkness around them. No words were needed. In the quiet of the dawn, they found peace in each other's presence, knowing that whatever lay ahead, they would face it together.

Chapter Fifty-One
Elara
Dinner is ser... interrupted.

Elara sat on the edge of her bed, the dim light from the small window casting long shadows across the stone walls. Her mind buzzed with thoughts of the scourge foxes, the cryptic warnings she had received, and the growing darkness within her that she still didn't fully understand. Tallin's words echoed in her mind;

"Not everyone sees you the way I do."

There was something in his gaze she couldn't ignore, something protective yet haunted. As much as he tried to act like he was in control, Elara had sensed his uncertainty. In the quiet moments between their conversations, it was clear that she had more power than he wanted to admit.

A knock at her door brought her out of her thoughts. She stood, smoothing her hands over her simple tunic, her heart picking pace. Tallin entered, his eyes meeting hers with that usual unreadable expression. He was back to being his composed state, though there was a tension in how he held himself that hadn't been there before.

"Meira has brought you some dresses for tonight's dinner," he said, stepping aside as Meira entered the room, her arms full of luxurious fabrics in deep blues, silvers, and black. She moved gracefully, almost silently, and laid them out on the bed without a word.

Meira caught Elara's gaze momentarily, her expression calm, always unreadable. Then she stepped back, her arms at her side as though awaiting further instruction.

"I'll leave you to get dressed," Tallin said, his voice steady but with an underlying tension. His hand rested on the doorframe as if he were about to exit quickly. "I'll leave Meira to assist you."

Elara watched him for a moment, weighing her decision. She could feel the balance of power between them shifting, and tonight, she decided. It would move further.

"No," Elara said firmly, standing taller. "You'll stay."

Tallin blinked, caught off guard. His gaze sharpened as if he hadn't heard her correctly, but Elara held his eyes, her stance unwavering. A slight smile appeared on Meira's face, but she hid it as quickly as it appeared.

"I've spent enough time being watched on your terms, Tallin. If you want to see me, you'll do it on my terms this time."

His mouth parted, but he didn't argue. There was a flicker of something in his gaze. Something akin to attraction. He nodded, stepping back into the room, crossing his arms, and leaning casually against the wall. Meira raised an eyebrow, clearly intrigued, but said nothing as she stepped aside to allow Elara room to inspect the dresses. Elara walked to the bed and ran her hands over the fabric. The dresses were stunning, fine silks and brocades, far more extravagant than anything she had ever worn. They were fit for royalty, and wearing them felt foreign and exhilarating. She selected a deep midnight blue gown with silver embroidery that shimmered in the low light. It was elegant, with a high neckline and long sleeves that hugged her arms. It reminded her of something a queen might wear. Without a word, Elara began to undress. She could feel Tallin's eyes on her, though he remained quiet. She could sense the tension in him, the way his breath hitched just slightly as she peeled off her tunic, revealing the smooth lines of her shoulders and back. The air between them crackled with unspoken intensity, but Elara didn't look at him. Not yet. Meira moved to her side, helping her undress. Elara felt her hands gliding on her as the material left her body. It sent a tickle of excitement through her, but she steadied herself, not wanting to show the pleasure it brought. Meira moved around to her front, blocking Tallin's view as she removed Elara's underclothes. Her hands brushed against Elara's breasts as she did, the dark of her skin a stark contrast to the white of Elara's. Both heard Tallin shift position to see what and how Meira was touching Elara. The two women risked a smile between each other, out of sight of Tallin. She slipped the dress over her head, adjusting the fabric as it settled on her body, and only then did she turn to face him.

"How does it look?" she asked, her tone even, though she could feel the heat of his gaze tracing her figure.

Tallin's eyes lingered for a moment longer before he spoke, his voice low. "You look... perfect."

There was a softness in his words that she hadn't expected, but Elara merely nodded, satisfied. She turned to Meira, who had kept her hand on the arch of Elara's back. She watched the exchange with quiet amusement.

"Thank you," Elara said, and Meira gave a slight nod in return before excusing herself from the room.

Once Meira was gone, Tallin straightened, gesturing toward the door. "Shall we?"

Elara nodded and followed him, her heart pounding with anticipation. This was new: dinner alone with Tallin in his personal dining room, no guards or audience. The idea of dinner alone with Tallin was charged with an intimacy that unsettled her, but she wouldn't let herself be rattled—not tonight. The dining room was smaller than she expected, though no less lavish. A long table stretched between them, with fine silverware and candles that flickered softly in the low light. Tallin gestured for her to sit, pulling a chair out for her. She did so, smoothing the fabric of her dress as she settled into the high-backed chair. He took his place across from her, pouring wine into their glasses with practised ease. For a moment, the silence between them was comfortable, almost companionable. Elara took a sip of wine, letting the rich taste settle on her tongue as she studied Tallin from across the table. He was composed, as always, but there was a flicker of something behind his eyes, something vulnerable that he hadn't entirely managed to hide. Just as she was about to speak, the door to the dining room swung open, and a young Night One strode in with an air of casual arrogance. His dark hair fell in loose waves around his face, and his smile was sharp, predatory. He was handsome like Tallin was, though there was something far more dangerous in his demeanour.

"Kaelen," Tallin said, his voice tight with surprise, though he remained seated. "What are you doing here?"

Kaelen grinned as if he had every right to be there. "I heard you were having dinner with our guest, and I thought I'd join. After all, it's not every day we entertain such... exquisite company."

Elara's eyes narrowed as Kaelen's gaze flickered to her, lingering a little too long for her liking. There was something predatory about him, something that put her on edge. She glanced at Tallin, whose jaw had tightened in irritation. Having spoken to Kaelen before, she knew he was feigning an introduction. She chose to let him keep their secret meeting just that.

"Kaelen," Tallin said firmly, his tone brooking no argument, "this is a private dinner."

Kaelen's grin widened as he sauntered to the table, pulling out a chair and sitting down without waiting for an invitation. "Come now, brother. Surely there's no harm in a little company?"

Elara bristled, her eyes locking onto Kaelen's as he looked her over, a smirk playing at the corners of his lips. It was clear what he was trying to do: push a wedge between her and Tallin. Elara wouldn't be so easily rattled.

She turned her attention back to Tallin, deliberately ignoring Kaelen's presence. "The wine is wonderful," she said smoothly, her voice steady. "Thank you for this."

Tallin's eyes softened as he looked at her, grateful for her calm. "I'm glad you're enjoying it."

Kaelen, sensing that his attempts to insert himself into the evening were failing, leaned back in his chair, his smile fading slightly. "Well, it seems I'm not wanted," he said, feigning hurt. He stood, casting one last glance at Elara. "But I'll be around should you change your mind."

With that, he left, the door closing behind him with a soft click. Tallin let out a long breath, his shoulders relaxing. "I apologise for my brother. His arrogance is... persistent."

"I noticed," Elara said, her tone light but her gaze serious. "But he didn't bother me."

Tallin nodded, though the tension in his jaw hadn't entirely disappeared. "He doesn't know you like I do."

Elara looked at him, her heart skipping a beat at the intensity of his gaze. There was more behind his words than just a casual statement. There was a deep feeling she wasn't sure she was ready to confront.

After dinner, Tallin rose and extended a hand to her. "Shall I walk you back?"

Elara hesitated for only a moment before taking his hand. They left the dining room together, silently walking through the dimly lit halls. The quiet between them felt intimate, a sense of understanding that hadn't been there before. When they reached her room, Tallin paused, his hand still gently holding hers.

"Goodnight, Elara," he said softly, his voice filled with unspoken emotion.

"Goodnight, Tallin," she replied, her eyes lingering on his for a moment longer than necessary before she slipped into her room and closed the door behind her. As she leaned against the door, her heart still racing, Elara couldn't help but feel that tonight had changed something between them.

Whatever it was, it left her both exhilarated and afraid.

Chapter Fifty-Two
Kayriss
South.

When the party awoke, the sun had barely begun to rise. They stirred from their bedrolls as the sky lightened to a pale grey. A cool breeze drifted through across weary bodies, carrying the scent of damp earth and the promise of the day's journey ahead. The mood among them was light, almost jubilant as if they could sense that their long trek was finally nearing its end.

Kayriss stretched her wings, the soft glow of dawn reflecting off their ethereal edges, as she and Isaac walked back up to the party. Isaac stood beside her, a faint smile playing on his lips as he watched the others pack their gear. Even the ordinarily stoic Grind had a slight bounce as he rolled his beard into a single braid.

"We've made good time," Kayriss said, turning to Isaac. "By midday, we should reach the city."

Isaac nodded, adjusting the straps of his bag. "And we'll finally be able to find out what the hell is going on," he said, his voice and stance filled with strength. "Though something tells me the Night One city won't be the most relaxing place."

Kayriss smirked. "We'll take what we can get."

The rest of the group gathered quickly and were soon on their way. As they walked, laughter echoed through the trees, banter flying back and forth as if they were on an adventure rather than marching toward an unknown fate. Granite even broke into song with Browntail and Cutlass, and their catchy songs were clearly caught.

"Think they have any decent food in this city?" Isaac asked with a grin, his gaze flicking toward Hooth. "I'm getting tired of dried meat and stale bread."

"I think food is the least of our troubles. I do not know what reception we face." Hooth responded dryly, his sharp eyes scanning the path ahead.

Isaac wrinkled his nose. "As long as it's better than those Frogmen."

Kayriss laughed, her voice light. For a brief moment, it felt like they were just travellers on the road with no particular destination, free from the burdens of prophecy, war, and the looming darkness that seemed to follow them wherever they went.

The mood shifted as they neared the outskirts of the Night One city.

The trees began to thin, the dense forest giving way to towering structures in the distance.

They saw it.

The black spire pierced the sky, its sharp edges glinting in the early morning light. The air grew colder and heavier as if the land warned them of what lay ahead.

A sealed tower, holding answers and another hu-man.

It rose like a monolith from the city's centre, impossibly tall and made entirely of smooth obsidian. Its surface gleamed with an unnatural sheen, reflecting the pale light of the sky. No windows, doors, or signs of life broke its surface. It was as if the tower had been carved from the heart of the world, black and impenetrable. A cold shiver ran down Serafin's spine as her gaze locked onto it, and she felt an overwhelming sense of foreboding.

The laughter and banter ceased.

Each party member fell silent individually as their eyes turned toward the tower. The weight of what lay ahead crashed over them like a wave, and the lightness they had shared moments before was replaced with a cold realisation.

This was it.

The last days of travel—their last campsite before the Night One city.

This was what they had been moving toward all along—the heart of the danger, the final push. Whatever awaited them in that city, in that tower, wasn't something they could laugh off or face without fear. This was their last step before plunging headlong into the unknown.

Kayriss tightened her grip on her staff and Isaac's hand, her wings twitching at her back. She felt Isaac move closer beside her, his usual playful grin replaced by a grim set to his jaw. She glanced at him, and their eyes met for a brief moment. No words were needed. They both understood.

"We're almost there," Isaac said quietly, his voice low but steady.

Walking a few paces behind, Serafin clenched her fists as she stared at the sealed tower. She had known this moment was coming, but seeing it now, looming over the city like a monument to everything they feared, made it feel all too real. She felt herself dry up inside as a dry wind tore through her. She felt a tug deep inside to return to the waters as if the tower threatened her. She pushed the feeling down, forcing herself to stay focused. Grind, always the practical one was the first to break the silence. "This changes nothing," he said, his voice firm. "We knew it would be dangerous. We keep going, no matter what."

Kayriss nodded, though her heart was pounding in her chest. "We've come too far to turn back now."

The group continued walking, their pace slower now, and they were more cautious. The landscape around them had changed—where the forest had been lush and green, the ground here was darker, the trees gnarled and twisted, their branches reaching out like claws. The city walls loomed ahead, dark and foreboding, with narrow streets leading toward the massive tower at its centre.

Isaac glanced at Kayriss, his expression grim. "This place feels... wrong." Kayriss nodded in agreement. "It's like the whole city is on edge."

This is where it all ends. The final push has begun.
No more turning back. No more doubts.
The darkness is waiting for them, and they will face it head-on.

PART THREE
The Sealed Tower

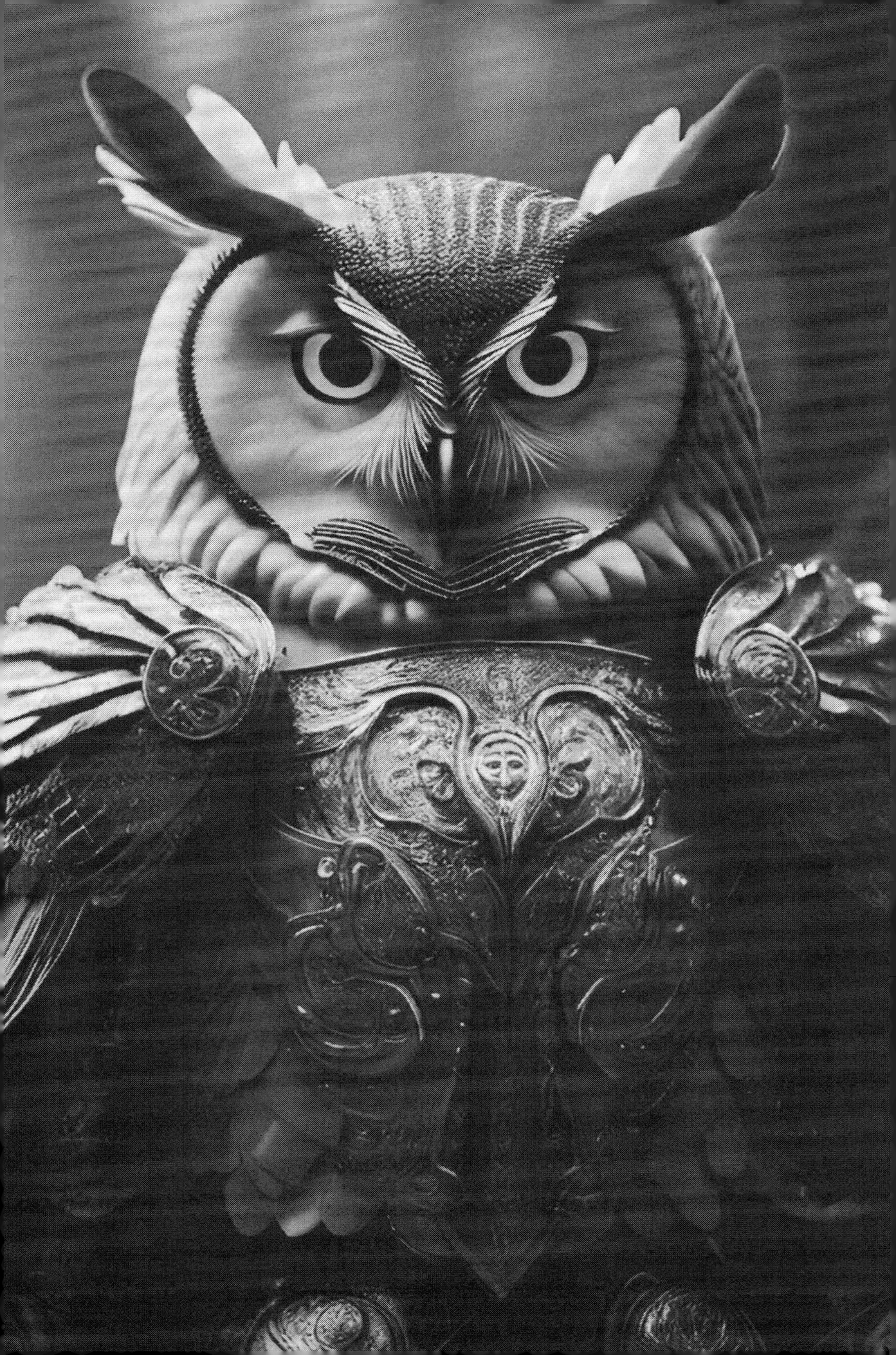

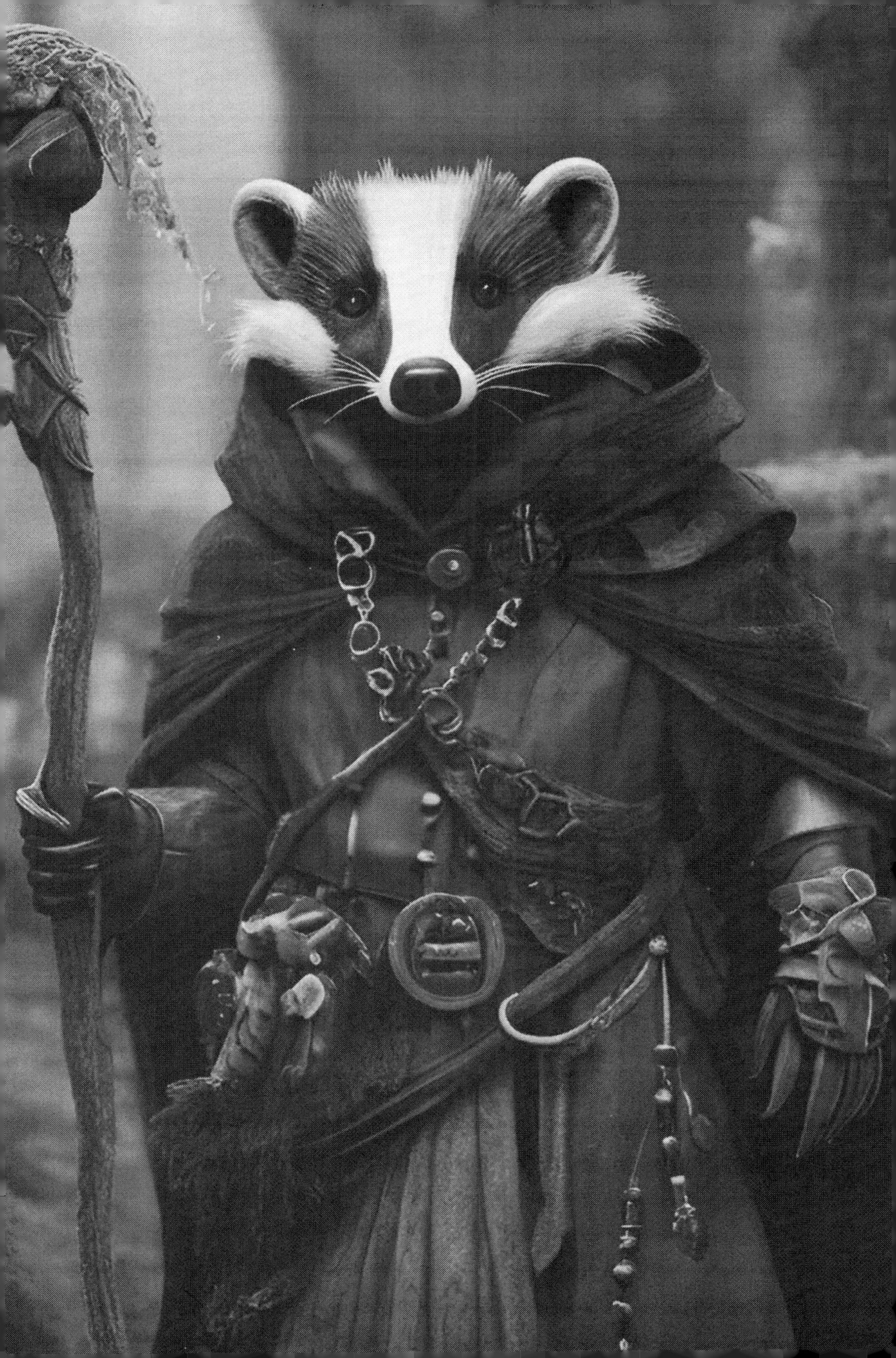

Chapter Fifty-Three
Tallin and Elara
The fracture of warmth.

The evening air clung to him as it blew down the corridor. Night Ones' passing acknowledged his presence, but as they moved away, they disappeared into gossiping shadows. Tallin tutted his disgust at them but knew where he stood, outside Elara's door, dressed in his dining finery, was the cause of their loose lips. The breeze was cool yet failed to soothe the simmering heat beneath his skin. Tallin strode through the narrow alleyways of the citadel, his hands shoved deep into the folds of his tunic, desperate to contain the trembling tension building in his fingers. His mind raced as it always did after any time spent with Elara, but now…? this was different. This time, the conflict between duty and emotion gnawed at him more ferociously.

Kaelen's voice echoed faintly in his head, a shadowy whisper growing stronger each day. 'You're slipping. This is exactly what I need.' Tallin could imagine him. Wide grinned and sharpened the knives of diplomacy. His pulse quickened as he tried to push the thoughts away, though they clung to him like a stubborn storm cloud. He knew, deep down, that Kaelen was right. He had promised himself he wouldn't let it get this far, keep Elara at a distance and maintain control.

Control was slipping through his fingers, and it had been for a while. He wouldn't admit it to himself. He replayed the evening in his mind. The warmth of her laughter, her eyes lit up under the candlelight, the quiet moments between them where words weren't needed. He had tried to remain distant, detached like he always did. He had even told himself that he didn't care, that his interest was nothing more than a fleeting curiosity. The truth was inescapable, now more than ever.

There was something about her. Something that gnawed at his core and stirred a warmth he had long buried. And that terrified him. Tallin's breath came faster as the truth settled in his bones. He liked her. He cared for her despite everything. Despite knowing that Kaelen was waiting for this, for his control to unravel, Tallin could feel the warmth blossoming in the corners of his chest, which he hadn't felt in years. It surged unbidden, wild and untamed. He clenched his fists, trying to quash it.

'You can't let this happen,' he told himself. 'You know where this leads'.

He had always prided himself on his ability to keep emotions at bay, to keep the cold, calculated edge that had served him so well. But Elara... Elara was a storm. A beautiful, unpredictable storm. No matter how much he tried to distance himself, the distance strengthened the pull whenever he left her side.

The voice whispered again, " Kaelen wants this," like a cruel reminder. He knows you're losing control.

Tallin stopped, pressing a hand to his forehead, his pulse pounding in his pointed ears. The warmth that rose inside him was equal parts terrifying and intoxicating. There was a small and treacherous part of him that didn't want it to stop. The part that craved her presence. The part that wished he had stayed just a little longer tonight.

His feet faltered, and he nearly turned back, the thought seizing him.

He couldn't. He shouldn't.

**

The door clicked shut behind her, and Elara leaned against it, the cool wood pressing into her back as she closed her eyes. Her heart was still racing, and every thud against her ribs reminded her of the evening she had just shared with Tallin.

What had just happened? She had told herself to stay guarded, to remain wary of the man whose intentions were as murky as a midnight sea. Tallin was no friend; he couldn't be. She felt that she had seen his kind before, men who wore their charms like armour, who hid their true selves behind a veil of mystery and smiles. An instinctual defence against the darkness. Tonight... tonight something had shifted. Darkness was becoming a light she hadn't thought possible. She pressed her hand to her chest, trying to still the warmth that threatened to spread through her. No, she told herself. Don't be a fool. She walked deeper into the room, the soft glow of the lantern casting long shadows on the walls. She needed to clear her head. She paced, feeling the tension between her desire to trust him, just a little, and the voice in her mind that screamed not to. She couldn't afford to be wrong about Tallin. Too much was at stake. She couldn't get caught up in the strange attraction between them.

Help her, something was there.

She could feel it. She had felt it from the moment their eyes met tonight. The silence between them had been heavy with an unspoken tension, the kind that made her stomach flutter in ways she hadn't expected. The laughter was alive and true. When he had left... she had stood there, her breath caught in her throat, wishing he hadn't gone so soon.

Her heart begged for the door to open. She begged for him to enter, to enter her. Could she even trust him? She couldn't. He was tied too closely to Kaelen, and if Kaelen had taught her anything, loyalty was dangerous. Tallin had his motives, his reasons for being around her. She didn't know what they were, but she knew enough to keep her guard up.

Still, the warmth wouldn't leave her. It curled in her chest, unsettling and unfamiliar. She had kept him at a distance for so long, trusting no one but herself in this strange new world. Tallin... Tallin was slipping through the cracks of her defences, which terrified her. Elara moved to the window, pressing her palm against the cold, dark glass. She gazed out into the night, her thoughts spiralling. She had fought against it for too long to let herself be vulnerable now. She couldn't afford to feel anything for Tallin. Yet, despite all her logic, she couldn't deny that something had shifted. A small, dangerous part of her wanted to believe that maybe, just maybe, she wasn't lost in this place. That she wasn't alone. That perhaps he could be trusted.

Trust was a luxury she didn't have.

She sighed, her breath fogging the glass. Whatever was blossoming between them, she had to stop it. She couldn't let herself get pulled into his game.

The warmth lingered, and she wasn't sure she wanted it to go away despite everything.

Chapter Fifty-Four
Kayriss
Next stop...

Kayriss crouched at the edge of the crumbling ridge, her sharp eyes scanning the vast, overgrown ruins that stretched before them. The remnants of the old hu-man world lay beneath her. Broken towers, shattered roads, and the occasional twisted metal skeleton of a building still standing against time's ruthless march. It had been centuries since the hu-mans had vanished, their civilisation swallowed by nature and silence. But even after four hundred years, their traces still lingered, like ghosts haunting a land that had forgotten them. She had found trinkets around the north but nothing she'd kept or needed. Here, it was everywhere.

She sighed, brushing a lock of her brown hair behind her ear as the breeze carried the faint scent of decay, moss, and the earth, reclaiming what was once unnatural. Here and there, the outline of an ancient road was still visible, the asphalt cracked and overrun with wild roots as though the forest had risen to devour the concrete remnants. A rusted road sign peeked through the tangle of vines, its faded letters unreadable but unmistakably hu-man. Each sign was a reminder of the world that had come before, a world long dead.

Kayriss turned her attention to the others. Granite stood nearby, his hulking form almost statue-like as he gazed at the distant skyline of the Night One city, now obscured by early morning mist and creeping shadows. The Night Ones lived there, nestled in their fortress of twilight, far from prying eyes. They were getting closer, but the most dangerous stretch still lay ahead. And Granite's plan... well, it was not without its risks.

At camp this morning, Kayriss asked the party what they thought. The pirates wanted nothing better than to 'avast the swabs' with a frontal 'aaaarrrrtack'. Hooth wanted to attack from the skies for obvious reasons, trying diplomacy from the air. He knew that Elara had been forcibly taken, and he wanted to avenge Ansel's assault.

Isaac wanted to leave the area with Kayriss; he was honest about that, but he sided with Granite, who said stealth against an unknown enemy was preferable. Edgar nuzzled his hand at his words, a clear gesture that he would stand by his master.

"Underground," she muttered, uneasy about the Mine Folk's idea. Granite had insisted it was the best way, the only way, to enter the city without being spotted. The tunnels... the thought of descending into them made her skin crawl.

Kayriss stood and walked over to where Granite waited. The others were gathered nearby, checking their gear, sharpening blades, and readying themselves for what was to come. None of them were talking, each lost in their thoughts, their silence an unspoken agreement. No one liked the idea of the tunnels.

"This is madness," Kayriss said quietly, standing beside Granite. "You're certain this is the only way?"

Granite turned to her, his stone-grey eyes steady, unfazed by her doubt. "We walk through those gates in daylight, we're dead," he said, his voice low and calm, like the rumble of distant thunder. "The Night Ones will see us coming long before we get close. We'll never make it."

"And the rats?" Kayriss countered, her gaze hardening. "You know that they are more than likely down there, yes?"

"I know. But it's the best of two evils." Granite said, though something in his voice suggested he knew better. "We've crossed worse things than a few rats."

Kayriss held his gaze, her instincts screaming at her to push back, to find another way. He wasn't wrong. She knew that. The Night One city was a fortress, its high walls and watchful sentries making it impossible to approach unnoticed. If they were to slip inside, it had to be under the cover of darkness and in the shadows where no one was looking. And the tunnels, no matter how vile the thought, were their best chance.

She looked back at the others. Isaac was sharpening his blade; his brow furrowed in quiet concentration. Serafin, sharp-eyed and restless as ever, murmured to herself, her hands moving along the metal of her twin blades. Both were decorated in various shells and dancing coral from base to tip of each point. Everyone else carried out their morning checks and readied themselves for what lay underground. They were all prepared for the fight ahead, but the tension in the air was unmistakable. They knew the risks. The rat horde. The darkness. The unknown is waiting beneath the earth.

Kayriss exhaled slowly, rubbing the back of her neck. "How far do the tunnels take us?" she asked, her voice softening as she shifted her gaze back to Granite.

"All the way, I'd surmise," Granite said. "If that map is right."

On the wall of a nearby piece of shattered brickwork was a poster depicting a mass of coloured, if faded, lines. They spiderwebbed across it, intertwining at more significant junctions.

"They must have been transit tunnels once, designed to ferry thousands of hu-mans beneath the city. Now, they were little more than forgotten pathways, overrun by nature, and worse," He said, his tone matter of fact. She shuddered, imagining what might lurk down there after all these centuries.

Kayriss didn't like relying on old maps, but she trusted Granite. He'd never led them wrong before. Still, her fingers tightened around the hilt of her staff, an unconscious gesture as the weight of her decision settled over her.

"We leave at sundown," Granite said, turning away from the city to face the group. "Get ready."

The others nodded, silent as ever, though the glances they exchanged told Kayriss they were just as uneasy about the plan. She caught Isaac's eye momentarily, and the unspoken question hung between them. 'Are you sure about this?'

Neither answered. Both wanted to run. Far, far away and collapse in each other's arms forever.

Kayriss moved away from the group, her feet carrying her to the edge of the ridge once more. Later, the sun would begin its descent, casting long shadows over the ruins surrounding them. She could feel the pressure building in her chest, the weight of command sitting heavily on her shoulders. As their leader, the final decision was hers, and once they entered those tunnels, there would be no turning back.

She knelt by a patch of wildflowers that had forced their way through a crack in the old road. They were small and delicate, their bright colours contrasting the decaying world around them. For a brief moment, she thought of what this land had once been, before the Night Ones, before the hu-mans had fallen.

How had they let this happen so totally?

It didn't matter. What mattered now was survival, and they couldn't afford to make mistakes. The Night One city held the answers they needed, held Elara, held the key to stopping whatever was, or could be coming, the key to everything.

First, they had to survive the dark beneath.

Kayriss stood, her mind made up. She would lead them into the tunnels despite her fear. Despite the rats.

The sun dipped lower as the day progressed, the light fading into the horizon. Soon, it would be time.

The darkness, as always, was waiting for them.

Chapter Fifty-Five
Tallin and Elara
Enter her.

The morning light filled the room as Tallin entered, and Elara felt his presence before she even saw him. It was as if the air shifted, thickened, and pulled her towards him despite their distance. The room, dimly lit by the pale glow of the rising sun, flickered shadows along the stone walls, but it wasn't the flame that illuminated the space.

It was him.

He was the storm rolling in, heavy with an intensity that both thrilled and terrified her. His weight filled the room, his energy pressing against her skin before he even touched her. Elara stood by the window, dressed in the garments left for her. Their soft fabric was pale grey, almost white, and fell loose around her frame. The gown clung where it should and flowed where it didn't. She had never felt more exposed, more vulnerable, even though she was covered. Her heartbeat quickened, not from fear but from something else, something deeper. It pounded in her chest, throat, and veins, and when she turned to face him, it was as if the world had stopped moving. He was a silhouette against the door, darkness etched into his every feature. There was no need for words, not here, not now.

Their eyes met, and that was all it took.

He moved toward her, slow at first, then faster, like the inevitable descent of night. His hands, rough and calloused from battles fought and scars earned, reached for her but did not yet touch. It was as if they traced her silhouette in the air, gathering her shape from the light and pulling it toward him. She felt the pull deep within her, a tug in her chest, and the moment their bodies were close enough to brush, the world tilted.

Her fingers, trembling yet sure, found their way to his chest. The fabric of his tunic was silken, dark as midnight, but beneath it, the heat of him surged. She could feel his heart beating, steady and slow, an anchor in the storm. Her touch slid lower, and he shifted, helping her, until the fabric fell away, and there was nothing between them but skin and breath.

They undressed each other without hurry, yet with an urgency that left no space for hesitation. His hands found the ties at her waist, the soft folds of her gown slipping down her shoulders, cascading like twilight, leaving her bare beneath his gaze. She stood before him, unshielded, and it felt like she had stepped into shadow, her pale skin catching the faint light that danced around them.

He followed suit, his clothes falling away like night devouring the last remnants of day. Every inch of him was darkness, muscles carved in deep lines, a body forged in both hardship and desire. He was the embodiment of the night, and yet, when his eyes met hers, there was light within them—a flicker, a spark.

The distance between them vanished, and when they came together, it was like the meeting of shadow and light. His hands traced over her skin, reverent but hungry, as if she were the first warmth he had felt in an eternity of cold. Her body answered, arching toward him, her breath quick and shallow as his heat seeped into her. She was the moon, pale and glowing in the face of his night, but she needed his darkness as much as he craved her light. They moved together in a silent rhythm, their bodies speaking in ways words never could. Each touch, each kiss, each press of skin to skin was a dance of opposites. Light and dark, fire and ice, strength and vulnerability. She felt herself dissolve into him, yet she somehow became more. More alive, more present, more aware of every sensation, the heat of his breath on her neck, the press of his hands on her hips, the way their bodies fitted together like they had been made for this very moment.

When the crescendo came, it was not an explosion but a slow, consuming wave, dark and deep, pulling them both under. It was the kind of darkness that didn't frighten her but comforted her as if being swallowed by it meant becoming whole. He was the night, and she was the light within it, and together, they existed in a perfect, fragile balance.

As they lay entwined, the room grew quiet again. The shadows lengthened, but the candle still flickered, casting its pale light over their intertwined forms. She could feel his steady and strong heartbeat, and for a moment, it was all that existed in the world. The storm had passed, leaving a quiet, unspoken promise in its wake.

**

Outside the door, footsteps echoed down the corridor, away from Elara's door.

Chapter Fifty-Six
Kayriss
Life will rise again...

The descent into the earth was slow and cautious as if the shadows were watching. Kayriss led the group; her footsteps light on the crumbling stone stairs that spiralled deeper into the old hu-man tunnels. The air was thick with the smell of dampness and decay, the walls slick with moisture that had crept in over centuries of abandonment. She could hear every drip of water, every scrape of their boots on the ground, magnified in the deep silence.

It had been hours since they'd left the surface behind, and the dim light of their lanterns and torches barely pushed back the oppressive blackness that enveloped them. The world above seemed distant now, almost like a dream. Down here, it was as though time itself had frozen. There was no birdsong, no wind, just the steady rhythm of their breathing and the muted echoes of their footsteps reverberating through the vast tunnels.

"Stay close," Kayriss whispered, her voice barely audible. Her hand rested lightly on the hilt of her staff as she glanced back at the group. Isaac was behind her, his expression grim, while Granite followed at the rear, ever-watchful. His hands traced the stonework of the hu-mans of old, impressed by their relative smoothness. The otters had taken up the middle, their cutlasses drawn and ready. Every shadow was pounced at, showing their readiness. Hooth walked just behind, clearly not liking the enclosed space. Kayriss could see his wings twitching as he walked, ready to respond to the first sign of danger.

The tunnels, had once been the lifeblood of the ancient hu-man city, were a labyrinth. The faded map in Grind's possession helped guide their way, but the age and wear of the parchment made their accuracy questionable. Some of the underground had collapsed over the centuries, leaving massive piles of rubble and twisted steel. Other sections were half-flooded, forcing them to wade through knee-deep water that smelled of rot. The walls were lined with strange, rusted tracks, once meant for transport machines but now long abandoned and buried under grime.

Kayriss hated it down here. The darkness was too complete, too final. She couldn't shake the feeling of being watched, like the tunnels were alive, waiting for them to falter. Worse than that, she could hear them—the faint, skittering sounds in the distance, always just beyond the reach of their light. The rats were down here. She knew it. They all did.

The rat horde.

She shuddered at the thought. They weren't the rats of the surface or of old; they were small, scurrying creatures that scavenged scraps in ruined cities. No, the horde was something far more sinister, more unnatural. It had been born of the dark, mutated and twisted by something long forgotten in these depths. Granite's stories spoke of their glowing eyes, razor-sharp teeth, and uncountable numbers. A tide of fur and fury that would tear through a city in hours. No one who had encountered the horde survived to tell more than whispers of it, except, she realised, the Mine Folk. Granite was embellishing the story for added drama and ready them for an attack.

"Kayriss," Isaac's low voice snapped her back to the present. "We need to stop. Rest."

She glanced over her shoulder at him, his face barely visible in the lantern's flickering light. He was right. They'd been walking too long, and the weariness began settling in. She could see it in the others, too. Browntail and Cutlass looked tense whilst still enjoying their adventure, their eyes darting at every shadow. Hooth's hands were shaking, though whether from fatigue or the constant strain of holding anxiety at bay, Kayriss couldn't tell. Hooth had hidden the otter chest at the entrance and vowed to collect it for them upon their return. That, at least, he was happy to be unburdened of.

"Here," she said, gesturing toward a hollow in the wall where the tunnel widened slightly. "We rest for a moment, but we don't stay long. Keep your weapons close."

The group moved into the alcove, the otters setting their backs against the wall while Hooth sat cross-legged, his eyes closed as he tried to regain his focus. Grind remained standing, his massive frame just outside the edge of the light, keeping watch. His silence was unnerving, but it was also comforting. Nothing would get past him.

Kayriss momentarily allowed herself to lean against the rough stone, her body aching from the long descent. She rubbed her temples, trying to banish the growing headache that pounded behind her eyes. The darkness down here wasn't just physical; it felt heavy and oppressive, as though it were seeping into her bones, clouding her thoughts.

"How much farther?" Isaac asked, his voice barely more than a whisper. His eyes flicked toward Grind, but it was Kayriss who answered.

"Grind said that there's a main passage ahead. It'll take us closer to the city. But we need to be careful. The deeper we go, the more dangerous it gets."

Browntail, usually the more optimistic of the otters, muttered under his breath, "Aaaarrr. As if it wasn't dangerous enough already."

Kayriss couldn't disagree. Something about the tunnels felt more wrong than even the ancient ruins above. It was as though the earth was hiding something from them, something it didn't want them to see.

Suddenly, Grind's voice cut through the quiet. "Movement."

Everyone froze, their breaths hitching in their throats. Kayriss' hand flew to her staff as she turned her head slowly, scanning the darkness beyond their lanterns. Granite had stepped fully into the tunnel, his eyes narrowed, his body tense. There was a stillness in the air now that came just before a storm. Until she heard it—a faint, distant sound—a soft skittering—too many feet on stone—growing louder.

Pitter... Patter... Pitter... Patter...

"Rats," Cutlass whispered her voice tight with fear.

Kayriss' heart raced. "Everyone up," she ordered, her voice sharp as a thorn. "Now."

The group scrambled to their feet, weapons drawn, lanterns swinging wildly as they prepared for the inevitable onslaught. Kayriss could feel the tension thrumming through them all like a wire stretched to its breaking point. The skittering grew louder, the sound of claws on stone echoing through the tunnels, coming from somewhere unseen. The walls themselves seemed to vibrate with the horde's approach.

"We run," Granite said, his voice a low growl. "Now."

Without hesitation, Kayriss led the charge, her feet pounding against the stone as they sprinted deeper into the tunnels. The sound of the rat horde echoed louder and closer behind them. The air was thick with fear, the scent of it mingling with the damp earth. She could hear the others following, their footsteps urgent, their breaths laboured.

They turned a corner, the narrow tunnel opening into a wider passage. The ancient tracks beneath their feet clanged as they ran, but there was no time to think or stop. The rats were coming.

Kayriss risked a glance over her shoulder, and her heart nearly stopped. In the flicker of the lantern light, she saw them. A wave of dark, shifting bodies, hundreds of eyes glowing red in the darkness.

Chapter Fifty-Seven
Tallin and Elara
Aftermath.

Elara felt a deep, overwhelming sense of defencelessness, yet a strange safety in that vulnerability. It was as if she had stepped into a void, letting herself fall but knowing instinctively that Tallin was there to catch her. Her heart raced with anticipation and fear, not of him but of the intensity between them. There was an ache in her chest, a pull that went beyond physical desire; it was the need to be seen, truly seen, and she knew he saw her in a way no one else ever had.

Her emotions swirled in an intricate dance of light and dark. The way his hands traced her skin sent waves of heat through her, igniting something deep within that felt primal and ancient. She was drawn to him in a way she couldn't explain, like the moon to the ocean's pull, inevitable and unstoppable. Yet, even as her body surrendered, her mind spun, caught between the thrill of giving in and the fear of losing herself.

Tallin, too, was a storm beneath the calm exterior. Though sure and steady, his touch was laced with a quiet desperation. She could feel how his fingers lingered against her skin as if he were memorising every curve, every detail, afraid it would vanish. He moved with purpose, yet there was an underlying fragility, a quiet longing he kept hidden beneath the strength he wore like armour.

He felt drawn to her light, not because it overpowered him, but because it complemented the darkness he carried. He also had an aching need, a hunger, not just for her body but for the connection that ran more profound than the physical. Being with her, touching her, felt like finding something he had lost long ago. She wasn't just warmth to his cold; she was a kind of salvation he hadn't realised he needed.

In those moments, they were both stripped bare, not just in body but in soul. Elara felt exposed, her emotions raw and unguarded, and Tallin, though outwardly composed, was breaking inside, letting her in where no one else had been allowed. It was a fragile balance... intense, delicate, and terrifying.

As they came together, the intensity of their connection only deepened. Elara felt her very essence being pulled into his, like light swallowed by shadow, but instead of being consumed, she felt more whole and more alive than ever before. She didn't fear the darkness in him; instead, she embraced it, feeling as if her light was finally understood.

For Tallin, each movement was filled with relief, as if he had finally found something eluding him, a sense of peace in the chaos of his soul. He didn't need to hide the shadows he carried because, with Elara, they weren't something to be feared. She accepted them, touched them, and in doing so, she illuminated parts of him he had kept hidden for so long.

When they lay together in the quiet after, their bodies tangled in the remnants of their passion, there was a stillness between them, but it was filled with meaning. Elara's heart slowed, the tension in her body easing, but the emotions lingered, raw, intense, and honest. She felt a quiet satisfaction, not just from the physical release but from the deep connection they had forged in the silence. Her mind buzzed with the weight of it all, but she couldn't shake the sense that something had shifted, something that couldn't be undone.

For Tallin, there was a quiet gratitude, a relief that washed over him like the calm after a long battle. He had given in to his vulnerability, allowed himself to be seen, and in doing so, had found something that soothed the unrest within him. There was still darkness, but it no longer felt like it defined him. He could be both dark and light with her, strong and vulnerable.

They lay in the stillness, hearts beating in unison, a delicate equilibrium between what they had been and what they had become. In the quiet aftermath, both knew they had crossed a threshold, and though neither knew what lay ahead, at that moment, they were bound by the unspoken understanding that light and dark could coexist, not in opposition but in harmony.

Chapter Fifty-Eight
Kayriss
RUN!

Kayriss' lungs burned as she ran, the narrow tunnel amplifying the pounding of her boots and the growing roar of the rat horde behind them. Her mind raced as fast as her feet, each second bringing the swarm closer. She had seen the hundreds, perhaps thousands, of glowing eyes swarming together, an undulating tide of fur, claws, and teeth. If they caught up, there would be no escape. The walls felt like they were closing in, and the oppressive air was thick with the smell of damp earth and ancient rot. Each turn of the labyrinthine tunnels brought a fresh surge of dread, and the feeling of being hunted was never far behind.

"Faster!" Isaac's deep voice echoed from behind, his steps heavy but sure. He was the only one who could match her pace, though the others were close behind. Kayriss glanced back quickly. Grind and Granites's faces were pale, beads of sweat lining their brows, dripping in rivulets down their beard braids as they struggled to keep up. Serafin was carrying both the otters, who seemed to be having a whale of a time as they bounced along in her arms. Hooth was part running, part flying, his wings aiding his speed as they flapped him forward. They all knew their weapons, such as the horde's numbers, would be useless against this threat of the horde's numbers. Kayriss, though winded, kept steady, her eyes fixed ahead, as always prepared for the worst. It wasn't enough. The rats were gaining on them.

"Isaac!" She called out, her voice strained. "They're too fast!"

He didn't need her to tell her that. He could feel the growing rumble beneath his feet, the thunderous approach of claws against stone. Every instinct screamed to fight, but this wasn't a fight they could win. They needed a plan—an escape.

Then she saw... a break in the tunnel up ahead, the faint outline of an opening in the stone wall, half obscured by vines and debris. She veered toward it without thinking, signalling the others with a sharp gesture.

"Here!" she yelled, praying the passage would lead them anywhere away from the horde.

Kayriss reached it and turned, beginning to cast a spell. Pulling thorns from nowhere, they burst from floors and ceilings, skewering many of the oncoming beasts. Her hands danced as spells flew. Vines encased some; mudflows engulfed others. Isaac was the first to reach her side, his massive hands tearing at the vines and old metal grating blocking the entrance. With a single heave, he ripped the barrier away, revealing a smaller tunnel beyond, barely wide enough for one person at a time.

"One at a time, go!" Isaac ordered, pushing the Mine Folk in first. They did not complain about this but lit the way forward.

Hooth followed, his large frame barely making it through. Serafin followed, her new otter friends almost annoyed to be walking again. Edgar bolted for the tunnel, his smaller form moving quickly into the dark. He hesitated long enough to glance back at the looming horde before diving through.

Isaac turned to Kayriss, his pulse racing. "You next?"

"No time," she roared, pushing him toward the opening instead. "Go!"

For a brief moment, he hesitated, his instincts battling against the idea of leaving her to face the rats alone. The calm, unshakable look in her eyes was all the reassurance he needed. Isaac nodded once, then slipped into the tunnel. He did not have to wait long, and he pounded his feet faster as Kayriss flew into the tunnel, a swoosh of dust following her.

As she flew in, she cast a spell upon spell, attempting to close off the tunnel entrance completely. Light blinked away as the tunnel filled with nature, their only light source, lanterns, and torches. There was no time for logical thought. She could hear the rats now, their claws scratching closer, the horde ready to burst through at any second. Kayriss' heart clenched but continued with all the spells she knew. Power coursed through her, filling her with an energy she had never felt before. A green light filled the tunnel, illuminating it almost completely. This was not of her conscious doing, but the light burst forth anyway, the feeling filling her, tingling every sense. She felt it deep within her. Something moved.

Life. Change. Rebirth.

Kayriss looked down at her skin, watching it drift in colour, undulating through nature's offerings. It finally settled on a white tone with a hint of green, unnatural to her but wild in nature. Her hair became thicker and more vine-like as she flew, moving with a wave of motion. Leaf-like scales burst forth from her shoulders and grew down her arms, embracing nature.

Landing, the ground shook as she took a stance of readiness and confusion, unsure of what was happening. A cascade of rock and debris collapsed, sealing the passage with a deafening crash. Dust filled the air, choking her as she stumbled back, but the sound of the rat horde, so deafening moments before, was gone. The barrier held. She thought she'd collapse with the effort for a moment, but Isaac held her steady before she knew what was happening.

In his arms, she knew she was safe. It was then that she passed out.

**

The group stood in stunned silence, the only sounds being their ragged breathing and the faint echoes of settling stone. Serafin rushed forward, her heart hammering in her chest as she moved next to Isaac and Kayriss.

Gasping, she looked at Isaac, who was in as much shock as she was. Kayriss had taken on a form more in tune with nature than she had before. He could still see who she was, but her colouring had changed. Her eyes were a fire of green, and the scales, in the form of leaves, drifted down from her shoulders to her wrists. Neither had words.

Grind stood beside the pile of rubble, checking its stability. He nodded to the group that it was as secure as it could be. The party joined him as he walked to Kayriss. No one had any words.

Kayriss was changing.

Chapter Fifty-Nine
Tallin and Elara
Betrayal Uncovered.

Elara had drifted to sleep in Tallin's dark arms. She'd felt happy as she fell. It was a blissful feeling, although there was a nagging feeling that she'd dived into a pool blindfolded.

She stirred in Tallin's arms at the faint creak of her chamber door. The room was still bathed in the moon's soft glow, its silvery light spilling through the high window. Tallin's arm rested behind her, his steady breathing telling her he was still deep in sleep.

Something felt wrong. She blinked against the haze of sleep, her heart quickening as the door slowly swung open. The figure that stepped inside was a shadow at first, tall, broad, and purposeful. Then, the moonlight caught his features. Her breath caught in her throat.

Kaelen.

Behind him stood two Night One guards, their black armour gleaming ominously, and a third figure lurking just beyond the threshold—a shadow, silent and watching. But there was no time to focus on it. Kaelen's eyes burned with fury as he strode toward the bed.

"Get up, brother!" Kaelen's voice cut through the air like a blade, sharp and seething. "On your feet." His voice was laced with both malice and joy at his find.

Tallin jolted awake, instinctively reaching for his clothes that lay at the bedside. Elara scrambled to sit up, the blanket slipping from her shoulders as she reached for clothing out of reach.

"What in the abyss are you doing?" Tallin growled, pushing himself upright. Kaelen's lip curled in disgust as his eyes flicked to Elara.

"What am I doing? No, the real question, Tallin my dear brother, is who have you done? I warned you about this. I warned you that defying our father would be your downfall. And now look at you. Bedding her?" He spat the last word, disgust thick in his tone. "You've sullied our bloodline with your weakness. You've betrayed our father's legacy."

Tallin's eyes darkened, and he took a step toward his brother, unashamed by his nakedness.

"Watch your tongue, Kaelen. Elara's done nothing wrong, and neither have I. You and Marus think you can control everything with your threats and your power, but you don't own me. I am not your puppet."

Elara's heart pounded as she slipped from the bed. She felt Kaelen's gaze oozing over her form, taking in every curve at its slender level. She pulled a thin robe over her shoulders, aware that it was not hiding everything she wanted. She could feel the weight of Kaelen's stare even as she moved behind the two brothers, her fingers trembling as she tied the robe shut. Kaelen's sneer deepened.

"Is that what you tell yourself? That you're still free?" He gestured to Elara, his voice dripping with venom. "You think she is part of your freedom? You've damned yourself and the prophecy along with you."

"The prophecy? Don't lecture me about the prophecy," Tallin shot back, his voice rising. "The words of people long gone. This is our world and no hu-mans could take it from us. Besides, you've never cared about it, Kaelen. You only care about power. About how you can twist it to your advantage. What Elara and I share has nothing to do with you."

"Nothing to do with me?" Kaelen barked a laugh, though it was devoid of humour. "You blind fool. You think you're saving her? Saving us? You've doomed us all! The prophecy speaks of a union that could doom our kingdom, not one that will save it. And you, of all people, have shattered us to death." His voice lowered into a dangerous growl. "And you've done it for her."

As Tallin took a step forward, fists clenched, Elara's gaze shifted to the third figure lingering in the doorway, her face half-hidden in the shadows.

But those eyes. Elara knew those eyes. Meira.

A cold wave of shock rolled through her. How long had she been silently standing there, listening to this unfold? Had she been part of this all along?

Tallin must have seen the shift in Elara's expression because he turned to look at the door. "Meira?" His voice faltered, confusion overtaking his anger. "What is this? Why are you here?"

Meira's face remained emotionless, her gaze icy as she stepped forward. "I serve the king, Tallin. As do you. Or at least, as you should have."

Tallin's face paled as realisation dawned. "You've been working with him...with them this whole time?"

Kaelen's smirk grew. "You thought you could stand against us alone? That no one else saw what you were doing? The prophecy requires sacrifice, Tallin. You've forgotten that. Meira understands. I understand."

He stepped closer, his voice dropping into a low, menacing whisper. "You were never meant to be the hero of this story. You were always meant to fall."

Tallin's muscles tensed, but the two Night One guards sprang into action before he could move. They seized him by the arms, forcing him to the ground, his knees hitting the stone floor with a harsh thud. He struggled, but the guards' grip was ironclad, unyielding. Elara gasped, rushing toward him, but Meira blocked her path, pushing her back.

"Kaelen, don't do this!" Tallin shouted, fury and betrayal etched into his voice as he fought against his captors. "You don't understand! This will destroy us all!"

Kaelen crouched to meet Tallin's gaze; his smile twisted with malice. "Oh, I understand perfectly. But you... you've always been too weak to see the bigger picture. That's why you'll never be king." He stood, turning his back on his brother.

Elara's heart raced, panic gripping her as she looked between the two brothers, desperation clawing at her chest. But her eyes kept drifting back to Meira, who stood watching, arms crossed, cold and indifferent.

How long had this betrayal been in motion?

Kaelen motioned to the guards. "Take him away."

The guards yanked Tallin to his feet, dragging him toward the door. Elara tried to step forward, but Kaelen's cold gaze stopped her.

He smiled at her then, a slow, cruel smile that sent a chill down her spine. "Oh, don't worry, Elara. You're coming too." His voice was mockingly sweet. "I wouldn't want you to feel left out."

Tallin struggled against the guards, his voice hoarse with desperation. "Kaelen, listen to me, don't do this. The prophecy…"

"The prophecy is mine to decide," Kaelen snapped, his patience wearing thin. "You've had your chance. You've chosen your path, and now, you'll face the consequences."

He stepped toward the doorway, pausing just long enough to glance back at the two prisoners before him, his smile turning darker, more malevolent.

"Throw them both into the mines," Kaelen ordered, his voice cold and final.

The evil smirk on his face was the last thing Elara saw before the darkness of the guards' hands closed in.

Chapter Sixty
Kayriss
The changes in Kayriss.

The campfire crackled softly, casting flickering shadows across the clearing as the party sat silently, gazes drawn to the figure lying motionless in Isaac's arms. Kayriss' chest rose and fell in shallow, rhythmic breaths, her face peaceful despite the chaos her body had undergone. Her once familiar skin was now pale, almost white, with a faint, ethereal green hue, like the bark of an ancient tree touched by moonlight. Once smooth, Her arms and shoulders were covered in intricate patterns of delicate but leaf-like solid scales. Her hair, dark as ever, spilt over Isaac's lap, but it seemed to shimmer with a hint of green as the firelight danced over it. And then there were her eyes, closed now, but when open, they burned with a fire green intensity that had unsettled them all.

Grind sat closest to the fire, his thick arms resting on his knees as he studied her with a mixture of wariness and concern. "I don't like this," he muttered, breaking the silence. "This... transformation. What in the stoneshite is happening to her?"

Granite frowned in thought, his eyes never leaving Kayriss. "It's some kind of mutation," he said softly, his voice laced with curiosity. "But not one I've ever seen. This isn't the work of dark magic or corruption. It's... different. She's changing, but not into something evil, I'd wager. It just isn't in her."

Serafin leaned back against an odd-looking seat, an antique from the old world. She leaned towards Kayriss, her lips curled in a half-smile, though it didn't reach her eyes. "Different or not, she's not the same Kayriss we knew yesterday. She's... something else now." She flicked her eyes toward Isaac. "You've been with her the longest, Isaac. Do you have any idea what's going on?"

Isaac looked down at Kayriss, his expression heavy with worry. He adjusted his grip on her, his hands tender as they brushed the leaf-scales on her arm. "I don't know," he said quietly, his voice tight with emotion. "She has always been so powerful. It's why I love her. But I assumed the power was just hers to command." He looked up at the others, his eyes pleading. "I think wherever she draws her strength from, it might be seeping into her."

Hooth knelt beside Isaac and Kayriss, his hands hovering just above Kayriss' altered skin. His brow furrowed in concentration as he studied the changes more closely. "It's like she's becoming... part of nature," he murmured, his voice thoughtful. "Look at her skin. It's like the bark of a tree, but still soft, still Elven. And these scales," he touched one of the leaf like patterns on Kayriss' shoulder, "they feel like they're alive, like they're growing." Hooth glanced up at the group, his voice more certain. "This isn't just a curse. This is something bigger."

Browntail squeaked as he took a swig from his flask. "Bigger, eh? That's what worries me." He wiped his mouth with his paw and squinted at Kayriss. "I've seen people change before, usually after some foul magic or alchemical concoction gone wrong, but this? This feels like the land itself has claimed her. Not sure if that's a blessing or a curse yet."

Hooth stood back, his feathers ruffling slightly as he watched her. His amber eyes gleamed with something like understanding, and he was going through that awareness in his mind. His beak clicked softly, a sound of thought. Isaac noticed, asking;

"Hooth, you've got the closest connection to nature out of any of us, being so close to Ansel. Can you sense anything? What's happening to her? Anything Ansel might have taught you?" The owl took a few slow steps back towards her, his taloned feet click-clacking on the stone floor. "I feel... the forest within her," Hooth said, his voice a deep rasp, almost like the wind through trees. "She is becoming one with the natural world. Her druidic nature is calling to her. For what reason? I cannot say. But mother nature moves like the river, always flowing. It has chosen her, or perhaps she chose it. But this transformation..." he paused, his gaze lingering on Kayriss' scaled arm, "it's only just beginning."

Grind let out a heavy sigh, rubbing a hand through his beard. Dust and the occasional pebble flew free from the braids, only to be snatched up by Cutlass. "That's all well and good, Hooth, but what does it mean? Is she going to be all right? Can she even fight like this? We can't have someone falling apart in the middle of a battle."

Isaac's grip tightened protectively around Kayriss, his voice steely. "She's not going to fall apart. Kayriss is stronger than all of us. Whatever this is, whatever she's becoming, she'll master it. I know she will." He looked down at her again, his fingers gently brushing a strand of hair from her face. It felt like a vine tendril, heavier than normal hair. "She has to."

Serafin nodded slowly, though there was hesitation in her eyes. "Isaac's right. Kayriss is a fighter. But we need to be cautious. This transformation, it could be dangerous, not just for her, but for all of us."

Grind stood, his eyes flickering between the members of the party. "So what's the plan, then? We just sit here and wait for her to wake up and hope she doesn't burn us all alive with those new fire-green eyes of hers?"

Hooth shook his head. "No. We keep moving forward. Whatever's happening to Kayriss, it's connected to all of this, and we need answers. Now, more than ever. If this is part of some greater power, some force tied to nature, then there might be others who can help us understand it."

"Assuming they don't see her as a threat and try to kill her on sight," Browntail muttered. Isaac glared at the captain. "That's not going to happen," he retorted.

Grind moved to Isaac, his heavy armour clanking as he stretched. "Then it's settled. We keep an eye on her, but we push forward. Whatever is behind her transformation, we'll find out. We'll rescue Elara, too, and then get the hell out of here."

The fire crackled louder, and for a moment, the group sat in silence again, the weight of Kayriss' condition hanging over them like a storm cloud. Finally, Hooth spoke again, his voice a low murmur. "Be ready for when she wakes. She may not be the same Kayriss we knew."

Isaac looked down at her again, worry clouding his gaze. Her pale skin shimmered faintly in the firelight, the hint of green glowing like a forest just after a rainfall. Whatever had happened, was happening, or whatever she was becoming, there was no going back now. All he knew was that he would stand beside her, and all they could do was wait.

Chapter Sixty-One
Tallin and Elara
Why...?

Elara was still reeling from the weight of Kaelen's betrayal, the iron grip of the guards who had seized Tallin, and the cruel command that would send them both to whatever hid below the citadel. There was one person whose betrayal cut deeper than all the others.

Meira. Elara stood by the window, her hands clenched into tight fists, her knuckles white with tension. The room felt colder, as though the warmth had drained from it the moment Kaelen and his guards entered, shattering the hope and love that had grown.

Meira stepped forward, her footsteps soft on the stone floor. She moved with a predator's grace, her dark hair falling in sleek waves over her shoulders, her face unreadable as she regarded Elara.

"You betrayed me," Elara said quietly, her voice shaking with barely restrained fury. "Why?"

Meira paused, a faint smirk tugging at the corner of her lips. "Betrayal? Is that what you think this is?" She folded her arms, her expression calm and detached. "It's not betrayal, Elara. It's survival."

"Survival?" Elara's voice rose, her hands shaking as she turned to face the woman she had once trusted with her life. "I trusted you, Meira. You were my friend. How could you do this? How could you side with Kaelen?"

Meira's eyes gleamed with something dark, something cold and calculating. "It's in the nature of the Night Ones to betray," she said, her tone as smooth as silk. "We aren't bound by loyalty or love, Elara. We are bound by power. We serve whoever holds it. And right now, Kaelen is the one with the upper hand."

Elara felt her heart twist painfully in her chest. "So, you abandoned Tallin? You abandoned me, for power?"

Meira laughed, the sound bitter and mocking. "Abandoned? Oh, you're still so naive, Elara. I didn't abandon anyone. I was simply... choosing my path. And right now, Kaelen looks far more likely to be the next king than Tallin ever will." She shrugged as if the decision had been simple. "But don't get me wrong. I kept Tallin as an option. Just in case things didn't work out with his dear brother."

Elara's stomach churned at Meira's callousness. The woman she had known, the woman who was the first to gain even the smallest of trust, was replaced by someone cold, pragmatic, and utterly ruthless. "You were playing us both," she said, her voice hollow with the realisation.

Meira's smirk deepened. "Of course I was. Do you think I'd tie myself to just one of them? I was always going to choose the winning side. Tallin is...well, he's charming, isn't he? Noble, good-hearted. For a Night One that is. And," she added with a wicked glint, "he knows how to make a woman feel very wanted."

Elara's breath caught, her chest tightening as Meira's words hit their mark. She could feel the heat of anger rising, her cheeks flushing with a mixture of hurt and fury. "How could you..."

"How could I? Let a Prince fuck me for his pleasure? Believe me, the pleasure was mine too." Meira said with a soft, predatory laugh. "You see, I was enjoying the real Tallin, the one who knows exactly how to touch a woman, how to make her forget the world. With his power. It's a shame you will only get that once." Her voice dropped into a low purr. "I'll never forget the way he felt... when he was inside me."

Elara's vision blurred with tears of rage. She wanted to scream, to claw at Meira's face, to strike her for every venomous word that spilt from her lips. More than anything, she wanted to tear down the walls of this twisted reality where loyalty was nothing more than a game and love was a weapon to be wielded against her.

Meira stepped closer, her voice soft and mocking as she tilted her head to look down at Elara. "You see, Elara, Tallin may love you in his noble way, but he belongs to no one. He's as much mine as he ever was yours. And now?" She smiled, a cruel curve to her lips. "Now he belongs to Kaelen. As do you."

Elara's hands trembled at her sides, her body rigid with barely controlled fury. "You disgust me," she hissed, her voice shaking with emotion. "I don't care what you say. Tallin is not yours. He never was."

Meira laughed softly, a cold, sharp sound that echoed in the empty chamber. "We'll see, won't we?"

At that moment, Tallin was allowed to dress. Slowly and never taking his eyes off his brother, he clothed himself with hatred burning in his eyes. The guards approached with large cuffs for Tallin's wrists, binding him into subservience. He said nothing as the guards shoved him away, their ironclad hands forcing him to march toward the doorway. Elara's heart wrenched as she tried to reach him, but the guards grabbed her roughly, pulling her back before she could even brush his arm.

"Tallin," she whispered, her voice barely audible over the sound of her pulse roaring in her ears. He didn't meet her eyes. He kept his head high, his face unreadable as he was led out of the room.

"Keep her quiet," one of the guards muttered, tightening his grip on Elara as she struggled. "The mine's no place for a princess to be making a fuss."

Meira stood in the doorway, her arms folded, watching with cold detachment as Elara was dragged behind. "Be careful, Elara," she called out mockingly, her voice like a serpent's hiss. "The mines can be very unforgiving. Just like Kaelen."

Elara glared at her, her heart burning with hatred and sorrow as the guards forced her into the cold, stone corridors. The darkness of the citadel seemed to close in around her, the weight of betrayal pressing down on her chest until she could barely breathe. As they marched toward the mine, where the darkness truly lay in wait, Kaelen's shadow loomed more immense, and Meira's cruel smile was the last thing she saw before the door to her old life closed behind her.

Chapter Sixty-Two
Kayriss
New life.

She leaned into him, pressing her forehead against his chest, feeling the strong beat of his heart beneath her. "But what if... what if you don't love me as much?" Her voice was barely a whisper, her greatest fear finally spoken aloud. "What if I'm not who I was?"

Isaac pulled her closer, wrapping both arms around her as though he could shield her from her doubts. "Kayriss, look at me," he said softly, lifting her chin with the edge of his fingers. "Nothing could ever change the way I feel about you. This..." He gestured to the faint changes across her skin, gently touching the new leaves on her arms. "This is just a part of the journey we're on. But you, your heart, your mind, your soul, are still the woman I fell in love with."

She searched his eyes, finding only love and sincerity there. There was no trace of hesitation or disgust, only a deep, unwavering affection. It warmed her chest, pushing away the icy grip of fear.

"Do you mean that?" she asked, her voice breaking.

Isaac smiled softly, his thumb brushing away a stray tear that had slipped down her cheek. "I've never meant anything more."

A breath of laughter escaped her, shaky but real, and she found herself leaning up to kiss him, a soft, tentative brush of lips. Isaac responded, pulling her deeper into his arms, the kiss lingering, filled with everything unspoken between them. She smelled of nature's morning, tasted like the freshest stream, and smelt like a meadow of flowers. When they finally pulled apart, his forehead rested against hers, his breath coming just as fast as hers.

"I don't care what happens next," Isaac whispered, his voice thick with emotion. "We'll face it together, whatever comes."

Kayriss nodded, feeling her heart swell with love for him, with gratitude that he was there, that he hadn't abandoned her in her darkest hour. She was still Kayriss, even if her body had changed. And Isaac still loved her, still saw her the same way he always had.

As they held each other, the faint sound of movement reached her ears, and she turned her head slightly. Across the tunnel, nestled in the corner, the two otter pirates, Browntail and Cutlass, watched them with soft, knowing eyes. Browntail gave them a slow, approving nod while Cutlass curled tighter into Browntail's side, their tails entwined, looking as content and warm as if they were lying in the heart of a sunny meadow rather than a cold, dark tunnel.

Kayriss felt a faint smile tug at her lips. Something was comforting in their quiet companionship, in the way they mirrored her connection with Isaac. For a moment, the world outside the tunnel didn't matter. It was just them—her, Isaac, and the two otters sharing a stolen moment of peace amidst the chaos.

As Kayriss rested her head back on Isaac's chest, feeling his heartbeat beneath her cheek, she knew that whatever changes had come, whatever changes were still to come, she would face them.

Isaac was with her, and nothing could take that away. She thought it best not to tell him about the changes she felt internally.

Of the life growing within her.

Chapter Sixty-Three
Tallin and Elara
Void.

Tallin's heart pounded as the guards pushed him and Elara down the jagged, spiralling stairwell deeper into the Citadel. The cold, wet air stung his lungs, and the flickering torchlight cast dancing shadows on the rough stone walls. Every step echoed, creating a symphony of ominous clicks and thuds. The narrow stairwell seemed to descend forever, plunging them into an abyss beneath the city, far from the watchful stars above.

Beside him, Elara walked with as steady, unshaken stride as she could, her hands still bound tightly in iron chains. Her sharp eyes flickered with rage and contempt as if she were angry at herself for allowing this to happen. 'She should have expected this,' she thought, running the scenario through her mind.

The guards, hulking figures in black armour, remained silent, their visors down, their weapons ready, ensuring no chance of escape.

Tallin leaned closer to her, his voice a low murmur. "I'm sorry this is happening to you. I never thought it would get to this." Elara saw the sadness on his face, an expression she hadn't used to seeing since she got to the dark citadel.

Many steps passed, and the group remained in silence.

"I've never been this deep before," he admitted, glancing around. The air grew heavier the further they descended, thick with the weight of secrets long buried. "I've never been in the mines."

Elara's gaze flicked to him, her expression unreadable. "That's because there are no mines, Tallin."

Her words hit him like a punch to the gut. He nearly stumbled on the next step, catching himself against the wall. "What do you mean? The obsidian mines are right below the tower, right? That's what they've been saying for years. The scourge foxes work the obsidian mines. It's why they remain so obedient. Their families mine, the ones above secure the city. It works for everyone!"

A grim smile twisted Elara's lips, though her eyes remained cold, hard. "That's the story, yes. The one you tell everyone. But it's a lie."

Tallin stared at her, bewildered. His voice came out harsher than he intended. "What are you talking about?"

Elara slowed, her voice lowering as the guards' attention wavered. "There are no mines, Tallin. Not for obsidian. They take the slaves for something else."

His stomach twisted. "Something that's worse than that?"

Her eyes locked onto his, and momentarily, he saw real, unhidden fear. "Nyxsarathryn," she whispered. They serve someone, something, called Nyxsarathryn."

Tallin's confusion deepened, and a chill ran through him. "Nyxsarathryn? Who... What is that? I've never heard that name before."

"You wouldn't have." Elara's voice was tight, filled with an edge of bitterness. "It's not a name any of the foxes are allowed to speak above ground. It's the name they whisper down here, deep beneath the Citadel. The name that makes the foxes tremble and too afraid to fight back. Nyxsarathryn must provide the obsidian. I'm just guessing here. This is your house, Tal."

Tallin's blood ran cold, a knot forming in his chest. He felt his known world crumbling. His whole life, he'd known of their way of doing things. It was a co-existence that worked for everyone. Deep down, he knew it was how the Night Ones kept power, but he'd also been lied to. "Why would they lie about this? To me??"

Elara's eyes grew darker, her voice low. "Because if all the people knew, there might be a revolt. You all think this is how it is, but it seems you Night Ones are the real ones being lied to." She let her words hang in the air, their weight suffocating.

Tallin's throat tightened. "Who... who is Nyxsarathryn? What is it?"

Elara shook her head. "I wasn't told. But it must predate the Night Ones surely? If you were under the assumption that it was a mine?"

Tallin's mind reeled as he tried to process her words. Not miners, not labourers, just servants to the real royalty. His entire life had been a lie, built on false promises and a history of deceit. This... this was madness.

Before he could ask more, the stairway ended in a comprehensive stone platform. A massive iron door loomed ahead, embedded into the far wall. It stood at least three men high, carved with intricate symbols and covered in chains. The door's surface seemed to pulse with an eerie, faint glow as if the stone was alive.

Tallin stopped in his tracks, his heart hammering in his chest. "What is this?"

Elara's face was grim as she looked at the door, her jaw tightening. "This must be where they are taking us. Beyond that door... that must be where Nyxsarathryn waits."

The guards moved forward, pulling the heavy chains from the door, their movements methodical, practised. They seemed almost robotic, not a word spoken as if they had done this a thousand times before. One of them grasped the iron handle and pulled. The sound of creaking metal echoed through the stone chamber as the door swung open, revealing nothing but darkness beyond it. A darkness so deep and unnatural it seemed to swallow the light from their torches.

Tallin felt his breath catch in his throat. He stepped back, his instincts screaming to run, fight, and do anything but go through that door. The guards were already turning to them, hands on their shoulders, shoving them forward.

"This isn't right," Tallin hissed, panic clawing at him. "This isn't what we were told!"

Elara's eyes met his, a flicker of regret passing through them. "It's never been right, Tallin. We just didn't know how wrong it was."

The door yawned wider, revealing a gaping maw of blackness as cold air rushed up from the depths below. There was no sound beyond the threshold, no hint of life or movement.

Only a void.

As the guards pushed them closer, Tallin's heart thundered in his chest, the ominous presence of the door suffocating him. This was it. Whatever was waiting for them beyond that door was nothing like they had ever imagined.

As they crossed the threshold, swallowed by the darkness, the weight of Nyxsarathryn's name pressed down on them like an invisible hand, pulling both deeper into the unknown.

Chapter Sixty-Four
Kayriss
The runaway.

Kayriss trudged through the thick air of the tunnel, her footsteps a slow, measured echo against the cracked stone beneath her boots. The stale, sour smell of decay permeated the London Underground tunnel, seeping into her lungs with every breath. It felt like ages since they had left the surface world behind when the city's last rays of sunlight had disappeared behind collapsing roofs and dark clouds. Her limbs ached, and the others fared no better. Weariness had settled into their bones, dulling even their sharpest instincts.

Behind her, Edgar shuffled, his leather armour rubbing against his flank. His breaths came in shallow bursts, a stark contrast to Captain Browntail's rumbling grumbles. The otter had walked at the back of the group, his large cutlass clutched in his paws. Despite his gruff attitude today, the Captain held the rear with a silent sense of duty.

Isaac muttered a prayer under his breath, hands constantly twitching to the hilt of his sword, while Hooth's soft feathers rustled now and then as his owl eyes scanned the dim path. Grind trudged near the front with his pickaxe glinting occasionally as it rested on his shoulder, and Granite followed silently. Serafin looked dry in the darkness, clearly missing the waters she lived in. Kayriss was happy to have her on their side, though, as she had proven both savage in battle and knowledgeable of the lands.

"How far?" Kayriss asked aloud, her voice cutting through the oppressive quiet.

"Deeper still," Grind replied without turning back. "The map said the tunnels under the citadel stretch for miles, though there's little telling how many of 'em are still passable."

Kayriss nodded, though she doubted he could see her in the gloom. Passable. The word had lost meaning the further they had descended. Twisted pathways, flooded tracks, and half-collapsed walls had become their new normal. Yet, this was the only way to Elara without alerting every Night One—the only way to rescue her.

A faint scurrying sound echoed ahead, and the group froze. Kayriss felt her heartbeat quicken, her fingers tightening on her staff. Rats. More of them.

Since they entered these forsaken tunnels, the infestation of vermin had been unrelenting. The rats had become a constant threat, diseased and corrupted by whatever foul magic seeped through the stones. Their red eyes glowing in the dark, their claws sharp as razors.

Kayriss raised a hand, her eyes narrowing as she peered into the shadows ahead. A flash of fur darted across their path, too quick to identify but enough to send a shiver down her spine.

"Not again," muttered Cutlass, her eyes glinting dangerously in the half-light. She had been more on edge since the rat swarm attacked, her eyes darting to Browntail at every opportunity.

Kayriss was about to signal an advance when the fur flashed again, closer this time, and this time... it was smaller. She blinked, her mind registering the movement. It wasn't the sickly, pale brown of a rat. This fur was a deep, fiery red.

A small shape leapt from the shadows, tumbling to a stop just before them. It looked up, trembling, its wide amber eyes locking onto Kayriss's with fear and desperation.

A child. No, a fox.

The fox cub couldn't have been older than ten. Her delicate face was streaked with grime, and her fur was matted with dirt. She was breathing heavily, her small chest rising and falling rapidly. Kayriss lowered her staff slowly, her instincts screaming that this was no ordinary encounter.

"Who are you?" Kayriss asked, her voice soft but firm.

The little fox hesitated, glancing at the others behind Kayriss. Captain Browntail had already lowered his weapon, suspicion flickering in his dark eyes. Isaac shifted as if ready to lunge. Grind's calm presence finally seemed to coax the child into speaking.

"I... I'm Ayleigh," the cub stammered. "I ran away. From them."

"From them?" Kayriss repeated, stepping closer.

Ayleigh nodded, wiping a tear from her cheek with a shaky paw. "The Goddess... Nyxsarathryn... she took my family. She has them trapped. All of them. The scourge foxes... she's keeping us under the citadel. I escaped, but they're still there."

Kayriss's heart sank. She had heard rumours of the scourge foxes, Wildlings from the lower realms who had a reputation for being thieves, bandits, and brigands. They were not scared children or families in chains.

"And you're down here... alone?" Captain Browntail asked, his voice low with disbelief.

Ayleigh nodded again, her eyes pleading. "I know the tunnels. I can help you. But... please... you have to help me get my family out."

Kayriss glanced back at the others. Grind's face was unreadable, his dark eyes flickering in the pale light. Hooth was silent, though his feathers were ruffled as if agitated. Cutlass's tail twitched while Isaac had gone still, his jaw clenched.

They had come this far, battled horrors Kayriss never could have imagined. But now, standing before this child, there was no question. Kayriss knelt, bringing herself to Ayleigh's eye level.

"If you help us," Kayriss said softly, "we'll help your family. I swear it."

The scourge fox cub's eyes widened with hope, and she nodded rapidly. "Follow me, then. I know a way to the citadel."

Without another word, Ayleigh darted into the darkness, her small form moving with surprising agility. Kayriss motioned for the others to follow, and soon, they were plunging deeper into the tunnel, the walls closing in tighter, the air growing more oppressive with every step.

The sense of dread grew. Kayriss could feel it, like a weight pressing down on her chest. The citadel lay ahead, buried deep beneath the earth, and with it, something...

Ayleigh moved with purpose, her tiny paws guiding them quickly through the maze of tunnels. As they descended, the darkness thickened, and strange, echoing sounds began to follow them. Unnatural whispers seemed to slither through the cracks in the stone, and Kayriss couldn't shake the feeling that they were being watched.

"They say," Ayleigh whispered, her voice barely audible, "that the tunnels under the citadel are cursed. Some who go down here... never come back."

Kayriss felt a chill run down her spine. She didn't doubt it. The walls seemed alive, pulsing with some unseen energy, as though the citadel was a living thing, feeding on the fear of those who entered its domain.

"We'll make it," she muttered, clenching her staff tighter. "We have to."

Even as they pressed forward, Kayriss couldn't shake the feeling that something far worse than rats awaited them in the shadows.

Chapter Sixty-Five
Kaelen
A King's panic.

    King Marus sat on his throne in the obsidian citadel, his fingers lightly drumming against the armrests as the flickering flames from the braziers cast wavering shadows across the walls. The council chambers, ornate yet oppressive, reflected the weight of the Night One kingdom. Dark banners embroidered with silver glyphs hung from the high ceiling, and the scent of burnt incense permeated the air. The elders of the Night Ones murmured among themselves, their whispered conversations filling the silence. Marus' mind wandered, caught in the web of his many burdens. Before he could lose himself in the labyrinth of his thoughts, the heavy iron doors creaked open, and a lone figure stepped inside. Kaelen, his youngest son, strode forward, his eyes sharp with an intensity Marus had grown used to—yet today, something felt wrong. The boy's gait was commanding; his jaw clenched tightly in a smile that screamed victory.

Kaelen knelt before him but said nothing.

"Rise," Marus said, his voice echoing through the chamber. "Speak your mind, Kaelen."

Kaelen stood but didn't meet his father's gaze. "I have done what needed to be done."

A cold feeling crept up Marus' spine, though he kept his expression impassive. "What is it you have done, my son?"

The council murmured louder now, their eyes darting between father and son. Sensing the tension thickening like smoke, Marus lifted a hand, silencing them all. "Out. Leave us."

The elders hesitated, their concern palpable, but obeyed without question and filed out of the room. The massive doors shut behind them with a resonant thud, leaving the King alone with his son in the dim light.

Marus' voice dropped into a low growl, all pretence of calm abandoned. "Kaelen, what have you done?"

Kaelen's face remained stone-like, but there was a flash of something in his eyes. Defiance, perhaps. "Tallin is gone. I banished him to the mines."

Marus surged to his feet, his obsidian-coloured cloak swirling around him like the night itself. "You banished him?" His fury crackled in the air between them. "Your brother? My eldest son??"

"He betrayed our blood," Kaelen retorted, his fists clenching at his sides. "Tallin laid with the hu-man woman, Elara. He defied the prophecy. He defiled your bloodline. Sullied it with her filth."

Marus froze, his rage suspended as if caught in time. His breath seemed to still be in his chest, and a dread unlike any he had ever felt seized him. Slowly, he sank back onto his throne, his hands gripping the armrests with white-knuckled intensity.

"Elara?" The name escaped his lips, barely more than a whisper.

Kaelen nodded. "I did what was necessary for the kingdom. Tallin's actions would have brought ruin upon us all. The prophecy warned us about their kind. And he laid with her. In your house." Kaelen almost spat the last words, emphasising his disgust. "So, I sent them both to the mines, where they belong."

Marus' gaze snapped up, his eyes wide and wild. His heart thundered in his chest as though it would tear itself free from his ribcage. "Both?"

"I sent Elara with him," Kaelen said, his tone carrying a hint of pride, as though he expected to be praised for his decisive action. "She is of no use to us now. Tallin is too weak to resist her. I rid us of the danger."

For a moment, the silence in the chamber was absolute, broken only by the distant crackling of the fire. Then, like the crumbling of stone, Marus slumped forward, his face twisting in disbelief. His gaze dropped to the cold, black floor, panic flashing in his eyes.

"Is she at least to be killed? Tell me she lives no longer, at least." His voice was barely audible.

Kaelen blinked in confusion, his brow furrowing. "Dead? No. I banished her, Father. That should be enough. I thought..."

Marus was instantly on his feet, his face twisted with a fury so raw it turned his pale skin ash. "You thought wrong!" he roared, his voice shaking the very walls of the citadel. He advanced on his son, eyes blazing like two dark suns on the verge of collapse. "You do not understand the forces you have meddled with. You have no idea what you have done."

Kaelen flinched under his father's wrath, taking a step back, but the confusion remained etched into his features. "I only meant to protect our people. The prophecy..."

"The prophecy means nothing without understanding," Marus snarled. "Elara is no ordinary hu-man, Kaelen. Her blood... Her mere touch could doom us all." He hesitated, eyes flicking to the shadows that seemed to press in from the room's corners. "Her blood is tied to the darkness that is below us. You have unleashed something far worse than you can imagine."

Kaelen's confidence wavered, doubt creeping into his voice. "But she is just a woman..."

"She is more than that!" Marus cut him off, turning abruptly toward the doors. "Tallin's foolishness may have doomed us, but you... your actions..." He broke off, his voice trembling with a fear Kaelen had never heard. "You do not know what you've set in motion."

Without another word, Marus stormed from the chamber, his obsidian cloak billowing behind him as he disappeared into the shadowed corridors of the citadel. The echoes of his footsteps faded, leaving Kaelen standing alone, his heart pounding as the weight of his father's final words sank in.

"You do not know what you've done."

Chapter Sixty-Six
Kayriss
The foxes' tale.

Kayriss moved silently through the crumbling tunnels of the old Lon-don underground network, her boots barely sounding on the cracked stone floors. The air was thick and heavy, filled with the scent of damp earth and forgotten history that she and the party were becoming accustomed to. Flickering lights from bioluminescent mosses had begun to cling to the ancient walls, casting eerie shadows that shifted and danced as they ventured deeper into the forgotten depths. Grind and Granite seemed more at home here, although the glow seemed ethereal and unworldly to everyone else.

At her side, Ayleigh padded along, her small fox form barely visible in the gloom. The scourge fox cub had a strange grace about her, unnervingly calm, considering the stories Kayriss had heard about her kind. Ayleigh's orange-tipped and sleek fur blended with the darkness, making it seem like she was more shadow than flesh.

They had been walking for hours, the silence between them broken only by the occasional water drip or the distant creak of ancient metal settling deeper into the earth. Kayriss welcomed this silence; the world above had become far too loud and dangerous. Down here, at least, there was a strange stillness… until Ayleigh spoke.

"When we become useless," Ayleigh began, her voice a soft whisper in the oppressive darkness, "we go to see her. Nxysarathryn."

Kayriss stopped in her tracks, the name sending a chill up her spine. She turned her gaze down to the small fox, her sharp eyes searching the cub's expression, though it remained unreadable.

"The goddess in shadow," Ayleigh continued as if it were nothing more than a bedtime story. "She takes us when we are no longer useful. We are never seen again after that."

Kayriss' brow furrowed. "What do you mean 'never seen again'? Does she kill you?"

"No," Ayleigh replied, her voice unnervingly calm. "She does not need to. She takes what's left of us, our essence, our will, whatever lingers when the body fails. She gathers us like stones for a mosaic, placing us wherever needed. We deliver obsidian to the Night Ones above, make them believe their kingdom thrives over a mine."

Kayriss felt her heartbeat quicken. The Night Ones, the creatures who ruled the darkened world above, believed their citadels stood upon rich veins of obsidian, a mineral sacred to them, used in their buildings and weaponry. The idea that it was all a lie, an illusion crafted by this dark goddess, unsettled Kayriss deeply.

"She is tricking them?" Kayriss whispered her voice tight with disbelief. "Nxysarathryn made them believe the obsidian came from beneath?"

Ayleigh nodded, her silver eyes reflecting the faint glow of the moss. "It keeps the Night Ones in place, gives them purpose, makes them think they are in control. But it's all a game to her. She craves control, always, and the Night Ones are just pawns to her."

Kayriss shivered, pulling her cloak tighter around her. The damp air felt colder now, and Ayleigh's words weighed heavily on her. "Control until the hu-mans come back," she muttered, remembering what little she had learned and knew of the ancient wars. The downfall of humanity was a mystery to most, a story told in fragments, dark magic, betrayal, and the rise of new powers in the ruins of civilisation.

"Yes," Ayleigh replied, her voice darkening. "She waits for them. For you."

Kayriss stopped, turning sharply to face the cub. Her breath caught in her throat. "What do you mean, me? I'm no hu-man."

"No, but you are their kin in spirit," Ayleigh said, her eyes glinting with something ancient and knowing. "You all came from them, didn't you? You were part of them. Long ago. And besides, you bring the greatest prize." She motioned towards Isaac.

Kayriss felt her pulse quicken as the cub's words seemed to echo through the tunnel, reverberating off the stone walls like a forgotten secret rising to the surface.

"We were much different, too, before the fall," Ayleigh continued, her voice barely whispering. "After the hu-mans... we were free to grow, to thrive, that was until we were found by her."

The druid's breath caught in her chest, the weight of this revelation hitting her like a tidal wave. She knelt beside the small fox, her face etched with sympathy and curiosity. "What happened to your families?"

Ayleigh turned her head slightly as if remembering something long buried in time. "At first, it was amazing. We were promised everything. But that is what she took." The small cub wiped her snout, brushing a tear from her cheek.

Kayriss felt the hair on the back of her neck rise. The air around them seemed to thicken as Ayleigh spoke as if the very stones of the tunnel were listening to her tale.

"But we were just a plaything, a means to an end for her," Ayleigh said, her voice growing softer, almost regretful. "Nxysarathryn took our nature and twisted it, feeding off it, using it as fuel. She brought the whole world down before. The fall of humanity... She wants to do it again." Ayleigh paused, her eyes narrowing. "That was her doing. She destroyed everything. Because she hates the hu-mans."

Kayriss sat back on her heels, her heart pounding. "But why? Why would she do that?"

Ayleigh's eyes flashed with something dark and ancient, a wisdom beyond her youthful appearance. Kayriss realised that this was historical, ancestral knowledge that had been drummed into her, and she wasn't sure how much was repetition. "Because she loves to gloat. She revels in her power. She enjoys reminding the world that it was she who brought humanity to its knees. Theat is was she that cut off its head. But now..." The cub's voice dropped to a conspiratorial whisper. "Now she wants them back. She wants hu-mans to return so she can destroy them all over again. She thrives on their destruction."

The tunnels around them seemed to close in, the darkness becoming almost tangible. Kayriss felt her stomach twist with dread, realising the goddess's control was deep and far-reaching. This wasn't just about the Night Ones, the druid's love for Isaac, or the remnants of the old world. This was about a force of pure malevolence that had orchestrated the end of an entire civilisation and now wanted a second chance to watch it fall again.

The druid's love for Isaac...

Kayriss realised that this demon wanted her love. Turning, she vomited violently in the darkness. Isaac was at her side in seconds, helping as he could.

"And you serve her?" Kayriss asked as she wiped her mouth. Her voice was barely above a whisper as if fearing the walls themselves might hear.

"I have no choice," Ayleigh said, her tone colder now, resigned. "I am bound to her will. She has my father. I am her servant, like all the scourge foxes. She pulls the strings, we obey. Or we die." The cub hesitated, then added quietly, "But I do not share her hatred. I do not revel in destruction as she does."

A silence hung between them for a moment, heavy with understanding.

Kayriss stood, brushing the dirt from her cloak. "And you're telling me this now because...?"

Ayleigh glanced at her, her silver eyes gleaming in the dark. "Because the path we walk leads directly into her hands. And I need you to know what's coming. You must understand the stakes... And I want my father back."

They walked deeper into the tunnels, the weight of their conversation settling over them like a shroud. The passages grew narrower, the walls closer, until they reached a chamber where the air felt colder, more oppressive. At the far end stood a massive iron door, chained and locked, as though the world itself had been sealed behind it.

Kayriss felt the energy shift around them, a malevolent force just beyond that door, waiting, watching. The chains were thick and ancient, as though forged in a time long before even the hu-mans had ruled.

Ayleigh stopped beside her, staring at the door with an intensity that sent shivers down Kayriss' spine.

"This is it," the cub whispered. "This is where she waits, but we can get in over there, where I got out." Kayriss reached out, her hand hovering just above the cold, rusted metal of the chains. Her fingers trembled.

"And if we open it?" she asked, though she already knew the answer. Ayleigh's voice was little more than a breath in the darkness.

"Then the true nightmare begins."

Chapter Sixty-Seven
Elara
Paths will collide.

Around the pit's edge were the scourge foxes, small, shadowy figures with orange fur caked with the underground grime. They were gathered in a circle, murmuring in voices too soft to comprehend, their tails flicking back and forth in a trance-like rhythm. The eerie glow from their fur casts a faint light on the pit, just enough to see their twisted forms.

"They're chanting," Tallin whispered, his voice barely audible. "What are they doing?"

Elara's stomach twisted as she watched the foxes. Their murmuring was hypnotic, their movements unsettlingly synchronised. The pit seemed to respond to them as if the darkness within was listening, growing hungrier with each passing moment.

Then, without warning, one of the foxes stepped forward, teetering on the edge. Elara's heart leapt into her throat as she watched the fox pause, its eyes unblinking, its body swaying slightly.

In one horrifying moment, it stepped into the void.

Elara gasped, her hand flying to her mouth as the fox disappeared into the pit. There was no sound of impact, no scream—just silence, as if the pit had swallowed it whole.

"What... what just happened?" Tallin stammered, his voice barely above a whisper. "This isn't... shouldn't be..."

Before Elara could answer, another fox stepped forward, mimicking the first. This one, too, without hesitation, tumbled into the abyss, vanishing into the darkness below. The foxes began to fall one by one, each stepping forward as if compelled by some unseen force, their murmurs growing louder as they plummeted into the pit.

Elara felt the terror rising in her chest, choking her. "They're... they're killing themselves," she managed to whisper, her voice trembling with disbelief. "Why are they doing this?"

Tallin shook his head, his face pale and strained. "I don't know. I don't know..."

The last foxes stepped forward, its small body poised on the edge. It hesitated momentarily, its eyes turning toward them, locking with Elara's. There was something in its gaze, something knowing, something... malicious. Then, without a sound, it fell.

Elara screamed, her mind reeling. "No! Stop!" But it was too late. The last of the foxes was gone, swallowed by the darkness. Her scream echoed into the void, bouncing off the unseen walls and disappearing into the abyss.

A sound came.

A low, rumbling growl, deep and guttural, reverberated from the depths of the pit. The sound made the hair on the back of her neck stand on end, that primal, instinctual terror kicking in.

Whatever was down there was awake now.

Tallin's grip on her hand tightened, his fear palpable. "We need to go. Now."

Elara couldn't move. Her legs were rooted to the spot, her eyes fixed on the pit. The growl grew louder and more distinct as if whatever was below was stirring, waking from a long slumber. Then, from the blackness, came the unmistakable sound of something… climbing.

"Tallin," she whispered, her voice barely audible. "Something's coming. I can't move."

The growl turned into a low, rasping chuckle, an inhuman, cold, and mocking sound. Elara's heart raced as scraping claws against stone grew louder and nearer.

From the depths, the first tendril of darkness emerged, a twisted, clawed hand, blacker than the void itself. It gripped the pit's edge, pulling something vast and monstrous from the abyss. A low, gurgling laugh echoed through the chamber, filling the air with its malevolent glee.

"Elara," Tallin said, his voice tight with panic, "run."

Elara couldn't move. She was frozen in place, her body paralysed by terror as the thing from the pit began to pull itself up, its massive form looming in the flickering light.

A voice. A laugh drew forth from the shadow itself. Deep and terrible, echoing from the darkness itself.

"Welcome. My child."

Chapter Sixty-Eight
Kayriss
Nyxsarathryn.

Kayriss led the way through the narrow tunnel, her palms scraping against the jagged rock as they crawled deeper into the ancient passages. Behind her, Isaac and the others followed silently, their breath ragged in the stale, claustrophobic air. The oppressive darkness clung to them like a shroud, and even though Kayriss was getting used to the close quarters of the underground, something about this place felt wrong, as if the earth itself was holding its breath.

"Keep moving," she whispered, though her voice sounded small in the gloom. Every inch they progressed, the weight in her chest grew heavier. She could hear the faint murmurings ahead now, low and rhythmic, like some dark chant carried on a cold, unseen wind.

Finally, after what felt like an eternity, the tunnel widened. The ground sloped upward, and a distant light's faint, sickly glow reached them. Kayriss quickened her pace, eager to escape the crushing confines of the tunnel. She pulled herself up and out into an expansive cavern and stopped dead.

A great chasm stretched before them, a pit of impossible depth, its blackness swallowing the feeble light. The murmurings were louder here, coming from the edge of the pit where figures were gathered, small, shadowy shapes that Kayriss recognised immediately: scourge foxes. Their amber eyes gleamed faintly in the gloom as they moved in eerie unison, their heads bowed, their voices chanting in a language Kayriss couldn't understand. Quickly, she cast her animal conversing spell, but nothing happened. The words remained foreign, dark and old.

Before her, the foxes began throwing themselves into the pit. The last one, without hesitation, teetered on the edge of the abyss for a heartbeat, then threw itself into the void. Kayriss felt her stomach lurch as she watched it vanish into the darkness, swallowed without a sound. She was too far, and their jump was too unexpected for her to assist.

For a moment, there was only silence, the murmurings gone, replaced by the vast stillness of the pit.

Then came the laugh.

It started as a low growl, deep and resonant, vibrating through the stone beneath her feet. The laugh built in volume, a terrible, rasping sound that sent shivers racing down her spine. Kayriss' eyes widened as something stirred in the darkness below, and the pit seemed to come alive.

Slowly, from the abyss, a massive form began to rise.

A pair of purple eyes, great, slitted orbs burning with malevolent light, emerged first from the shadows, gleaming like twin stars in the blackness. Then came the rest of it: an enormous obsidian dragon, her body coiled with impossible grace as she pulled herself up from the depths.

Nyxsarathryn.

Her vast, serpentine body was covered in glossy black scales that shimmered like glass in the dim light. Laced between the obsidian plates were streaks of deep violet, veins of power that pulsed like molten lava beneath her skin. The scales along her spine were jagged, like shards of broken crystal, and her massive and leathery wings unfurled from her sides with a sound like stone grinding against stone. Her breath rattled the air as if the earth trembled in her presence.

She was terrifying and beautiful, a creature of immense, dark power. As she rose higher, her long and curved claws dug into the edge of the pit, and her massive head turned toward the figures at the edge of the chasm.

Kayriss's heart pounded in her chest. She had heard of Nyxsarathryn, the Goddess in Shadow, from Ayleigh, but the story did no justice to the sight before her. The dragon's eyes glowed with an intelligence far beyond any mortal's understanding, ancient and cold. Her presence dominated the cavern, a force of nature made flesh.

Then Kayriss saw them, two figures standing frozen at the pit's edge. One was a woman, hu-man, her face pale with terror. The other was a Night One, his dark eyes wide as he tried and failed to move the woman. They stood as if trapped in a nightmare, unable to escape the dragon's gaze.

Nyxsarathryn's great head loomed over them, her purple eyes fixed on the woman. Like the grinding of ancient stones, a low, rumbling voice rolled from her throat.

"Welcome... my child."

The words dripped with a terrible mockery, and Kayriss couldn't see Elara's face from this distance, but she could feel the horror radiating. The woman, Elara, was frozen in place, her body rigid as if held by invisible chains.

Kayriss' breath caught in her throat. "No..." she whispered.

Beside her, Isaac clambered out of the tunnel, his face pale as his eyes took in the sight before him. He froze, staring at the great dragon that had pulled itself from the pit.

"Nyxsarathryn," Isaac breathed, his voice barely audible. "Gods..."

Kayriss glanced at him, fear mingling with desperation. She could see the shock on his face, the disbelief. Unlike this, none of them had truly believed the stories of the Shadow Goddess. Now, standing before her, there was no denying the horror of what lay beneath their world.

Nyxsarathryn shifted her great wings, the leathery sound echoing through the cavern as her gaze lingered on Elara. The Night One beside her tried to pull her away, but his efforts were futile. The dragon's eyes were locked on her, a predator watching its prey.

Kayriss felt the weight of the moment pressing down on her. Elara was in terrible danger. They all were. She turned quickly to Isaac and the rest of their party, her voice sharp and urgent.

"Prepare yourselves!" she hissed. "We don't have much time."

Isaac's hand was already on the hilt of his blade, his eyes never leaving the towering form of Nyxsarathryn. The rest of their group moved with practised efficiency, weapons drawn, eyes wide with fear but determined. They had come too far to turn back now.

Nyxsarathryn's laughter echoed through the chamber, a sound so cold and filled with malice that it made Kayriss' blood run cold. The dragon lifted her head slightly, the violet veins pulsing across her dark, obsidian body.

"You cannot run," Nyxsarathryn rumbled, her voice filling the cavern. "There is no escape. You are mine now, little ones. All of you."

The darkness seemed to close around them, the shadows growing thicker as Nyxsarathryn's presence filled the space. Kayriss' heart pounded in her chest, her breath coming in short, sharp bursts.

From the depths of the pit, another sound filled their ears. Something else began to rise.

Kayriss tightened her grip on her staff, her eyes darting from the looming dragon to the pit's edge, where the darkness writhed and churned.

Something terrible was coming and they were standing in the heart of it.

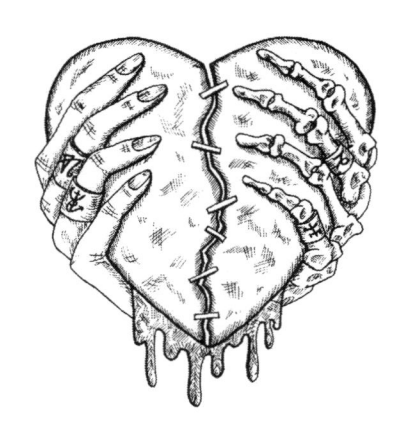

Chapter Sixty-Nine
Elara and Kayriss
Hope fades.

"

Below her, Elara saw the new party of mixed characters, one of which she recognised in her soul. Another human. A male. He was standing with a motley group of animals and humanoids who were readying themselves for battle.

Kayriss and the others were moving into position, their weapons drawn, eyes wide with fear and determination. Isaac, Kayriss, Granite, Grind, Browntail, Cutlass Serafin and Hooth are ready to fight to save her. But before they could strike, the ground trembled, and from the pit below came a sound that made Elara's blood run cold.

A soft chittering, like a swarm of insects. But it wasn't insects.

Pitter... Patter... Pitter... Patter... Pitter... Patter...

Rats—hundreds, thousands—swarmed up from the darkness below, their eyes gleaming in the dim light. They moved as one, a tide of writhing, squirming bodies surging toward the group.

Granite was the first to react. He charged at the swarm with a roar, his hammer swinging wildly as he tried to crush the vermin beneath his feet. There were too many. The rats crawled up his legs, biting and clawing, pulling him down.

"Granite!" Kayriss screamed, but there was nothing she could do. Grind was already running to his aid, but the swarm engulfed the younger Mine Folk in moments. Granite's roar turned to a gurgling scream as the rats overwhelmed him, dragging him to the ground. His body was buried beneath the tide, his struggles growing weaker until there was only the sound of gnawing and the crunch of bone.

Elara's stomach twisted in horror. She couldn't look away as Granite's form was consumed, eaten alive by the ravenous swarm. The sight of it, the grotesque, merciless death, made bile rise in her throat. She wanted to scream, but the terror choked her.

Nyxsarathryn's presence boomed over the chittering, her command unspoken yet absolute. The rats stopped, their eyes glowing as they lined the pit's edge, their bodies twitching, ready to attack at the dragon's order.

"Do not move, little play things," the dragon commanded, her voice carrying a terrifying authority. *"Unless you wish to join your friend in the rat's stomach. Chomp chomp..."*

Kayriss and the others froze, weapons still drawn but useless in the face of Nyxsarathryn's power. Isaac's knuckles were white around the hilt of his sword; his eyes locked on the dragon as if trying to calculate some impossible way to defeat her. There was no way out. The rats waited, twitching and chittering, their hunger barely contained.

Nyxsarathryn shifted her grip on Elara, turning her attention toward Isaac. Her eyes gleamed with something wicked, something darkly amused.

"Step forward," she purred, her voice as smooth as glass. *"Isaac."*

Elara's heart skipped a beat. How did she know his name? She could feel the dragon's malevolent intent wrapping itself around them like a noose, tightening with every word. Isaac hesitated, glancing at Kayriss and the others, but there was no choice. Slowly, he stepped forward, his face set in grim determination.

Nyxsarathryn tilted her massive head, her violet eyes narrowing with satisfaction. *"Here,"* she said, her voice a dark, mocking whisper. *"I made you something."*

With a flick of her claw, she threw Elara toward Isaac.

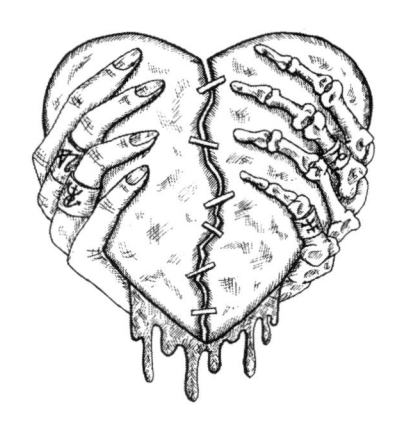

Chapter Seventy
Elara and Kayriss
Darkness is here.

Elara barely had time to scream before she crashed into him, knocking them both to the ground. Isaac's arms wrapped around her instinctively, breaking her fall as they tumbled across the stone floor. The impact left her breathless, her body trembling with shock and fear.

The moment Elara and Isaac collided, something happened.

It started as a low vibration beneath the stone floor, barely perceptible at first, but it quickly grew. Isaac's arms had instinctively wrapped around Elara, and as their bodies touched, skin against skin, a pulse of dark energy rippled out from them. The cold, lifeless stone beneath their feet began to hum and then shudder.

Like distant thunder, the rumble was soft at first, but it built rapidly, shaking the entire cavern. Dust and small stones fell from the ceiling, and the edges of the pit trembled as if something deep below had stirred in response. A few rats lost their grip and tumbled backwards, disappearing entirely.

Nyxsarathryn paused, her violet eyes narrowing as her massive head tilted slightly. Her attention suddenly fixed on Elara and Isaac.

"There. My little Darktouch has set the wheels in motion. Soon, the human spirits will return from the alter realm where they went when they all died out. Where I sent them." The dragon hissed, her eyes gleaming with sadistic delight. *"Then I can torment them all again."*

Her purple eyes glinted with glee.

For a heartbeat, everything went still. Then, the ground beneath their feet heaved violently as though the ancient, dormant power of the earth itself had awakened. Rats fell in number as they tumbled to the floor. Hooth took flight, scooping up the two otters from the shaking floor.

Kayriss gasped, stumbling backwards, her staff clattering to the floor as the rumbling intensified. Still holding Elara, Isaac glanced confusedly at her, then back at the dragon. His grip tightened protectively around Elara out of instinct, but he, too, was shaken. The floor beneath them felt alive, like some force had been unleashed, something neither understood. The air in the cavern changed. It became heavy, oppressive, charged with the sensation that something had shifted, something fundamental, something wrong. A deep, unsettling sense of dread swept the entire chamber, gripping everyone present. Nyxsarathryn's amused expression faltered, her eyes darkening as she observed the sudden disturbance.

The rats stopped moving from the pit's edge, their twitching bodies frozen in eerie stillness as if awaiting a command they did not yet understand. They, too, seemed jolted by the shudder, and they looked around bemused at each other. Even the shadows seemed to pull back, wary of whatever had just been set in motion.

The silence that followed the rumbling was suffocating, as if the world had taken a breath and held it.

Isaac's gaze flicked between Elara and the floor beneath them, his brow furrowing in confusion. "What... what is this?" he whispered, his voice barely audible over the lingering tremor in the stone.

Elara, her heart racing, could barely find words. She could feel it, the energy coursing between them, the strange, electric charge that seemed to hum through their skin and into the very bones of the earth. It wasn't just magic. It was something far older, something primal. And it felt as though it had been waiting for them.

"I... don't know," she whispered, her voice trembling. Her hands were still pressed against Isaac's chest, and she could feel the same power pulse resonating through him. It was terrifying and overwhelming, a force they couldn't control. "But I think... we've done something. Something terrible."

Nyxsarathryn hissed, the sound sharp and full of anger. *"What have you done?"* she growled, her wings shifting, her massive claws scraping against the stone as she moved toward them. The ground rumbled again, but this time, it wasn't her doing; it was the chaos power from Isaac and Elara, surging uncontrollably beneath the stone.

The ominous feeling grew, wrapping around them like a suffocating fog. The sense of something being torn, ripped open, was palpable as if reality had been wounded.

Kayriss staggered backwards, eyes wide. "Something's wrong," she said, her voice tight with fear. "Something's breaking... this wasn't supposed to happen."

Isaac and Elara stood frozen in the centre of the chaos, the hum of power between them growing louder and more insistent. It felt as if they had become the eye of some vast storm, and everything around them—Nyxsarathryn, the cavern, the world itself—was being drawn into the vortex.

With a deep, resounding crack, the floor split beneath their feet.

A jagged fissure raced through the stone, snaking out in all directions, as though the very foundation of the earth was breaking apart. Nyxsarathryn recoiled, her enormous body shifting back in surprise, her wings flaring wide as she let out a low, furious growl.

"You fools," the dragon spat, her voice filled with cold rage. *"You've torn the veil. You don't even know what you've done."*

Elara's heart pounded in her chest as the total weight of the situation crashed over her. The fissure beneath them pulsed with an unnatural light, a profound, violent energy that seemed to seep from the earth. She could feel and sense that something beyond their understanding had been unleashed, and whatever it was, it had changed everything.

"You were supposed to fall for each other," Nyxsarathryn continued. She was furious with an anger unleashed from years of planning ruined. *"You've betrothed yourselves to others! You are the wrong halves!"*

Isaac stared at the crack in the ground, horror dawning on his face. The energy between them had calmed slightly, but the damage was already done. Whatever spell they had completed, whatever ancient force they had awoken, was now loose in the world.

Around them, the rats stirred again, their eyes glowing with a renewed, more sinister light. The air was tense, and even the dragon seemed uncertain of what would come next.

Kayriss, now standing with her staff back in hand, whispered, "Life as we know it... it's been torn. Everything is about to change."

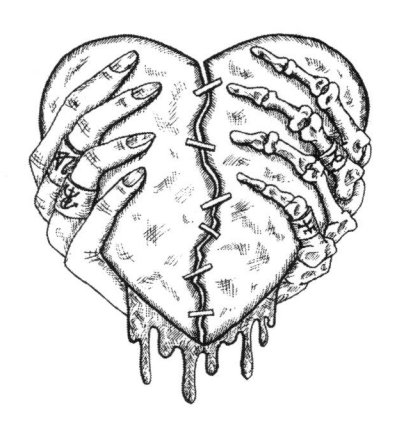

Chapter Seventy-One
Nyxsarathryn
Fury unleashed.

The air in the cavern was thick with tension, the lingering rumble of the earth beneath Elara and Isaac still reverberating through the stones. All eyes were now on Nyxsarathryn. The great obsidian dragon loomed above them, her violet eyes blazing with fury. The ominous crack in the ground pulsed with unnatural energy, but even that seemed insignificant compared to the raw rage radiating from the dragon.

Nyxsarathryn's gaze flicked between Elara and Isaac, her lips curling back to reveal rows of gleaming teeth. Her body coiled like a snake preparing to strike, obsidian scales shimmering with a faint, menacing glow. The vast cavern seemed to darken around her, the shadows deepening as if the very air recoiled from the creature's fury.

"*You fools,*" she hissed, her voice low and venomous. "*You've torn apart what was carefully woven for centuries.*" Her eyes narrowed, locking on Elara first, then Isaac, her rage palpable. "*I was so close... so close to restoring my dominion over the human filth. And you... you... have ruined everything.*"

Still reeling from the pulse of power that had erupted from their touch, Elara felt the full weight of Nyxsarathryn's words. Her heart hammered in her chest as the dragon's fury washed over her, suffocating in its intensity. She had never felt so small, so powerless, in her life. Isaac stood beside her, sword clenched, but even he seemed frozen in the face of the dragon's wrath.

Nyxsarathryn's enormous head turned slowly, her gaze settling on Kayriss. The dragon's eyes gleamed with sudden, dark understanding. Kayriss took an instinctive step back, gripping her staff tightly, her breath catching in her throat.

"*And you,*" Nyxsarathryn growled, her voice laced with a vicious kind of satisfaction. "*You hide a secret from them. From all of them.*" Her violet eyes bore into Kayriss as if peeling away layers of her very soul. "*But not from me.*"

Kayriss froze, dread flickering across her face. "*Say nothing, dragon...*" It was a threat that made even the mighty dragon stop in her tracks for just a moment.

Nyxsarathryn then let out a sound that was half growl, half laughter, a terrible rumble that shook the air. "*You carry his child,*" she bellowed, her voice echoing through the chamber. "*Isaac's child.*"

The words struck Isaac like a blow. His eyes widened in shock as he watched Kayriss's hand instinctively reach her stomach. She hadn't had time to tell him; there never seemed the right time... Kayriss looked over at him, half fearing that he would be angry or leave with this new human woman—someone his race, someone that didn't look like nature was invading her very body. The dragon's words rang out with a terrible certainty. Around them, the others stood in stunned silence, eyes darting between Kayriss and Isaac, all looking equally bewildered.

Nyxsarathryn's massive head tilted, her mouth curling into a cruel smile. *"How delicious. A child born of forbidden blood, conceived in defiance of the natural order. Another nail in the coffin of the world you all seek to protect."*

Kayriss's heart pounded as the weight of the revelation settled over her. Her body trembled, not from fear of the dragon, but from realising what this meant for her, Isaac, and their future. She had never felt more vulnerable, more exposed.

"And now you know. Now you realise what you aberrant mutations have done," Nyxsarathryn sneered, her voice dripping with mockery and hate. *"Such a fragile thing, hiding in plain sight. A mistake, just like the rest of you."*

Isaac looked at Kayriss, his mouth opening to speak, but the words were stolen from him by the dragon's oppressive presence.

No words were needed.

Amidst the terror of the looming dragon, as the cavern trembled and shadows clawed at the edges of their world, Isaac's gaze found Kayriss. Everything else fell away for a moment: the rumbling earth, the dragon's fury, and even the dark fate unfolding around them. His heart swelled as he looked at her, standing firm despite the danger. The flicker of light danced across her face, illuminating the fierce determination in her eyes, and in that instant, all he could feel was love, pure and undeniable. It was as though the chaos had no power over him, no meaning, except that it brought him closer to her. She was his anchor, the bright, undeniable force in a world spiralling into darkness. And though death lingered in the air, Isaac realised there was nothing he wouldn't face for her, nothing that could make him look away from the woman who had become everything to him.

Kayriss knew in that briefest of seconds that he was there for her, no matter what.

In those moments, Nyxsarathryn's attention shifted, her gaze moving toward the rising figure of Tallin, who was beginning to stir. He groaned, pushing himself up from the cold stone, his hand pressed to his head where Nyxsarathryn had knocked him unconscious earlier. His eyes flicked around the cavern in confusion, finally landing on the towering form of the dragon.

The moment Nyxsarathryn saw him regain consciousness, her fury reignited. Her violet eyes flared, her body coiling as if preparing to strike again. *"And you,"* she spat, her voice a thunderous roar that echoed through the chamber. *"You pathetic wretch. You were supposed to be my tool, my weapon to shape the Night Ones. But you've allowed yourself to be ruined by weakness... by her!"* She gestured toward Elara with one enormous claw; her teeth bared in disgust.

Tallin, still dazed, tried to stand, but his legs wobbled beneath him. He opened his mouth to speak, to protest, but Nyxsarathryn cut him off with a deafening roar that shook the cavern walls.

"You ruined everything!" the dragon bellowed, her rage boiling. *"All of you! I had centuries of planning, of manipulation, and you... you mortals have undone it in a single moment! Do you have any idea what you've unleashed? What you've brought upon yourselves?! I was just wanting my playthings back so I can break them again. You mutants were nothing, but now? You'll feel the same wraith."*

The floor rumbled beneath them again, but it wasn't from any spell this time. It was from the dragon's fury, her power shaking the very foundation of the earth. Her great wings unfurled, casting a shadow over the entire cavern as she reared back, her eyes blazing with pure, unbridled hatred.

With a savage growl, Nyxsarathryn turned her gaze upward. Her massive clawed hand shot toward the ceiling, her talons wrapping around a jagged stalactite as easily as a child might pluck a flower. Heavy and sharp stone formation snapped free with a loud crack, sending dust and debris falling to the cavern floor.

The others watched in stunned horror as Nyxsarathryn lifted the stalactite high, her intention clear. Kayriss's heart lurched in her chest as the dragon turned toward her, her eyes blazing with murderous intent.

"*You,*" Nyxsarathryn hissed, her voice dripping with venom. *"I will crush you and your bitch child first."*

Kayriss barely had time to react. Nyxsarathryn, with a snarl of rage, hurled the jagged stalactite through the air, aiming directly at her.

The world seemed to slow as the enormous spear of rock hurtled toward Kayriss, the deadly point gleaming in the dim light. Isaac screamed her name, but there was no time.

No time to move, no time to defend.

Kayriss raised her hand, eyes wide in terror as the shadow of death descended.

The world she knew...

...ended.

Chapter Seventy-Two
Isaac
Sacrifice.

The world seemed to slow as Nyxsarathryn's roar echoed through the cavern, her massive claws ripping the stalactite from the ceiling with terrifying ease. Isaac barely had time to register the deadly shard of rock, jagged and sharp, as it hurtled toward Kayriss. His heart slammed in his chest, and in that instant, everything else faded away... the dragon's fury, the tremors beneath his feet, even the suffocating dread that hung in the air.

All he could see was her.

Kayriss stood frozen, her wide eyes reflecting the looming shadow of death as the stalactite cut through the air. Isaac felt something deep within him ignite, a primal, desperate instinct. His mind filled with only one thought:

Save her. Save them both.

Without a second thought, he moved.

Isaac's muscles screamed in protest as he pushed off the ground, flinging himself toward Kayriss with all his strength. His body crashed into hers just as the stalactite came barrelling down. He caught the fear in her eyes, the shock as he threw her aside. His arms wrapped around her, his only desire to protect her, to shield her from the fate that awaited.

For a fleeting moment, their eyes met, his filled with love, hers wide with disbelief. He wished he could have told her everything he felt, that at this moment, as the world crumbled around them, she was all that mattered. He wanted to talk about the child growing inside her, about how much hope it had filled him with.

There was no time.

The force of the impact sent Kayriss tumbling to the ground, and for an instant, Isaac knew he had done it.

He had saved them, but then the searing pain hit.

The stalactite slammed into his back, its jagged edge tearing through muscle and bone, driving deep into his body. The world around him exploded in agony, a white, hot, searing pain that stole the breath from his lungs. He gasped, the taste of blood filling his mouth as his legs buckled beneath him.

Isaac collapsed to the ground, the weight of the stalactite pinning him in place. His vision blurred, dark spots creeping at the edges as the life drained from his body. Even as the pain coursed through him, his mind remained on

Kayriss. His heartbeat not with fear but with love. For her, for the child, he hadn't known was growing inside her. His hand reached out, trembling, to where she lay only feet away. He wanted to touch and feel her warmth one last time, but his strength was fading too quickly. "Kayriss…" His voice was weak, barely a whisper, but he prayed she heard him.

Kayriss turned, her face etched in horror as she scrambled to her knees, crawling toward him. "Isaac, no… No!" Her voice cracked, filled with disbelief and raw pain as she saw the jagged stone piercing his body, the life slipping from his eyes. Isaac's vision was clouding now, and the world was growing dim around him. He could barely feel the pain anymore, only the distant echo of it. His body was heavy and growing colder by the second. Through it all, he forced a smile for her. It was a small, fragile thing, but it held all the love he could no longer speak.

"I… I'm sorry," he whispered, his voice broken, his chest heaving with shallow breaths. "I… I had to…"

Kayriss's hands wrapped around his, her tears falling onto his bloodied skin. Her voice was a choked sob. "I'll heal you… Hold on."

His heart ached at her words, but there was no time left. He could feel it slipping away, like sand through his fingers. All he could think about was the child they had created, the future he wouldn't be there to see. He had saved them, hadn't he? They were still alive. That was all that mattered.

"Live," he whispered, his eyes struggling to stay open, his gaze fixed on hers. "For… for both of you…"

Kayriss wept as Isaac's hand slipped from hers, the light in his eyes fading as his last breath left his body. His chest stilled, the warmth of life quickly draining from him, leaving only cold silence. Kayriss stared at him, her heart shattering into a thousand pieces. The man she loved, the father of her child, lay before her, his body lifeless, a sacrifice made in the face of the impossible. She felt as if the world had been ripped out from under her, her soul torn apart by the sight of Isaac's broken body. She screamed a raw, anguished sound that echoed through the cavern. Even in her grief, something else stirred within her. A spark of rage, of unyielding fury, lit deep inside her chest, spreading like wildfire. Isaac's sacrifice would not be in vain. The child he had given his life to protect would live.

Her hand clenched into a fist, and she felt the power. It surged through her like a rising storm, flooding her veins with heat and raw energy, far more than she had ever felt. Grief, love, pain, and fury all swirled together, fueling the magic that crackled around her, making the air hum with potential.

Nyxsarathryn had turned her head, her great violet eyes narrowing as she realised what was happening. The dragon, who had been filled with smug triumph moments ago, now regarded Kayriss with a new wariness.

Kayriss stood slowly, her eyes locked onto Nyxsarathryn. She was no longer trembling or afraid. Her magic surged within her, crackling in the air, building in strength. She raised her head, staring into the eyes of the dragon who had stolen everything from her.

"You've made a terrible mistake," Kayriss whispered, her voice low, trembling with power.

The air around her began to shimmer, and the ground beneath her feet trembled as she gathered her strength. Her magic was building, ready to be unleashed. Nyxsarathryn growled, sensing the power shift. Kayriss didn't flinch, her grief transforming into something unstoppable.

This fight wasn't over, and she would make sure Nyxsarathryn paid.

Chapter Seventy-Three
Kayriss
Vengeance.

The air around Kayriss hummed with new and untamed energy, the pulse of life surging through her veins. The grief that had shattered her heart was now fuel for something deeper, something primal. Nature called to her, wrapping its arms around her soul, whispering ancient truths into her ears.

Isaac's lifeless body lay at her feet, but the earth was alive beneath her, rumbling, restless. She could feel the ground like it was her flesh, feel the roots below stirring as her magic blossomed. The world began to shift around her, and the cavern trembled as if bracing for what was to come.

As Isaac lay there, flowers, grass and life sprung up under him, laying his lifeless body on a blanket of nature.

Kayriss closed her eyes, letting the magic take hold of her. She felt herself becoming one with the natural forces that surged through the air and earth, her body no longer just her own but an extension of something far older, far more powerful. She could feel the rhythm of the trees, the pull of the vines, the surge of growth and decay all around her.

Her wings, once delicate, began to expand. They stretched outward, the soft veins replaced with vines that twisted and spiraled, thick and tangled, alive with movement. They grew wider and larger until they spanned the entire cavern, a living tapestry of emerald leaves and twisting roots. They whispered with the sound of wind through a forest, crackling like dry branches and rustling like grass in a storm.

Kayriss's hair, dark and loose, began to lengthen, thickening into long, twisting vines that seemed to have a life of their own. They coiled and twisted like serpents, woven with leaves and blossoms, some blooming with brilliant colours, others darkening with the shadows of her grief. They slithered down her shoulders, each vine moving as though alive, swaying in rhythm with the earth's pulse.

Her skin turned pale, a glowing alabaster white, but there was something else beneath it, something green, like the first hint of spring beneath the melting snow. Veins of shimmering emerald light threaded through her skin, pulsating like sap in ancient trees. Her hands elongated, her fingers growing into sharp, thorned claws, wicked and natural, like the talons of a great predator.

She was no longer Elven.

She was nature's wrath incarnate, an elemental force of the earth itself.

Kayriss opened her eyes, which now glowed with a fierce green light, and her voice thundered through the cavern, commanding all life around her. "Rats!" she called out, her voice vibrating with the primal language of the wild. "You are free; turn against the one who enslaved you!"

Now released from Nyxsarathryn's dark control, the horde of rats swarmed as if hearing their true master for the first time. The massive horde moved like a flood, black bodies twisting and writhing in unison. They turned their beady eyes toward the towering dragon and rushed forward with a chittering chorus, their teeth bared, claws scratching against the stone as they surged up Nyxsarathryn's obsidian scales.

Nyxsarathryn roared in frustration, thrashing her massive tail as the rats climbed her body, biting and gnawing at her with relentless fury. Though they were not powerful enough to truly harm her, their sheer number overwhelmed her. They covered her like a living blanket, swarming over her wings, legs, and long snout, snapping at her eyes, tearing at her scales.

Kayriss watched, feeling the power building within her still, the transformation taking its true hold. The rats gave her time, biting and clawing at the dragon, buying her the precious moments she needed. Nyxsarathryn, distracted, flailed and struggled against the tide of creatures, her roars echoing through the cavern like the thunder of a coming storm.

Looking down at everyone left standing, she motioned with a now-clawed hand down the tunnel her party had entered. It became illuminated, with fireflies appearing from nowhere to guide their path.

"Friends. You must leave. It is not safe." She said, her voice sounding like nature's very essence.

Grind grabbed Ayleigh, who had become distraught at her missing family, and barrelled off down the tunnel. Hooth moved to Isaac's side, grabbing his bow and quiver that had scattered from his back and took to the air, firing at the dragon to give the party more chance to escape.

Cutlass leapt and bounded up to the hole, but when she arrived, she realised Browntail was missing. Turning, she looked frantically for her captain and saw him leaping over the devastation towards the stumbling Night One. Rocks fell for the ceiling as he darted between them, one crashing down close enough for Cutlass to scream out loud in panic. As Browntail got to Tallin's side, he rifled through his pouch, finding a small piece of metal. He jammed it into the handcuff lock and worked fervently to unlock it.

"Come now lad, we may be needing you. While I work on these, pick me up and maybe get us the hell out of here?"

Tallin was still groggy, but the otter made sense. He hoisted him up and dashed Elara's side. He reached her as another stalagmite fell from the ceiling. Again, Cutlass roared in panic; her small voice lost among the deafening roar of Nyxsarathryn.

Edgar, however, was at Isaac's side, lying next to his fallen master. Kayriss could feel the sadness emanating from the dog. She looked towards Tallin, realising they were the last few in the cavern.

"Night One. You have seen the truth of this world. Take Edgar with you. Do not let any more of the world's life suffer."

Tallin nodded and pulled the reluctant dog away from the body. Searfin snatched the screaming Cutlass as the remaining people bolted for the hole.

Kayriss looked down. Granite was dead. Her Isaac ripped from her.

Kayriss felt the final pieces of her transformation snap into place as the dragon struggled and rage burned like a fire within her. Her wings unfurled fully, casting shadows of vines and leaves across the stone. Now a crown of writhing vines and thorns, her hair reached past her hips, alive with the hum of magic. She felt the earth beneath her feet, the roots deep below, and the wild power of the natural world flowing through her like a river at flood. She rose in height. Two... Three... four feet taller. She was now no longer simply Kayriss, the druid. She was something more ancient and fiercer, a spirit born of the forest, of the earth's untamed might. She could feel the world's heartbeat within her, a steady, powerful thrum that drove her forward.

Nyxsarathryn finally ripped the rats from her face with a snarl, her violet eyes blazing with fury. She saw what Kayriss had become, her massive body coiling with rage. *"You dare stand against me?"* she roared, her voice shaking the very walls of the cavern.

Kayriss's voice rang out, calm and assertive, echoing with the voice of the wild. "I am the earth beneath you, Nyxsarathryn. The wind that whispers through the trees. You will not destroy this world."

With a single, mighty beat of her wings, Kayriss took to the air, vines spiralling in her wake like the roots of ancient trees tearing free from the earth. She soared upward with a force that shook the cavern itself, her wings cutting through the dark like blades of nature's wrath.

Nyxsarathryn hissed in fury, lashing out with her tail, but Kayriss was too fast. She flew straight for the dragon, the air crackling with the power of her magic, and slammed into Nyxsarathryn with the force of a hurricane.

The impact was deafening. The ground shook as the two forces collided, Kayriss's elemental strength crashing against the dragon's ancient might. Their bodies tumbled together, vines twisting and coiling around Nyxsarathryn's obsidian form as Kayriss pushed with all her might.

With a roar of effort, Kayriss surged upward, driving the dragon back. Nyxsarathryn let out a guttural scream, her claws scraping at the stone as she tried to anchor herself, but Kayriss was relentless, pushing her higher and higher.

The cavern's ceiling cracked and split as they crashed upward, stone and dust raining down as the force of their battle broke through the earth itself. They burst through the ceiling and into the open sky, the cold morning air rushing around them.

For the first time in eight hundred years, sunlight bathed Nyxsarathryn's obsidian scales, but it was not the light that was triumphant—it was Kayriss. Her vines lashed out, rooting into the dragon's wings, tearing at her scales, and with a final, mighty push, Kayriss threw Nyxsarathryn up into the sky.

The dragon screamed as she was hurled away, her massive body spiralling out of control, crashing into the outskirts of the Night One city above. Kayriss hovered in the air, her wings beating slowly, her glowing green eyes locked onto the dragon as she crashed into the earth below.

Nyxsarathyrn glowered at Kayriss, her sharp teeth glinting in the sunlight. Kayriss knew now she had the power to finish it.

Nature itself was on her side.

Chapter Seventy-Four
Grind
Sunlight.

Grind's heart pounded in his chest as he scrambled through the crumbling tunnels, the weight of Granite's death still fresh in his mind. The stench of blood and death filled his nostrils, but there was no time for mourning. Kayriss was up there, facing off against Nyxsarathryn herself, and all he could do was lead the others out of this collapsing labyrinth.

His legs burned as he pushed the remaining party members forward, Elara, dazed but alive, and Tallin, barely keeping up, still nursing the wounds from his earlier skirmish. He was also carrying an otter dressed as a pirate working diligently on his cuffed hands.

Isaac was dead... Granite was dead... Too many had fallen, but they'd be next if they didn't move. The tunnel walls shook with the force of the battle raging above them, sending rocks tumbling down like hail.

"Hurry!" Grind shouted, his voice hoarse from dust and despair. "This whole place is coming down!"

Behind him, Elara stumbled, her eyes distant as if still trapped in the darkness of Nyxsarathryn's pit. Grind grabbed her by the arm, dragging her forward. "We don't have time to freeze now! Kayriss needs us to make it out!"

As they moved, they realised that they were being followed.

Grind cursed life itself. They were in no shape to deal with the rats again, but no pitter or patter came. Gingerly, around the corner, a skulk of scourge foxes peered at them, not knowing where they'd be safest. Ayleigh ran to them and into the arms of her father. She motioned for them to run with the party, and they nodded, unsure of the weird collection of human kids in front of them.

Finally, they burst out into the open air from the underground network. Grind skidded to a halt, gasping for breath. The sky above was ablaze with violent clashes of green and violet light, the storm of power so fierce that even the very clouds seemed to part for it.

There, high above, Kayriss, now transformed into a spirit of nature, fought the obsidian dragon Nyxsarathryn in a battle that dwarfed anything Grind had ever seen. Kayriss's wings were a mass of vines, leaves, and raw life energy, while the dragon was a nightmare of black scales and violet fire. Their power clashed in bursts that sent shockwaves through the sky, and with each impact, the ground beneath Grind's feet trembled.

"Gods above," Tallin muttered, his voice thick with awe and fear. "She's... fighting that thing." He blinked against the light, not used to being in the sunlight without his visor.

Grind could barely speak, the sight above him paralysing in its grandeur. The dragon's tail lashed through the air like a whip, but Kayriss dodged with the grace of a hawk, her body glowing with the strength of the earth. The two titanic beings collided again, the force sending a tremor through the ground.

Grind watched, helpless, as Kayriss flung vines at Nyxsarathryn, attempting to bind the dragon's wings. For a moment, it seemed to work. The dragon roared in frustration, pinned down by nature itself. But then, with a vicious snarl, Nyxsarathryn tore free, snapping the vines like threads.

The dragon's maw opened wide, unleashing a stream of violet flames toward Kayriss, who barely managed to deflect them with a shield of swirling leaves. The fire scorched the sky, filling the air with the acrid stench of burning life, and the battle only seemed to intensify.

"We have to do something," Elara said, her voice shaking with terror. "We can't just stand here!"

Grind clenched his fists. "What can we do? That's not a fight for us."

The earth cracked beneath their feet as if in answer, reminding them how close this battle was to ripping the land apart. The massive aperture in the ground where Nyxsarathryn had first emerged yawned open nearby, its jagged edges glowing with the residual magic of the dragon's power. In the distance, Grind could see the towering silhouette of the Night One's Obsidian Citadel, a grim, foreboding spire of black stone looming over the horizon. Internally, he was glad that they hadn't got that far.

"This is where it all leads, isn't it?" Grind muttered, his eyes flickering between the Citadel and the battle. "It all comes back to them. The Night Ones." He looked over at Tallin, who was shielding himself from the sun's brilliance, clearly not used to being above ground without cover. Elara ripped a length of cloth from her clothing and allowed Tallin to cover his eyes from the brightness. Grind noted that she was helping him, her captor, in his hour of need.

The ground shook again, and Grind's attention returned to the sky. Kayriss had managed to land a heavy blow on Nyxsarathryn, sending the dragon spiralling downward. The creature crashed into the earth, its obsidian scales cracking under the force. For a brief moment, it seemed like Kayriss might have the upper hand.

With terrifying speed, Nyxsarathryn reared up and lashed out, her massive jaws closing around Kayriss's wing. The dragon's fangs sank deep into Kayriss's living flesh, and Grind's stomach twisted as a sharp scream of pain echoed through the air. Kayriss's wings faltered, her radiant light dimming for the first time.

"No!" Grind shouted, taking an involuntary step forward as if he could somehow reach her. "Kayriss!"

The dragon roared in triumph, violet flames licking at her wounded foe, but even as blood dripped from the gaping wound, Kayriss did not fall. Instead, a furious burst of green energy erupted from her body, pushing Nyxsarathryn back and forcing the dragon to release her hold.

Wounded but not defeated, Kayriss rose higher into the sky, her form trembling with power. She pointed a single clawed hand toward the massive aperture in the earth, the entrance to the dragon's domain.

"You will not escape again," she growled, her voice echoing with the force of the wind, the trees, and the very earth itself.

With a mighty gesture, Kayriss called upon the rocks and soil, pulling them from the very bones of the earth. The ground began to shift and move, the mouth of the pit narrowing as stones rolled into place, sealing the opening shut. Nyxsarathryn, realising what was happening, let out a furious, deafening roar. The dragon's wings flared, but before she could take flight, a massive boulder slammed into her side, knocking her back into the depths.

The rocks closed in around her, faster and faster, until only a narrow slit of light remained. Nyxsarathryn's violet eyes glared out from the darkness, filled with pure, undiluted hatred. The dragon screamed one last curse at Kayriss as the final rock slid into place, sealing her into the earth.

Silence fell over the battlefield.

Grind collapsed to his knees, his body shaking from the sheer intensity of what he had just witnessed. The world around them seemed to hold its breath, afraid to move in the aftermath of such devastation.

Kayriss floated slowly back down to the ground, her wings folding behind her. Her body was battered and bloodied but still standing. Her glowing eyes softened as she touched the earth beneath her, sealing the last remnants of the pit.

Grind could see the Obsidian Citadel looming nearby, dark and ominous, a reminder that the battle was far from over. Nyxsarathryn had been wounded, but she was not dead. Whatever she had planned, whatever the chaos caused by her spell going so cataclysmically wrong, would be revealed.

For now, there was only quiet… the quiet after a storm.

Kayriss, still in her elemental form, walked toward Isaac's fallen body, her steps slow, heavy with grief. She'd shrunk to her usual height but kept all the new additions to her form and features.

Isaac's body had been brought out of the cave by an undulating mass of flowers and grass, a natural carpet lifting her fallen love. The wind whispered through the trees as she knelt beside him, her fingers brushing against his cold hand. Grind swallowed hard, his heart aching as he watched the woman who had just saved them all crumple to her knees beside the man she had lost.

He watched his friend burst into the tears of a heart wrenched open.

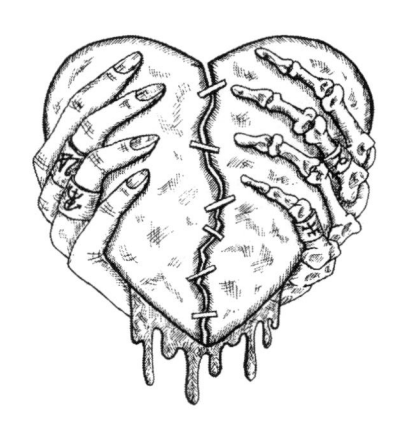

Chapter Seventy-Five
Kayriss
On the wings of grief.

Kayriss knelt next to Isaac, his body mostly covered by a blanket of woven nature, the fatal wound hidden from view. The wind tugged at her wings as if urging her to take flight, but she could not move.

Isaac was gone, and no healing magic she could muster would ever bring him back.

The world before her had never felt so vast, so empty. Every beat of her heart seemed like a cruel mockery, echoing through the hollow space where he used to be.

Her hands trembled as they reached up, holding her stomach as if cuddling the growing child within. It was too early for movement, but it felt warm still, the last remaining vestige of her Isaac. His warmth, his life, it had slipped through her fingers. She could still feel his touch, still hear his voice telling her not to worry and to live, but now, that voice was silent. The weight of his absence crushed her, making it hard to breathe, hard to stand. The sky felt a bleak grey, the earth beneath her feet cold and indifferent.

"Kayriss." Grind's voice came from behind her, steady but thick with sorrow. He was always the rock, always the steady one. His rough, battle-worn hand rested on her shoulder, but she felt nothing. "I'm sorry. I... I know it doesn't change anything, but we're here."

"Isaac wouldn't want this," Hooth added softly, his golden eyes filled with shared pain. His feathers were ruffled from his own failed attempts at comfort. "He loved you, Kayriss. So much. He died for so that you could live. You both could."

Loved. Past tense. The words sliced through her, sharper than any blade. Her voice cracked, hoarse and broken, as if every breath was a betrayal. "He's gone. He's just... gone."

Serafin stepped forward, her red hair glowing faintly in the sunlight. "We'll get through this together. You're not alone."

"Alone?" Kayriss laughed, a bitter, hollow sound that felt foreign on her lips. "You think... you think any of you can understand?" Her voice rose, breaking under the weight of her despair. "He was everything! He was my anchor, my hope, my..." Her words choked off in a sob, and she crumpled to the ground, unable to hold herself up any longer. Her wings dragged in the dirt, limp and useless. "He was going to be her father..."

Browntail knelt beside her, his voice low and filled with regret. "Isaac loved you with everything he had, Kayriss. He was your first mate. And if he were here, he'd..."

"Stop!" She shrieked, her voice raw. "Stop saying his name like he's just... gone on a journey. He's dead. He's dead, and there's nothing... nothing left of him. Not even me." Her tears fell freely now, spilling onto the earth beneath her, mingling with the dust and the memory of a life that had vanished in an instant.

Grind knelt beside her, his grief etched into the lines of his face. "You're still here, Kayriss. We're still here. Don't... don't leave us too."

She was already drifting away. The world around her was a blur, a muted roar of voices and sorrow that couldn't reach her anymore. The gaping hole in her chest, where Isaac had once lived, was too vast, too deep ever to be filled. The others meant well, but they didn't understand. They couldn't. Their words were dust on the wind, lost before they could touch her heart.

She could still see Isaac's face in her mind. His eyes were always so full of life, so full of hope. His touch was so warm and tender.

How could the world continue without him? How could she?

Her body shook with sobs as she stood. She didn't want to hear their voices anymore. She didn't want their pity, their understanding, their sympathy.

They weren't Isaac. They never could be.

She spread her wings, the aching, heavy weight of them unfamiliar in her new form, as if they no longer belonged to her. The wind caught beneath them, and she hesitated for a brief, agonising moment. Without a word, she launched herself into the sky.

"Kayriss, wait!" Hooth shouted after her, but his voice was lost to the wind. He took flight, but her enormous wingspan dwarfed his own. He realised there would be no catching her, however much he wanted to.

Her tears blurred her vision as she soared higher and faster, the earth a distant memory below her. She didn't care where she was going. She didn't care about anything anymore. All that mattered, all that had ever mattered was gone. She flew with reckless abandon, her wings cutting through the air as if she could outrun the pain as if she could escape the crushing weight of her grief.

The sky swallowed her, the clouds closing around her as she disappeared from view, a lone shadow against the endless horizon. The others watched, helpless, as she vanished into the distance, her cries carried on the wind until there was nothing left but silence.

In that silence, Kayriss was alone.

Devastatingly alone.

That is until Kayriss found her.

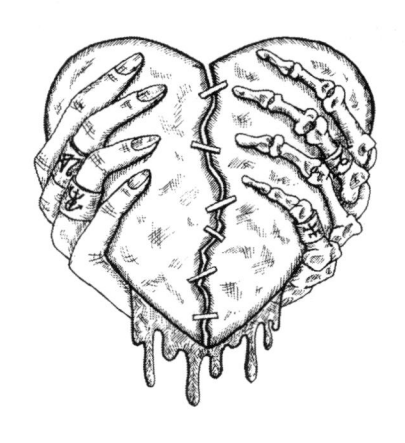

Chapter Seventy-Six
Everyone
The aftermath.

Grind stood at the edge of the shattered battlefield; his broad shoulders weighed down with exhaustion that went deeper than bone. All around him were craters and desolation where the two behemoths had fought.

The wind that had carried Kayriss away still lingered, cold and indifferent, but now there was only silence. The loss of Isaac and Granite had carved a hollow place inside him, a pit that threatened to consume what little hope he still had left. His mission to save his home was now complete. Gone would be the rat invasion, so that, at least, was one thing.

He looked at his friends, at the remnants of their broken company, and felt the weight of their grief pressing down on him like the weight of mountains. Kayriss, the heart and spirit of their group, was gone, and with her, part of them had been torn out. Isaac, the hu-man had fought by their side and travelled each road. He, too, was gone. Granite, the stalwart shield, had fallen at the exact moment as Isaac, and their loss felt like they were left exposed to a world that seemed intent on devouring every shred of light they clung to.

A strangled sob drew his attention, and Grind turned toward Browntail, the once-proud pirate captain now crumpled in grief. He held Cutlass, his first mate, in his arms; the female otter's body racked with tears. The bond between him and Cutlass had been unshakable, and Grind saw they were more than just the ship's crew. They were more than a brotherhood forged in blood and sea, but now, even Browntail's strength faltered under their loss.

Cutlass was trembling, her sobs tearing through the quiet like shattered glass. "I... I can't do this, Captain... I can't... not without Kayriss... Isaac... Granite... Not after everything."

Browntail's paw stroked Cutlass's fur gently, his eyes red but dry, his grief too deep to shed more tears. "We keep moving forward, lass," he whispered, though his voice held none of its usual fire. "They would have wanted that... even if it kills us."

Grind swallowed the lump and looked up at the sky, where Hooth circled restlessly. The white winged owlling had been scanning the horizon since Kayriss had flown off, hoping, praying, that she would return. She was too fast, too far. He had lost her.

Hooth's screech echoed through the darkening sky, filled with anguish and frustration. "I... I can't follow her," he muttered when he finally landed beside Grind. His feathers drooped, wings dragging on the ground in defeat. "She's gone... and I don't know if she'll ever come back."

Grind put a hand on Hooth's shoulder but had no words of comfort. He had nothing left but an empty ache where his heart had once been.

Nearby, Ayleigh sat on the ground, knees drawn to her chest, her tear-streaked face hidden in her arms. The young fox had endured more than anyone her age should have. Before all this, her home, her family, and her life were distant memories, and now the weight of uncertainty was crushing her.

"I don't even know if my mother's still alive," Ayleigh whispered, her voice broken. "I only know these few that made it out. Where are the rest? What if... what if they're all gone, too?"

Grind knelt beside her, his hand resting gently on her back. He didn't know what to say. He didn't have the answers she needed. All he could do was be there, as broken as the rest of them, a tether in the storm.

Tallin, the Night One who had once been their enemy, now stood before them, his eyes hidden beneath the blindfold he had chosen to wear since stepping into the light. His tall, shadowed form was shrouded in regret. He had once been a part of this darkness, a believer in the lies that had bound his people to cruelty.

"I'm sorry," Tallin said, his voice a low rumble filled with remorse. Though he could no longer see, his head bowed in shame. "Everything I believed, everything I was taught... It was a lie. I've failed you all and can never undo what I've done."

Elara, who had once distrusted him more than anyone, stood beside him now, her expression sombre but not unkind. She had seen something in him that he couldn't see in himself. A chance at redemption, perhaps, but it would be a long road.

"We've all lost more than we can bear," Elara said softly, glancing at the others, her green eyes filled with a quiet strength. "But this isn't the end, Tallin. Not for any of us."

Tallin nodded, though it was clear the weight of his past would hang over him forever. "I'll help you... however, I can. I owe you all that much."

Grind gave a faint nod, acknowledging the offer, but his mind drifted. The air felt strange and heavy, with an unspoken tension that hadn't existed before.

Something had shifted.

Serafin, the Oceanid, stood a short distance away, her sleek form shimmering in the sunlight. Her deep blue eyes were locked on the distant city of the Night Ones, her brow furrowed in confusion. "Something's wrong," she murmured, more to herself than to the others.

Grind looked up, following her gaze to the city that had once been Tallin's home. His stomach twisted as he saw it. Thin tendrils of purple mist, barely visible, seeped from the ground around the city's borders, winding like poisoned veins through the earth.

"What is that?" Hooth asked, his voice tight with unease as he stepped closer to Serafin, eyes narrowed on the strange mist.

"I don't know," Serafin said, her voice a quiet tremor. "But it's spreading."

Grind felt his heart sink, a new wave of dread washing over him. The purple mist pulsed faintly, like the dying embers of some terrible flame, but there was a malevolence to it, a creeping, insidious force that seemed to be reaching, grasping, hungering.

"What does it mean?" Ayleigh asked, wiping her tears as she gazed at the city in the distance.

Serafin's gaze never wavered from the mist. "I don't know... but whatever it is, it's not over. Not yet."

The wind picked up again, carrying with it the distant cries of the city below, a faint echo of what was to come. The shadows were gathering, darker than ever before. Grind knew, at that moment, that their journey was far from finished.

The end was still out of sight.

Veiled in a purple mist.

Epilogue One
King Marus
The mist in the midst.

"You do not know what you've done," King Marus snarled, his voice low and trembling with fury. His sharp gaze bored into Kaelen, who stood frozen in the grand obsidian chamber.

Marus's voice echoed off the black stone walls, every syllable dripping with the weight of ages, with the fury and despair of a ruler who was seeing the threads of fate unwind. The air in the chamber was thick with tension, and the shadows themselves seemed to close in, oppressive and cold.

Before Kaelen could respond, Marus turned, his long, black cloak billowing behind him like a stormcloud, and rushed out of the council chambers of the Obsidian Citadel. The doors slammed shut behind him with a finality that rattled the ancient halls. Marus's heart thundered in his chest, every step urgent, every moment too precious to waste on regret. The looming catastrophe he had feared for so long was upon them, a prophecy unravelling, and all the warnings and preparation had been in vain.

He sprinted down the narrow corridors, his mind racing faster than his feet. He needed his guard—his Royal Guard, the finest warriors of the Night Ones, the only ones trained for what might come. He needed their protection. The clack of his boots against the stone floors echoed through the darkened passages, and as he approached the council's quarters, he saw the wide, black-clad figures of the councillors emerging from their rooms, drawn by the sound of his urgency.

"My King!" one of the senior councillors called out, but Marus waved him away, his face a mask of grim determination.

"No time. Arm yourselves!" he commanded as he burst into the Guard's barracks, his deep voice reverberating through the chamber. "It's happening."

Without a second's hesitation, the Royal Guard leapt into motion. Their gleaming, dark armour clanked as they swiftly donned their plates, swords, and halberds, their faces grim and resolute. There was no need for questions; they had been trained to protect their king and his standing in this world, though none had ever been called upon to do it.

None of them truly believed the prophecy—none, except for Marus.

The king himself took his armour from the racks, the blackened obsidian heavy in his hands, and fastened the plates with swift, practised motions. His crown sat heavy upon his brow, but today, it felt like a burden more than ever before. The armour was tight against his body, but the weight steadied him. His fingers brushed the hilt of the black-bladed sword at his hip, a weapon handed down through generations of Night One kings, its edge imbued with the darkness of their realm. But would it be enough against what had been unleashed?

What was also handed down was the knowledge of terrors past. The prophecy was more than a fairytale to keep order in the Night One's favour. It was a truth that should never see the light of day.

His captain, Vorn, a towering figure clad in obsidian-black armour, approached him, the visor of his helm still raised. "Where do we go, my King?"

Marus's eyes darkened as he turned toward the winding staircase that led deep into the heart of the Citadel. "We go to the Doors."

The Royal Guard, eleven of the most battle-hardened warriors under Marus's command, fell in behind him as they descended into the lower depths of the Citadel. The winding stone stairs spiralled downward, lit only by ancient braziers' faint, flickering blue flames. The deeper they went, the colder the air became, the ancient power of the Citadel pressing around them like the weight of forgotten sins.

Those doors had been an entry to the mines for centuries, only opened to shove in the scourge of foxes and traitors. The legends of what lay behind them were spoken of only in whispers; stories told to frighten children, and warnings given to the foolish. Marus had always known there was truth in the tales; now, the truth had come for them all.

As they neared the bottom of the staircase, the cold became bitter, biting into their skin even through their armour. The great metal doors that stood at the base of the Citadel loomed into view, doors that had once been unbreakable, sealed by chains older than the Night Ones themselves.

Those doors were broken open. The heavy iron was twisted and shattered like something had torn them apart. Beyond them, a darkness that was more than just the absence of light crept forward, a malignant, living thing.

The guards stopped, their breath shallow, as a sound began to echo from the void beyond the door. It was low, at first, then rising in volume: laughter—a deep, guttural, malevolent laugh that seemed to curl around them, seeping into their bones, making even the bravest among them falter.

Marus's heart pounded, but he stepped forward, his sword in hand, its edge gleaming in the dim light. He could feel it now. The presence, hunger, and malevolent intelligence that had been lurking in the depths for untold centuries was now free.

A creeping, oozing mist was slowly undulating its way towards them. It crept and curled up from the darkness, sliding across the floor like a tide of poison. Like a living plague, thick and cloying, its tendrils slithering across the ground with the slow inevitability of death itself. It reeked of decay, rot, and forgotten graves as though it carried the breath of the countless dead in its foul, choking fumes. The mist writhed like serpents of shadow, seeking out life with an insidious hunger, curling around anything it touched, draining warmth and hope in its wake. It whispered of despair, its movements languid yet unstoppable, like the creeping advance of a disease that rots from within. In its swirling depths, there was the faint echo of laughter. It was cold, hollow, and devoid of mercy, the embodiment of death's cruel embrace, waiting to claim all that lived.

Vorn stepped up beside him, the other guards at the ready. "My King, what is this?"

Marus did not look away from the open doors, his voice steady but grim.

"It is the end of everything, Vorn. What lies beyond those doors was never meant to see the world again."

The purple mist thickened, swirling like a living thing, carrying the stench of decay and death with it. From the black void beyond the door, the voice that had laughed now spoke, low and thunderous.

"Foolish King," it hissed. *"You cannot stop what is already begun."*

In the darkness beyond the doors, a figure began to take shape, a towering silhouette of shadow and malice, its eyes burning with violet fire. The mist coiled around its feet, spreading wider, reaching hungrily toward the Citadel.

Marus tightened his grip on his sword, his jaw clenched. The weight of his crown had never felt heavier. His ancestors had locked away this, the terror they had buried.

Now, it was awake and from the figure came a whisper, as cold as death itself, reverberating through the hall.

"You are too late."

With those words, the battle began.

And so did the fall of the Citadel.

Epilogue Two
Emberlynn
The kindling.

The cave was a mouth of silence, gaping and still, save for the whispering crackle of wind and snow's thick, endless descent. Outside, the world had become frozen, but deep within the cave, it was heat... smothering, searing, blistering.

Kayriss lay on the rough stone floor, her skin damp with sweat, muscles taut with an agony that clawed through her body like wildfire. Her wings, tattered, fragile things now, twitched with every contraction, brushing the cold stone beneath her. The pain came in waves, not unlike flames licking at dry wood, catching, consuming, and leaving nothing but ash.

Her breaths were shallow and sharp like embers sparking to life only to die again. She was alone, utterly and completely alone, save for the relentless burn in her belly. The forest had always spoken to her, the trees, the rivers, the animals, her kin, but now, all was distant and muffled, as though the earth itself had recoiled from her.

From this.

The child inside her moved, and Kayriss gasped, feeling the fire within ignite once more. It felt like her bones were breaking, splintering into shards of molten glass. Every heartbeat sent another ripple of flame through her body. Her fingers clawed at the stone floor, nails scraping against the rock, but there was no relief, no coolness to temper the inferno raging within her.

She was alone, not by choice.

When the whispers from the grove had spoken of death and life entwined, she had known the path before her. But she had not known it would be this. The fire of creation, of birth, was cruel, crueller than the forest had ever shown her.

She screamed, a sound like a beast caught in its final moments, guttural and raw, as another surge of pain tore through her. It felt as if the fire inside her was trying to claw its way out, a beast made of flame and ash, ravenous and unforgiving. Her body trembled, and the cold stone beneath her did nothing to soothe the blaze within.

The cave was dim, the flickering of distant moonlight barely reaching its jagged walls. Outside, snow fell in thick, silent sheets, covering the world in cold silence, but within Kayriss, there was only heat, an unbearable, unrelenting inferno.

Her wings flared out once more, and the membrane singed at the edges from the internal fire that threatened to consume her. The forest had abandoned her, and the spirits of nature no longer whispered in her ears. She was left with nothing but the flames, the child within, and the searing, solitary agony.

She couldn't hear anything over the pain thumping in her head, leaving her more alone than she ever felt.

The final contraction came like the collapse of a burning house, with walls crumbling and beams falling. Kayriss gasped, her body arching in a spasm of pain so intense she thought she might shatter.

Then... the release.

There was a cry. It was small, piercing, like the first crack of flame in a quiet night. It filled the cave, echoing against the cold stone as the newborn child slid into the world.

Kayriss lay there, her body limp, drained, as though the fire had consumed all it could and left her nothing but cinders. Her breathing came in ragged bursts, her chest heaving. She barely had the strength to reach out, trembling fingers brushing the tiny form now wriggling beside her.

The child was warm. So, so warm. Too warm.

Kayriss blinked, eyes struggling to focus. The babe's skin was flushed, a deep, unnatural red, as the fire within Kayriss had not left her but had been passed on, kindled in this new, fragile form. The heat of her anger and sorrow passed to the tiny package she'd delivered. Her daughter's tiny hands flexed, and for a brief moment, Kayriss saw a flicker, a faint shimmer, like a spark dancing in the air.

The child let out another cry, this one softer, but beneath it, Kayriss could hear something else—the faintest crackling, like the first hints of a firestorm.

She pulled the child close, her breath shallow, as the snow continued to fall outside the cave. The heat radiating from the child was unmistakable, unnatural. This was no ordinary birth. Kayriss did not know what she had brought into the world, but the fire was not done.

Not yet.

This baby was something more, something ancient, something feared.

Kayriss closed her eyes, her body trembling with exhaustion. Her wings, now limp, curled protectively around the newborn. The flames within her had quieted, but the embers still smouldered. The cave was quiet again, save for the soft crackling that seemed to come from the newborn's breaths, a sound that echoed in the silence like a warning. Outside, the snow continued to fall, thicker now, heavier. The world was cold, but inside the cave, there was heat—the warmth of a mother's love.

Kayriss looked at the baby born from such sorrow, such death, and she felt the heat of the child against her chest, warming her from within, though the fire no longer felt like hers.

It was the child's now.

This little... tiny... phoenix child.

To Be

Continued...

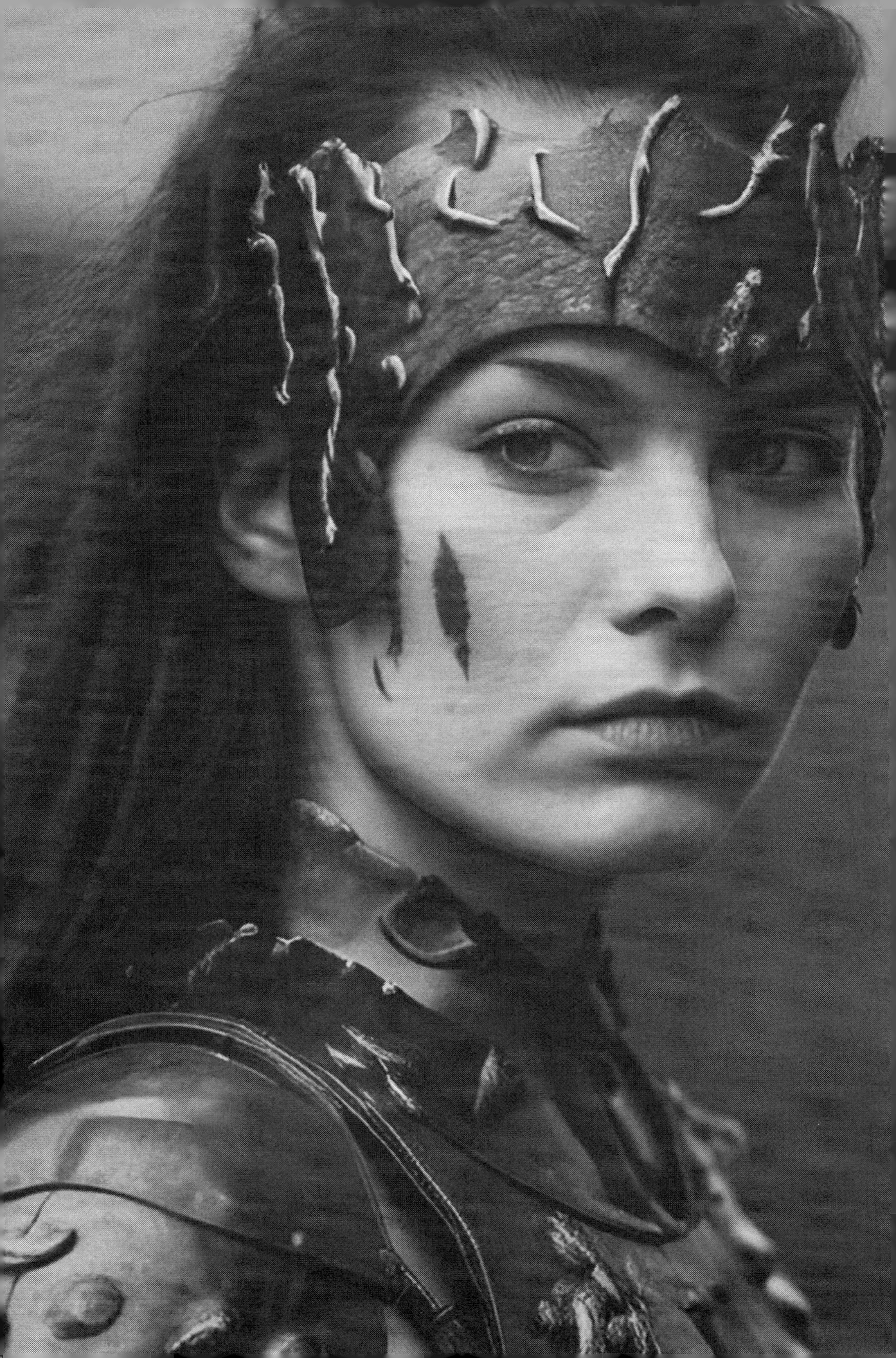

Appendix One
Swear Words of the New World by Race

Mine Folk Swear Words*

Shiteslate
Basalt brain
Stonecurse
Flintsplitter
Quartz quibbler
Marble mauler
Chisel chewer
Shard shitter
Bouldertosser
Cobble cougher
Pick dullard
Rust bearded Fool
Stoneskull
Magma mouth
Dust choked drudge
Cracked anvil
Copper blooded coward
Dirt eater
Weak armed whetstone
Brass bearded buffoon

Granite grumbler
Gravel gnasher
Rockrotter
Pebblepiss
Slagspitter
Dustdrinker
Brick biter
Rubble wretch
Siltstain
Cragcrapper
Mossbacked crag dweller
Tunnel tumbler
Ore for brains
Cave coddler
Sludgefoot
Rotten quarry dog
Sagging shaft
Shattered pick
Forge fumbler
Cave maggot

Otter Pirate Swear Words**

Blubberbait
Soggy furred / feathered Scoundrel
Clamshell cracker
Fish gutted fool
Bilge burper

Barnacle bottom
River rotter
Kelp sniffer
Scurvy whisker
Splinter tail

Night One Swear Words***

Shadow spawn
Blood rot
Skullbane
Worm licker
Hellmarked
Filth blood
Wormspawn
Stone brain
Honor thief
Grave walker

Void kissed
Curseborn
Nightcrawler
Soul thief
Darkheart
Shadowless
Light lover
Skin rot
Dull blade
Fate broken

* The author bears no responsibility for reactions received if used in the real world.
** And ESPECIALLY not these ones!
*** These? Wash your mouth out immediately.

Appendix Two
Trigger Warnings

While this work is a work of fiction, it covers some aspects that some readers might find disturbing or triggering. While it is not meant to upset, below is a complete list for you.

Dubious consent
Domineering presence
Powerplay
Animal death

If you are dealing with some aspect of your life that is upsetting, please reach out for the help you need.

Appendix Three
A picture of beauty

Fanart by Amy Cancetty

Amy is a 20 year old aspiring illustrator.

She was born at 22 weeks gestation with brain damage along with other additional needs and faced prejudice all throughout her life. She is a self-taught artist with an inspiring artistic flair that deserves recognition.

I am a very proud author to be able to help this young lady achieve a dream of having her work published in a book for the world to see.

This is her interpretation of Kayriss going through the changes she faces.

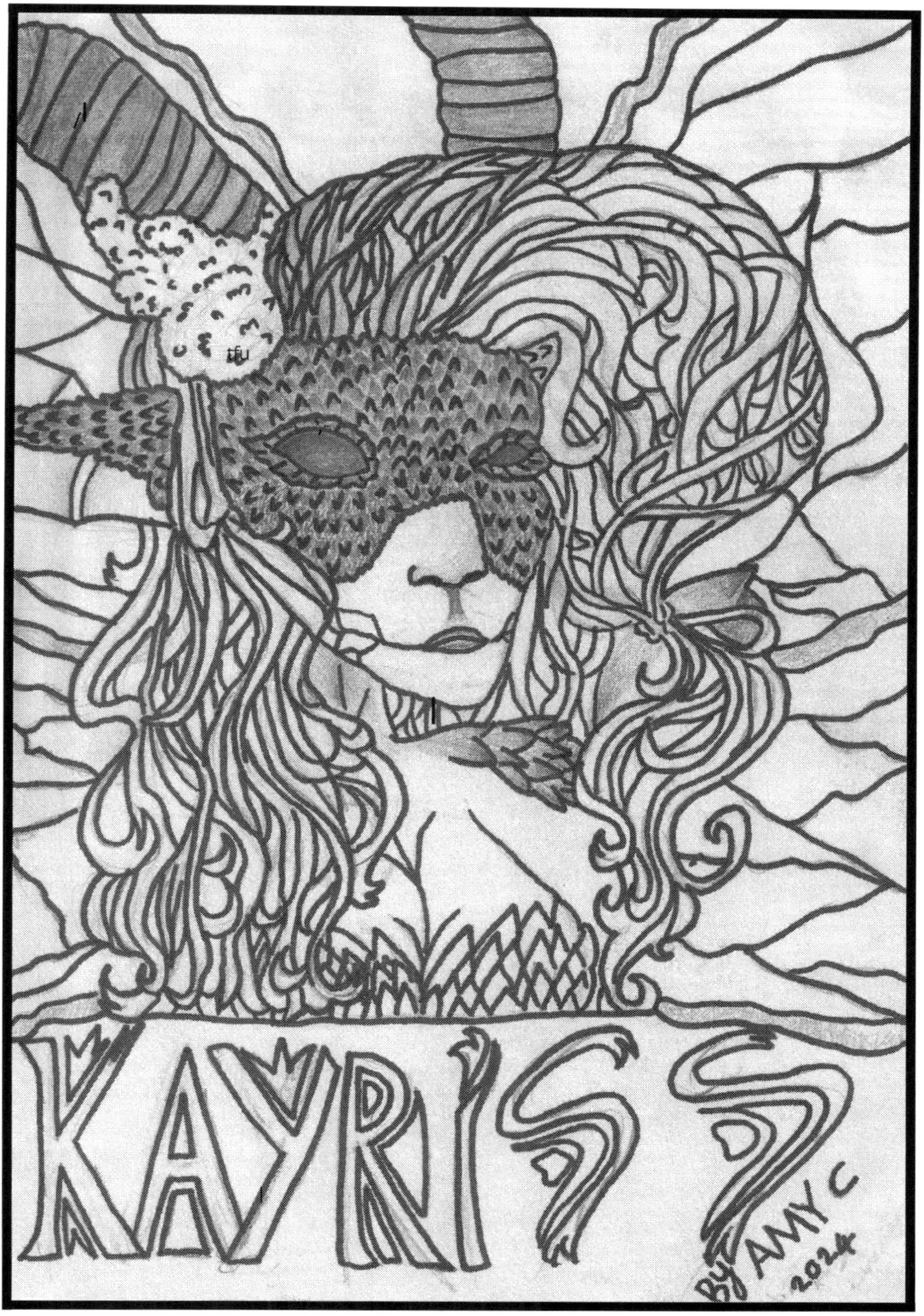
KAYRISS
BY AMY C
2024

Printed in Great Britain
by Amazon